HOOKED

Hooked

Frank A. DeFilippo

iUniverse, Inc.
New York Lincoln Shanghai

Hooked

Copyright © 2005 by Frank A. DeFilippo

iUniverse books may be ordered through booksellers or by contacting:

iUniverse
2021 Pine Lake Road, Suite 100
Lincoln, NE 68512
www.iuniverse.com
1-800-Authors (1-800-288-4677)

Yes, but no. This is a work of the author's imagination. Names, characters, places and incidents are either conveniently imagined or used fictitiously. To that end, this work is written to protect the innocent as well as the guilty. The author's intention is solely to provide entertainment and enjoyment. Any resemblance to actual persons, living or dead, is entirely coincidental.

Manuscript was prepared for iUniverse by CLS Business Services, cheryl@initialweb.com

ISBN-13: 978-0-595-34017-0 (pbk)
ISBN-13: 978-0-595-78805-7 (ebk)
ISBN-10: 0-595-34017-2 (pbk)
ISBN-10: 0-595-78805-X (ebk)

Printed in the United States of America

For my daughter Daniella,
Who learned to write at my knee.

Man in all the world's new fashion planted
That hath a mint of phrases in his brain.

William Shakespeare
Love's Labor Lost

Acknowledgment

My thanks to S. Ronald Ellison, Esq., my friend and attorney, who read the manuscript of *Hooked* for legal sufficiency as well as any lapses that I might have taken from common sense and my usual good taste. And to Mike Weiss, my long-time friend, author and winner of an Edgar Allen Poe Award for his own fine hand at mystery writing, who read the manuscript approvingly and with encouragement. And finally, to Mike Wellbrock, executive producer and colleague at WBAL-AM (1090) in Baltimore, who coaxed and coached me through trials, errors and exasperation with my [naughty word] computer, and to Cheryl Lightner, of CLS Business Services, who helped to organize this tub of alphabet soup into a presentable format.

I could not have imagined the sartorial *shtick* without the guidance of Allan Flusser's indispensable *Clothes and the Man* and *Style and the Man*, two books that not only have helped to fashion my own wardrobe but also assisted in draping the fictional and well-suited Richard E. Dart.

And a wink and a nod and a couple of well-chosen words to the dozen or so literary agents who considered but rejected the manuscript, but my thanks to the several who, nonetheless, had kind words of encouragement to plod on.

CHAPTER 1

▼

Under a bluebird sky, on a primeval bog known as the Eastern Shore of Maryland, the body of Sollie Stein was discovered face-up in a duck blind with one of his prime parts surgically removed and stitched into his mouth. The discovery was made, on a telephone tip, by the very same agents of the Federal Witness Protection Program who were supposed to protect Stein from even so much as a common cold. The coroner's report said that Sollie Stein died of a shotgun blast: it should have said that he talked too much.

Howdy. My name is Richard E. Dart, ace hunting-dog investigative reporter, raconteur and, some would say, all-around wise-ass. And right now, I'm assessing how I feel about something I might have helped to do. I get the willies every time I think about it. I'm a sucker for new assignments, and I was hooked right away. I could already smell the musty stench of cheap whiskey on damp wood and the reek of thousands of bladders in the rusting porcelain troughs that spelled relief. The oozing vomity aroma added still another layer of olfactory abuse that even a tank truck of Lysol couldn't erase. But nobody had warned me about dismembered body parts, especially Sollie Stein's clipped cock. Still, it was good to be home, back in Baltimore again.

I'd been on vacation when the city room plot was hatched, found out about it via a terse note on my computer terminal in the Washington bureau of *City Press* upon returning from two weeks in Chatham on Cape Cod. I'm 45, divorced, moderate to cynical. I don't work out or jog, which doesn't seem like very much fun because I've never seen anyone smiling while they're doing it. I'm comfortable being out of shape. At 150 pounds, squeezed into a 5'9" frame, I watch what I eat, keep lean and mean. I've been a reporter for nearly 25 years, my latest assignment the White House after eight years abroad in London and Moscow. It's always a bitch to uproot and leave, no matter how inviting the next stop might be. But from a reporter's point of view, I had the world by the balls.

Baltimore's Block is not exactly Mr. Rogers' neighborhood. Nonetheless, I was chosen to become the Boswell of the Block, chronicler of the erogenous zone that stretched across the underbelly of Downtown Baltimore like a cheap carnival runway, an X-rated strip of nightlife, where the menu was over-priced champagne, watered-down whiskey and blue-plate special blow jobs. In the Block's high times, the offering also included an occasional dose of the clap. None of the meat-market practitioners had the Good Housekeeping seal of approval stamped on her rump.

The Block was conventioneers' heaven and, in simpler times, Legionnaire's disease could often be cured with a shot of penicillin. Here, pot-bellied Rotarians from Iowa and flush-faced Kiwanians from Kansas could live out small-town fantasies at big-city prices. The Block is a seedy patch of real estate where testosterone and estrogen happily co-exist. But herpes and AIDS had unstarched a lot of one-night commandos, made monks of the formerly adventurous. These days, an exchange of bodily fluids could be lethal.

I was a generation removed from actual legwork, but nevertheless still retained a healthy appetite for doggedness. How long it would take to regain my legs was a matter of engaging my mind to the assignment. I'd paid my dues, made my way up the rungs of journalism reporting the excesses of the high and the mighty and the ministers of influence in capitals across the nation and around the world. Now I was going from the White House to an outhouse. The juxtaposition was amusing. They both stank. One exuded the perfumed smell of corruption; the other gave off the disinfected stench of every bodily orifice. But I knew I was still a damned good bird dog. And retracing the footsteps of my young days as a hard-assed political reporter, tempered by time, travel and experience, is what I would do for laughs, even if the assignment didn't include a paycheck. The face of Baltimore had changed as well as the faces of those who govern it. But the rules of politics are still the rules of the marketplace.

One thing hadn't changed. The man who presided over the news room of *City Press* like a manic Machiavelli was a hunch player as well as a hard-boiled son-of-bitch with a secret soft center like a Twinkie. Marry politics and economics, follow the money, and more often than not there'll be a hell of a story at the end of the chase. Usually he was right. I'd always been Buck Mulligan's favorite reporter. He'd hired me right out of college when I wasn't sure what I wanted to do, taught me the trade and turned me loose like a bloodhound on a long leash.

I've been hooked every since. Mulligan was mad as hell over losing me to the higher callings of foreign capitals and national politics. Now Mulligan wanted me back, insisting that I'd been playing to royalty long enough, time to get back to the fundamentals. I'd left the newsroom of *City Press* when the music of the business was the slap, slap, slap of Teletype machines and the choppy clatter of antique manual typewriters. And now I'm returning, full circle, to the eerie silence of computers and everyone's radioactive glow.

Mulligan was a rumple of a man, half hidden in a nimbus of smoke. Four packs a day—two Camel, two menthol, as if one took the edge off the other. Mulligan had a genius for feel. He was all glands, none of that "cogito, ergo sum" crap. Run with the wind, let your naked tool hang out. Buck had come up the storybook way, copy boy to police reporter to city editor. Too much education ruined reporters, Buck believed, because the more education a reporter got the more he'd stop and think. Thinking slowed down a reporter's reaction time. Mulligan had only one instruction for every reporter, whether it was a society beat diva or the police blotter jockey: "Smoke 'em out, kid."

I get a kick out of being a reporter. I have a healthy disrespect for just about everything, especially authority. And a newsroom is one of the few places I know of that is run by the inmates, a room full of misfits that could survive together no where else. Newsrooms are unhappy places. Show me a happy newsroom and I'll show you a dull one. And I confess I have a weakness: clothes. I like fine suits accented by collar pins, silk pocket squares, Kruggerand-scale cuff links and suede shoes, all of which may seem out of place in a business where entitlement to spitting on the floor is considered a fringe benefit. But, one man's joy is another's psychiatrist's couch. Returning to the newsroom was like being reborn. Local politics has a sassy flavor and panache that makes my heart tick like a taximeter and makes the White House and Capitol Hill seem like meeting-places for insurance adjusters. I'd been a prisoner in the White House press room long enough to know that I wanted out and back where politics is a touchy-feely business and not just ten-second sound bites and fluffy handouts. Covering the White House is a daily game of walking through the big gate, reporting to the pressroom and waiting for the administration's human trumpet to blast the party line at the morning briefing. Then back to the lounge until he returns to announce that the lid is on and it's time to go home. Washington is a company town whose only business is the company. Detroit manufactures cars, Delaware produces chemicals, and Washington manufactures itself.

Even though jetting around the world on Air Force One is surely a smoother ride than lurching on the Baltimore METRO, it was good to be back in the old city with the new look. Baltimore has rewards of its own—Little Italy, the crab houses, good private schools, inexpensive housing and, most of all, a place to call home and finally plant roots. In the time I'd been away, I'd been divorced and Baltimore had been rebuilt, christened by the ogling national media as renaissance city. It's harbor was now decorated with municipal Tinker-toys—mirrored hotels, million-dollar condos, needle-nosed fish tanks, world class yachts, twin ballyards, expensive restaurants and America's largest yogurt stand, Harbor Place. When I first came to work at *City Press,* the harbor was lined with rotted shed-piers and the flotsam—or is it jetsam, I can never keep the two straight—of Baltimore's storm drain system. Now, in good weather, the harbor is a walk across the street from the grungy *City Press* building and an environmentally friendly lunchtime pleasure. In the roaring junk bond days, even Donald Trump's yacht came calling.

Two blocks north of the miracle mile, and next door to City Hall, stands the Block, a shrinking row of century-old office buildings and storefronts whose upper floors showed the smudges of age and the crusted droppings of pigeons. At street level, the Block seemed to be mimicking the Vegas strip. A garish canyon of thermonuclear neon beckoned visitors with eye-popping fireworks of wiggling asses, twirling tits and disappearing G-strings. The signs had names—Miami Vice, Pleasure Dome, Trocadero, the Kit Kat Club, Gayety, Bermuda Triangle, Pandora's Box, and the most famous of all, the Two O' Clock Club, whose star stripper had no need for surgically enhanced breasts and who had once been the mistress of a famous governor. She'd undressed before more men than the entire chorus line of Ziegfeld Follies.

She was equally famous for her one-line object lesson: "Eat, eat, eat. Doesn't anybody fuck anymore?"

The obscenity law that governed the Block contained this codicil: Gravity could pull a G-string no lower than mid-thigh. On a night when a member of the vice squad's crotch police just happened to be in the audience, the star and proprietress of the Two O' Clock Club, wanting to give her admirers more bang for their bucks, wriggled and writhed and drew her skimpy sequins below her knees. The next day in court, when she saw whom the judge was, she told her lawyer that his services would no longer be necessary. She was fined fifty dollars and dismissed.

The peelers, as they were known in the trade, had names such as Tempest Storm, Thunder Thighs, Fabulous Faye, Betty Boobs, Tender Loins, Little Red

Writhing Hood, Deep Throat, Belle of the Ball, Lady in Waiting and Jaws. Jaws was a specialist, celebrated in the Block's kinky circles as a "humdinger." A humdinger is able to open her mouth wide enough to encapsulate a man's balls, and then hum like hell. It was a different kind of a trip. One stripper, the Body Politic, even had a graduate degree from a major university.

The hawkers and pimps stood in their doorways or sat on stools inviting passers-by—"We got whatever ya want, buddy"—into the dim, dank cellars of mystery where the musicians seemed to know only two songs—"A Pretty Girl" and "The Stripper." A mayor and a state senator had once played the saxophone in Block bands. The most melodic musical note on the Block was the rim shot, kind of a punctuation mark to the mocking forward groin thrusts of the real deal.

The prostitutes and the strippers trafficked freely on Baltimore Street in the shadow of the Police Department headquarters building, a mausoleum that could only have been designed by Albert Speer. Many of the street ladies would have done themselves better to wear sack dresses instead of the skimpy skirts and too-tight nipple-popping spandex tops that they considered showcases for their jugs. At show time, they vanished into the dark caves of smoke and booze where the only lights that shone were spotlights that limned stretch marks and pleats of flab on the performers. Time and hard knocks had treated many of them unkindly.

Mulligan's decision to recall me from Washington made sense, although under the rules of the game we played I'd never admit my delight. I know politics. I know the City. And I know where more bodies are buried than the U.S. Office of Graves Registration. Turn over any rock and I can identify the snake by name and political affiliation. The Block had lived by politics. Now it might die by politics.

The matter of whether the Block would remain a part of the local culture, at least in lore and conversation, was now in the hands of the voters. The life-or-death issue had been forced onto the Ballot in November by a born-again Christian public official who had vowed, as part of his recent covenant with the Almighty, to sanitize the city, beginning with the Block. He was asking the people of Baltimore to choose between sin and salvation by voting to eradicate a major sentimental institution where many of Baltimore's teen-age boys and bachelor-party grooms had achieved their rites of passage into manhood in the loamy opening of their choice, loins or lips or even a palm lubricated by Jergen's Lotion.

The twin pressures of development and demand for downtown office space had already forced several show bars to relocate uptown and away from the winking eyes of liquor inspectors and the police. This movement pattern, in itself, caused several city officials to oppose the referendum. They argued that the strip joints are easier to patrol if they are contained in one location instead of spread out indiscriminately across the downtown area. Doing away with the Block would only multiply the problem.

The forces eager to preserve the Block were also gathering. They included not only the bar owners, of course, but also a number of well-placed lawyers of the politic court variety, the major domo of Baltimore politics and several members of the city's police department. This alliance, as much as any other matter, not only amused me but added zest to the assignment as well.

In my early days, I was from the "holy shit" school of reporting, as in, "Holy Shit! What a story," kind of a scatological "Gee Whiz!" But time and creeping cynicism had dulled the hard edge of wonderment and lively innocence of knowing what a headline could do to an errant or vendible politician. Now crime and corruption were so commonplace that nobody seemed to give a damn anymore. Besides, television had transformed the game of reporting into a trivia contest.

The danger of most police reporters is that they become city editors. It had happened with Mulligan. Mulligan was famous for manufacturing crime waves, always ready to make his own little war if he had someone handy to take the pictures. Mulligan was also notorious for headlines. When it was learned that a man in the suburbs was abusing dogs, City Press screamed: DOG DACHAU FOUND IN COUNTY. And Mulligan once violated an agreement with the police by printing the names of 40 homosexuals who had been arrested in a raid on the men's room at a public park long before gays were coaxed out of the closet. When one of Mulligan's uncloseted victims committed suicide, the Mayor of Baltimore announced that *City Press* had killed the hapless homo. So when Mulligan ordered me to a meeting to discuss the Block assignment, I could write the speech I was about to hear. I'd heard it many times, many years ago.

"Don't be afraid to get your hands dirty, kid. And be careful not to soil your pretty clothes. But I want every one of these bastards, on both sides. Especially the guys who run those dumps, and the public officials who protect them.

"We want to play this one big, every day. I want names, because names sell papers and the more names there are the more papers we sell. The names of every guy who ever got a hand job and the names of every hooker who ever sucked a dick. The faggots, the maggots. And if you have time, check the queer bars. Might as well get them, too. And I want those fucking politicians. No fucking excuses. And no wasting time. And take a good, close look at that born-again asshole who found God in a bottle. Something about him's not right. Now get going. Smoke 'em out, kid."

The beauty of Mulligan was that his speech hadn't changed in 25 years. Everybody knew it, and everybody knew it was pointless to argue. When I walked out of the glass cubicle that was Mulligan's office, there was a wave of relief that I acknowledged with a wink, because I'd decided not to challenge Mulligan's assumptions. It would, as always, have pissed him off for the rest of the week. There are times when Mulligan could give an aspirin a headache.

CHAPTER 2

▼

I'd learned from Sollie Stein that on the first day of every month, for nearly a year, Anthony "Tony Scar" Scarlatti would climb into his shiny black Oldsmobile for the drive from Philadelphia's South Side to the Block in Baltimore for a meeting with Stein. Stein was the proprietor and license-holder, along with his wife Zelda, of the Palace Bar, and unofficial spokesman for the twenty-four other bar owners, peep show film operators, tattoo artists and pornography dealers on the Block. Stein had assumed the role of elder statesman upon the mysterious and highly publicized disappearance of Lord Julius Salisbury.

"Sollie, if I didn't love ya, I wouldn't bust my ass like this," Stein recalled Scarlatti saying. "Give me a break. Bend a little."

"Tony, bunky, you can have anything you want. The best champagne, the best blow job in the house, but not my bar," Stein would say.

"What, and lose my virginity," Scarlatti would laugh.

Scarlatti was in charge of acquisitions and mergers for the Terrachio family of Philadelphia. He'd become annoyed with Stein. Gaetano Terrachio was an impatient man, up in years, used to having his own way. He'd spread his influence and his organization across the Greater Philadelphia area and into New Jersey with such terrible swift force that no truck could move in or out of either territory without paying tribute. It was said that in his youth, Terrachio preferred a .45 caliber automatic as his weapon of choice. He was a big man who could fire it without a kick. Once, in a showdown with the Anastasia family, he confronted the rival's gang of workers on the docks of New York: "You tell Anastasia he fucks with any of my boys he gets this." Terrachio pulled the .45 from his damp armpit, waved it. The message was delivered. The Terrachio organization had already branched out into entertainment, having taken over—in a manner of speaking—several nightclubs in Philadelphia, Atlantic City and Cherry Hill. Gaetano Terrachio now wanted a piece of the action in Baltimore.

Stein remembered Scarlatti as a bully, mean as hell, built like a jukebox, thick from top to bottom. When he was mad, his eyes blazed like quarter-inch drill bits.

"Sollie, I'm getting sick of this shit. We're offering you top dollar for this box of vomit you call a club. Gimme a break. Waddaya want. The boss got a thing about people who say no, and the thing goes bang! Get what it mean?"

"Loosen up, Tony, baby, When I decide to put the 'for sale' sign up, you'll be the first person the real estate agent calls. Until then, no fucking deal."

I'd always heard that the Block was controlled by the mob. The mob wished it were true. The Block was a terrific generator of cash, not only from the perverts and the curious out-of-town, one-night dipsticks, but also from the rental fees for the jisim-stained rooms in the basement and the crash pads and gambling rooms upstairs. The girls contributed their share, too, in the form of percentages.

Gaetano Terrachio may have been Sicilian at heart, but his mind was as American as money. He had an idea, why he wanted to buy into the Block.

Terrachio needed a laundry, more precisely one with rinse cycle. So the Block and the mob seem like a heavenly-made match, like cement shoes and the East River, like a kiss on the cheek and a Stiletto in the back, like chalk stripe suits and Borsalino hats. Cross Terrachio and you sleep with the sushi. The wonder is that the courtship took so long.

So move over Sollie Stein, or so Terrachio thought, and enter the gang that couldn't shoot straight: Donald Peter "Large" Contino, 65, of Chicago; Francis Anthony "Tony Balls" Puglese, 70, of Elmhurst, IL; Frank "Baron" Barone, 65, of Miami; Ecco Fast Eddie" Catore, 83, of New York; Izaak "Red" Silver, 78, of Miami; Angel "Gus" Prince, of West Hollywood, FL; and the man fronting the scheme of alleged potential skimming and scamming, Stanley B. Botnik, 50, of Hollywood, FL, former carnival worker from Massachusetts and front man for the Lucchese organized crime family. And meet "Tommy," last name unknown, who traveled from Philadelphia to Baltimore to torch the rival Pandora's Box. Last name or not, Tommy was paid $20,000 for the assignment. Silver, a bookmaker for most of his life, took credit for arranging the bonfire, thus putting Pandora's Box out of operation for twenty days and sending a stern warning to Sollie Stein.

With *Godfather 111* and *Goodfellas* knocking 'em dead—you'll forgive the expression—on DVD and cable, it seemed like just the kind of business arrangement Michael Corleone might have dreamed up to decontaminate the family's ill-gotten millions from gambling and prostitution now that he's gone legit.

Only this time, the money Terrachio intended for the wash involved, extortionate credit transactions, robbery, interstate transportation of stolen property as well as gambling—small potatoes, rough-and-tumble, back-alley kinds of crimes in the new mob social order's higher forms of enterprise such as cocaine and women.

The story of Terrachio's good intentions for the Block is a study of money in motion. And following the money requires a Rand McNally Road Atlas of the United States. In the winter, January to be exact, in Florida where it's warm and Terrachcio vacations, a light bulb went off in Terrachio's head the way they do in the comic strips. He met with some gentlemen from the brotherhood, Dominic "Large" Contino, Donald Puglese, Sam Barona, Izaak "Red" Silver and Thomas J. Parson and discussed the purchase and operation of a bar on the Block in Baltimore, Sollie Stein's to be exact, because it was one of the biggest and brassiest.

During the discussions, it was suggested that Sollie Stein's club could be used by Contino, Puglese and Barona to sanitize funds they obtained in Illinois and Florida through their gambling, loansharking, robbery and interstate stolen property operations.

Family values, being very much the same all over, presume that it is first advisable to seek approval from the patriarch.

So before the purchase money for Sollie Stein's club would be forthcoming, Barona and Parson traveled to New York to obtain the approval of Ecco "Fast Eddie" Cattore—a boss in the Lucchese crime family, to operate the bar. For his nod of approval, it was agreed that the Block entrepreneurs would show their appreciation to Cattore, now 83, diabetic and hard of hearing, by endowing him with a share of the profits.

In the demiworld of the mob, cash is king. Here it is necessary to shift the genealogy to another family tree in another state. Some of the money for Sollie Stein's would find its way east from Chicago, where Contino was the kingpin of a gambling syndicate. In Chicago, Contino, along with Donald Puglese and eight others, were operating betting and gambling parlors in at least sixteen different locations where bets were accepted by telephone on sporting events such as football, basketball, baseball and boxing.

Contino was the organizer and leader who made all the important decisions. He had authority over the management and supervision of the offices used for the accepting of wagers by telephone. He informed players betting large amounts of money of the telephone numbers to be used for placing their wagers. He provided the schedules of games on which bets would be accepted, and paid and collected the winning or losing wagers with certain persons. Each of the locations did at least two thousands dollars a day in bets—all illicit cash.

Next the road to the Block in Baltimore would detour to North Miami Beach, where Contino, Frank Barona, aka Sam Vincent, Thomas J. Parson, and five others were operating a series of business enterprises that generated huge sums of dirty money—A New Hocke Shoppe, Lance European Imports, Inc., Twilight Video, Inc. The entrepreneurial efforts involved robbery, moving stolen goods, "gray market" automobiles, financing loansharking operations, wire fraud, gambling and "sham" thefts of automobiles to collect insurance. The enterprise also involved the employment of "juice men" who enforced the collection of loans, usually at three percent interest a week, or one hundred fifty six percent a year.

A quick demonstration of arithmetic involved an original loan of five thousand dollars that grew to twenty one thousand dollars, representing principal an unpaid and accumulated interest of three percent a week which the lenders tried to collect by implicit threats of violence and other criminal means to cause harm to the person and property of the unfortunate borrower.

Terrachio's cash flow charts also explained that the "gray market" car scheme functioned through an elaborate arrangement of electronic transfers of money from Deutsch Sudamerikanische Bank in Miami to at least seven banks in Hamburg, Germany. The seven transfers involved nearly four hundred thousand dollars a year. A "gray market" automobile is a foreign car that does not comply with U.S. emissions standards. They are purchased abroad and resold in the U.S. at prices lower than those offered by authorized distributors. Titles for the illegal imports were obtained by submitting false documents to the Texas Department of Motor Vehicles through a dealership called VIP Automotive, Inc. One such import, Terrachio explained, was a 1980 Rolls Royce Bentley Limousine. Stolen merchandise that was moved across state lines included Baume and Mercier, Patek-Phillipe and Rolex watches. And one "scam" theft of an automobile involved the removal of a 1984 Excalibur Roadster from its Hollywood, FL, parking place so the owner could collect insurance.

The money reserved by Terrachio from his newly acquired partners in Florida and Illinois would be deposited in bank accounts in amounts of less than ten thousand dollars in most cases to avoid IRS reporting requirements. Thus, the paper trail that would begin in Illinois and Florida would end in personal and business bank accounts in Maryland in a complicated series of currency and check transfers—United National bank of Miami, a Block account at Universal National Bank in Hollywood, FL, and a Block account at Gibraltar Bank of

Maryland. From the Florida accounts the money would travel upstream to Balti-more, mostly in cashiers checks totaling nearly two million dollars, through a man named Eli Morrelli, and other money in cash and checks from Contino, Puglese, Barona and Prince. The return trip would take the money to an account at Universal National Bank of Florida. The pixie dust, hundreds of thousands of dollars, would be shuffled through bank accounts in Florida and Maryland with intermediate stops on the books of Terrchio's Block account.

The revenue enhancement scheme at Sollie Stein's was intended to have a two-fold effect: It would increase the book value of the club at the same time it would provide a sly opportunity for skimmed cash. But the main mission was still the stated purpose of turning illegal money into legitimate currency. Terrachio had reasoned (correctly) that it would be simpler to have a cash register. But used to getting his way, Terrachio hadn't counted on Sollie Stein being the bullheaded old fart that he was.

When the first of the month rolled around again, Scarlatti materialized at his usual time as if he were a RoboCrook programmed by a computer chip. This time he looked meaner than ever. No small talk, right down to the business of a final offer. But Sollie knew this day would finally arrive, and he took the precau-tion of inviting a friend. Captain Joseph Nelligan, head of the police depart-ment's narcotics squad, emerged from a dark corner and pulled up a chair facing Scarlatti.

"Look, grease ball, we don't want any fucking outside wops coming down here and muscling our people," Nelligan said. "This is our fucking territory and it stays that way. You wanna live you stay in Philly and play with your Goddam cement shoes. You fuck around in Baltimore, three thousand cops and a lot of pissed-off people are gonna chase your dago asses clear back to the Pennsylvania line and you just might die along the way. Sollie, here, runs a nice clean business, from a business point of view. Some accountant wants to come in here and get ulcers on his dick, that's his business. Sollie works for me. The hookers work for me. You as much as take a piss in this town, I know about it before you zip up your fly. Now go back to Cream Cheese city and tell Terrachio to mind his own fucking business and we'll all live happily ever after."

Scarlatti pushed back his chair, stood up and spat on the floor: "Mudfuck, I'll see you again, real fucking soon."

I'd heard the story first-hand from Stein. I'd known Stein casually from the early days as a knock-about of several political fringe figures and a heavy contrib-utor to campaigns. Stein had retired with his glaucoma and his pacemaker, to live in fat city in a penthouse condo in Boca Raton when he wasn't back in Baltimore visiting his kids. I'd called Stein and arranged an interview on one of his infrequent visits. Stein was willing to talk only because he thought the way they beat the Philadelphia gang that couldn't shoot straight was a fucking riot. Stein, unfortunately, did not have the last laugh.

"Everybody, including you know-it-alls in the press, always assumed the mob controlled the Block," Stein said. "Shit, the Block was a mom and pop operation, and those assholes from Philadelphia couldn't break their way into jail if you gave them blowtorches. Salisbury had their number. He arranged a lot of local protection to keep the Block strictly a local institution. He did the city a favor and they fucked him for it."

Lord Julius Salisbury was a legend. He was also a mystery. He'd earned the name "Lord" because that's what he was—the overlord of gambling in Baltimore and boss of the Block where much of it took place. With the help of the police, Salisbury kept the Block clean, trouble-free and homegrown. The police got their rewards, too, for keeping outsiders exactly that way—out. But something went wrong, somebody switched signals. The Feds had busted and convicted Salisbury for bookmaking and wire fraud. On a tip that he was going to lose his appeal and go to jail, Salisbury disappeared in the middle of the night like a ghost in a graveyard, jumped bail, skipped off owing his lawyer $50,000. But only after arranging to sell his nightclub to his girlfriend, a slinky number who was a featured dancer before she went on Salisbury's personal payroll. At the time, the street talk was that Salisbury made his get-away in a horse van. Every so often, there'd be a report of a Salisbury sighting in London or Paris or even on a *kibbutz* in Israel. Most guessing had Salisbury re-potted to Canada. To this day he has not been heard from.

"Trouble with those thugs is that they don't know anything but guns," Stein said. "You disagree with them, you don't do business with them, the first thing they think of is shoot. Their dicks are bigger than their IQ's. Point is, the Block was our bread and butter. Started off as theaters way back when. Then little bars and liquor stores on the East Side moved in and they graduated to sin and sex and show business and watched the profit margins grow. It's as American as a dollar bill, the best traditions of capitalism."

Sollie Stein and his cohort of entrepreneurs were the children of immigrants, first generation East European Jews who were born in the row houses of East Baltimore around the Johns Hopkins Hospital and along corned beef row near the Lloyd Street synagogue, the oldest Jewish house of worship in America. As young boys, they had worked hard after school at such jobs as selling newspaper, packing boxes in the shipping rooms of the large garment manufacturers in the great industrial buildings that are now fancy loft apartments, and bagging cheap wine in the family liquor stores that seemed to be on every corner of East Baltimore. Some made it to college, even law school. Stein, among others, stuck with the family liquor business, prospered, and at the outbreak of World War II, got into the business of boosting the morale of America's fighting men.

For it was during World War II, the boom years after and all through the Korean War, that the Block reached the peak of its fame and celebrity as a contributor to the fighting spirit better than Bob Hope or any USO troupe. Baltimore was an important transportation center, and all the ships at sea and every train rumbling up and down the East Coast were carrying cargoes of GI's just itching to get screwed, blooed and tattooed, as the old saying goes. Baltimore was a favorite port of call, a city of flanks and shanks, haunches and paunches, where Jacks and Jills let freedom ring if only for five minutes and to hell with the Fuhrer. The best of the bevy was a tan-skinned beauty, Ayisha, who had worked her way across the Mediterranean from Algiers to France, sold herself in the bars and clubs of Cannes and Nice before the war, and now found herself on the Block as part of a cultural exchange that Lord Salisbury had negotiated when one of his dancers infected a judge with a gonococcus bacterium, causing a sniffle, if you will, and had to be reassigned to a distant duty station. Ayisha was the source of her own legend. The actor Orson Welles had years ago thrown a $100 bill on a bar table in Nice to claim her talents for the night.

The Block was actually two blocks, two sides. It was a subculture, a freak show of bag ladies and dwarfs, of motorcycle jockeys who hadn't changed the oil under their fingernails for two months. It was *Carnevale* in Rio, Mardi Gras in New Orleans, the Combat Zone in Boston, North Beach in San Francisco, the Great White Way, the Rockettes in pasties and G-strings, a line of rotten crotches and sagging blubbery tits that, in the sobering glare of daylight, could unstarch even the horniest old goat. The Block, in its surreal way, also made great campaign commercials.

As part of my get-acquainted research, I'd previewed the first of a planned series of television commercials at a local station before it went on the air. It was short, simple, to the point. The camera zoomed in slowly on a sign, a gyrating rump of lights, until they exploded into a pinwheel of color and finally dissolved on a beautiful young girl of about fourteen staring into an open doorway below.

The solemn voice of the narrator intoned: "What's a nice girl like her doing in a place like this. Vote to send her back home. Vote yes on Question Six. Paid for by Citizens for a Christian Baltimore."

I'm not usually a soft touch when it comes to political commercials. I'd watched too many politicians let television do their dirty work for them. But this was like a kick in the groin with ski boots. What the ten seconds lacked in subtlety they made up for in overtones. It was the milk-carton campaign of missing kids plugged into television. The commercial also conveyed the unmistakable smack of anti-Semitism, as if every teenage hooker who ever took it up this ass or had needle-tracks on her arm was the white slave of some greedy Jewish businessman with an overripe Kewpie-Doll wife and a condo in Boca. What's more, the kid in the commercial was too pretty to work on the Block.

I've learned enough about computers not to trust them. But when *City Press* offered to install a terminal and modem in my house I didn't resist. I could store information, access the wire services, file stories without getting out of bed. Except that I wouldn't store information. Too many weasels in the newsroom. As a joke, I asked for an unlisted password. It wasn't taken as funny. In the bad old days, too many reporters were on the payrolls of politicians. Besides, I like to keep what I know to myself. I'm old fashioned that way. I still prefer to work with a cheap ballpoint pen and a notebook, even have my own cockeyed system of shorthand. I don't even like tape recorders because they intrude upon interviews like a third brooding presence. But I understand all of that "misquoted" and "out of context" crap well enough so that often it's smart to make and save tapes of controversial exchanges. I've trained myself to remember, because I've discovered that the best way to loosen tongues is to take out a notebook and pen and never use them unless it's absolutely necessary. The other principle of journalism I swear by is, always be nice to secretaries. That and reading upside down.

I like to roam and rattle around in wide-open spaces. The house that I'd bought was a brick Georgian number in move-in condition in a leafy section of north Baltimore called Roland Park. The house was large and bright, east-west exposure for maximum sunlight, updated and filled with gadgets by the previous owners who were transferred out of town to a higher calling (and presumably a higher salary) on sudden notice. I got lucky. The only agreement I had to make, and that with my fingers crossed, was that I wouldn't stain the bleached oak floors dark. The computer was installed in the den that I planned to use as an office. I am neat, fastidiously so. I live alone, technically, except for frequent overnight cuddles with Shelly. The cleaning lady comes once a week. My marriage did not survive my assignment in Moscow and the rigors that were required in that restricted outpost long before Glasnost and the dissolution of the Republic. We'd lived and worked practically in quarantine in a building that was set aside for American correspondents. We saw the same fifty people every day and social-ized with the same fifty people every night. Nowhere to go, nothing to do except for the ritual trips to Helsinki to load the larder with Western goods. Occasion-ally there was an invitation to an embassy party, the Hungarian embassy being the most coveted. It had the best kitchen in all of Russia. My driver was a KBG agent, my translator was a KBG stoolie. We were told to assume that our apart-ment was bugged. To communicate privately in our own apartment we wrote notes to each other, and then burned them. Four years of this collective life was enough. We'd had too much of each other with no escape time. When we returned to America we decided to call it quits after 15 years and no children. Marriages that are made in heaven often do not survive here on earth.

CHAPTER 3

▼

So far, my research showed that Citizens for a Christian Baltimore was the front group for the man who was masterminding the campaign to wipe out an important piece of Baltimore's living history, like imploding the Bromo Seltzer tower or leveling the Washington monument at Mount Vernon Place. Yet no one had been able to link him to the movement conclusively.

Charles Sharkey had the ashen look of a week-old cadaver. His skin was too taut for his bones and his clothes were too loose for his frame, like sagging sails on tall spars. Sharkey's thick glasses gave him the appearance of a bullfrog peeking through a cake of ice. He was a union of Ichabod Crane and a calculator. For inside his great dome of a head was a mind that raced over numbers the way a Chinese waiter rattles off carryout orders and a brain the devised creative schemes of deceit and great cunning that would've been envied in a Medici palace. Eradicating the Block was the latest. And it was ingenious, because Sharkey was conducting his campaign against sin and sex with government money, legally, above board and strictly by the book. The Block had suddenly become valuable real estate because it practically hugged the harbor. And to make way for new office buildings that would house even more lawyers, accountants, stockbrokers and real estate agents, the Block would have to yield. Sharkey was the Elmer Gantry of the anti-Block lobby.

Sharkey had a shady reputation of awarding lucrative city construction projects to favored contractors without the nicety of competitive bids even though the law required them. He accomplished this dipsy-doodle by creating an extra-legal device known as construction manager. Technically, the job was not construction. He executed the old reverse English in the name of progress and speed in a city that had developed a reputation for getting this done in a hurry. The latest project was a new city office building that would wipe out a third of the Block.

My first interview with Sharkey was a how-do-you-do session over a tote lunch in Sharkey's City Hall office. I'd invited him to lunch at Paisan's, in Little Italy, a favorite wee-hours dinner spot with the Block crowd, but Sharkey declined, saying he preferred working lunches at his desk. I'd observed Sharkey from a distance at meetings and briefings and before committees of the City Council. He was slick, self-assured, always in command of his subject. I'd also spent time in the *City Press* library punching up microfilm and riffling through musty old clippings. But in that reliquary of molding newspapers, resting place of wars, floods, fires, great reputations and outrageous deeds, where Hitler rested in the same filing cabinet tomb with St. Elizabeth Seton, there was precious little information on Sharkey. I'd come to the right place, the morgue. Sharkey might just as well be a platter of cold cuts. That's the way he apparently preferred it. Little was known about Sharkey beyond his bureaucratic wizardry and the fact that he had convinced the mayor to sponsor an annual sunrise revival meeting for Baltimore's business community which attracted three thousand boardroom pinstripers who came as much to be seen as to pray. God and mammon competed for attention at this festival of heavenly commotion. In truth, God might just as well have called in sick.

Sharkey was as slippery as a fresh-caught flounder, not above reproach but just beyond reach of it. Sharkey was known for never communicating by memo or rarely issuing his wishes by phone. When he had information to impart or a deal to design, he usually escorted the recipient of his instruction to the men's room. There, in the echo chamber of municipal-tan tile, he checked every stall to make certain there were no occupants. And, when satisfied, Sharkey turned on two or more faucets full force and repeatedly flushed a commode to make certain his voice could barely be heard over the waterfall of gushes and never recorded by an electronic eves-dropping device. No one had ever laid a glove on Sharkey although several prosecutors had tried.

I entered the world of Charles Sharkey, an office as stern as its occupant that conveyed the sense that the universe truly is governed by accountants and lawyers and not by poets and metaphysicians—the personal computer, reams of paper everywhere, volumes that bespoke the law, a desk and another work table, a sofa, the flags of America and Baltimore, and a Bible on a coffee table that was open to the Book of Revelations. On the Block, I thought, prepare to meet thy maker had a meaning other than omens of Apocalypse.

I exchanged handshakes, lifted the back of my suit jacket, adjusted the knife-blade creases of my trousers and lowered myself into the designated chair with body language that must have suggested the image that I was about to sit on a pole. I never cross my legs and try not to lean against the back of a chair for fear of encountering a wrinkle. Every day I dress to kill. Today I'd defied the laws of gravity and business. I'd chosen a double-breasted chalk stripe suit to show who was in charge. And I accented it with a white broad cloth cutaway collar shirt to complement the crisscrossing of the double-breasted lapels. Antique Florentine cuff links fastened the half-inch of linen showing below the coat sleeves. Patterned over-the-calf socks led to glistening Ferragamo wing tips to complete the presentation. Style is being comfortable in your own skin. You either have it, or you don't. But Sharkey didn't seem to give a shit. For all he could care, I could be wearing a jock strap and sneakers. Sometimes I wonder why I bother.

"You want to talk about the budget," Sharkey said, attempting to set the tone for the discussion as well as to define the boundaries of the meeting.

I hadn't taken out my notebook yet, partly to relax Sharkey but mainly because I wasn't sure there'd be anything to write.

"The construction budget," I said.

"There is no construction budget as such," Sharkey said. "Construction projects are funded by bonds which are approved by the voters."

I could see that I was knocking him dead, succeeding beyond my wildest fantasy that the goo-goo dream of a truly open government, hell-bent on keeping the public force-fed with information, was about to come true.

"You have a list," I said. "I'd like to see it.

Sharkey never blinked behind his Coke-bottle-bottom eyeglasses.

"We'd have to put one together, and that would take some time," Sharkey said.

Blah, blah, blah. On, and on, and on. I was annoyed. The city was spending millions of dollars a year on bricks and mortar projects and there was no accounting of it to the press or the public. What's more, it was evident that Sharkey was not used to dealing with reporters. For the first rule of the game is that the harder you make reporters work for their stories the meaner they become. Sharkey meandered on about how the city was progressing and how tourists were coming in all colors, shapes and sizes, slung to their Nikons and camcorders, from all over the world to visit the miracle mile of Baltimore's harbor, to Ooooooh! Over their French fries and Aaaaaah! Over their Haagen Daazs.

Sharkey praised the mayor for holding the tax rate down and gave a gold star to the Department of Public Works' Special Services Division for making the city, at least the part the tourists see, function like a set of Lionel Trains in the FAO Swartz window at Christmastime. It was the municipal line strung out. The mayor and the city were one and the same. Attack one and you attack the other. I could see that a space was being reserved for me on the enemy's list of those who disagreed that the two were permanently joined at the hip.

I knew I was getting nowhere, not a snowball's chance of collecting even a snippet of information about anything but Sharkey's spiritual agenda of smite and smote, of locusts and frogs, of Sodom and Gomorrah, and born-again bullshit of believing its possible to put aside a lifetime of hypocrisy, hug a tree and be saved. In the pit of my stomach I knew I would walk away clueless. Worse, I'd have to report to Mulligan that my notebook was blank. I thought as I stood to leave, Sharkey's as slick as they say. He wasn't even intimidated by my CEO in-charge suit. I'd decided half way through the interview to resort to plan B: Work the edges until they close in on the center. Reporting is all slipping and sliding. You either learn to skim on silver skates or you fall flat on your ass.

I'd learned from Sollie Stein that two years before my return to Baltimore, the federal government had created a Strike Force on Organized Crime. In fact, twenty such little armies of crypto-fascists had been established across the country, and Baltimore was one of the nation's major cities to be so blessed as to have a strike force of its very own operating under the direct command of the U.S. Justice Department and accountable to no one but the attorney general himself. The Baltimore unit was under the direction of Robert Krall. I'd checked him out. Krall was an undistinguished lawyer who got the job by sucking up to the rich and powerful in the Administration. Krall had spent a lifetime sniffing the hem of power as a mid-level career bureaucrat at Justice. If you closed your eyes when he walked you could almost hear the stomp of jackboots goose-stepping across the plaza outside Krall's courthouse office. In his new job, Krall was like a hog in slop. He finally had recognition and power. Underline power.

The files at *City Press* revealed that one of Krall's first official acts was to raid Pandora's Box. Among the articles that were confiscated from the bar near the cash register was a framed picture of the owner, Broadway Brown, with his arm around the governor Maryland. The picture, it was learned, was one of hundreds that had been taken at a million-dollar fund-raiser for Governor Marshall Goodwin. To Brown the picture was a memento: To Krall it was evidence that the Mafia in Maryland was Jewish, not Italian. Krall made certain that the picture received the public attention he believed it deserved.

Brown screamed as if he'd been bitten where it hurts by one of his hookers.

"The fuck ya think ya spend a hunnert dollars to go to an affair like that for. Ta eat a fucking corned beef sandwich? Ya go to be seen, get close to the main man. The picture says I was close."

The picture was impounded and ordered sealed as evidence by a judge who had been appointed to the bench by Governor Goodwin to ease him out of the way when, as state's attorney, he'd threatened to launch an investigation into owners of pinball machines. Many of the owners were reconstructed slot machine barons with close ties to the Block. Now that slots were illegal in Maryland, the parasites took their profits from school kids instead of housewives.

My Ferragamo wing tips crossed the marble threshold of Paisan's restaurant shortly after midnight. By then, the families and fun-couples were gone and the glitteriest restaurant in Little Italy was transformed into a massive pasta palace for the underside of Baltimore. The first person I saw was Tony Russo, a small-time operator with a big-time mouth, whom I'd known from my early days as a regular customer at Paisan's. Russo had appointed himself the unofficial *maitre d'* of Paisan's. Russo had done time at various stages of his career as bookmaker, one of Baltimore's outstanding numerologists, and fencer of hot items. Most recently he had unloaded a modest fortune in bootleg food stamps on two frequent customers who came permanently attached to badges that bore the unmistakable emblem of the FBI. On another gig, he sold a gallery of stolen paintings to undercover agents of the Baltimore Police Department. Russo had made a colorful career of appearing almost annually in Circuit Court on charges of bookmaking. He had just been busted again.

"The Nazi's in the other room," Russo boomed my way. "He's taking pictures with his tie clip. Sonofabitch shoulda been a U-boat commander."

What the hell's he talking about, I asked myself in the corner of my brain that processes mental questions. Then I asked aloud the same question of Russo.

"The Nazi. Krall. The gangbuster," Russo said.

Holy shit, I thought. Damon Runyon in one room, and the Terminator in the other.

"Have a great night," Russo said.

"Thanks, but I have other plans," I said.

I was ushered into the largest of four dining rooms and seated three tables from Krall. I ordered an Absolut on the rocks and linguine with white clam sauce, easier on the system late at night than larding my stomach with heavy tomato sauce. I remembered that Paisan's was a favorite of Spiro T. Agnew before he got caught with his fingers in the tambourine. He ate the same thing on every visit, linguine with clam sauce. The thought made me want to change my order. Presidents and candidates validated their campaigns at Paisan's—Jimmy Carter ordered chicken cacciatore, Ted Kennedy veal. At Paisan's they serve macaroni, not the trendy crap that resembles a box of crayons, but real honest-to-mama spaghetti with made-from-scratch marinara sauce. These days, the difference between macaroni and what is called pasta is three dollars a pound.

I'd learned, too, that the word had been quietly passed by the State Police to keep Governor Goodwin out of Paisan's because the place was under surveillance and its phones were tapped. And the object of much of the federal affection was no other than Russo himself, not so much of whom he was but more because of where he might lead.

I glanced at Krall, Krall glowered back. Although neither of us would admit it, each of us had hoped to catch the other's eye. Krall was bigger than he appeared in the *City Press* photo file, kind of square like a refrigerator. He had sandy-colored hair, close-cropped, cut in the regulation style probably right out of the Justice Department grooming manual. His suit was three buttons, his shirt white button-down, his tie narrow black knit. He looked more upholstered than dressed. Krall's most remarkable features were his gray cat's eyes and the divot in his chin. Add to those a curlicue scowl that resembled an anthropomorphic potato chip. The rest of his beefy face was an expressionless blank on a field of flesh the color of raspberries. I got a silent case of the chills.

Krall whispered to his wraith-like companions, got up and wormed his way through the checkerboard of tables, heading in my direction. The needle on the prick alert in my mental circuitry shot into the red zone.

"I've been meaning to call you," Krall said, uninvited but nonetheless slouching into a chair at my table.

"Same here," I said.

"Must be a big deal you're working on, bringing a class act like you back to Palooka Ville," Krall said.

"Same old drill. Cover every story the same. Start at point A and don't quit until you reach point Z. Then you start over again, kind of what you do," I said.

I was trying to be cool, indifferent, keeping the edge off my voice and looking more into my three fingers of vodka than into Krall's smoky squid eyes. But we both knew that the conversation was more like two dogs circling and sniffing, trying to decide whether to fuck or fight.

"I have a hunch I know what you're digging into," Krall said. "Maybe we can make a deal, work together, trade information, help each other."

In every reporter there's a cop close to the surface struggling to get out. It takes a mean streak to restrain the raging beast. I'd known a few reporters over the years who were closet cops, getting their jollies working with the police, just to get a break on a story about a drug bust. To me, that's just as bad as being on some politician's payroll.

"No deal," I said, looking up from my drink and into the fog of Krall's eyes with all the firmness I could fake. Now I was mad and heading for pissed off.

"I'd have been disappointed if you'd said anything else," Krall said. "But suit yourself. There are other ways. Like subpoenas and grand juries. See Russo out there? I'm gonna haul his ass before twenty one of his peers and have him squirming so much that he'll be tap dancing and doing bird calls and I'll be calling the tune. When the time comes, I'm gonna play that little greaser like a five-string banjo."

"Jesus, just what I've always wanted to do when I grow up, a chance to be a cop," I said. "Worse yet, a fink. Thank you for the chance to make my dream come true."

The karma here was definitely bad. I was losing it and making an enemy at the same time. That third, invisible eye in the center of my head called insight told me not to piss off Krall.

All of which began to make me wonder about Russo. Trouble was, Krall and I were in the business of asking questions, not answering them. But the big difference between our occupations, I realized, is that prosecutors have subpoena power and reporters don't. A reporter can go only so far and then he's left with his pecker in his hand, pissing in the wind. Not a chance of peeking at tax returns, doing net worth's, bugging telephones, destroying families and wrecking reputations or forcing friends to snitch on friends. Those are the real powers of a prosecutor. I had a bad case of subpoena envy.

My linguine arrived, piping hot, sending up tendrils of steam, along with a second Absolut. Krall gave me a last gray stare and put out his hand.

"I hope you'll reconsider our talk," Krall said. "It could work well for both of us."

I said nothing. But the part of my brain that often counsels me not to be an asshole was telling me now to shake his hand, which I did. I plowed into my pasta.

I took another long look at Krall and the two copies he was with. There was something sleazy about most feds. You could tell by the way the lapels puckered that they wore cheap suits, some of them left over from the golden age of polyester, and their feet were shod in shoes with soles that resembled snow tires. I could imagine the cuddly Berettas snuggled in the damp cups of their armpits. Half the feds ended up on the take from people they were investigating, and the other half wound up scrambling their brains because of the double lives they led. They never grew up beyond cops and robbers except that now they were playing with real guns and other people's lives. Funny, I've heard people say the same thing about reporters.

I scanned the dining room. It was filling with diamonds and beehive hairdos and overripe bosoms straining against too-tight gauze. The men came and went in twos and threes, loose at the collar and wearing half-pound diamond pinkies that sent out shards of refracted light, looking like overweight bouncers and bottle-weary bartenders. And the women who were lucky enough to be escorted had the indifferent look of, Christ, anything to pay the bills. It was the Block in miniature, a lifescape of flanks and shanks, eye bags and puffy faces that looked as if they had been shaped out of Silly Putty and accented with too much mascara and painted-on lips. A fog bank of smoke hung over the room at just above head-level, diffusing the cones of light shooting up the walls. Almost every Italian restaurant I'd ever been in had either a mural of a gondolier poling on the Grand Canal in Venice, or a fresco of the leaning tower of Pisa that was out of scale and tilted too much. Paisan's had both. For the refugees from the Block, the day was ending almost as it had begun—in dim light and thick smoke. All in all, not a bad nightfull. I decided I'd better get to Russo before Krall applied the rubber hose of justice. I went home and laid my head down to sleep the sleep of the innocent.

I get up every morning and eat my Shredded Wheat just like everybody else. That and orange juice. But first the important work of the morning. I dress to kill every day. I'm partial to blue and gray, conservative, you might say, but I add panache to the look with carefully chosen accents. My closet is as big as my bedroom. The suits hang two inches apart on double racks, the kaleidoscope of ties, yards and yards of silk, are hung on a rack with fastidious precision, and the shoes are arranged in pairs, each stuffed with cedar shoe trees. And the shirts are on hangers, grouped by colors. Some day I'll have to take inventory.

Now showered and shaved, I'd put out a dark gray worsted suit, bespoke by Huntsman on Saville Row, that I'd had made when I was assigned to London. I prefer English tailoring to the slouch cuts the Italians are peddling. With the suit I paired a white broadcloth shirt with a straight three-inch collar (no starch) and punctuated it with a burgundy club tie (woven, not printed). To add sass, I poked a white linen square into the breast pocket and completed the medley by slipping into black Allen Edmonds cap toe shoes over maroon polka dot knee-high socks. My idea of a Saturday afternoon of fun is poking around Paul Stuart's in New York.

I'd decided to let my fingers do the walking. On the way to the office, I took a detour to the Municipal Building across Lexington Street from City Hall. The first floor of the hollow granite block contained the property tax office, which was alive with citizens settling back taxes and overdue water bills. Since I'd worked the City Hall beat years ago, the entire system had been brought into the computer age. Back then, bills and records were stored in boxes at a municipal warehouse and were, for the most part, treated as trash. Now, anyone can come in and follow the simple instructions attached to the half dozen computer terminals on the long counter and punch up the records for any piece of property in the city. Which is what I was about to do. With the arrival of computers, a lucrative sideline developed for real estate entrepreneurs. They tracked like scavengers properties that were to be put up for auction unless taxes were settled by an assigned date. Tax sales had become a marketplace for mischief.

I slipped on my horn-rimmed half-eyes and the blurry screen came into focus. Tap, tap, tap and a few more taps, and I completed the task of booting up the three hundred block of East Baltimore Street. One by one, the properties scrolled by—300, the Gayety Club; 301, Pandora's Box; 302, Bermuda Triangle; 303, Two O'clock Club. And on, and on and on. At first, I noticed nothing unusual. All taxes were paid, the water bills, too. No outstanding violations, everything up to code. Then a pattern began to emerge. All bills were sent to the same address in the 400 Block of East Redwood Street, the financial district of Baltimore that was squeezed between the Harbor and Baltimore Street, half a block from the *City Press* building. I continued pulling up addresses from the guts of the municipal mainframe. The same was true of the 400 block of Baltimore Street—all bills were sent to the same owner, Investors Joint Venture. Holy shit, I thought. No wonder Sharkey's giving them a fit.

My next stop was the courthouse, a block up the street from the Municipal Building. As a young reporter, I'd learned my way through the "grantor" and "grantee" books in the land records division of the City of Baltimore, where all sales and purchases of real estate were recorded. I used to joke that, if all else failed, I could search titles for a living. It was headachy work.

The room resembled a library except that every book looked the same, was, in fact, the same. Addresses, prices, dates, buyers, sellers. One by one, I slid the heavy gray ledgers out of the metal racks and onto the nearby work tables. The ledgers told the history of Baltimore the way a Monopoly Board is kind of a guided tour of Atlantic City. Block by block, they showed cultural and social movements, and neighborhood-by-neighborhood they documented entire migrations. They showed the Jewish migrations from the east side of town to the west, with the German Jews always one step ahead and socially removed from the East European and Russian Jews. And as the Jews crossed town, they were replaced in the row houses around the buttery-domed Johns Hopkins Hospital by blacks. Later, many blacks abandoned the poorest side for better homes on the west side. For there are really three black Baltimore's—the young and the old, the rich and the poor, the east side and the west side. The line of demarcation is Charles Street, and the two worlds never meet. Little Italy was stable as were the old German neighborhoods of South Baltimore. Generations lived and died in the same houses.

The three hundred and four hundred blocks of East Baltimore Street were spread out over dozens of volumes. I sampled several. Investors Joint Venture began assembling properties in the late Forties and early Fifties when the war had made merchandise scarce and many of the actual stores went out of business and were converted into show bars. One by one, they were picked up at fire-sale prices and assembled into a formidable jigsaw of real estate, all rental properties, that covered two long blocks and several crossover properties in the center of a decaying city. Clothing stores, liquor stores, office buildings—some still with their frou-frou ornamental ironwork fronts on upper floors—had morphed into strip joints, adult video parlors, sex aid stores, a couple of hot dog and deli stands and the ever-present bail bond office to rescue drunks and troublemakers from a night in the tank. The Art Deco White Tower on the corner, with is hockey-puck hamburgers, had been designated an historic landmark, an amusing juxtaposition. Cultural anthropologists and social historians would some day examine the Block's ruins the way tourists and archeologists follow the winged phallus to poke around the lava-banked whore houses of Pompeii, only to discover that lust was no different in 79 A.D. than it is today.

I rarely get excited, but my heart was going pitter-patter. My notebook was filling up and the camcorder in my brain was recording impressions. I was just about ready for my first meeting with Mulligan. Buried deep in my Burberry, I almost tap-danced down the steps as I left the courthouse with only one more piece of string to gather before I had the real estate angle tied up. I worked my way down Calvert Street to Redwood and right, around the corner, to 415. The directory showed that Investors Joint Venture was located on the fourth floor. So, too, was the insurance agency of Joseph Frank, the impresario of Baltimore politics. Holy shit!

I sneaked into the *City Press* building on a back elevator to avoid Mulligan for now. I went directly to the library and spent two hours reading the molding brown clippings in a drawer labeled Joseph Frank. Status in a newspaper morgue is having a drawer all of your own. Many of the by-lines in the file were mine. As a young reporter, I'd covered Frank at the peak of his power. Now I was busy filling in the blanks of my years away.

CHAPTER 4

▼

Frank collected bright young Jewish lawyers the way some people collect stamps or baseball cards. And he got them elected to the City Council and the state legislature not only as a source of personal power and patronage, but also as a reminder of how far Jews had come in Maryland. One of his brightest was now governor. Frank had wrested political power from the Irish ward-heelers and muldoons, and was now a Jewish political boss in a state and city where Jews had been prohibited from holding public office until 1824. As a young man on the make, Frank had been a professional boxer. Now he was rich, gray, distinguished. His thick face was set on broad shoulders and dropped off to a bow tie that he wore as kind of an explanation point! It was said that Frank had once beat a man to death with his bare fists in a bootlegging incident. But if he had, newspaper files and police records of the event vanished years ago, presumably by the hand of one of his political factotums or a reporter his payroll. Frank now had everything but respectability.

Frank subscribed to the primal view that politics and economics make perfect bedfellows. The best marriages are made not in heaven but in political clubhouses. The rules of politics are the rules of the marketplace. You play the percentages. In elective politics, patronage is a system of rewards and punishments. Frank formed his insurance agency after helping his friend, Peter D'Anunizio, become mayor. He prospered on city insurance contracts. Frank was given control of the city health inspectors, while a friendly rival for political power had an iron grip on the liquor board. Together they bought a linen supply company whose tablecloths and napkins could be found in most restaurants and bars wishing to avoid being shut down for breeding roaches or serving watered whiskey.

Frank's favorite saying was, "democracy in action." And to Frank, democracy in action didn't come cheap.

Frank's home base was his powerful political organization, the New Deal Democratic Club, whose army of bosslets and precinct workers populated the city as well as many of its government agencies. The club met on the first Monday of every month, and its annual victory ball was a political and social event that had taken on a life of its own. On election day, Frank could put thousands of workers on the street at $25 each. The so-called "walk-around money" was assembled in cash from the sale of jobs and from candidates eager to pay for a slot on Frank's many sample ballots. An assistant state's attorney's job during Frank's suzerainty carried a price tag of $5,000, and a spot on a palm card cost anywhere from $2,000 to $5,000, depending upon the district and the intensity of the competition. Another way of generating cash was to print duplicate sets of sequential tickets to fundraising events. When the fundraising reached the desired level, Frank would pocket the additional money and report the duplicate tickets as unsold. The cash was stored in safe deposit boxes, away from the peering view of the IRS and any investigating auditors who resented Frank's political practices. On the Sunday before an election, Frank's ward captains and precinct leaders traveled from across the city to New Deal's headquarters to pick up the money that would be paid to his workers for their election day services. And on the return trip, half the money would mysteriously disappear in the very deep pockets of the leaders before any of it reached the b'hoys on the streets. Frank winked at the deception.

But in later years, the arrival of television and the access to decent jobs had greatly diminished Frank's influence, and with it his power. Men who were making $1,000 a week in the steel mills and auto assembly plants were not about to give up a day's pay to mope at the polls for $25. And government itself had helped to weaken political organizations by assuming the many dependencies the clubs had served in bad times. Political clubs were the welfare agencies of their days, when the currency of the times were buckets of coal and baskets of groceries.

It is an article of faith with me that an ignorant editor is a happy editor. Tell them nothing until the information is ready for print, and short of that tell them as little as possible. I was reluctant to brief Mulligan, but I had to account for my time.

"Whatcha got, kid?" Mulligan said from the phlegm bucket of his throat.

"Nothing much, yet," I said.

I deliberately tried to conceal my excitement over the real estate discovery, because Mulligan would want to rush into print before the puzzle was assembled. By itself, it was not such a great story. Working a story such as this is like eating an artichoke, peeling it apart leaf-by-leaf, layer-by-layer, until the prickly center is exposed.

"Found a lot of buildings that Joe Frank owns," I said. "Now I've got to find out what it means."

"Chrissake, kid. It means he owns a lotta buildings and collects a lotta rent," Mulligan said.

My faith in my judgment about editors was confirmed. Mulligan was basic. Crime was the primal scream. Give him a murder or a bank robbery and he'd cover it like a blanket. But the dynamics of politics and the nuances of government eluded him. All politicians are crooks, and that was that. It never occurred to Mulligan that not all crooks are politicians.

"You're wasting time, kid," Mulligan said. "Get to work on the crooks. Smoke 'em out, kid."

It had worked. I revealed as little information as possible. Mulligan asked for no more than he got. Which was unusual. He must have missed his bran muffin this morning.

Every morning at eight o'clock, Frank heaved his considerable hulk onto a chair at Bickford's cafeteria on Calvert Street, on Court Square, and waited for the crowd to gather for the thrill of being seen in the shadow of the great and the near great. One by one and two by two, lawyers, accountants, city council members, state legislators, ward captains, coat-tailers, has-beens and never-would-be's drifted in before heading to work, and soon several tables were jammed together and filled like a huge groaning board. Until his election as governor, Marshall Goodwin had been among the ritual visitors. It was an hour of good-natured banter and repeated old tales of political hi-jinks, nothing very heavy and surely no dark political mysteries. Frank knew what everyone else was thinking. No one knew what he was thinking. Frank had a mind like a computer designer: Everyone made a piece of the computer, but he was the only one who knew how all of the pieces fit together.

I stepped into Bickford's for the first time in fifteen years. Frank, as well as several of the old-timers, signaled recognition immediately. Frank made a grand fuss, gestured expansively as if he were an eagle about to take off, welcomed me to the banquet table of coffee and Danish, introduced me to the newcomers in his circle of loyal serfs.

"You're a big shot, now," Frank said. "Whatcha doing back here at square one?"

"I missed you," I said.

In a sense it was true. I enjoyed the high life, the perks and the status offered by Washington and the world at-large. But I was never happier as a reporter than when I was covering local politics. The White House, the Washington bureaucracy, were impenetrable, virtually uncoverable, a life of handouts, official statements, of artificial events and plastic people. City politics was real—colorful people, ethnic neighborhoods, local bars and political clubhouses where they drank beer from pitchers and ate Polish sausages and sauerkraut—the kind of places where, if you walked in and yelled "Bunky," twenty people would turn around to acknowledge the call. Baltimore was a whole city on catarrh. Hardly anyone spoke Harvard English, but instead it was a tongue almost devoid of vowels, as if the natives were trying to convert six diphthongs into a language.

"I'm flattered," Frank said. "For that, I'm buying you breakfast."

Frank was always ready to buy as well as to be bought.

I remembered years ago when frank was persistent about having lunch. I finally agreed. We entered the Emerson Hotel dining room, sat at a table for two next to a potted palm. I assumed the tree was equipped with a listening device. Near the end of lunch, over ice cream, Frank reached into his shirt pocket and pulled out a roll of $20 bills as thick as his fist.

"Buy yourself a couple of suits," Frank said. No doubt about it. He knew my weakness.

"Put it back in your pocket," I said.

"No strings attached," Frank said.

"If you don't put that back in your pocket, I'm going back to the office and I'm going to write a story saying that you tried to bribe a reporter," I said.

I hoped the potted palm was listening.

When, one-by-one, the crowd began drifting off to begin the day's work and the tables were nearly empty, I eased down several chairs, closer to Frank.

"I'm fascinated by your real estate holdings," I said. "Why those lice bins, and not a fancy office building or two."

Frank also owned the very building we were sitting in. Once, when Bickford's raised the price of coffee by a nickel, Frank ordered his real estate manager to raise Bickford's rent by $50 a month.

"It's my retirement portfolio," Frank said.

"The way Sharkey's moving the bulldozers in, there won't be anything left for your retirement," I said.

"I win either way," Frank said.

Now he had me.

"Sharkey's only going as far as I let him," Frank said. "I'll tell you a story some day if I ever have to."

"Don't leave me standing on my tip-toes," I said.

"We'll see," Frank said.

We left Bickford's together and headed in different directions.

Frank and Goodwin's lives had intersected when one was on the way up, the other on the way down. As a lawyer, Goodwin made a living representing the whores and pimps on the Block. His critics claimed that, as governor, Goodwin had learned his morals from his clients. Goodwin's uncle owned the Club Miami, and his cousin was the bail bondsman around the corner. In a more tight-assed time, the police swooped down on the Block and arrested all the strippers. Goodwin appeared in police court at midnight and argued that the state's obscenity law, as it had been applied in this case, was unconstitutional. The judge agreed and overturned the law.

I'd watched Goodwin's early career progress, but I was reporting from London when be became governor. Goodwin had since cut his ties to Frank, but honored the political separation only in the breach. He dealt indirectly with is old patron through a third-party arrangement of patronage and cash for political services rendered. Nothing had really changed except the appearance, which in politics is all that really counts.

I'd heard that gifts arrived at the governor's mansion like peppercorns on Michaelmas day. There were golf clubs and suits by the dozen, vintage wines to line the climate-controlled cellar that had been a gift from friends, whites and reds in bottles musty with age, and even a sauna that had been installed at the expense of some hapless chap seeking favor. Add to the boodle watches for the wrist and pocket, shirts by the box and ties by the dozen, whiskey by the case and books that went unread, cuff links that bespoke Marylandia, and turkeys and hams and crates of Rock Cornish Hens to fill pantry and freezer. The good life came occasionally by delivery truck or courier, but mostly in person.

Sollie Stein had confided that there was one habit Goodwin couldn't break. He loved to shoot crap.

CHAPTER 5

▼

I called Shelly and asked her to meet me at Paisan's. I'd met Shelly Klein when she worked in the White House press office while attending law school at night. A dangerous liaison, some might say, in fact did say, but one that nonetheless flourished on Air Force One and the press plane on those lonely weekend trips and long junkets abroad. We both understood conflicts of interest and observed a very thin line that separated our work. She'd wanted to get out of Washington and hunker down in a medium-sized law firm in a medium-sized city. When I was yanked back to Baltimore, Shelly asked if I wanted company. She'd never married, was fifteen years younger than I, and had Cindy Crawford legs that went all the way up to her shoulders.

I entered Paisan's on a whiff of competing aromas. Tony Russo was presiding over a bowl of chicken tortellini soup as if he were waving a baton in front of the Baltimore Symphony Orchestra. It was a genetic feature of most Italians that if their hands were tied behind if their backs they would be unable to talk. Russo parked at the same banquette every day, his gerbil eyes in command of the doorway, afraid to miss a customer coming or going. Russo was a gossip. By day, Paisan's was a different establishment, filled with judges, lawyers, businessmen and an occasional office or birthday party of giggly women in a side room.

"What's shakin', Tony, baby," I said.

"My dick," Russo said.

"With considerable effect on the Richter scale, I'm sure," I said.

"What the fuck ever that means," Russo said.

"It's a compliment," I said. "Anyway, I understand there's a big game once or twice a week up at Pandora's Box,"

"What I hear, too," Russo said.

"Anybody interesting come to play?" I said.

"Hear that, too." Russo said. "But I've never been there. Dice ain't my thing, as the court dockets will show."

Holy shit! Sollie Stein's got a finger on the governor, too. Stein had been one of a handful of businessmen who were encouraged, expected to pay occasional tribute to Goodwin for his intervention and protection whenever necessary. Usually they visited unexpectedly, so there were no records of phone calls or appointments, and they patiently waited their turn for a private visit. And in the sanctum of his office, they expressed their loyalty and friendship in cash, nothing so crass as white envelopes, but a simple wad of bills tightly bound by a rubber band. The unencoded cost of most visits was $5,000. Goodwin's dice money.

"The Nazi was here again the other night," Russo said. "The word's out he's fishing to connect the governor to the Block and put the whole fucking bunch out of business."

The sudden jerk in my stomach muscles said that Krall had gotten to Russo first.

The main dining room was nearly full, and Shelly had been seated, nursing a glass of white wine, on a banquette against the wall facing the room. The back of her head reflected in the mirror behind her. She resembled the face on the matchbook that said, "Draw me and win a free art lesson." She had great zoomers to boot. If I had to pick a word to describe Shelly, I'd choose ripe. She was wearing a suit of black wool crepe over a white silk blouse with a bow, a simple antique gold pin resting on the curve of her left boob. I leaned over and kissed her lightly on the lips, then sat down and signaled the waitress for an Absolut on the rocks.

"Having a good day," I said. "Things are beginning to come together. Joe Frank owns the whole damn Block. There's a demolition derby going on up there that he says he can stop anytime he wants to."

"From what you say, Frank's got something on everybody," Shelly said. "Does the file include Sharkey?"

"Frank implied as much," I said. "Told me he's got a secret he's keeping until he needs it."

"That could be a bluff to throw you off the scent," Shelly said. "If Sharkey controls the fate of the property, Frank's going to protect him, not hurt him."

"You're thinking like a lawyer," I said.

We'd been scanning the menu while talking. When the waitress returned, I ordered a fish stew of muscles, scallops and shrimp for Shelly along with a second white wine.

Me, I like messy food, tasty peasanty stuff that feels as if you've inhaled half the kitchen when you're finished. So with my second Absolut, I ordered *bruchetta* as an appetizer and *pasta e ceci*, the Italian equivalent of soul food.

"But what if Sharkey double crosses him," I said. "Remember, Sharkey's off the deep end with all this sanctified bullshit of his."

"Remember, you told me Frank's specialty is knowing how all of the pieces fit," Shelly said. "I'm going to follow the bouncing ball on this one."

The food arrived. I dipped a spoon into Shelly's fish stew. It was thick and rich, heady with olive oil and spices. My *bruchetta* was crunchy and tasty, and one among other reasons I always carry a pack of Altoids. And the *pasta e ceci* was a thick version, with chopped *fettuccini* and chick peas in a rich tomato sauce smoothed with cream. It was to die for, four stars in the food chain.

I paid the check. As we worked our way through the restaurant, I waved to Russo, cupped one hand to my ear and the other to my mouth, body language that said I would call him. He winked. Trouble was, Russo's phone was probably radioactive.

Outside, I walked Shelly to her car, a stone green Saab 900 turbo.

"I may need a lawyer tonight," I said. "My place?"

"I'll bring the Annotated Code of Maryland, all three volumes," Shelly said.

I headed for my Volvo 850 GLE and pointed it uptown.

To preserve the myth that independence strengthens relationships, Shelly bought a high-rise condo about eight blocks from my house. Aside from living together, it's supposed to be reassuring to know that if things turn sour you won't be out on your ass on the street. So we honored the convention by having separate digs, though each was stocked with the other's likes and needs and quick changes. We'd never discussed marriage. But everybody's into biological clocks these days, so I'm sure the time will arrive when I'll be called upon to make a serious choice. I have nothing against marriage. It's just not very high on my list of fun things to do.

CHAPTER 6

▼

I often wonder why I like being a reporter. At first, it was the writing, fresh out of college with a head crammed full of shit about writing great books and whom shall I model myself after, Hemmingway or Flaubert? Shall I write long sentences or short ones, or backwards should I run them the way they used to do in *Time* Magazine. Writing looks easy. Nothing to it. Just put one word after another and on your best days try to be all nouns and verbs. The greatest sentence ever written was only two words long: "Jesus wept." But after they give you enough weather stories to write, shovel enough garden club handouts your way, or you spend six months on rewrite building murder stories and taking dictation from police reporters on deadline, you wish you were back in college writing book reviews and essays on how I spent my summer and using big words you know you'll never see again except in the dictionary.

Or is it the flatulent self-importance of being in the vortex of world events? A newsroom is wired to the world. If a spy satellite spots a nail puncture in a tire on a Russian army truck in Siberia, you know about it first. It's nice to know that you know about it first, and that knowledge by itself causes many reporters to float on their own gases. Seeing your name in print two hundred fifty thousand times a day isn't bad for the glands, either.

Could it be the chase? The same curiosity that impelled Watson and Cricks into the laboratory? Or the same sense of adventure and wonderment that drove men and women to the moon and beyond? In the news universe, no two stories are the same, no two days are alike. Every day is a new direction. When you wake up in the morning you never know what you'll be doing or where you'll be going. Worse, you never know what the people you cover will be doing. Reporting is an antidote to boredom, therapy for the restless. Life is more about journeys than destinations.

It could be argued, too, that reporters are like policemen on the corner: Get caught and your name is in the paper. After all, names make the news. So is it the lofty soar-with-the-eagles mission of correcting wrongs, making the world a better place to live, ferreting out the wicked and the corrupt, being a social worker without portfolio and behaving like a general pain-in-the-ass? You bet. Some of that, too.

The power of the press is no empty phrase. To many, it's raw power—the power to intimidate, threaten, cajole, to watch grown men wriggle and writhe, their eyes begging for mercy, knowing their asses are in a sling and a quarter of a million people will read about it the next day.

Journalism is not an adult profession. It is a trade in which it is possible to see how close to the surface the child in all of us is. Some reporters fancy themselves cynics. Others enjoy being viewed as just plain pricks. I suppose the sum total of every reporter is measured in pieces of all of the above.

Krall had been quiet lately, which meant his investigation, so far, had turned up little or nothing. Usually, when the feds are onto something, lawyers begin bragging about the clients they've signed up and leaks begin finding their way to newspapers and television stations. Mulligan had said nothing about phone calls or news tips. But, then, he might not, just to test me. The grand jury had been meeting for weeks, but no star witnesses, no great revelations, none of the serious breaches of grand jury secrecy that were usually committed by the prosecutors themselves. Russo's lips flapping the breeze, when they were not cooling hot soup, were the first hint I'd had that the great behemoth of the federal system of justice might be stirring in a way that heightens bladder activity among its likely targets.

Local cops do not like federal law enforcement officials if, for no other reason, than they are called law enforcement officials. Cops are cops, and that's that. They are arbiters of family feuds, referees in neighborhood rumbles, friends in time of need, ticket-giving, club-swinging apple-stealers. Federal law enforcement officials are college boys with degrees in criminology, accounting or law. Local cops do not appreciate the feds stepping into their territory so it appears as if local cops are not doing their jobs, which most of the time they are not.

My appointment with Captain Joseph Nelligan had been postponed twice, the first time because his ace undercover agent got snuffed by another of his narcotics agents in a colossal screw-up, and the second time because he was supposed to be out of town. Now I was being ushered into Nelligan's office, one of those glass boxes with slatted blinds to keep words in and eyes out.

Nelligan was a bully, a big man with a nose like a truffle snuffer, full of veins and craters, and hands the size of Smithfield hams. For a man of his age and station in life, Nelligan appeared very well haberdashed in good cloth, not your average work-a-day galoot who has to moonlight to pay the kids' doctor bills. The suit must have been custom tailored. The artillery in his armpit didn't reveal the telltale bulge that most cops wear like a third shoulder blade. He seemed too perfumed for what he was, out of context with himself. Cops should not exude the sweet smell of success in the same way that senior executives seem to say, Hey! Look at me. I've made it. Nelligan was tough because he came up the tough way, busting junkies in shooting galleries, chasing hoods in piss-stained alleys, losing his own identity to become a link in a drug chain, never knowing if he'd return to collect another pay check. Nelligan had achieved the rank of captain by doing what he does best—surviving. Nelligan waved me in.

"Been a long time," Nelligan said.

"Been a long time since I've covered a police story," I said.

"Fuck off, Dart. You're not covering a police story any more than I'm a delegate to a national political convention," Nelligan said.

"I'm covering you and Krall," I said. "That make's it kind of a police story."

"What the fuck's Krall got to do with me," Nelligan said.

Bulls eye, I thought. Let the games begin.

Nelligan ranted, raved, cursed, gestured, his index finger giving a mighty prod to an imaginary asshole named Krall.

"Krall's a fucking bootlicker who's kissed enough ass to pave the streets of East Baltimore," Nelligan said. "He's a law-book ninny who wouldn't know a bank robbery from a hopscotch match."

"This is my fucking town," Nelligan said. "If Krall wants to play sheriff of Mayberry, he'd better think twice. He messes with any of my people on or off the force, I'm gonna cut his balls off, sew 'em in his mouth and send him back to the Justice Department C.O.D."

"Just thought I'd mention it," I said.

Krall must be getting close to something—or someone.

As in the comics, a light bulb went off over one of my memory circuits. I recalled that Sollie Stein had mentioned that Nelligan had lust in his heart for one of the strippers on the Block, that she was his eyes and ears. Nelligan knew everything that went on five minutes after it happened.

Nelligan calmed down, probably regretting that out of habit he'd lost his cool in the presence of a reporter. He tried to recover by talking about the old days when one or two drug lords supplied the city and the hard stuff was confined mainly to black Zip Codes.

"Now the white shit's coming in by the boat load and the whole fucking city's sniffing nose candy," Nelligan said. "Makes the job tough."

I decided the timing was wrong to try and muscle Nelligan with hardball questions. Better to work the edges a little more and give Nelligan all the space he needed. My pyloric valve sent a synapse to my brain that said the penalty for pissing off Nelligan could be severe. I'd remembered stories about Nelligan planting drugs in cars of people who'd crossed him just so he could bust them.

I stood up, tested the dimple in my macclesfield tie, adjusted and buttoned my navy blue double-breasted jacket, shook the Smithfield ham that Nelligan extended and thanked him.

When I arrived home, Shelly had already let herself in, changed into a pair of jeans and one of my blue denim shirts. I planted a wet kiss on the back of her neck, a tender spot just below her left ear. She quivered and got goose-bumpy for a second. She'd stopped by Eddie's supermarket and picked up a prepared dinner—two large slices of vegetable lasagna and Caesar salad. From the wine rack in the kitchen I withdrew a bottle of Chianti Machiavelli. But first, decompression time. A couple of Absoluts for me, a white wine or two for Shelly.

We eased out onto the sun porch, glasses in hand, where Shelly had created a love nest of wicker and fern that resembled a California wine bar. Not exactly my taste, but a small concession to the interior designer hiding inside of Shelly. The Crayola sky to the west hung in the air like a gallery of painted kites. From my porch on the hill it was possible to sample Roland Park, a scramble of architecture that rejects the cookie cutter the way that baloney resists the grinder. No two blocks, no two houses were the same. They came in as many flavors as Baskin Robbins—red brick Georgian, yellow clapboard, aged brown shingle, white stucco, even Wedgwood blue aluminum siding. Roland Park is the oldest planned community in the country, dating back to the 1890's. It is controlled by an association with strict by-laws about what can be done to properties, and it receives a grant from the city to maintain its streets. Until the long arm of the law reached out and declared segregation off limits, Roland Park was as white as Wonder Bread, among the most haute Republican Zip Codes in America. I'd once declined to live in a building because the owner refused to rent to Jews.

"I met with Nelligan today," I said. "The guy makes my skin crawl."

"It's the part of you that has a built-in resistance to cops," Shelly said.

"More than that," I said. "The guy's been on the force twenty years, puts on this Irish macho tough-guy act for me, and I agree he's one tough mother, for no reason at all. He still hangs around the Block when he should be counting the days 'til gold watch time, and the word is he has the hots for a young hooker. Claims he runs the Block, keeps it straight and clean. Now I ask you, why is he so worried about Krall, unless he's going to get fingered?"

"Keep your eye on the hooker," Shelly said.

"In intend to, tomorrow night," I said.

"Keep it in your pocket, or you might get a sniffle," Shelly said.

We both laughed.

We finished our drinks, went back to the kitchen where Shelly popped the lasagna into the microwave. She divided the Caesar salad onto two plates, applied the croutons and dressing. I pulled cork on the Machiavelli and poured. If the person who came up with the idea of freshly prepared take-home food dinners ran for president, he (or she) would get my vote even though the Chinese were generations ahead.

Before we went to bed, Shelly and I took a shower together. I got the soap right where I wanted it and proceeded from there.

I bopped by the office late the next day to see and be seen, to check my mail and messages. The mail was slim, the usual assortment of news releases, notices of press conferences and invitations, all of which were urgent to somebody but not one that meant a damn thing to me.

The little red voice mail light on my phone was winking at me. I picked up the receiver and activated my messages. The first was from a candidate for political office who said he had some information for me. I wrote down the number along with a notation to return the call later. Next was my barber calling to say he had to cancel my appointment tomorrow. Shit. I get a haircut every two weeks whether I need one or not. Then came a reminder that I had an appointment with my dentist two days from now. The next message got my attention.

"Dart, this is a friendly warning. Fuck off or you're dead meat."

I didn't recognize the voice. I played it a couple times over and still no hint as to who the disembodied baritone belonged to. But that was part of the game, too, and I shouldn't have expected a calling card along with the threat.

Basically I'm a pacifist, not a coward, mind you, but someone who'd rather walk away than risk having his features rearranged. I've had my share of close calls, though, like the time a candidate for governor lunged at me, threatened to kick the shit out of me and run me out of the state. What made him even madder was that I stood there grinning and taking notes. He ordered his bodyguards to "get" me, but they thought better of it. I declined the protection the police and the longshoremen's union offered me. The next day, I wrote a story about the threat, and that was the end of his candidacy.

Another time I was sent to cover a meeting of Teamsters officials during an especially violent strike. They got a kick out of scaring the hell out of me, which didn't take much. And along the way, I politely declined *City Press's* invitation to cover the war in Viet Nam. There was, too, the threat from a black political boss that was delivered by a black reporter.

"Don't fuck with him," I was told. "He's a thug. He'll rub you out."

I never worried much about the politicians. They talked a lot, all bluster, but did very little. They were too concerned about their images and their own asses to think like street fighters or back alley punks. Sure, they could've called in a chit, given the assignment to a tough on the take, but they knew that if they fucked over a reporter they'd be taking on the whole newspaper fraternity. It's kind of like shooting a cop. The whole police force comes out. Besides, threats from politicians were mostly bluffs. They usually didn't care what you said about them as long as you spelled their names correctly.

The gauge on my adrenalin pump raced into overdrive. This call was a challenge, the test being whether to listen to the voice or to play dumb and plunge on. I decided the caller was trying to learn as much about me as I was curious to know about him. Understanding limits and knowing how far to go is part of what reporting is all about. I tossed a coin in my head and the play dumb side won.

I tap, tap, tapped on the word processor next to my desk, fed it my password and sucked up my message file. It said: "See me. Mulligan." I pointed my brown suede Ferragamos toward Mulligan's corner of the world, where he perched like a benign Buddha in a blue-gray haze of incense. The Camels were going full blast like an open-hearth smoke stack.

"Word's out your kneecaps are about to become an endangered species," Mulligan said.

"You must have gotten the same message I did," I said.

"Means you're onto something," Mulligan said.

"Not quite sure what I'm onto yet," I said, "but a lot of the wrong people are getting uneasy."

"Smoke 'em out, kid,' Mulligan said. "By the way, I'd like to see some copy soon."

"You'll get it as soon as I do," I said, saluting and cracking my put-on smile.

The twirling tits and wiggling asses were blinking their day-glo messages in the fading twilight along the Block. Outside of Pandora's Box was the usual assortment of maggots, a doorman in a studded leather jacket warming his hands around a Styrofoam cop of coffee, a couple of his pimply-faced pals with tattoos and a woman in a T-shirt with jugs as big as basketballs. They sprang to attention as I approached. "We got whatever ya want, buddy." Including the clap, I thought.

Inside Pandora's Box, the mood was blue lights on silver Spandex. The dancers now resembled aerobics instructors more than the elegant Lily St. Cyrs and Sally Rands of the past in their long sequined gowns and floor-length white boas. And the music was no longer supplied by a live trio of saxophone, piano and drums. More than likely it was Neil Diamond or James Taylor on tape. One thing had not changed through the years, though. On the Block the expression "Go fuck a flagpole" had a literal meaning. Every strip dance act ended with the performer in the raptures of mock orgasm while engaged in passionate union with a vertical pole, humping the giant phallic symbol in panting hydraulic motions with the insides of her thighs and the breadbasket of her loins. Being able to fake an orgasm was a critical condition of employment on the Block.

The long wooden bar was sticky to the touch and had the fenny smell of an overused wipe-up rag. Its surface was scarred with cigarette burns. The rows of bottles behind the bar stood like silent sentinels whose true colors seemed diluted by the introduction of water to their contents. Along the bar, a half dozen men, mostly middle-aged, sat with that I-just-messed-my-pants smile on their faces. They were being worked over by hostesses in peek-a-boo shorty nightgowns with their chocolate cherry nipples and Velcro bushes teasing through the gauze. And you could watch the practiced hands kneading stiff bulges in the men's pants.

I stood beside a bar stool, ordered a Heineken that I would drink from the bottle. I was immediately joined on the next bar stool by a hostess whose job it was to keep me company. For this pleasure she expected a large tip.

"You the law?" she said.

"No, I'm not." I said. "My name's Richard Dart, and I'm looking for Faye Madison."

"I'm Fern," she said. "Faye will be back soon. Meantime, will I do?"

The bartender overheard me asking for Faye and was now eyeing me with a look that said watch out. Soon, a barrel of a man in oversized polyester plaid waddled over and introduced himself as Broadway Brown. Broadway recognized the name from my by-line in the old days. Broadway wanted no trouble, spent fifteen minutes making happy talk, then offered me, with his compliments, the specialty of the house—Fern's cupid-bow lips wrapped around my throbbing Johnson.

I protested. But the same curiosity that killed the cat got the best of me, too.

Fern took me by the arm and led the way down a narrow flight of stairs. We were in a room with a single overhead bulb and a dirty rumpled sheet on a Sonny's Surplus cot.

Fern sat on the cot, her face six inches away from my erogenous zone, her tongue flicking matter-of-factly and fully prepared to fellate.

"Come on," Fern said. "Unzip."

"No thanks," I said. "Give me your phone number. I'll call you tomorrow."

"Broadway will get mad if I don't take care of you," Fern said.

"Just tell him I said I have a headache," I said.

Shame on Broadway. He'd tried the oldest trick in the hat to get blackmail material on me. But I'd gone along with Fern as kind of a guided tour to find out first hand the stories I'd heard about the Block's celebrated pleasures. When Fern and I emerged upstairs, Fern gently shook her head no, and Broadway's smile quickly folded into a troubled, oh, shit! Look.

Faye, as promised, had returned from her walk across the street to visit a girl friend in one of the neighboring meat lockers. Fern introduced me and moved on to the next promise of the evening, giving Faye the eye-sign that said heads up. On the Block, body language was an expensive way to talk. Faye was a soft, pretty blond, incredibly cool, kind of a Barbie Doll spun-honey look, almost as pretty as the girl in the Citizens for a Christian Baltimore television commercial. I could see through her gossamer gown that all of the parts fit just right. Faye looked as if she stepped right out of a wet dream. Nelligan's hard-on for Faye was understandable, but what, for crying out loud, was her attraction to him?

"You were asking for me," Faye said.

"I was," I said. "And seeing you makes me glad I did."

I thought of the old *Pal Joey* line, "Treat a lady like a whore, and a whore like a lady."

"That's nice to hear once in awhile," Faye said. "So what can I do for you?"

"Can I buy you a drink," I said.

"No thanks," she said to an offer that usually led to part of her night's take-home pay. Her receptors had picked up Fern's warning, and I could see that my moves were being shut down fast. I decided to head directly for the bottom line.

"Then you can tell me about Joe Nelligan," I said.

"I can tell you about Joe Nelligan in one word," Faye said. "Goodbye."

Close up, Faye was as cool as a burpless cucumber, calm and collected. Never quivered, moved a muscle. Her eyes were wide open and her pupils were set at full aperture. She never blinked. I'd bet my favorite cuff links that under the gauzy sleeve in the cup of her arm that was hooked on the bar to prop up her chin like the Thinker was a telltale pin cushion of needle tracks.

I was batting somewhere down the charts at about the same average as the bat-boy for the Baltimore Orioles. The only score I'd made tonight was what I didn't want to do, and that was to be permanently inscribed on Nelligan's shit list. As I pointed toward the door, I knew Faye would be heading for the phone as soon as I was out of view.

The bartender gave me his best fuck-you look and said, "You'd settled for the blow job you'd been better off."

Outside the air was clear and crisp and my lungs were grateful for the flushing after and hour of pumping second hand smoke. Two policemen strolled by, swinging their clubs, locally called "espantoons," and joking with the low-lifes clumped around the doorways. I wanted to call Shelly, but trying to find a phone booth on the Block that didn't smell like the inside of a urinal was like searching for a hymen in Pandora's Box. So I walked two blocks to *City Press* where my car was parked anyway.

"I'm still a virgin, but I may need delousing," I said when Shelly answered her phone. "I lost something else, though. I'm out of the neutral zone, probably fair game for Nelligan. Talked to Faye, but she wouldn't talk back. And sure as hell, Nelligan knows by now she had a visitor, if not from her from Broadway. I wonder if Turnbull & Asser makes bulletproof shirts. But probably the worst thing Nelligan can do right now is to try and rattle me. Better he lets me be his blood-hound and see what I come up with before he tries any rough stuff."

"What's Faye like," Shelly said.

"She's a class act," I said. "Out of place in the bar and with Nelligan. My guess is, she's flying on something and I'll bet you a tie to a tennis racquet that Nelligan's the source. It's the only way he could keep her hooked on him."

"No bet," Shelly said.

I told Shelly that I was tired and going to my house tonight, alone with a couple of drinks and the puzzle shifting around in my head, waiting for the male pieces to couple with their female mates. I liked the image.

CHAPTER 7

▼

Charles Sharkey's demolition derby was proceeding right on schedule. He announced that a new municipal office building would go up on the site of a parking garage across the street from City Hall. What he neglected to say, right up front, was that that the design of the building would also consume an adult bookstore and the fleabag office of a bail bondsman. I thumbed through my notebook. The garage and the two other buildings were owned by Joseph Frank.

I was beginning to understand why Frank said Sharkey could go only as far as he let him. Sharkey also conveniently neglected to reveal the financial arrangements for the purchase of the garage, saying only that the details were being worked out.

Almost coincidental with the announcement of the new building, the anti-Block commercials began airing on television as if one action was reinforcing the other. And the baroness of beer, a wealthy brewery heiress, Pauline Schmidt, continued her weekly Sunday night radio broadcasts assailing Frank as a corrupter of city politics and a whore master who enslaved young women in a life of sin in his many underground bordellos on the Block. Frank loved the attention. Frank responded to Mrs. Schmidt's screeds predictably every Monday morning with quotes from Shakespeare, assembled for him by one or more of his bright young lawyers. The attacks made Frank a figure larger than life, for if power is the appearance of power, such heightened mystique gave Frank a dimension that few political entrepreneurs ever achieved. At the peak of his power, Frank controlled a majority of votes on the City Council, enough to propel or block any piece of legislation at the snap of his bow tie. From his perch in the visitor's section, if he wanted a bill passed he signaled by rubbing his eye (yes), and to kill a bill he rubbed his nose (no). When the publishers of a major Baltimore newspaper wanted to build a new plant in a design that required the closing of a city street, they sought out Frank to arrange the votes for a zoning exception. The First Amendment blushed.

Sollie Stein arrived in Baltimore as the guest of the federal government upon invitation by subpoena *duces tecum* that was signed by Robert Krall and dated the first day of Passover, proving that God has sense of humor even if Krall didn't.

"Bastard's are starting," Stein said. "Party's beginning. I've been subpoenaed to testify before the grand jury. Don't know what the fuck they want with me. I'm old, sick, been outa town for years.

"What they want," I said, "is to scare the shit out of you so you'll sing interesting little ditties about your friends and former playmates."

"No fuckin' way," Stein said.

"Don't ever say that," I said. "In politics, never say never."

I wanted to see the subpoena. Stein said, "Trust me." Stein hadn't been wrong yet.

The phone call was informational. Stein knew the rules of the game and he hadn't said "off the record." I assumed I could use the snippet of information, but I would never reveal my source. It was time to meet with Mulligan again, this time with story in hand. I went to the deserted *City Press* newsroom at night, sat down at a computer terminal and began tapping out a lead paragraph.

> "A special federal grand jury has begun issuing subpoenas in what is believed to be an investigation of the Block in downtown Baltimore and related activities such as gambling, prostitution and narcotics.
>
> The subpoenas were signed by Robert Krall, head of the special Federal Strike Force on Organized Crime that is assigned to Baltimore, according to informed sources.
>
> Krall did not respond to repeated phone calls to comment on the nature or scope of the grand jury investigation, nor was it possible to confirm directly through is office that subpoenas has been issued for witnesses to begin appearing before the grand jury.
>
> However, it was confirmed by at least one person close to the investigation that subpoenas have been issued and the grand jury will begin hearing testimony within a week.
>
> The investigation is believed to center on Baltimore political power broker Joseph Frank and his one-time protégé, Governor Marshall Goodwin.
>
> There were also indications that federal prosecutors have met unofficially with other fringe figures who are not directly related to the investigation in their efforts to begin gathering information."

The story continued for twenty more paragraphs of background. I flashed the story to Mulligan's terminal with the words "URGENT AND CONFIDEN-TIAL" blazing across the top. My heart was ticking like a cheap alarm clock.

Early the next morning, the trembling phone shook loose the sleep that had gathered me up in watery layers of ambiotic innocence. I had been, as they say, dead to the world.

"Did I wake you up, kid? Sorry." It was the ratchet of Mulligan's voice coming up from the tar pit of cigarette toxins.

"Krall's onto your story, threatening you with a contempt citation if it runs" Mulligan said. "You sure of what you've got?"

"Yes, I'm sure of what I've got," I said. "How in the hell did he find out about it in the first place?"

"Computer virus," Mulligan said. "Computers are about as private as a public shit house. Somebody must have seen it and tipped him."

"Go with it, Buck. I'll be there in an hour," I said.

The paper hit the streets, the shit hit the fan.

"GRAND JURY PROBES BLOCK," the banner headline screamed. "Boss Frank, Gov. Goodwin believed targets," the subhead spelled out. It was vintage Mulligan.

On the sidewalk outside the courthouse the television trucks were gathering like the scene of a RecVan rodeo, their satellite poles shooting skyward ready to beam back to home base live shots of Krall. The steps were swarming with report-ers of every stripe—print, radio, TV. The television photographers had set up their tripods in a semicircle of three-legged Cyclops, and the still-shooters from the papers were slung to their Nikons like tourists waiting for the perfect shot before rushing to catch the bus.

I slid by unnoticed and worked my way down to peek into Bickford's. Frank was holding court as usual, surrounded by his loyal trenchermen, ready to stroke along with the sharks in time and tempo, as if nothing had happened and he was simply anticipating the coming of Thanksgiving or the first day of spring.

Frank seemed to see me through the plate glass window. He never flinched, only gave me a tight smile that I took to mean that he would deal with me at the right time.

I moved quickly down to the Block. The morning shift stood around in sin-gles and in clumps reading *City Press*, looking dazed and dumbfounded as if the sky had fallen and the cash register clinked for the last time and the years of peace and payoffs were all for nothing now that the feds, Charles Sharkey and a smart-ass reporter seemed to be working like ferrets to eradicate a way of life that kept people in food and shelter and off the welfare rolls. Even the cops were pissed.

The cobweb of wires and cables that connected telephone exchanges across the city was crackling with conversations among lawyers and clients—retainers, fees, subpoenas, Fifth Amendment, lapsed memory, Krall, motherfucker (used interchangeably with Krall), but most of all, what the fuck do they want with me? Shit happens.

It is the nature of grand jury investigations to, literally, scare the shit out of people, the innocent as well as the guilty, the piano player in the whorehouse as well as the whores themselves. And once in the sanctum of the grand jury room, there are no lawyers, no rules. Just a court reporter, two, maybe three prosecutors, who work the good-cop, bad-cop routine and twenty one of your peers who look the way you'd expect them to look. Bored. Bored silly. A life, a family, a career is in their hands, and for the most part they'd rather be home drinking beer and watching television. A prosecutor has rarely lost a case before a grand jury. The trick to appearing before a grand jury is to wriggle and writhe, slip and slide, work the room and find a friendly face then play to it. Most of all, look sincere, fake it if you have to. Shave the truth, dissemble, let the memory do the old dipsy-doodle, but never lie unless you're sure you're the only one who knows the answer. Perjury is the only crime you can commit before a grand jury. Knowing about a crime is not a crime. Lying about it is.

I arrived at *City Press* in time to learn that a second battalion of reporters had been dispatched to the State House in Annapolis, thirty-five miles away. Governor Goodwin had scheduled a news conference to respond to the suggestion that his name had been linked to the investigation of the Block. His advisers were stunned by the news, but on second thought shouldn't have been. Only the governor knew the truth. There had been rumors for months that Goodwin was on the Justice Department's hit list along with several other governors. Now he was about to face the music. And the truth.

I watched on the newsroom television set as Krall appeared before the thicket of electronic equipment on the courthouse steps.

"It is the policy of this office to neither confirm nor deny any activity by the Special Strike Force on Organized Crime, or any grand jury that might have been empaneled for whatever purpose. The story that appears in today's editions of the *City Press*, therefore, may or may not be true. But whatever the case may be, such journalism is the height of irresponsibility and a compromise of the secrecy of the grand jury process and of the system of justice in America under which a person is innocent until proven guilty."

Against a chorus of shouts, Krall refused to answer questions, spun around and was swallowed up by the huge brass doors of the courthouse.

Screw you, I thought, as I strutted toward Mulligan's office looking like a peacock but feeling like a lion. Krall could deny and denounce and scream like an angry gangbuster, but attention was exactly what he wanted. He was anxious for the word to get out so the guilty would begin feeling their blood pressure rise and their sphincters tighten. I almost wretched at the thought of doing Krall's work, but that was the nature of the business.

"Nice work, kid," Mulligan said.

"Thanks, Buck. I needed that," I said, bowing low and sweeping the air with an expansive gesture of my arm.

"Krall's screaming his ass off," Mulligan said. "Talking about subpoenaing you to find out your source, then turning around and trying to make a deal to work together."

"I've already turned down the offer to become one of his stoolies," I said.

"I know. That's why he's coming to me," Mulligan said.

An intern said the wire services were beginning to transmit the story of the governor's news conference. I excused myself, said I'd be right back.

True to everything I remembered and had heard about Goodwin, he was as slippery as an eel. He denied any connection to the investigation. He criticized prosecutors for being on a fishing expedition, and in the process besmirching the good names of public officials as well as of private citizens. Goodwin criticized the press for creating a witch hunt. He criticized everybody but himself. "Shocked and dismayed" was his favorite phrase whenever he was trapped.

"Have you received a letter advising you that you are under investigation?" Goodwin was asked.

"No, I have not," Goodwin answered.

"Have you been subpoenaed to testify before the grand jury?" Goodwin was asked.

"No, I have not," Goodwin answered.

"Will you testify if you are subpoenaed?" Goodwin was asked.

"It's been my policy since I've been governor not to respond to hypothetical questions," Goodwin answered.

And so on.

Persons who are under investigation are usually not subpoenaed because they will simply invoke the Fifth Amendment until they are wheezing for breath. Or, they might even demand immunity, in which case they can't be prosecuted. Prosecutors usually try to deal up, make an arrangement with a little fish to hook them a bigger fish. It is only at the later stage of an investigation that the objects of a prosecutor's affections are sent letters advising them that they are "targets" of an investigation. The paper chase takes weeks, sometimes months. Prosecutors assemble newspaper clippings. They obtain court orders to tap telephones. They interview friends, business associates, sales clerks, bartenders, restaurant owners and, finally, they subpoena the accountant and a bundle of tax returns. A net worth study reveals that income and lifestyle are out of synch, one is far beyond what the other would normally allow. Then comes the offer to sit down and chat, which is declined. Finally, the sum total of information is packaged as evidence and presented to the grand jury, which votes for indictment. Goodwin was off the hook for the moment.

Tony Russo, drumming a paradiddle on the table with a fork, feigned surprise to see me. It was impossible to slip by the sentinel of Paisan's.

"Got a lotta nerve, showing your face in broad daylight," Russo said.

"You're the only person I'd put my life on the line for," Tony baby.

Paisan's was a medley of sights and sounds—rattling plates, tinkling forks, popping corks and the roil of conversation that collided mid-air in the low-ceilinged room and ricocheted off the walls and kept coming at you like the chattering of an Uzi. If you want a quiet, private meal, go someplace else.

"You got *minestrone* for brains," Russo said. "One fucking day, one fucking story, you got the whole town pissed off at you. Frank, the governor, Krall, Nelligan, the whole fucking Block. They could give you a dose of AIDS they would."

I didn't laugh because I didn't think it was funny. Russo knew what was coming down, probably had a part in it, which is why I was here. That and to eat. Russo had a nose that could pick up airborne messages and an ear that could monitor more conversations at one time than a CIA satellite. These snippets he assembled into compartments of information that he dispensed from his station by the door at Paisan's.

"Tony, I need some help, some guidance," I said. "Just a couple crumbs of information."

"The fuck you come here for, so they can spot me," Russo said.

Russo had a point. He was so fixed to the spot on the banquette, impossible to miss, that anyone seeing him would see me. I had to take my best shot.

"Safest place you can be, right out in the open," I said. "Nobody'd ever believe we'd sit here like this and talk about high crimes and misdemeanors. Besides, everybody knows we're buddies from the old days and you like to bullshit. No notebook, no pen, off the record."

Russo squirmed, looked around the room and said: "Ask."

This I had to back into instead of getting directly to the point.

"What's Krall after?" I asked.

"After that shit you wrote today, you come here to ask me that," Russo said. "I thought you knew it all."

"Was I wrong?" I asked.

"Made interesting reading," Russo said. "You'll be in a lot of scrapbooks."

"So tell me then, what's Krall after?" I said.

"Sonofabitch is dumber than dog shit," Russo said. "Must have a law degree from the place in Florida that advertises on matchbooks that for twenty five dollars you can get a diploma. Wants to be a hero, but doesn't know how. Doesn't know a fucking thing about politics, who the players are, how they play."

"How do you know that?" I asked.

"Got an invitation, phone call, from a couple of his goons, probably the two look-alikes he's always in here with—they always work in pairs so they can lie for each other—wanna know if I'll sit down with them in a hotel room and discuss public corruption. Cute. They take you to a hotel room, make you feel like you're being protected, then the turn around and fuck you by leaking it to the press, worse, making you a witness. They say they want names, who's who, shit like that. Told them I appreciate the invitation but I'm busy. Said there are other ways, but they'd like to do it the easy way and would like my cooperation as a citizen. Told them nobody I know is corrupt, and even if they were it wouldn't be public. That pissed them off. Said they'd be in touch."

"Subpoenas are flying like snowflakes in December," I said. "You get one?"

"Nope," Russo said.

"Stick around the house," I said. "They always come by registered mail, return receipt requested. When the mailman can't find you, the marshals will."

Time to quit for now, take it a step at a time, don't push too hard, make the man nervous. I'd gotten more out of Russo than I expected. Krall will probably do even better. Russo's weak spot is that he likes to hear himself talk, show off how much he knows rather than appear that he's in the dark. I asked if I could buy him a drink. He declined, I thanked him and made my way into the main dining room.

My Absolut arrived as if by telekinesis. I said to hell with cholesterol, at least for the moment, and ordered risotto, a rich, creamy rendition with seafood. My taste buds were grateful for the treat.

Russo understood nothing about investigative techniques. Decoding what he said suggested that Goodwin's argument about Krall being on a fishing expedition was closer to the truth, for now, than even he believed. Having a list of names was one thing. Knowing how to connect them took more insider knowledge than painting by the numbers. But eventually, prosecutors could get their wits together, piece-by-piece, by laying out a theory and chasing it whether it's right or wrong. They had all the time in the world and the federal budget to spend on it.

Russo was to the prosecutors what clover is to hogs. That they fingered Russo was evidence enough that Krall and his gangbusters were starting at square one, hoping a slip of the lip would give them a tuna bigger than Russo. Russo floated on his own gases, the source of his own momentum, a small-time neighborhood gambler who talked about big league buddies. My guess was that Krall would offer to help Russo with his gambling problems in exchange for information on his playmates. You talk, you walk. That's what friends are for. If he were of no use, they'd throw him back in the water.

Back at *City Press*, the red eye on my voice mailbox was winking its urgent tremulo.

The voice in the box said to call Mr. Stein as soon as possible.

Sollie Stein sounded as nervous as a debutante at a Junior League tea. He'd learned the kind of information that could get a man in trouble. Governor Goodwin had asked a middleman to arrange a meeting with Joe Frank. It was a meeting that neither wanted but both needed.

"Had to tell somebody," Stein said. "Through the grapevine, waddya think. The two of them are hip deep in shit and they're not gonna talk? They got enough on each other to sing longer than the second act of *Aida* and they're not gonna talk?"

Nothing comes between good friends like good money. Goodwin and Frank had had a falling out over money. Not money that passed between them or that one owed the other, but money that Frank publicly claimed to have accepted in exchange for political support. It was hilarious, we agreed, a real fucking comedy of errors, almost as funny as Milton Berle and Bob Hope when they played the clubs on the Block.

A couple of governors ago, Frank had demanded a judgeship for a relative as the price for his backing. When the tailor did not arrive for a fitting of the robe, Frank felt betrayed, became annoyed. He was, after all, in the business of handshakes and understandings. Politics is an occupation that is built on winks and nods and one in which good politicians stay bought. So on a Sunday night around election time, Frank decided not to get mad but to get even. He summoned a few reporters to his headquarters suite in the Emerson Hotel and played a scratchy tape recording of voices that were supposed to be his and the governor's agreeing that $50,000 in cash had been passed to Frank. About the only words that were clearly discernable were "fifty" and "thousand." The rest of the conversation was muffled and fuzzy, as if faucets were running and toilets were flushing. To this day, questions linger about whose voices played the parts of giver and taker. But Frank's little morality play backfired. The tape was impounded by the state's attorney as criminal evidence, but only a few days later disappeared from his safe and eventually landed in the office of the Internal Revenue Service, courtesy of a rival political boss to whom the state's attorney owed allegiance. The IRS forced Frank to pay taxes on the $50,000. And Goodwin and several others broke from the Frank organization and joined the ranks of the governor. It was the beginning of Frank's decline and fall.

"Meeting's set for Eddie Pomeroy's Roadhouse, way out Pulaski Highway," Stein said. "Eight o'clock next Tuesday."

Holy shit! I thought. Holy shit! Stein's got to be out of his fucking mind telling me this, knowing what I do for a living. But I was never one to look a gift source in the mouth.

Stein explained that Eddie Pomeroy was a cousin who was thrilled by the high honor that his establishment was being paid and just couldn't keep his fat mouth shut. As if who's talking. The nappery in Pomeroy's roadhouse also bore the unmistakable black identification stamp of Frank's linen supply business.

On the second floor of Eddie Pomeroy's is a room that looks as if someone had thrown a hand grenade into a New Orleans whorehouse. It is a special room, hidden from the public, for special customers. Entry was up a separate flight of stairs, advance notice required. Only Eddie Pomeroy knew who was coming and when. The room is heavy with maroon velvet, dark wood and brass lamps. It is a room where the rich and powerful can meet in private, and on such occasions Eddie Pomeroy himself serves as bartender and waiter to protect the privacy of his customers. Eddie Pomeroy's Roadhouse got its name because of its location on a major highway heading north to New York. But it was more than a roadhouse. On the floor below was a first class restaurant that prospered on thick steaks and quality seafood, well worth the drive. Eddie Pomeroy had come a long way from the Block.

Between now and Tuesday, my sphincter would tighten and my bowels would loosen.

CHAPTER 8

▼

The election-day referendum on the Block was closing in on Baltimore like a menacing noose. Charles Sharkey torqued up the tension a few notches. The little-girl commercial was sending its tetchy message through thousands of television sets thirty times a day at a cost of one $1,000 to $3,000 a showing. Sharkey had sent a letter to all of his revival-meeting companions asking for money and support. And he was trying to mobilize the fundamentalist preachers in the area to use the power of their pulpits to overcome the opposition of the infidels. A copy of the letter arrived anonymously in my mail slot.

"There is a sinister force in our beloved city that is more evil than Satan himself," the letter said. "It is corrupting our political system and poisoning our youth in the name of Mamon. Christ drove the money changers from the temple and they have found refuge on the Block. They have powerful allies in high places. I need your help and all of the help you can rally to drive the anti-Christ out of Baltimore. There will be a candlelight rally at Memorial Stadium on Sunday, September 3. Please join me in this important mission in the name of everything that is decent and Christian."

One man's joy is another's psychiatrist's couch. Some people get their jollies wearing their morals on their sleeves, if there are such things as morals. These days the only absolute is vodka. Charles Sharkey was the kind of man who would take a Rorschach test and accuse the doctor of showing him dirty pictures. I slipped the letter into a drawer, convinced it was not a story as it stood by itself. If I can ambush Goodwin and Frank at their meeting, that's the story, and the Sharkey letter will be a "meanwhile," several paragraphs down.

I phoned Shelly and asked her to meet me at my house that evening, my turn to pick up dinner. At Eddie's, I bought a pound container of lump crabmeat, a couple of lemons and two beefsteak tomatoes. If I weren't up to the Z in Alzheimer's, my memory said there was a bottle of Freemark Abbey Chardonay in the wine rack, the perfect companion for the crabmeat. A sensible dinner after today's risotto. I put the wine in the freezer for a quick chill.

Shelly arrived in high dudgeon and low neckline that touched all bases like a grand slam homerun. She also had on that stern don't-mess-with-me look that she wears to the law firm's weekly partnership meetings. They must teach it in law school. She was as taut as a furled umbrella. The antidote to Shelly's heebie-jeebies, I'd learned, is a dip in a cool glass of wine and a change of clothes, not that I wanted her to trade the neckline for one of my shirts that hung on her like an oversized Mumu. Unless she wore it with no undergarments or slacks. Then a man's shirt on a woman's body becomes high fashion. That and no bullshit for about ten minutes while she let it all out, non-stop. I sucked on my Absolut while Shelly sipped her wine.

"Before you tell me anything," Shelly said, "a letter arrived in the office of a client, who'll remain nameless for the time being just to keep the story clean. He called to alert us and find out what the hell it's all about. First thing that came up at the partnership meeting was you and me. I pointed out that we're consenting adults, that we know the boundaries and limits. And I also reminded them, in case they'd forgotten, that the firm's job is to represent out client and not to play peeping Tom."

That slimebucket Krall, I thought. Wondering who in the hell the client is. I knew about most of them, but scanning my mental Rolodex offered no clues of a connection to the Block. A surge of hot acid shot up my esophagus. I was wondering if Krall knew about Shelly and me and was setting us up.

"This town gets smaller every day," I said. "What do you think happened to me today? First, I got a call from Sollie Stein saying the oddcouple, Joe Frank and Goodwin, are meeting next week. Then, I shifted down to visit Russo, and it turns out that Kralls's *gauleiters* are trying to con him into sitting down for a little polite conversation. Now this. So far, I'm on enough shit lists to paper the newsroom—Nelligan's, Frank's, Goodwin's, Krall's, Sharkey's and everybody who owns one of those fornicatoriums on the Block. And while we're compiling lists, let's not forget the threatening phone call that I'm not sure was a threat."

"What we are looking at here," Shelly said, "is a serious case of subpoena envy" A wicked grin crossed her face and I knew she was winding down.

"At some point Krall's got to go to the Justice Department and show that he's building a case," I said. "True, they've probably given him permission to do a little exploring, some forensic proctology, if you will. But sooner or later they're going to want to see some hard copy. Either that or I'm a naïf."

"The RICO anti-racketeering statute's very broad stuff," Shelly said. "It covers practically anything from parking tickets to grand larceny. Originally, it was aimed at people whose names end with vowels. Then it was broadened in interpretation and application to include corrupt public officials who defraud the public of honest government."

"Christ, I'm sure glad you went to law school," I said. "Honest government is probably an oxymoron, and most people would say corrupt public officials is, too. But are there any definitions, or parameters, or is it a case where if they think you're guilty you are and most times they can find something embarrassing, if not compelling?"

"That's about it," Shelly said. "It used to be that a person was guilty until proven innocent only in administrative law. Now it's the case with criminal law, too. They destroy a person with headlines and subpoenas."

The truth was, only Frank and Goodwin knew if they were guilty. And the truth would probably be bad enough.

I took the tub of crab meat from the refrigerator and distributed the moist lumps equally on two plates, garnishing them with four lemon wedges each. I washed the two beefsteak tomatoes and began surgery with a serrated knife. Shelly preferred hers in wedges, I liked mine in slices. On the compatibility charts not a very serious matter, but Freud no doubt would have discerned something *Oedipal* in my preference for round slices. To the tomatoes I applied salt and pepper, garlic powder, chopped basil and a sprinkling of olive oil. The trick to this salad was to sop up the juice with crusty bread, say *ciabatta*. The Chardonnay said how-do-you-do to the crabmeat in my mouth and the two got along just fine.

It was a hot-sheets night. Shelly and I slipped into bed. The only thing that was on was the red eye of the security system. Under the covers she was soft and smooth. Her inner thighs were concave, like a dancer's, and running my fingertips along them was like stroking the silk lining of a fine suit. We touched all of the pulse points. We nibbled at each other, our hands moving knowingly and purposefully in and around the important parts until she inserted me into the dampness of her loins. The vaginal wrench gripped me. ZIPPITY-DO-DAH! The white heat of my tool flashed into Shelly as she moaned her acceptance and ground her groin into mine to deepen her own spasm of pleasure.

Whoever said dreams are postcards from the subconscious had it almost right. My dreams arrive mostly uninvited. There's one that comes around frequently in which I'm either running or being chased. And another in which I'm searching for something I never find. Like the dream in which I spent all night looking for my car only to remember at about dawn that I'd hitched a ride to a party with someone else. Or another, when I was in a room full of documents searching for a piece of information I never found. One thing I like about my dreams is that they're never threatening, only tiring. I interpret them as being an extension of my day job, the hunt, the chase, the pursuit. I even work at night.

I wake up every morning with a smile just to get it over with, to paraphrase W. C. Fields, and that's kind of the way I look at politics. You learn to wink at it, view it as a comic opera, and if you don't you could end up with a serious headache.

Friday is get-away day. I zippered by my Barry Bricken slacks over Alan Flussser shirttails, blue end-on-end with white tab collar, added a red ancient madder tie and topped it off with a navy Ralph Lauren blazer. Traditional, but indispensable, a uniform that'll take you anywhere.

This Friday was also a troubling day. I like to avoid leaving fingerprints on a story or a source. Should I share my information about Frank and Goodwin with Mulligan? Mulligan's problem is that he'd begin talking about a big story coming up, want to send an army of photographers and blow the whole gig. On the other hand, I could go out there alone and play peek-a-boo and get my ass busted by a couple of gorillas, worse by Goodwin's state troopers. The two things I hate most are pain and poverty. The other choice is to go by myself, low-key, be a gentlemen and a scholar, and take my chances. I decided to give myself the weekend to think about strategy.

I don't like surprises. At *City Press*, Broadway Brown was waiting for me, unwilling to tell Mulligan why. His silence exposed me to certain interrogation, which violated the way I like to operate. I wish to hell Broadway had phoned instead. I took Broadway to a conference room down a hallway, out of sight, sat him down and poured two cups of coffee, black.

"Must be important," I said. "The middle of the morning is your sleep time, not the point on the clock for you to make social calls."

"Like to talk off the record, if I can," Broadway said.

Off the record was a phrase I didn't like to hear, but in certain instances, such as this one, I would put aside my high standards and professional objections in the interest of gathering information that might produce a good story. I agreed.

"Important's not the word," Broadway said. "It's my ass. Remember the picture they took, the one of me and Goodwin at the fundraiser? Found its way out of a courthouse safe and into the hands of a television reporter. Nobody knows how. He's been around, trying to talk. So far I've dodged him.

That fucking Krall again, I thought.

"Now Nellgian's all over my ass, saying I'm drawing too much heat. I oughta get out of town for awhile," Broadway said. "You know how reporters think. What the fuck should I do?"

I tried to appear cool and thoughtful at the same time I was attempting to conceal the look that said I was about to mess my pants out of sheer joy.

"What we have here, Broadway, is a case where a reporter is illegally in possession of state's evidence," I said. "Now, that's a crime. Sooner or later your reporter is going to realize that and he's going to panic. And what do you think he's going to do?"

So much of my life has been spent around lawyers that I can turn it on and sound like one at the drop of a codicil. God, I was good. Here was Broadway getting $250 an hour advice from a reporter who was playing Louis Nizer. Broadway wouldn't know the difference between a tort and a wart, just as most lawyers wouldn't know the difference between an *umlaut* and an omelet. But there is a kind of symmetry between journalism and the law, a natural progression that leads a lot of reporters to law school. I never went because I like what I do. Broadway must have been scared shitless for him to come and see me, probably more terrified of Nelligan than afraid of Krall. Krall could make life miserable, Nelligan could make it end. And doing what I do does not exactly endear me to people. Broadway must have decided I was the least threatening.

"Tell me, for Chrissake, what's he gonna do?" Broadway said.

"He's gonna to try and get it back in the safe, because he knows as long as he has it he's committing a crime," I said. "And as long as he can't get it back in the safe, the person who gave it to him is in trouble, too."

"So what do I do?" Broadway said.

It was playing out just as I'd hoped. Broadway took the hook.

"If I were you," I said, "I'd march right up to Krall's office with a lawyer and file a formal complaint, show him you know the scam that's coming down. Tell him you're going to file a petition with the court demanding that he 'show cause,' which is fancy law school language for 'explain,' how it got out of the courthouse in the first place. Then if it shows up back in the safe—Bingo!—you've got him by the balls and you're off the hook. If it doesn't, you still have him by the balls because he doesn't have the picture."

Carrying it off was an exercise in ballsmanship, and I wondered if Broadway had a pair of stones big enough to jiggle in Krall's face as well as the brains to do it.

The saying goes that opportunity rarely knocks twice. But here's a case where it not only did a paradiddle on my door, but it also performed inviting cartwheels before my disbelieving eyes. The older I get, the more I'm convinced that what goes around comes around. Now it was my turn. In the Jewish religion there's a series of *mitzvahs*—good works—and the most rewarding are those that are done anonymously, when the recipient doesn't know who's performing the deed. It's kind of like that in politics, too. The pleasure is doubled when the weasel in the trap doesn't know who set it. Fuckers anonymous. I was on a role. I decided to push from another direction, see how long my luck would hold out, even if giving advice bent the rules of the trade.

"Can't Nelligan help you?" I said. "He's got a tin badge just like Krall and probably knows a hell of a lot more."

"Nelligan's out of the question," Broadway said. "He's still pissed that Krall's nosing around in our business, he considers his territory. No messing with the feds right now, wants to wait 'til they fuck up then he'll come down on them if they so much as spit on the sidewalk."

"What's he afraid of?" I said. "He claims he runs the town and anybody who crosses him gets busted one way or another."

"Beats the shit out of me," Broadway said. "Personally, I like peace and quiet. Let Nelligan do it his way."

"What about Faye?" I said.

"Gotta go," Broadway said.

In journalism, as in life, you can't win them all.

"Go see Krall," I said. "Do what I suggested and let me know."

In the reporter's code of honor, off the record usually meant working the story from another source. Other than Broadway, there were two more prospects. The television reporter, and eventually Krall. In the long run, I'd probably have better luck fucking over Krall than hassling another reporter with all of that bullshit about protecting his sources and honoring the First Amendment. Besides, he'd be shielded by a battalion of company lawyers filing motions to prevent publication of a story about the picture because he was guilty as hell of illegally possessing criminal evidence. For the last laugh, he'd get beat out of his own story. God, I love this job.

Shuffling through my mail, I found a long white envelope that looked as if it had been typed the way kidnappers address ransom notes. The typewriter was manual, the type ragged, uneven, kind of like manic Guttenberg. No return address, of course, and my name misspelled "Drat" instead of Dart, intentionally, I assumed. Inside was a large sheet of white paper with one line of type: "Since you such a ferret, check out Joe Frank's son."

I knew Joe Frank had a son, the "Dauphin," they called him, an amiable airhead who had to be pushed through law school but who did very little in the way of lawyering. If he was to inherit the Frank machine, the end of organization politics was clearly in sight. Milton Frank had neither the talent nor the disposition toward power and money in the way that his father was obsessed by both. Now just who in the hell was tossing me another marshmallow, leading or misleading me in the direction of a harmless playboy because of who his father happened to be? Often anonymous tips don't pan out, the handiwork of somebody who has a personal grudge, a disgruntled bureaucrat or political hack. But in this business, the rules of the road say you check everything, especially when the name is Frank.

Often the easiest way to find someone is to let him find you. It was nearing lunchtime and my body clock indicated that I was getting hungry. I phoned an acquaintance from the old days in the court clerk's office, Mickey Miller, a political fringe figure in the Frank organization, and got a quick rundown on Milton Frank. Nothing very exciting, all normal stuff—he liked fancy clothes, fancy women, fancy cars—except that he ate lunch every day at the Bay City Café at Fells Point. Whatever turns you on. Hunch playing was part of the job. I checked the photo file for an updated look at Milton Frank. I left *City Press*, pointed my internal compass east toward Fells Point on the harbor front, a newly gentrified area where baby boomers have rehabbed Eighteenth Century row houses that were once the homes of seafarers, condos are going up in abandoned tobacco warehouses and college kids come to frolic on Saturday nights in a joyous jumble of neighborhoods where winos sleep in doorways next to parked Jaguars, Benz's and turbocharged Saabs. Fells Point's narrow streets are cobblestone, its sidewalks are brick and the streetlights are antique and supposed to make sentimentalists break out into a chorus of "The Old Lamplighter." The aroma of baking bread from the H&S Bakery ovens suffused the neighborhood like urban perfume. Until the trendies discovered Fells Point, it was a run down ethnic neighborhood of Greeks and Poles. At Broadway market, the *pirogues* are homemade, and the sausage casings are stuffed before your very eyes. As Bismarck observed, never watch sausage or laws being made. I was familiar with one, not interested in the other. Down the block were a couple of Greek restaurants, the Acropolis featuring live music and gamey belly dancers. Jimmy's Restaurant was a local institution where judges and young lawyers ate inexpensive lunches shoulder-to-shoulder with the locals.

Bay City Café arrived in Fells Point only lately, after the tight-assed yuppies set up housekeeping in the new colony of townhouses and marinas that were rising up from the urban rubble. The café took its place in the lineup of hangouts along with the Waterfront Hotel, Bertha's, the Admiral Fell Inn and Pierpont's. The café was beginning to fill up, but even without a reservation I managed to get a very visible table that gave me a panoramic view of the entire room, especially the doorway. One of the first things I noticed was the Frank laundry mark on the table linen. To carry out the café's carefully cultivated frou-frou image, sounds that I discerned belonged to Vivaldi rounded off the rough edges of tinkling cutlery and the gathering hum of lunchtime chatter. The place was done up in mauve and pink, with napery to match, and every table had a bud vase with a fresh flower in it. It was as if the owner(s) had read a book on how to appear classy and current. Bay City Cafe was a pleasant cookie-cutter look-alike right out of Bon Appetite.

A waitress materialized. With a flourish of self-mockery, I ordered an iced tea, thinking it best to forgo my usual Absolut in the interest of decorum. Drinking and driving could not only be lethal. They could also be material for a set-up. Let a pissed-off politician see a reporter having a lunchtime drink, and all of a sudden the word spreads that he's an alcoholic. Or a clandestine cop on a private payroll can see that the offending reporter is stopped, told he can't walk a straight line and escorted to headquarters for an embarrassing night in the tank. And that was only a warning. Along with the iced tea, I ordered a cold seafood salad of crab, shrimp, muscles, scallops and squid.

My lunch and my prey arrived in my line of vision at about the same time. Holy shit! My adrenalin pump charged into high gear. Holy shit! Bottom fishing for information is usually its own reward, but rarely pays bonuses. Coiled on the right arm of Milton Frank, looking serene and business-like in one of those power suits women wear in boardrooms and lecture halls, her hair pulled together into a professorial poof on top, was Fern, the lady of the night whose lips had been ready to accept my Johnson only hours ago. That fucking Joe Frank, I thought. Once he tried to get the goods on me with a bribe, and now only recently he tried to bring me down with a blow job. And Broadway was doing his dirty work. Whoever wrote me the one-liner about Milton Frank knew where he was coming from, as the saying goes.

Milton Frank's eyes panned the room from behind tinted lenses. Finally, they locked in on mine. I smiled and gave him a chest-level wave; he responded with what I decoded to be a fuck-you sneer. Milton Frank had the furrowed look of a man who could laugh at almost anything but himself. He turned and guided Fern to a corner table without the help of a *maitre d'*, a gesture that I assumed meant the table was on reserve for him every day. He was obviously happy being bored by repetition.

I returned to my seafood salad with little appetite, but force-fed myself anyway. The sprinkling of capers and diced garlic gave the dish its earthy zest. I checked my right trouser pocket to make certain I had a tin of Altoids. I didn't want to offend Milton Frank and Fern with dragon breath. I ordered a coffee, high test, to wash down lunch, and along with it asked for the check. Both arrived and the account was settled with a credit card. Mulligan would eventually get the receipt, so I mentally thanked him for lunch.

Finished, I folded my napkin with the Joe Frank insignia facing up, turned on my sense of irony and headed in the direction of Milton Frank and Fern. It was easy to see that I was as welcome at lunch as a roach crawling up the wall.

I extended my hand.

"Richard Dart, Milt, how are you," I said.

His hand didn't move.

"You really don't give a shit how I am, so why ask," Milton Frank said.

He also had no intention of introducing me to Fern, so I introduced myself to observe how she would handle it.

"Milton knows you were in the club," Fern said, "so don't try to fake it."

"Mickey Miller called and said you were checking me out," Milton Frank said. "Maybe you can scare the hell out of politicians, but I'm a lawyer. You mess with me and you and that rag you work for are gonna be in court and I'm gonna end up owning you and the paper."

Milton Frank had the personality and the wit of a crash dummy. The point was, the tipster who wrote the note probably only wanted me to know that Milton and Fern were an item and the Frank connection to the Block went deeper than real estate. I strained to figure out what else I could learn from seeing these two taking their sex act public.

"You heard the latest lawyer joke?" I asked. "There's a guy trapped in an alley by a lawyer, a murderer and a mugger and he has only two bullets in his gun. What should he do?"

I paused. Milton Frank didn't blink.

"Shoot the lawyer twice," I said.

"You're not only a pain in the ass, you're a comedian, too," Milton Frank said.

"Well, it was certainly nice seeing you two," I said. "Nice being seen—and obscene."

"Stay out of my life," Milton Frank said.

Now that Milton Frank and I had been formally introduced, the story of the Block was becoming a family affair. He had an office on Calvert Street, in a tall building a few steps from Bickford's, around the corner from the Block, which was more than likely owned by Joe Frank, too. I'd have to check it out. But what the hell was he doing displaying Fern on his arm, other than the obvious. Now don't get me wrong. Fern was a good looker, a little chipped around the edges, maybe, but still attractive. And the way Milton Frank looked at her, you could tell that her birth control pills were working overtime. Besides, the way she turned out for lunch, Fern could have been selling health care plans or timeshares instead of herself. No one would know the difference unless they actually saw her in the club, kind of like the Mayflower Madame who led a double life. But here was Milton Frank, swapping bodily fluids with an anonymous list of night crawlers who could be carrying around all sorts of dangerous little bugs in their moist parts. The thought of it was like being thwacked on an erect body part with the blunt edge of a butter knife.

Reversing the question—what the hell was Fern's fixation with Milton Frank?—was equally amusing. I know when I'm out-haberdashed, but this was not one of those occasions. Milton Frank preferred shiny suits of gaudy hues, narrow ties and long shirt collars, an admixture of decades where nothing was in proportion. Lapels and ties should be approximately the same width, and the length of shirt collar points should correspond. His attempt to approximate the "mob" look assumed the appearance of a *pachuco* in a zoot suit. Was it money? Was it love? Surely it couldn't be lust, because Fern must have had all the offers she could handle. Even nymphomaniacs who own liquor stores need a rest once in awhile. But serial screwing isn't always enjoying it, and going through the motions doesn't always involve lust. Could be there's something to that. Maybe Milton, with his shiny suits and tinted glasses, turned her on. Maybe he's the lust in her life. Or maybe it was her way of feeling important or maybe needed, compensating by day for what she did at night. Perhaps Fern suffered an abused childhood. And I did not want to overlook the possibility that maybe, just maybe, Milton treated Fern with a great deal of tenderness, something that did not come with her job on the Block. I had the feeling that Joe Frank would not consider this a marriage that was made in heaven, or even at the local synagogue. These are the eternal verities that reporters ponder. That and the metaphysical question, why do people park on driveways and drive on parkways. Maybe some-day I'll give up reporting and take up forensic proctology.

CHAPTER 9

▼

In journalism, as in life, you cast your bread upon the waters and hope to get Oreos and Fig Newtons in return. The weekend was easing closer, but before I began to decompress I wanted to stop by *City Press* one more time. Preventive journalism, I called it. Technically, there are no weekends in the news business. News happens when it happens, not on reporters' schedules. And there are weekend newspapers that keep the presses rolling almost around the clock. Who's to stop a train wreck or a plane crash, or World War III, for that matter, because some dandy-assed reporter has scheduled a dinner party or has theater tickets?

And I've known a president or two who decided on the spur of the moment to take off for home late on a Friday afternoon—a favorite punishment of Lyndon Johnson's—sending two hundred fifty reporters and an equal number of wives into snits and fits. Worse was keeping a full press plane sitting on a runway until past midnight on a Sunday for the return trip to Washington, arrival at Andrews Air Force Base at 6 A.M., bused back to the white House without even time to shave and shower before starting work again at 8:30 A.M. I can recall attending the White House Correspondents' annual black tie dinner when, after Johnson's speech, his press secretary announced that the president would be leaving for his ranch in Texas in half an hour. None of the traveling press had so much as a toothbrush. We got off the press plane at 6 A.M. in Austin, looking like a flock of drunken penguins in our wrinkled tuxedoes. Only strong marriages survive the White House beat. World War II was declared on a Sunday night, and John F. Kennedy was gunned down on a Friday afternoon. Even the death of Christ is commemorated on a Friday. So what's sacred about weekends?

There is a certain point you reach in story chasing when there's nothing that can be done to alter its outcome except to sit back and watch it happen. I had the sinking feeling the minute I eased into my parking space alongside the *City Press* building that I should have gone home instead. In the newsroom, Mulligan was screaming for my head and the winking light on my voice mail was competing for my eye. I have always subscribed to the wisdom that, "whose bread I eat, whose wine I drink, his song I sing." I decided to deal with Mulligan first.

"Nice of you to stop by once in awhile, kid," Mulligan said.

"Nice of you to notice that I do," I said.

"Nobody likes a smart ass," Mulligan said. "Instead of wisecracking your way through another day, how about sitting down at your computer and writing me a story. Been a long time since our readers heard from you."

"Trust me, Buck, a couple more days and you'll have all the story you want," I said. "I've got roof." Roof is a catchword reporters employ to describe a story that'll blow the roof off.

"Chrissake, kid, you been screwing around for days and all I've seen is one story," Mulligan said. "This isn't a goddam ballet class. Get your ass moving."

I backed out of Mulligan's cubicle, feigning that I was gagging on the toxins of his second-hand smoke, which I was. What offended me more than tarring my own lungs was that every time I met with Mulligan I had to send the suit I was wearing to the cleaner to restore it to an environmentally acceptable condition.

Back at my desk, I signaled my phone that I would accept the messages in its computer chip memory. The first was from Shelly, saying that she'd take care of dinner and meet me at my house. Another was a wrong number. Another was a computerized telemarketing service from a bank in Iowa offering me a pre-approved VISA card. And finally, the high pitched tremolo of Sollie Stein's voice, sounding as hollow as if he were talking through the Harbor Tunnel, or worse, on one of those $9.95 Taiwanese phones that have the sound quality of two tin cans on a length of waxed string. My pyloric valve began to flutter. I could taste the acid rising in my stomach.

I let my fingers do the walking and clicked off the seven digits of Stein's unlisted number, listening to the computerized blips of the touch-tone buttons play something that sounded vaguely like "my dog has fleas."

Stein answered after the second tremble.

"Sollie, baby, what's shaking," I said.

Stein went right to it, no small talk.

"Meeting's off," he said. "Eddie Pomeroy called, said the word came down it'll be a no show."

"You sure you've got it right?" I said.

"Couldn't be any more simple," Stein said. "Meeting's off."

Smart hunting dogs don't stop and ask for directions. I smelled a case of the old dipsy-doodle. This was a set-up. The question was, who's the bait and who's going to get caught in the switch. Stein was soon to be the guest of the grand jury. I was the bloodhound on the case. I was convinced the meeting was still set for Tuesday. If I show up, they'll have found their leak and Sollie Stein might just as well turn up his pacemaker and stand in front of a microwave oven. Death by microwave. I wondered if there'd ever been a documented case. If I don't show up, Mulligan will hand me my ass for not coming up with the story I promised him. What a way to spend a weekend, worrying about who's coming to dinner with Joe Frank.

"Sollie, while you're on the phone, you heard anything from Krall or his goons lately," I said.

"Got a call two days ago, some U.S. Marshall, told me to keep my calendar clear for a trip downtown on a day's notice," Stein said. "The guy who called said they'd been slowed down by some procedural bullshit."

"Stay in touch, Sollie," I said. "Let me know when you have your coming out party."

Procedural bullshit. That could be anything from instructing the grand jury or not yet receiving clearance from the Justice Department. What a minute! What if Broadway followed through on what I'd suggested? What if he'd gotten Krall so rattled that the rhythm of the investigation was disrupted, left Krall squirming so that he needed time to figure out how to slip through the noose? Holy shit! Maybe Tuesday won't be a blank page in my life after all. In the reporting game you make your luck.

I caught the next elevator down and sprinted from *City Press* up to the Block. My heart was ticking like a taximeter on a rainy day in Manhattan. I stopped to decelerate before stepping into the twilight zone of Broadway Brown's club. In the fading late afternoon, the thermonuclear light show of neon ladies bumping and winking their wares across the second stories of the Block's clubs gave passers-by day-glo complexions of pink, blue, cantaloupe and lime. In the doorways were the usual collection of society's square pegs, a stud muffin in a leather jacket, an overripe melon of a woman flicking her tongue across a half acre of lips and the same barker I'd heard before, "We got whatever ya want, buddy."

I took a deep breath and crossed the threshold into the miasma of Pandora's Box. There, in the blue-gray fog of smoke and dim lights, the hostesses were lounging over cigarettes and sodas. They'd not yet changed from their jeans and T-shirts shirts into their peek-a-boo work clothes for the evening. Faye and Fern were not among them. An occasional trilly laugh floated out of the tight little circle of sorority sisters. A lone drinker sat at the bar nursing a bottle of Budweiser while a pneumatic-looking hostess stroked his crotch and brought his gland to life. Somewhere in the dark a speaker pumped out Ella Fitzgerald's "Lady Be Good." I'd seen the bartender before, the pleated face that said go ahead and try, and hands the size of catcher's mitts to back up the look. The place smelled worse when it was empty than when it was full of people, the competing odors of smoke, musty wood, urine, disinfectant and perfume. I'd been in swamps that smelled better. None of the ladies made a move toward me. They probably knew who I was from my previous visit. Either that or they figured I was the crotch police.

Do I deal with the bartender or approach the ladies? Trying to do business with the ladies would be a waste of time. They'd get playful, cute but uninformative, probably start licking their lips, stroking their hands, standing Coke bottles in their crotches, doing deep-breathing exercises, the universal language that needs no interpreter. My guess is they'd probably been instructed to never say anything to anyone. The bartender's another matter. By now, Broadway probably knew I was here. The bartender more than likely hit a button somewhere under the bar that sent a pulse to a buzzer in an underground room that Broadway called an office. That stunt's in all the gambling and mob movies. Is this art imitating life or the other way around? Go figure.

There's no point in trying to reinvent the wheel when the wheel's lying right there in front of you. The buzzer did its trick and the person of Broadway Brown heaved his considerable hulk in bolts of plaid through a doorway that opened from the very same flight of stairs that Fern had led me down for some heavy slurping.

"Dart, good ta see ya," Broadway said. "How's my favorite reporter."

"Broadway, you ungrateful shit, I give you free legal advice and you don't even have the common courtesy to call me back as I asked. What the fuck gives?"

"Was gonna call, no shit," Broadway said. "What'll it be, coffee, tea or a slice of Vickie?"

"Thanks, but no thanks," I said. "I don't eat, drink or screw while I'm working. Tell me what's with Krall."

"This is off the record," Broadway said.

"Off the record doesn't mean a damn thing when other people know about it," I said. "Make it background. That means I don't use your name or attribute the story to anyone but sources." That neat bit of dissembling seemed to satisfy Broadway.

"Did like you said, called my lawyer, Arnie Schuster, and went up to see Krall," Broadway said. "Kept us waiting an hour, but when we finally went in and laid out our story, the sonabitch went crazy. Accused us of obstructing justice, impeding an investigation, tampering with the grand jury, you name it."

"What about he picture," I said.

"I asked, show me the picture and I'll get outa your face," Broadway said. "He refused. Schuster said we're going to court, and Krall said we couldn't do that because he's in charge of the investigation, not us. So Schuster gets to him real good when he said, keep your calendar open next week because you're gonna see what it's like on the other side of the table."

That explained why Sollie Stein was told to be ready for a grand jury appearance on a day's notice. Krall was now on hold and had to delay everyone else, including his own grand jury. And nothing aggravates a grand jury more than moping around all day in a stuffy hearing room, eating greasy carry out food supplied by a local deli on a meal allowance that a bureaucrat in Washington decided was adequate to feed twenty-one of his so-called peers.

"Broadway, baby, I'd like to know the minute a hearing is scheduled," I said. "No two ways about it. Until then, *ciao*."

I was anxious to see my squeeze. Shelly and I usually celebrated the weekend with a split of champagne on Friday just to say goodbye to the dippy crap we'd been through all week, hers the tangle of the law and demanding clients, mine dealing with the thousand and one assholes it takes to put together a story. I slouched the two blocks back to my parking space, relieved that I had a back-up story to cover my ass, slid into the Volvo and headed north to the greenswards of Roland Park.

The Jones Falls Expressway was the usual car strangled spanner, chock-full of Jags, Benzes, Hondas, Toyotas, Turbocharged Saabs, even an occasional American-made car, most of them these days with vanity license plates and phone antennas. I often wonder what conversations take place on those adult toys. Are they talking to girl friends and mistresses? Dictating letters to secretaries? Doing big deals the way they do in TV commercials? Calling weather or a local radio talk show? Or are they simply calling ahead to their wives to have a martini ready in fifteen minutes. It all looks very self-important.

The JFX is a moonscape of craters and pocks, a straight shot from downtown to the suburbs, twelve miles long at best. But the twelve miles can often take forty-five minutes to an hour, especially on Friday when everyone's rushing home to crawl into jeans, a cold drink and whatever else is handy. My exits, either Coldspring Lane or Northern Parkway, were intermediate ramps, no more than ten minutes from downtown, the beauty of Roland Park. Having no car phone, I flipped the radio from FM and music to AM and mayhem, from Bizet to bizarre.

"A prison inmate who won early release after convincing a judge of how much he missed his family beat his mother to death with a statue of the Blessed Mother just two days after being freed....Four men were gunned down on North Avenue in what police said was a drug-related shootout. Two men were killed, one was taken by helicopter to Shock Trauma in critical condition and the fourth is in serious but stable condition at University Hospital. Police are searching for a man carrying an automatic weapon who escaped on a motorcycle....A woman prison guard was shot in the head in broad daylight in front of her West Baltimore home after taking her grandchild to school. Police have no suspect or motive....This brings the total number of gun-related deaths to forty-nine so far this year, third highest in the nation after Detroit and the District of Columbia....Things go better with Coke....Funeral services were held for seven-year-old Randy Jarvis, who was sexually assaulted, stabbed several times and choked to death. Police have a suspect in custody who has a long record of sex-related crimes, including sodomizing a four-year-old girl....Televangelist Jim Bakker's appeal has paid off. A federal court has ruled that the judge who sentenced him to forty-five years in prison was prejudicial and has ordered a review of the sentence. The ruling said that if federal guidelines had been followed, Bakker should have received a sentence of no more than twelve years....Double your pleasure, double your fun, chew Wrigley's Doublemint gum...."

I'd reached my boring point. Crawling along the sluiceway at 15 MPH was not my idea of life in the fast lane. And if patience is a virtue, I'd probably be condemned to the slowest-moving traffic circle in hell. I veered off at Falls Road, up past the stern white Methodist church and the Burgee Funeral Home and across the street the SPCA headquarters with the grazing goat and next to it the large municipal recreational park, and hung a right at Thirty-sixth Street for maybe a longer but more picturesque detour through Hampden. Hampden is an old industrial section of Baltimore, a Lavern and Shirley kind of Palookaville, where row houses co-exist with ancient textile mills, hardware stores and auto repair shops. Hampden has its ups and downs, is built on hills and in valleys that curve and swell like a Tinker Toy horizon. The antique flagstone mill buildings follow the contours of the Jones Falls that used to carry dyes and other carcinogens to its emptying point in the Baltimore Harbor. Much of Hampden is under the JFX. Hampden is heavily working class, religious, patriotic and whiter than Wonder Bread, a mill town of migrants from West Virginia and Southern Pennsylvania. It is the home of skinheads and Methodists and, once, when a black family took up residence, a few bricks persuaded them to relocate before anyone could say blockbuster. There's a small storefront bar in every block, sometimes two or three, where they still serve boilermakers—dollar shots and nickel beers— and the Hampden VFW posts answers its phone, "The Foxhole." Hampden is strictly for the locals. Outsiders had better be there on legitimate business and get it over lickety-split. Hampden is also strictly by the rules, and there are two no-nos for outsiders who stray into Hampden: Never ogle a young woman, and never enter a local bar. The exceptions are the Café Hon, Mame's and McCabe's, where outsiders and celebrities from the three nearby television stations have limited amnesty, and the Rotunda shopping center, a reconstituted insurance office building where baby-boomers from downtown and local shoppers eye each other warily among the supermarket foodstuff and avoid each other in the downscale shops. Hampden folks come in two flavors, young and old. There appear to be no middle-agers. The young dress like punk rockers and hip-hoppers, and the old are double-knitters left over from the golden age of polyester, who dress as if they're appearing on "Bowling for Dollars."

Hampden's main drag is Thirty Sixth Street, a strip of storefronts, carry outs and eat-ins—the New Systems Bakery, a Rite Aid, a couple of bridal gown shops, an appliance store, a wall covering shop, and the durable Café Hon, a down home testimonial to gentrification. Most remarkable about Hampden is the number of craftsmen who hang out their hand-lettered signs—roofers, auto mechanics, painters, cobblers, television repairmen, scissors grinders, an army of handymen making their way doing society's dirty work. Hampden is Ku Klux Klan country, a white warren in the center of the city that is butted on three sides by black neighborhoods. The Hampden Democratic Club is a mainstay of city politics. Its members subscribed to the notion that white is right and vote that way in a city that's majority black.

Hampden is joined at the hip to Old Roland Park, rediscovered by upward bound stock brokers and bank junior vice president, the gateway to its uppity neighbor, Roland Park. I hooked a left off Thirty Sixth Street onto Roland Avenue, an architectural dazzle of mismatched houses painted in a palette of colors that resembled a Benjamin Moore display case. A few more blocks, a few more minutes, and I'd be home in my leafy grove surrendering to a weekend full of vim, vigor and vodka.

"....Now for a look at traffic, then the weather....A three-car pileup at the end of the JFX has traffic stalled all the way back to the downtown area. Police are on the scene, and tow trucks are ushering vehicles to the shoulder. A lot of rubber-necking going on. The road should be cleared in about fifteen minutes. The belt-way is clear both ways, but the outer loop on the west side is beginning to slow down at the usual trouble spot at the three bridges....Now, the weather. A high pressure system is bringing us mild temperatures and light breezes. The temp is sixty-eight, the wind at five miles an hour. The weekend looks great, with more of the same. Saturday, the highs could reach seventy, and Sunday not quite as warm with highs in the mid-sixties. By Monday, it'll begin clouding up, with showers by late afternoon....For minor aches and pains associated with arthritis, more doctors recommend...."

I felt kind of like the weather, stuck somewhere between a Bermuda High and a Mississippi Low. The story of the Block and its priapic past had more loose ends that a plate of linguini. Christ, what a comic-strip line-up, as funny as Dick Tracy and his gallery of misshapen mutants—there's Charles Sharkey, Joe Nelligan, Sollie Stein, Tony Russo, Joe Frank and don't forget Joe Frank's Beagle-browed son Milton, two hookers named Faye and Fern, Eddie Pomeroy, Broadway Brown, the governor and Dick Tracy himself, Robert Krall. The only discernable connection was the Block, each one of them feeding off the trough for his own peculiar need, strange bedfellows bouncing on the same sheets in a cosmic fuck-a-thon that, if televised, would raise more money than Jerry Lewis and all his kids with those horrible diseases. Or better still, put it on an X-rated pay channel in hotels, motels and inns and watch the occupancy rates shoot through the Dow Jones average. Hey! We've got rooms galore, three stars in the Mobile Travel Guide, a piano lounge, and an indoor swimming pool with a whirlpool for your aching traveler's ass. But most of all, we have virtual reality television that does everything but deep breathe and cuddle your cock for you. Let dirty channel television do its thing, then you do your thing, whatever's your pleasure. All for $4.95, charged to your room. Another $4.95 will get you an inflatable Faye or Fern, anatomically correct, your choice, and a tube of Vaseline, the next best thing to being there. And here I was, practically in the sack with them, trying to sort out the riff from the raff and assemble them into a snapshot of our town that I could present to Mulligan and the 250,000 loyal readers of his family newspaper. Somewhere out there there's an inkblot with my name on it.

I swung my two tons of Swedish sheet metal into the driveway behind Shelly's car, and in a single fluid twist popped the gearshift into park, cut the ignition and grabbed my briefcase. Up the steps and into the house, I headed for the kitchen where I found Shelly already dressed down, sculpted into jeans and one of my shirts knotted at the front. Shelly's kisses were moist, not the open-throated wet kind but full and moist with her lips parted just enough to let some tongue slide through and tickle her teeth. Out bodies were clamped together, saying I missed you, and all of the parts fit just right and seemed to stand up and say hello at once. I could do this 'til the cows come home.

But hello's being what they are, we unlocked our limbs and smiled as I spun to retrieve a bottle of *Proseco* from the refrigerator and get the weekend underway. I uncorked, poured, toasted the Block and asked what's for dinner. Shelly had picked up two cooked lobsters and Caesar salad, which married well with the *Proseco* and the bottle of Robert Talbot chardonnay that would lubricate dinner.

"Gotta hunch I'm about to have my ass handed to me," I said. "Do I follow through on a tip that I'm now told is off, or do I pretend it never happened. If I go ahead, Sollie Stein's liable to get tossed back into the water and I could get hurt. If I don't, I might blow a big one."

"You make it sound like a problem in metaphysics or nuclear engineering," Shelly said. "Like whether the cosmos began with a big bang or did it really matter if Einstein couldn't tie his own shoes."

"Maybe Shakespeare was right," I said. "Maybe they should shoot all the lawyers. Except the one I might need if I get messed up by Joe Frank's goons or Marshall Goodwin's Janissaries."

Shelly sparkled, standing with her back to the picture window, the sinking sun back-lighting her bottle-blond hair into a haloed frame of honeydew. If I had my Nikon handy, I'd take her picture. I kept telling myself that politicians don't mess with reporters. The last time a reporter was reduced to particles was years ago in Arizona when his ignition got itself wired to several sticks of dynamite by the mob's demolition crew. And only recently, a Spanish reporter in New York was diced into sushi for getting to close to the cocaine trail from Columbia. But that's on the home front. War's different.

"Maybe you should give up reporting and get into the adult world," Shelly said. "There's publishing. You could become a book editor. You could go back to school, get an MBA and become a takeover artist. How about political consultant or press secretary? While we're at it, where's the book you've been threatening to write for the past twenty years."

"I could do any of the above," I said. "But would you still respect me in the morning."

One thing I'd learned a long time ago is how do deal with a lobster. A lot of people attack the tail with hardware such as knives or scissors to try and remove the meat when it's really as simple as snap, crackle, pop. Tear off the flippers, insert your finger into the opening and push. Out slides the tail, meat intact. While Shelly distributed the Caesar salad, I separated appendages from lobster carcasses, uncased the tails and cracked claws, doing the dirty work before we ever sat down to eat. We'd already finished the *Proseco*, so I pulled cork on the chardonnay, a rich buttery wine that even the lobsters would enjoy, reward enough for the sacrifice they'd made so that we could feast.

"Maybe you're right," I said. "Maybe the child in me is too close to the surface and I ought to give up this kid's game, maybe teach, that's it, teach other kids how to stay kids by becoming reporters."

"And Shakespeare said they should shoot lawyers," Shelly said. "In his day, the last refuge of a scoundrel was patriotism. Today it's journalism. Screw up in public office and you no longer go to jail. You're rewarded with a political column, or a talk show. Better still, an analyst on television. Even get rich by writing books about the crimes you committed. Richard Nixon made more money writing books that he ever made as a lawyer or politician. Ronald Regan got to be president partly by writing a newspaper column. Haldeman, Erlichman, Colson, John Dean, Jeb Magruder, even Spiro Agnew, they proved that whoever said crime doesn't pay didn't know squat about politics or the American system. Even Henry Kissinger. He thinks he's still secretary of state with that syndicated newspaper column of his. Turn on a political convention or tune in the world and what do you get? Some washed up, tinhorn politician jerking his ego off. If they know so much about politics, how come they're not still in office. And they should shoot lawyers? Wash your mouth out."

Shelly was on a roll, unwinding.

"Lawyers are living proof that not all crooks are politicians," I said. "It's a fact of life that lawyers have to learn to live with. Everybody thinks all lawyers are crooks, except their own. Their own is okay. All the others are crooks. When you see a lawyer with his hands in his own pockets you know it must be pretty cold outside. In court, in divorce or whatever, there's always a winner and a loser. Every loser hates his lawyer. The winner hates the loser's lawyer for trying to screw him. The loser hates the winner's lawyer. Lawyers send bills based on time. And there's always the thought, how come it took so long? He could have done it in half the time. Lawyers are bloodsuckers, that's why they ought to shoot them."

The fun of it was that we both knew how to yank each other's chains, score points yet keep it light. If you can't do that and still laugh and be friends, end it.

In love as in life, it's important to know when to hobble and when to gobble. Shelly and I coiled in the middle of the big bed, queen-size, extra firm mattress for better bounce and fewer squeaks. Our tongues played mischievous games while our hands roamed among the mounds and curves under the tented cotton sheet, the north, the south and every stop along the skinny-dip trail. The smoothest part of Shelly's body, probably any woman's, for that matter, was her inner thigh, like the finest fabric, an infant's *tush*, an American Beauty rose petal, silky to the tactile test. The kneading accelerated along with low moans of heightened nighttime promise. Slowly, Shelly drew me into her holy of holies and we coupled like two spoons. Against the steady rocking and rolling, we smeared each other with moist kisses. Suddenly we both stiffened at the same instant, my body releasing its flash of heat into the dampness of Shelly's groove tube, squeezing out the last leak of pleasure. Wunderbar! The big O simultaneo!

"I love being in you," I said.

"I love your being in me," Shelly said.

After a few minutes of lying still in a huddle of spent cellulite and letting the pounding subside, I withdrew myself and we both headed for the bathroom and the Jacuzzi, where I'd already stashed two glasses and the remainder of the dinner wine. In the bubbly warmth of the tub we drank our wine and fondled each other as our bodies became heavy and ready for sleep. We dried each other with oversized towels, lingering to make certain the fun parts were good and dry. Back in bed, I heard clocks ticking in my head. Clocks ticking as in the weekend racing toward and end. Clocks ticking as in Tuesday closing in on me. Clocks ticking as in Broadway Brown's picture and the grand jury probe. Several time bombs ticking at once, old time spring-wound clocks by Westclock and Big Ben with radium dials and big bells with hammers for alarms. The ticking grew closer and more metronomic, and I knew I was sinking into the boozy haze of alcohol-induced sleep. My whole life ticked to the tock of somebody else's clock.

Morning arrived at 9:05 when a slat of sunlight caught my eye like a silver Thunderbird. I bounced out of bed and headed for the shower, but not before I peed and shaved. In the steamy shower I lathered up part by part. I thought of the soap commercial that claims its product is good for all two thousand body parts, even the gentle parts. After rub-a-dub-dubbing for five minutes, I rinsed, dried and stepped into a pair of boxer shorts.

By now, Shelly was awake. I sat down on her side of the bed and stroked her cheek.

"How'd you like to do something exciting today," I said.

"Which clothing store?" Shelly said.

I was becoming predictable, but that's part of living together. If two people can't read each other after all these years, then someone's not paying attention to the shorthand lessons. Love is being comfortable with someone.

"I was thinking Washington, Alan Flusser's new shop, then maybe dinner at Paul's."

"It's a good thing there's a bribe attached," Shelly said. "Dinner'll turn me on every time."

CHAPTER 10

▼

Along Connecticut Avenue, from Rhode Island to about Eighteenth Street, a fellow in search of decent threads can drop a swatch of serious money. There's the Polo Shop, Britches of Georgetown, Brooks Brothers, J. Press and now the Flusser shop up on Jefferson Street. A bit farther uptown is Alexander Julian's boutique. All of these stores are heavy with dark wood and leather and bright brass fittings in the look of those daunting British men's clubs or maybe Daddy Warbucks' proper library or maybe even a showcase tack room.

Flusser was one of my favorites, along with Ralph Lauren. While Lauren promoted the old money look of Newport and the elegance of Fred Astaire, and the better department stores traded on Armani and Hugo Boss, Flusser was an advocate of the Savile Row look of fine gentleman's tailoring. I'd learned early in life that the first principle of dressing well is knowing how you want to look. Flusser and Lauren, especially the Purple Label, were my heroes. Zegna and Kiton aren't exactly shabby, either.

Flusser himself is an admitted dandy. In the Flusser store there's an air of easy opulence, of highly polished wood and oriental carpeting beaten to just the right threadbare look of shabby gentility. His clothing comes in two flavors, readymade and bespoke. Flusser's readymade shirts are among the best, fine broadcloths in bold British stripes, spread, rounded or straight collars adaptable for wear with or without a collar pin. Anyone not willing to plunk down $150 or more for a readymade shirt should not be in Flusser's shop. Suits are another matter, starting at a minimum of $2,000 for custom tailored, known for their painstaking detail and thousands of hand stitches with real silk thread, not the plastic stuff that doesn't grip the fabric. Following the style of Savile Row, single-breasted suits are nipped at the waist and double vented. Flusser's suit trousers have no loops because he frowns on belts, but all are equipped with inside buttons for braces. Braces button, suspenders clip. The trousers, all pleated, have cuffs with tiny lead weights sewn in to assure the pant a proper drape.

I was in textile heaven, head-to-thread in bolts and swatches. First the shirts. I selected a blue, double-track-stripe broadcloth with French cuffs and spread collar. Next a cornflower blue voile, French cuffed. This was followed by a horizontal white pencil strip on blue end-on-end ground, again French cuffs, of course, and finally a blue mille-raie stripe, one spread and two with standard three-inch straight collars. If it's blue, I own it.

On to the suits. The tailor spent an hour-and-a-half taking my measurements, including such important details as where do I carry my wallet and what items, i.e., glasses, pen, etc., do I usually carry in my inside jacket pockets. And always the all-important question—on which side do I dress, to the east or to the west. He concluded that my right hip was one-quarter inch higher than my left, and that my right arm was one-quarter inch longer than my left. Of such anatomical discoveries is a bespoke suit made.

Now to the swatches. There were six-by-six inch squares of fabric, plain and fancy, stripes and plaids, checks and nailheads, barleycorns and tweeds, gabardines and seersuckers, fine woolens for blazers, and even cashmere corduroy. There were other woolens, too, in Tuscan ivory, olive and black, cashmeres in deep navy blue, lambs wool and soft camel, grays in tones of slate and coal, broad stripes, chalk stripes, pin stripes, browns the color of tobacco and autumn flowers, plaids in hues of putty, smoke and dusty green with touches of plum, big plaids, little plaids and plaids in between. The palette of fabrics boggled the eye. From the swatches I selected two, one a muted glen plaid with a teal windowpane pattern that could be dressed up or down, depending upon the environment or the occasion. Marry this with a solid shirt, the cornflower blue that I'd just bought, and a red and blue paisley tie, slip on a collar pin for a precise look and, watch out Doublemint twins. The second suit was a dark blue with alternating fine stripes of red and medium blue, an unusual look that caught my eye and would add a little contrast in my closet to the rows of dark blues and grays. Total tab: $4,550. What the hell, I did this only twice a year. I decided to quit before my eye wandered to the tie table.

While I was getting my jollies over the tactile quality of the fabrics, coddling, fondling, rubbing, the lush wooly squares, Shelly had returned from her own grand tour of Connecticut Avenue shops, toting a bag from Saks Jandel and a box from the Polo Shop. It was getting on to the suicide hour, too early to drink, too late to do anything else, but I figured it would take us a good half hour, at least, to work our way down Connecticut Avenue, stash the car and present ourselves at Paul's.

For Shelly and me this was a homecoming. When we worked at the White House, we ate here often. Paul's is in one of those fish bowl buildings on Connecticut Avenue, an escalator ride above street level, a large room of dark wood and brass railings, where male bonding is a high ceremony. The table linens are white and crisp, and the tables are arranged for maximum exposure, a vanity fair of who's who and who's not.

Paul greeted us with a flourish of hands and a gush of hyperbole about how good it was to see us, how well we looked and, Miss Shelly, you're more beautiful than ever. Paul looked like an overweight deli counter man, a corn husk of hair sprouting on each side of his head, which was as bald as an egg. Paul was a legend in Washington, the ultimate power broker, working the room, playing the tables like three dimensional chess, seating friends within chatting distance, placing enemies at opposite sides of the room banishing political fringe figures to the back of the room near the kitchen, out of view, reserving his showcase center table for the reigning political heavyweight. Paul also had a fondness for gambling and had once been busted at a poker table with a group of other dirty old men.

"Paul, you're just as full of bullshit as ever," I said."

"You should know, Dart, bullshit is what makes the world go 'round and pays the rent," Paul said.

Paul guided us to a table just off center stage, not a bad position for two people who hadn't been here for awhile, but, then, early Saturday evening isn't exactly power lunch time. When Paul seats you, you know you've been put in your place.

I ordered the usual, Absolut for me, a bottle of Flora Springs Sauvignon Blanc for Shelly, which I'd later help to polish off.

"Anymore suits, you're going to have to build an annex to the house," Shelly said.

"It'll thin out around tax deduction time, when the Goodwill truck comes around," I said.

We scanned our menus, searching more for inspiration than food. More often, I'd rather have a bowl of chili than one of those precious presentations of *nouvelle* cuisine, three pea pods and two carrot strips splayed around a splinter of fish swimming in a pool of mango salsa. But Paul made no pretense of running a health spa. He served real food for real appetites, huge portions, the best chicken matzo soup in the District. For people with bad stomachs and government-issue ulcers, Paul even had something called potted chicken. At Paul's, if you wanted steak you got a slab the size of Utah. If you wanted crab cakes, you got them by the pound. Shelly settled on the Rockfish, I chose crab cakes, both broiled, both with asparagus.

In the corners and crannies of power such as Paul's, the White House press room and the galleries of the House and Senate, mine was a fairly recognizable face. I'd even been on "Meet the Press" and "Face the Nation" a few times. Looking around the room, my eyes caught an occasional acknowledgement, a smile here, a wink there, sometimes even one of those chest-high truncated waves.

It had been a long day.

"Time to hit the pot," I said. "Make room for a second drink."

"I'll follow you and detour to the ladies room," Shelly said.

Having attended to business, we rejoined in the lobby where we were deliberately intercepted by Paul.

"None of my business, but some folks are very unhappy about the way you're poking around the Block," Paul said.

"How the hell do you know about that," I asked.

"Gambling's a tight little fraternity, the betting, the lay-offs, the bookies, the juice men, I know 'em all," Paul said.

At first, I didn't make the connection, then suddenly it hit me like a George Foreman punch. In the news business, as in life, what goes around comes around—more often than not with a vengeance. Paul was faking it by talking about gambling.

The world knew, and I knew, that Paul had had a very public romance with a celebrated stripper a third his age. And in working the circuit, she'd probably picked up word to avoid Baltimore because it was hot, hot, hot. She'd probably told Paul, who put two and two together—my unexplained reassignment to Baltimore and trouble on the Block under the by-line of Richard E. Dart. Besides, the story of the investigation had been picked up by television. With satellites, uplinks and downlinks, television now assumed one of the properties of God: It's everywhere at once.

"Got nothing to do with you, Paul," I said.

"Got something to do with some friends," Paul said.

"I'll remember that," I said.

At the table, our food was waiting under burnished domes that resembled hubcaps. I sipped my second Absolut as the waiter removed the hardware and poured wine for Shelly. Something else caught my eye. The ubiquitous logo of Joe Frank's laundry was stamped in a corner of the underside of the tablecloth. Holy shit! I held up the corner for Shelly to see. She puckered and gave one of those low whistles and arched her eyebrows in the universal language of disbelief.

"So much for anonymity in another town," I said.

"You're about as anonymous as the Washington Monument," Shelly said.

We ate silently. The crab cakes were luscious, huge, moist, no binder, broiled to golden glory. And Shelly affirmed that the Rockfish lived up to the star billing of those she'd had before on many occasions. No desert, thank you, just black coffee and the check. On the way out, Paul was not at his usual station, so another awkward encounter was avoided.

Close to 9 P.M., we approached the Russell Street gateway to Baltimore, the antic sculpture of red-and-black ironwork with the huge letters B-A-L-T-I-M-O-R-E stacked on their sides, end-on-end, pointing skyward, and the winking beacon on the guidepost cracking tower of the pyrolysis plant—a fancy environmentalist name for an incinerator—and the roadside flower bed with its park bench emblazoned with the booster slogan, "Welcome to Baltimore," to which some spray paint Michelangelo had appended the local term of endearment, "Hon," turning the line into kind of a civic lovesong, "Welcome to Baltimore Hon"—without the requisite coma. In the town by the crabflats that bills itself as the city that reads, the merry prankster with the aerosol can was long on soul but short on grammar.

At home again, I poured a brandy and removed my new shirts from their bag. I studied them again, pleased with my purchases, knowing they would get gentle care at T. C. Wing, in Old Roland Park, the last remaining Chinese hand-finished laundry in Baltimore. None of that acid lye detergent and mechanical folding for my shirts. The last time I had some shirts done at a commercial laundry, I refused to wear them until the Wings returned from vacation to redo them. The brandy was kicking in, warming my giblets. I hit the pillow sleeping. Shelly was already out. Shopping's hard work, if its done right.

Monday morning, seven o'clock. Time to wake up and smell the decaf. Shelly had already gone when the clock radio began barking the news at me. After performing my morning functions, I went to the closet to make my most important decision of the day. I chose a classic gray pin stripe, married it to a pink mini-check shirt with a tab collar and a black grenadine tie, four-in-hand knot, dimple centered and precise. To the breast pocket I added a pouf of windowpane-overlaid handkerchief that picked up the grounds of the shirt and tie. Rarely am I out haberdashed. If I lived in Dundalk and worked at Sparrow's Point, I wouldn't have to worry about crap like this.

I am sometimes in error, but never in doubt. I thought that if God didn't want me to win a Pulitzer Prize, why did he create the Block and assign me to preside over its decline and fall? I directed my feet to the sunny side of the street, headed straight for the office, lickety-split, feeling all verbs and nouns, full of riffs and obbligatos and syncopated rhythms and waterfalls of words ready to pour out of my bubble machine computer in pursuit of truth and justice. Those and the story that Mulligan was demanding. If I got the story I was after, it really wouldn't matter whether it was on the front page of *City Press* or on the back of a box of Fruit Loops. It would have dancing girls in the lead and lots of other good stuff up front, guaranteed to make several lives uncomfortable if not downright miserable.

At the office, the first order of business was coffee, black and strong like my heart, from the printers' room on the fourth floor where they had a half dozen pots going at twenty-five cents a cup, the profits intended for the union pension fund. Back at my desk a floor below the coffee pots, I thumbed through the weekend's accumulation of mail and other junk paper when it caught my eye. Another case of the hoo-ha's, another one of those anonymous number 10 envelopes with the ragged type, my name again deliberately misspelled D-R-A-T. Another single line of type on an 8x10 sheet of white paper: "Fuck off or you're dead meat." My correspondent may have a limited vocabulary, but whoever it was got right to the point. Another Maalox moment. I could feel the anxiety band tightening around my head. Again the conundrum: Was I being tested or should I take my mail seriously? Next time it might be a plastic bomb. On a story such as that of the Block, the threat could come from anywhere because everyone affected had something to lose, not the least among them me. Could be Frank. He'd done it before, murdered a guy with his oversized fists and beat the rap to boot. Frank had the most to lose. Could be Sharkey, the Jimmy Swaggert of the anti-Block movement. But when the story is parsed, I was actually helping Sharkey's cause. Maybe there's something I don't know, a Rosebud somewhere. Everybody has one. I'd already ruled out Broadway Brown, not his style. Broadway's clumsy, but in his own way forthright. The manner in which Broadway operates, he'd let me have it straight to my face, like a shot of redeye and a slab of raw beef. Nelligan's a possibility, a good one, too, because he regards the Block as his personal real estate and Faye as his number one bimbo. How about my good buddy Robert Krall. Wouldn't put it past the asshole, the feds and their disinformation bullshit and their undercover crap. Nope, Krall's high up on the list. I thought, what the hell, let's find out.

It was too early for Broadway to be at the bar, but I knew the name of the street where he lives. I let my fingers do the walking through the crisscross directory, came up with the address but the phone number was unlisted. I decided to call in a chit from an old friend at the telephone company, something naughty, maybe even unethical. But that's what friends are for. I explained. He protested. I squeezed. He resisted. I pushed. He choked and relented. Half an hour later I had the number. I dialed and accomplished what sounded as if I'd brought Broadway back from the dead. His ratchet of a voice would have made a death rattle sound like Laurence Olivier reading Shakespeare's Richard II.

"Dart, Broadway. Sorry about the wake-up call," I said.

"The shit, for me it's the middle of the night. How the hell'd you get my number, and what the fuck's so important a man can't sleep?" Broadway said.

"Any word from Krall yet?" I asked.

"Christ, it's Monday morning. Lawyer's don't work weekends, they play golf," Broadway said.

"If I don't hear back from you by the end of the day, I'm assuming he's stonewalling," I said.

"Assume what the fuck you want and lemme go back to sleep," Broadway said.

"See you in the funny papers," I said.

I punched in the password, entered my computer, slugged the story "pix" and began tap, tap, tapping my way into Mulligan's heart.

"A critical piece of evidence in the grand jury's investigation of the Block is missing from the special prosecutor's safe in the federal courthouse and is believed to be in the possession of a Baltimore television reporter, *City Press* has learned.

The evidence is an 8x10 photograph of Governor Marshall Goodwin and Broadway Brown that was taken at a $100-a-ticket fundraiser for Goodwin and displayed prominently in the Block bar Brown owns, according to sources familiar with the investigation.

The photograph was confiscated during a recent raid on several bars on the Block, including Pandora's Box that was conducted by members of the Federal Strike Force on Organized Crime under the direction of Special Prosecutor Robert Krall.

Krall had asked that the grand jury be impaneled to investigate possible connections between prominent political figures and organized crime. Among those linked to the Block are political boss Joseph Frank and his one-time protégé, Governor Goodwin. Frank is a major downtown property owner whose portfolio includes every building on the Block as well as other buildings in the business district.

The photograph is alleged to be in the possession of Art White, an investigative reporter with WACK-TV, according to informed sources. White is known to have been asking questions of law enforcement officials and other political figures about the photograph and Broadway Brown's connections to the governor.

At the same time, Krall has been unwilling to produce the picture of the two men, leading to speculation that it has actually been removed from Krall's office safe.

Meanwhile, legal dueling over the whereabouts of the photograph has slowed down the work of the grand jury and the appearance of prospective witnesses before the panel has been delayed indefinitely

Illegal possession of criminal evidence as well as tampering with evidence are crimes punishable by fines and/or imprisonment.

According to persons familiar with the disappearance of the photo, attorneys have threatened to obtain a court order demanding that Krall produce the picture as proof that it is still in his possession and locked away in his safe...."

Another dozen paragraphs of background and the piece was finished. I decided to delay sending the story to Mulligan's file until late in the day to limit the chance of exposure, leaks or tampering by in-house weasels. Krall would not be a very happy camper when the first edition hit the streets tomorrow. With a predictable political twitch, he'd threaten contempt citations, search for leaks in his office and within the grand jury, scream about the integrity of the grand jury process being violated, when, in fact, the disappearing evidence had nothing to do with the grand jury. Krall's a polecat. But as a reporter, I'm not supposed to think that way because such a seditious attitude will color my judgment. Worse, never talk that way. In case I'm ever sued for libel or slander, and the aggrieved party was able to find one person to whom I made such an observation, they could prove malice, the heart of any libel case. That's why I smile when I write. Smiling puts me in an ironic mood. Still, Krall's a polecat and a public figure to boot, so he'd have a hell of a time proving damages when he's his own worst enemy. He'd end up suing himself.

Writing not only brings out the WOW! in me, but it also heightens my appetite. Disappearing until later in the afternoon seemed like the best way to avoid Mulligan's bear-trap office. It was one of those bright honeysuckle days for which Baltimore is famous, so I decided to walk to Marconi's for lunch. Marconi's is a

Baltimore institution, a white row house on a dingy downtown Baltimore street, halfway between a former USO building and St. Alphonsus Roman Catholic Church. Its owner has a jewelry store across the street. One block away is Park Avenue, one of Baltimore's mean streets where blacks and Asians study each other warily and the site of the first racial demonstration in Baltimore in 1959, when black high school students picketed a Chinese restaurant.

Trouble was, I never got to Marconi's. Just because I'm paranoid doesn't mean somebody's not following me. But on my stroll down Calvert Street I was intercepted by the intimidating presence of Joseph Nelligan, who insisted that I have a sandwich with him at one of those little greasy spoons that look as if they specialize in salmonella or E-coli. It was an offer I'd have been a damned fool to refuse. Besides, I had the impression that nobody ever said "no" to Nelligan. We slid into a wooden booth that was tacky from dampness, murder on creases. I studied Nelligan's tented hands on the table. They could have been classified as deadly weapons. He had knuckles the size of golf balls. His nose was a purkey pink gristle-goo of blackheads and divots. I still regarded his station in life and his overall drape in expensive tailoring a curious juxtaposition that I would keep on file in the appropriate memory circuit. Without consulting a menu, I ordered tuna on toast and iced tea instead of the cold poached salmon I'd had my mouth set for at Marconi's. Nelligan the bad stuff, coffee and a ham and Swiss on rye, enough salt and preservatives to render him as embalmed as King Tut.

"You've been hassling Broadway Brown. I don't like surprises. What's coming down?" Nelligan said.

It was clear that this was no ordinary pop quiz.

"I never compromise a source," I said.

"Broadway's not your source, he's mine, all mine. When I say shit, he squats. When I say talk, he screams. And when I say quiet, he clams up," Nelligan said.

"Then ask Broadway what his problem is," I said.

I could see Nelligan's gorge rising like a rod of mercury in a thermometer. He had the flush-faced look of an angry man who was about to pop the blood pressure cuff, and the vein at his right temple began doing a rhythmic cha-cha-cha as his face tightened.

Nelligan said: "Dart, let me draw you a finger painting so there's no confusion. This is a nice town, a quiet town, and I like it that way. The Block's a treasure, part of the local culture, and in my book it deserves the same kind of protection as the Baltimore Museum of Art. And I aim to see that it gets it. So all of a sudden a tight-ass reporter, name of Dart, blows into town and begins causing a fuss. Between him and a law school suck-up named Krall, the shit starts flying and a lot of people are becoming very unhappy. Now that's where I come in. It's my job to preserve the peace and enforce law and order. So what's a guy like me supposed to do about a guy like you who's disturbing the peace?"

"Everybody has a job to do. You do yours and I'll do mine, and if there's a conflict it means we're both doing our jobs well," I said.

That was heroic talk and well-wrapped bullshit. Nelligan knew it, I knew it. The truth was, that beneath my splendid sartorial armor I was ready to mess my pants. There were as many ways as Heinz had varieties that Nelligan could put the screws to me, some of them very painful and disfiguring, others embarrassing and threatening to my job security. Pain was not very high on my tolerance list. Nor was wearing my scrotal sac up around my Adam's apple. I am not a very good liar.

Our food arrived just in time to deflect the conversation, or so I thought.

"Look, wise-ass, I don't handle backtalk very well and I don't handle people who don't cooperate very well, either, you really wanna know," Nelligan said.

I picked up half of my sandwich and bit off a manly chunk, hoping if not to delay the conversation to at least throw Nelligan off stride by altering the cadence of the interrogation. I couldn't very well tell him about the story of the picture when I hadn't even shown it to Mulligan yet. First thing Nelligan would try would be a deal with Mulligan and have the story killed. And Mulligan, being a former police reporter, was not above trading off a story for the promise of another, like a drug bust or a grizzly murder, the kind of crime beat lunacy that makes Mulligan's heart go pitter-patter. Besides, it's not ethical. I just wouldn't tell Nelligan as a matter of principle, mainly because I don't like cops. Especially this one. The Constitution says, "We, the people," not we, the cops.

"Tuna tastes oily. They don't use the good white stuff," I said.

Even though Nelligan was wolfing down his sandwich without missing a breath, he managed to talk around the dough-ball of rye in his mouth.

"I don't think I like you," Nelligan said.

Another day, another shit list. The tone and the measured cadence of Nelligan's statement conveyed an unmistakable peal of doom. In journalism, as in physics, equal forces of pressure applied against each other produce a center of force of exactly zero. Neither of us was getting anywhere, although I'd say Nelligan had made his point more convincingly than I had. We both finished our sandwiches in contrived silence. Nelligan ordered another coffee and a slice of apple pie with vanilla ice cream, the kind of lunch that comes with a side order of angioplasty. I'd like to see the results of this guy's next cholesterol test. Maybe clogged arteries will get him first.

I asked for the check. Nelligan protested. I insisted. The rules of the game are that reporters always pay when they're having lunch with sources. Even former sources, which is what I expect Nelligan was about to become. We fussed over the check, small as it was, one more time before I paid and we walked out into the bright honeydew afternoon, smelling like the grease in the deep-fry stove.

"Start looking over your shoulder," Nelligan said.

"Always do," I said.

I double-timed it back to *City Press*. After the roughing up I'd just gotten from Nelligan, I was in no mood for chicken shit from Mulligan. I went over my story of the missing picture one more time to smooth out any rough edges and zapped the copy to Mulligan's computer terminal with the word C-O-N-F-I-D-E-N-T-I-A-L spread across the top like an open invitation. Saying confidential to a computer is like posting the word "private" on a public toilet. We all played the game, though, knowing that confidentiality would be honored only in the breach. Before the story hit the streets, six editors and the layout person would see it, call attention to the piece, pass the word to everybody in cyberspace to punch up a story slugged "pix" and have a read. After half an hour, my computer screen fluttered the words "Come see me. Buck."

I slouched my way through the obstacle course of desks toward the glass box from which Mulligan presided over the newsroom. As I approached the door, Mulligan was torching up a cigarette, sending up curlicues of lazy smoke. Just my luck. Between Mulligan's smokestack and the grease at lunchtime, this suit was headed for the cleaner as soon as I could get if off my back. Too bad I can't dry clean my nasal passages.

"Nice story, kid, you sure of what you've got?" Mulligan said.

"Double sure. Checked it twice, just like the rules say," I said.

"Krall's gonna go apeshit when it hits," Mulligan said.

"We've been down that road before," I said.

"Anybody else out there know about this?" Mulligan said.

"Not up until a half hour ago when it left my computer. Christ knows what's happened or who's seen it since then," I said.

It's one of those newsroom clichés: You can tell a reporter by his source. I've often thought the opposite is true as well: You can tell a source by his reporter. Nobody knew it but me, but I was actually giving Broadway Brown a certain cachet. True, I'd nudged the plot line along a little, but only out of enlightened self-interest. Imagine. A bar owner doing the old ju-jitsu on the special prosecutor, halting a grand jury investigation and maybe even getting Krall reprimanded in court or even fired. Is this a great country or what?

Usually Mulligan behaves like a man with too much fiber in his diet. Today he was a pussycat, surprisingly calm and receptive—no questions, no doubts, no combustible comments. Most times he'd lob a zinger at me just to get a rise. He read the story again, tapped a couple of keys, and then sent it to computer heaven or wherever the stuff is stored and processed for publication.

Mulligan said: "Okay, kid, see you on page one. Get a good night's sleep. It might be your last one for a while."

Class dismissed. I went to the men's room, whizzed, washed my hands and face and called it quits for the day.

CHAPTER 11

▼

The clocks were ticking again, doing their sprung-rhythm dance of metronomic monotony inside my head while my heart thump, thump, thumped in a kind samba counterpoint against my rib cage. This would be the longest twenty-four hours of my life, a sleepless night of shucking and shamming with myself over whether to play peek-a-boo with Joe Frank and Marshall Goodwin and plant the kiss of death squarely on dear old Sollie Stein's pink cheeks. Stein, after all, has been a trusted friend and the best source I had. Signifying's worse than lying. I had to resolve this moral divide, the eternal tug between passion and reason.

Is a life worth a story? Hell, no. What did I really care if Frank and Goodwin were up to their hips in sheep dip, sucked up in the great vortex of the federal justice system. One lined his real estate portfolio with the gains from city insurance contracts and blackjacked restaurant linens; the other lived off handouts and second story crap games. Together, the two of them were like a symbiotic circus, antagonists on the record, but behind the peel-away layer as thick as the thieves they were in the interest of mutual survival.

Journalism is like politics: It gets you from here to there. And in one, as in the other, you make up the rules as you go along. As a reporter, I'd committed my share of tasteless deeds in the name of the public's right to know. I'd forced quotes out of grieving mothers whose children had just been barbecued in house fires. I'd hassled widows of policemen killed in drug deals gone sour. And once or twice, maybe more, I'd even misrepresented myself on the phone. All the while presenting a gloss of indifference and nonchalance on the outside, ready to puke on the inside, standing there as rigid as a robot, taking notes like a Kelly Girl steno. Reporters move in and out life people's lives without ever making a connection.

I tossed and turned, mashed the pillow, tried sleeping on my right side, left side, back and stomach, unable to block the demons and goblins that were invading my nightmares. On the other hand. On the other hand, if Frank and Goodwin were dipping their fingers into the public tambourine, shouldn't the parliament of voters be told about it and let them be the judge. After all, the public is a higher authority than Robert Krall, or Joe Nelligan, for that matter. One way or another, the truth, like pregnancy, will out, and the chips will scramble into an amazing Rorschach of patterns. In the scheme of things, Sollie Stein was really small potatoes—in Yiddish, a *schlepper*, to keep the metaphor clean. Maybe, just maybe, I was overstating the case. Sollie Stein should have been named Macbeth. He was killing my sleep.

Morning on the Block is simply a time of recycling yesterday, a seamless place where today is tomorrow as well as the day before. Change on the Block comes in the form of faces, not events. A stubble-faced man in Che Guevara fatigues, an unfiltered cigarette dangling from his sunken cheeks, hosed down the sidewalk in front of Pandora's Box, cutting off the stream frequently for pedestrian traffic, the sun glinting little oil-slick rainbows. A puffy-eyed mother-of-all-matrons, with skin the color of Velveeta, in a psychedelic muumuu and white beaded boots, leaned against the frame of Polack Johnny's sausage stand, teasing a Styrofoam cup of coffee with tiny sucking sips, suggesting that it was too hot to handle, which it probably was. Beer trucks, soda trucks, liquor trucks and other purveyors of goods and services were lined up curbside like a fleet of Red Cross vehicles delivering maintenance doses of the vital fluids that would get the Block through another night of surrogate sex.

By morning, the Block is an important pathway across downtown Baltimore. On good days, the young professionals toting their endangered-species brief cases walk to glass towers of offices from the newly gentrified neighborhoods of East Baltimore and Fells Point. Lawyers swagger with assigned self-importance across Baltimore Street to the several courthouses in the area as well as to the police headquarters holding tank to liberate clients with Budweiser headaches. And buses making the downtown loop spit their exhaust contaminants into the air we breathe, which makes the function much easier because it can actually be seen. An interesting turn of the screw these days is that the Block is noisier and livelier by day than it is by night.

The electricity of the airborne message told me that this morning would be like no other morning on the Block. On racks and stacks across the city, the first edition of *City Press* was hitting the streets, ready to jump-start the criminal justice system as well as the hand that turns on my goose bump switch.

Evidence Photo Missing
From Court House Safe

Krall Threatened,
Reporter Suspected

With his usual gusto and gritty flamboyance, Mulligan got the headline and the sub-head just right, telescoping the essence of the story into four simple lines, which is what a headline is supposed to do. That and sell papers.

I strolled a deliberate course on and around the Block, watching as walkers scooped up the papers. It's ironic, but in the world of instant communications, newspapers are often beaten on their own stories—picked up by the wire services, zapped by computers and satellite dishes to radio and television stations to be heard and seen before they're even on the streets. A case in point for why afternoon newspapers have all but vanished.

Broadway Brown was a sudden celebrity, having achieved, by my hand, his ephemeral slice of fame. A small clump of what I guessed to be reporters was gathering in front of his bar. The hose-man in the fatigues was having a playful time at crowd control, holding the invaders back with a fine spray of water. And the woman in the muumuu was conducting business as usual, with little success that I could discern. I thought, poor fucking Broadway's still dead to the world and has no idea what's in store for him. My conscience was clear. I'd warned him.

Reporters are mischief-makers at heart, and after a hard night's work I was ready to have some fun. I walked over to the growing cluster of reporters and staked a territorial claim on the perimeter of the circle. It was a full two minutes before anyone discovered me.

"Hey, look, it's the main man himself, all dressed up like a Brooks Brothers' cut-out," a voice said.

"Give us a fill," another voice said.

"Sorry, I don't talk to reporters," I said.

It's true. Reporters are the last ones to realize there's no law saying that people have to talk to reporters. Most times, they're better off if they don't, especially when a reporter says he wants to get your side of the story just to make it fair.

Talk and you're fucked for sure. So it's an article of faith with me that I never talk stories with other reporters.

"Tell us where Broadway is," a disembodied voice said.

"Christ, if I knew would I be here?" I said.

"You probably got him stashed somewhere," a voice said.

"Pretty big stash, try to hide a lump the size of him," I said.

"Need pictures," a photographer said.

"Ever hear of enterprise journalism? Try it sometime," I said.

"Hey, butthead, who's the stoolie?" a voice said.

"Gotta go, gang. See you in the funny papers," I said.

Catch-up journalism is no fun. It says you lost. There's nothing worse in the job than having to scramble for a new angle or rewrite somebody else's copy. And it's especially hard on television reporters because they need pictures to write the words to, which I've always thought was kind of ass-backwards. The first law of television is making the words match the pictures. As a result, a lot of important material gets left out because they don't have the right pictures to go with the facts.

I wish the weather were as predictable as Krall. When I arrived in the newsroom I could see that Mulligan's cubicle was smoky and overcrowded with bodies that didn't resemble the reporters I knew. Before I could evaporate, Mulligan saw me staring and with a grand overhead flourish waved forward in the manner of an executioner summoning his victim.

The gentlemen seated around Mulligan's desk were not exactly the building custodians. One was Krall, the other an attorney for WACK-TV. Krall's face, gray eyes and divot chin, was the original blank slate, an asset, I suppose, in his line of work as well as in poker or lying. James Greene, esquire, was tall and gray, smooth and distinguished, known around the city for his polished demeanor as well as his steel-trap mind, whatever that means.

"These gentlemen have a problem they'd like to discuss with you," Mulligan said.

"Be a pleasure," I said.

"Who was your source?" Krall said.

"You know I can't divulge that," I said.

"You've libeled my client and everyone of its reporters," Greene said.

"This can be resolved if Mr. Krall can produce the picture," I said.

"I can get a contempt citation," Krall said.

"There's a law in this state that says you can't force me to reveal a confidential source," I said.

"My station's concerned that you've destroyed its credibility as a news organization, and that's actionable," Greene said.

Blah, blah, blah, blah. This could go on forever. Trouble is, we've become such a litigious society that it's impossible to take a leak without a lawyer first checking the law books or conducting an environmental impact study. And Krall's a real piece of work, sitting here lying through his fucking teeth. The guy in the middle is Greene. He's got a point, but that's not my problem. Nobody trusts reporters anyway. Still, they're a notch above lawyers. Funny, sitting here listening to one news organization talking about suing another, while the real weasel wouldn't know how to deal with the truth if it jumped up and kicked him in the ass. I was about to commit an act of piracy.

I said: "Mr. Krall can clear this up by producing the picture, and when he does I'll be happy to write a retraction, which I'm sure Mr. Mulligan will be very unhappy about printing."

Krall's Adam's apple bobbed as he swallowed. I had him by the balls and he knew it, and I'd just put them in a vice and began tightening it ever so slowly. Greene, by his silence, seemed to be enjoying our tetchy little roundelay even though his presence was more to protect his employers at WACK-TV in the event of legal action than to assert any threat against *City Press.* I decoded his statement about libeling the entire staff of reporters as an attempt to cozen me into revealing the name of the reporter with the purloined picture. Nice try.

Mulligan's impatience worked effectively as either a shield or a sword. On this occasion, he lowered the cutting edge by standing and announcing an end to the meeting that had been as productive as a group therapy session with a good psychiatrist: Nothing very much happens, but it makes everybody feel better.

Krall's the only person I've ever imagined who could sit and strut at the same time. On his way out, Krall gave me that bad-ass, flat-faced look of his.

Krall said: "Next time we meet it'll be on my turf and my rules."

"You threatening me, 'cause if you are, I'm taking notes and I'll see you in the funny papers," I said.

"That was off the record," Krall said.

"You say off the record first, not to cover your ass after you've screwed up," I said.

Greene stepped between us.

"Gentlemen, let's lower our voices and our blood pressures. We all have some soul-searching to do."

The voice of reason often resembles a pennywhistle calling the children in from play. The socket in my mental circuitry that processes rational thought obliged me to hear it, heed it, while at the same time I sensed that Krall's receptors were picking up the same message. Krall clammed up, I backed off. End of discussion.

I was beginning to bump into myself. The same people, the same dog-chases-tail connections were propping the story up like bookends. Time to poke under another corner of the rug. As usual, the voice mail was twinkling like a red firefly. Before I dealt with the unknown, I remembered I hadn't seen Shelly for a couple of days and lunch at Paisan's would be a welcome reprieve from the clash of events and egos. She agreed, said she'd meet me there.

I instructed the voice mail to deliver my messages, which revealed the following intelligence: The voice of Joseph Nelligan allowing as how he did not like surprises or assholes who held out on him; The Alan Flusser shop with the news that my suits would be ready for a preliminary fitting one week from today; Broadway Brown complaining that I'd fucked him real good, please call; a reminder to attend *City Press's* annual seminar on its 401(k) investment plan; that strange gurgly voice again warning (final) that I would be carved up like hors d'oeuvres unless I backed off the Block; and an invitation from Charles Sharkey to meet with him at my convenience. Let the shithead wait a day or two.

Entering Paisan's, I was not denied the announcement of my arrival by the brass-band voice of Tony Russo, who was seated at his customary banquette conducting triage on the restaurant's patrons. Never has anyone owned so much as Russo to the interior designer who arranged the furniture in Paisan's

"Had any visitors lately?" I said.

"Krall's bozos still trying to get me in a hotel room for some small talk," Russo said.

"I'm listening," I said.

"Told 'em last time I volunteered I ended up in Korea," Russo said.

"What are you hearing on the streets?" I said.

"Mostly about you and your stories. You gotta be dumber than dog shit, messing with that crowd, 'cause you got everybody pissed off from the court house down to the cop on the beat," Russo said.

"Taking my chances," I said.

"Tell you what I did hear on the street. Heard some people gonna go right to the top at the Justice Department to try and stop Krall and his investigation. Word is they got something heavy on some people close to Krall they figure could be embarrassing if it got out. They're talking right now to the attorney general. Now, don't be stupid and ask the next question, 'cause I learned from you never to reveal my sources," Russo said.

Holy shit! The crossfire's getting thick and here I am without a flack jacket. Somebody's in trouble and getting desperate. What Russo's saying had to be a legal maneuver fashioned by one or more of the lawyers who had clients who were caught in the investigation's undertow. Going to the top is risky business, more of a delaying tactic than anything else, but it could also be a signal that somebody's guilty or willing to talk or both.

"Russo, you're a sapphire in the rough. Gotta go. Watch your ass and keep me posted," I said.

I stepped into the main dining room and scanned the horizon of heads for Shelly. She was seated at a table between four spaghetti eaters on one side, and a fried calamari and a bookmaker's salad, the menu's tribute to Russo's occupation, on the other. I kissed her on her left cheek and slid into my chair.

"Now that you've got everybody's attention, what are you going to do for the main event," Shelly said.

"That was the warm-up before Sinatra. Just getting started," I said.

"Thought you'd want to know, most of the lawyers in the firm are betting with you that the picture's not in the safe," Shelly said.

"Krall's a dork, clumsy enough to screw up his own investigation. The only value the picture has to a reporter is to force an interview with Goodwin so the public will make the connection between the governor and the Block. Big deal. Whoever doesn't know it now will know it soon," I said.

"There's a strategy in law that says, if you've got the facts, argue the facts. If you haven't got the facts, just argue. Strikes me that Krall hasn't got much and he's trying to build a case through the media," Shelly said.

Our waitress arrived, as if on cue, with a glass of white wine and an Absolut, even though I was planning to order iced tea. But, what the hell, a good story is always cause enough for a reward.

Shelly order the grilled veal *pallard*, and I decided on *tonnarelli frutti de mare*—homemade noodles with shrimp, scallops, mussels and calamari, sauced with white wine, tomatoes and garlic. The food of the gods.

"You're probably right. As soon as he gets the picture episode behind him and resumes the grand jury investigation, we'll get a daily dribble of leaks about who's being subpoenaed and who's saying what to the jurors," I said.

"Trial by leak," Shelly said.

"Another trick is to move the grand jury from its meeting room upstairs and out of sight down to a main court room which is in the full view of the press," I said.

"Then there's the trail of guilt they create by subpoena *duces tecum* when they begin calling for income tax returns, documents, whatever paper they can get their hands on. That's why *duces tecum* is called 'screw 'em and take 'em'," Shelly said.

The waitress looped our plates under our chins, Shelly's still sizzling, mine sending up vapors of garlicky steam guaranteed to unblock any clogged sinus passage or other orifice.

"During one grand jury investigation, Krall actually smuggled a key witness into the post office in a mail truck and up through the loading dock area to a freight elevator that took him to the court house section of the building," I said.

"All's fair in love and grand jury investigations," Shelly said.

"Another caper was, they met with a cooperative witness at a motel in the suburbs, one of the guys who helped do Agnew in, same as they want to do with Russo. Must go on all the time. Christ, I'd like to see the Justice Department's bill for hotels and motels. Probably look like the entire department's shacking up at lunch time," I said.

"They're all too tight-assed," Shelly said.

"Show a little respect for the truth police," I said.

"While it's fluttering through my mind, tonight's the big night, your moment of truth. What are you going to do?" Shelly said.

"I'll let you know when I decide," I said.

"Nobody likes a smart ass," Shelly said.

"*Moi?* You know I never make decisions until the last minute. No different in this case," I said.

Actually, I hadn't thought about the meeting for a while, and I wished Shelly hadn't brought it up. Now it'll be on my mind the rest of the day.

I ordered two coffees and the check, which I settled with plastic and would pass on to Mulligan. In journalism, an artful expense account is considered the highest form of creative writing. Shelly replaced the smudge of lipstick that was now imprinted on her coffee cup and we were ready to leave.

On the way out, Russo gave me a farewell shot.

"You didn't find her on the Block, did you?" Russo said.

"She's too expensive for the Block," I said.

The elbow in my ribs said cheap shot. Out on the sidewalk, I told Shelly I'd call her when I decided what to do about tonight. That was a playful little lie.

I was playing for time and I knew it. They don't conduct sensitivity sessions in newsrooms, so being a pain in the ass comes with the territory. My motto is Humphrey Bogart's zinger from *Deadline USA*: "Those are the presses, sweetheart, and there's nothing you can do about it." The real thrill of being a reporter is following a story wherever it goes. This story was no different.

Evening was lowering its shades. In the rearview mirror, the sun slid under the horizon like a giant ripe peach as I headed east on Pulaski Highway, over a bridge that, for some reason in Baltimore, is called a viaduct, old Route 40 on the map, part industrial, part commercial, part residential—all working class Baltimore where the men came home from the factories and plants and sat on white marble "stoops" in their undershirts and drank National Bohemian beer from quart bottles wrapped in paper bags. Route 40 was in the history books, though. It was the main road that United Nations diplomats traveled by car between New York and Washington before I-95 was built. During the early Sixties, every Saturday for several years, Third World diplomats formed motorcades and headed north on Route 40, demonstrating and kicking up a fuss along the way because white merchants refused to serve them food in their segregated restaurants in that primeval outpost known as East Baltimore. The clashes became especially nasty when local civil rights activists in search of headlines joined the diplomats.

But that was then and now is now. Tooling along at about 45 mph was all that a respectable car would tolerate on the moonscape of potholes and swollen seams of Route 40 without creating in the driver a fear of dropping his undercarriage as well as his giblets.

Now, under the protective coloration of darkness, I was within a chip shot of Eddie Pomeroy's Roadhouse. I eased up on the RPM's to an acceptable cruising speed so as not to miss eye-checking a single car. I rolled past the front of Eddie Pomeroy's and saw nothing that raised the appropriate hairs on the back of my neck. I executed an illegal U-turn and slipped by the roadhouse from the other side and still no fortune cookie. Shit. Now I was forced to check the parking lot in the rear of the restaurant where the same driveway was both entrance and exit with no other escape. I raised my eyes heavenward and invoked the benediction of the patron saint of reckless reporters and fools. I entered the driveway slowly, cautiously, as if I were driving over a bed of nails. I approached the lot and executed the necessary right turn into the first row of cars near the stairs that led to the private entrance. Moving at a petty-paced speed, I checked license plates and cars on both sides of the aisle, not a familiar tag or a limo in view. I turned left, then left again, into the second valley of cars, my eyes and neck working as if I were watching a tennis match at Wimbledon. Again, no fucking luck. Right turn, right again into the final canyon, working and perking, watching and waiting, sneaking and peeking, until finally my radar eyes picked up a clue that every reporter who ever covered a police beat recognizes: Three radio antennae and oversized tires on an unmarked government-issue four-door Ford. No wonder there wasn't a limo in sight. Goodwin might be traveling in an unmarked State Police car. The plain-clothes driver was behind the wheel reading a newspaper by the beam of an overhead light.

He looked up, I looked over. He sprang out of his car and appeared in front of mine. If I'd tried for a speedy get-away, he'd have been flatter than a tortilla in Tijuana. I wondered if this oversized *pistolero* was a one-man welcoming committee for every customer who entered Eddie Pomeroy's parking lot. Whatever, he certainly got my attention. We glowered at each other, acting like two Sumo wrestlers, circling and snarling, one waiting for the other to lunge. I rolled down the window, asked if there was a problem.

"No problem. We had reports about addicts ripping off expensive car radios and cell phones. Just a precaution," he said.

Bullshit. The man never showed a badge, never identified himself. Then suddenly it hit me like a kick in the groin with ski boots. This guy must be the advance man, sitting here, making sure the way was clear or, if necessary, using his police radio to warn away the second car, the one carrying its precious cargo, if there was trouble at the destination point. I'd be willing to bet my press card, which I didn't show either, that as soon as I pulled out he'd be on his two-way laying down some heavy police talk in numbers that translated into something like "stay in holding pattern, will advise." Common sense being the first rule of reporting, I decided to politely buzz off.

I smiled, he smiled, I rolled up the window, he stepped aside. I made a mental note of his car's license number. I squeezed the accelerator ever so gently and eased out of the parking pad, into the driveway and onto Route 40 where I parked beside a diner about a block down the road that gave me a wide-angle view of Eddie Pomeroy's Roadhouse and driveway. Stakeout journalism, it's called, playing the cops' own game, is about as exciting as watching paint dry.

It was now half past the magic hour of eight o'clock, and there was still no sign of Goodwin. The other problem was that I wouldn't know Joe Frank's car from a Harley Davidson. I was playing a hunch on something I'd learned while covering the White House, watching the Secret Service hundreds of times with their armies of advance men, walkie-talkies, scout cars and the rest of their code name mumbo-jumbo. After the shootings of the Kennedy Brothers, Martin Luther

King Jr. and George Wallace, some of that high-tech, one-on-one protection had to have found its way down the security chain to state capitals. A sandwich and a cup of coffee sounded like a terrific idea, but I was afraid to abandon my lookout post.

I have a low boring point, and I was rapidly reaching it. Another half hour went by when, suddenly, out of the distant shadows and into the white night of the overhead streetlights cruised a tan twin of the government-issue Ford on the parking lot. Same porcupine antennae, same heavy-duty, hug-the-road black wall tires. Only this copy had two men in the front seat. Holy shit! From this distance I couldn't be certain that the man in the passenger seat was Governor Milton Goodwin, but I'd bet my gambling limit of a nickel on it. Again, I took down the license number next to the one I'd recorded earlier. Holy shit! They were a single digit apart—ZXY 735 and ZXY 736. What are the mathematical probabilities of that ever happening except that in this case the two cars were probably assigned to the governor's motor pool even though both had alphabet soup for license numbers instead of the regular State Police tags.

It was time to stop playing a one-man gang and get the hell out of here. As hunch-playing goes, not a bad night. I had two choices. Either run the numbers through the Motor Vehicles Administration public relations office and let them forewarn the governor's office. Or, drive to Annapolis and check the parking lot at the governor's mansion. If my assumption was correct, by now the first cop had already told the second cop who told the governor that there'd been someone snooping around the parking lot who did not comport himself like an ordinary customer looking for a parking space.

At home, I pushed the play button on the answering machine and heard Shelly say: "If you weren't going to kiss me, why'd you keep me standing on my tip toes?" She knew where I'd gone.

I ate an apple, poured some brandy and headed to the shower for a thorough delousing. Undressing is less fun than dressing, no fun at all, come to think of it. There are no tough decisions on color or purpose, accessories or style points, no dandy peacock strutting in front of a full-length mirror, no unfolding of crisp linen, no washed and starched feeling—just hang it up or toss it in the hamper. But I'll get even in the morning. In the shower, the glow of the brandy on the inside and the heat of the steam on the outside enveloped me into a damp drowse, half asleep, half bluesy, in the thermal waters pulsating in a steady stream from my shower head, brought to me courtesy of the person who planned the waterworks for the City of Baltimore more than a hundred years ago.

In bed, with the television set on, I watched the eleven o'clock news: "There's grim news tonight for newborns in Baltimore....Eighteen in a thousand will not live to be a year old. That startling statistic is contained in a new nationwide report on infant mortality. Baltimore has the third highest number of infant deaths of any major city in the nation, following the District of Columbia and Detroit. The alarming increase is attributed to drug use and the high incidence of teenage pregnancy in the city....On the bright side tonight, Baltimore has been voted an All-America city, one of ten in the nation to receive the honor. It's the third time in the past twenty years that Baltimore has been designated an All-America city. The mayor will pick up the award at the White House next week....Crime stalks the streets like a menacing plague. Earlier this evening, a six-year-old girl was accidentally shot to death, the innocent victim of gunfire in a drug deal gone sour. Little Annie Sowell was playing on the sidewalk when a bullet from an automatic weapon ripped through her chest and slammed her into the brick wall of her West Baltimore row house home, leaving her dead next to her doorstep. Police have a suspect in custody....The weather after these messages...."

The miracle of modern electronics is that you can tune out the world without getting out of bed. Zap! Take that, and it's gone—no more murders, no more doomsday statistics, no more war, floods, famines, even better, no more weather reporters with their smarmy jokes or homilies about what to wear the next day. Television has so trivialized the news that it's desensitized us to hard times and bad breaks. Now the programmers even want to televise executions. The little girl with her lungs blown away is just another piece of celluloid. I tried to cheer down. I turned off the lamp, rolled over on my right side and slowly slid down about three levels of subconscienceness into the black hole of sleep. Happy trails.

Every little cock likes to think he has to crow to make the sun rise. Morning is my time of day, full of vinegar, creative juices charging, synapses sparking, my wardrobe waiting and cereal ready to go snap, crackle, pop in my face. The sights and sounds of morning are wake-up calls for the day, flushes, gushes, brushes, rushes, a Vanity Fair of stroking and ego-jerking aimed at a central point between woman's navel and knees.

From the closet I pulled an off-navy chalk stripe suit along with a regimental tie in alternating inch stripes of navy, burgundy and yellow. The shirt, a body of light blue and white stripes set off with white French cuffs and collar, showcased the jaunty look of navy and burgundy striped braces. Add to the medley burgundy polka dot over-the-calf socks, black cap toe shoes and a peek-a-boo of white pocket square with a burgundy border and—if, as Shakespeare said, clothes make the man, then I'm well-suited to be the person Willie had in mind.

I'd returned Charles Sharkey's phone call, and he said it'd be all right if I stopped by to see him on the way to *City Press*, had something he said I might be interested in. At City Hall, I entered Sharkey's chamber of horrors, where numbers are crunched and computers decide whether school kids get new textbooks and how many times a week trash will be picked up. Government is in the quality of life business, and one fucking guy with a dime-store degree in accounting sits here with the power to alter the way we live and how much tax we pay for the privilege of surviving on the cusp of urban disaster. Already they've cancelled the rat patrols and next to go are community recreation centers, dumping kids on the streets to play stickball in $100 gym shoes and do drug deals to pay for them. Occasionally it helps to make a reality check.

I was directed to the same chair that I sat in the last time I visited Sharkey, careful to lift the back of my suit jacket and straighten the creases of my pants as I lowered myself into sitting position. Looking around, nothing very much had changed, same stacks of print outs, same rows of law books, same flags. Sharkey looked as gaunt and cadaverous as ever, like he was a serious candidate for a toe tag. If I were Sharkey, I wouldn't by any green bananas.

"Nice day, nice of you to stop by," Sharkey said.

"Ditto to both, but you obviously didn't invite me here for a weather report," I said.

"True, I didn't. But I have something here that I think might make a nice story," Sharkey said.

"I'm all ears, eyes, too, if necessary," I said.

Sharkey said: "First, I'd like to thank you for the help you've been, for the stories you've written. You've helped the cause by showing the trail of corruption and illicit activity that leads from the gutter right to the top. If we can't trust the officials we elect and the people who help elect them, then we have a terrible mess on our hands, a mess that we must clean up by eliminating the sources of corruption…."

Often the mind can absorb only as much as the seat can endure. I couldn't believe my fucking ears, not so much what I was hearing as much as what he was saying. I wanted out of here, fast. Sharkey truly believed he was doing God's work. This tin-horn Elmer Gantry dragged me to his office for a lecture on the manners and morals of public officials, conveniently forgetting that he's one of them, treating me like a partner in the work of his polyester paradise, proving once again that God must love assholes because he surely made enough of them, not to piss HIM off, of course.

"Mr. Sharkey, no disrespect intended, but I'm not part of your package, not doing what I'm doing for the same reason you are. Now, you said you had something I might be interested in," I said.

Sharkey handed me three sheets of paper, stapled together, and said: "What you're holding is a list of twenty five developers who're interested in putting up office buildings where the Block now stands. That's valuable real estate that'll add millions of dollars to the tax base of the city. There's a great opportunity waiting out there. It's called progress."

Holy shit! I thought, the guy's not only leading the crusade against the Block, he's already secured its replacement. Doing God's work doesn't come cheap, but turns out to be an urban land grab as well. Now he even has the developers and their money behind his ban-the-Block telethon, a lot of the same money that's usually laid off on the politicians who are trying to save it. I wondered how much they'd contributed directly to Sharkey's slush fund to pay for the commercials. In politics, as in baseball, it's called covering all bases. Shrewd sonofabitch, smart as they say, all right, Sharkey has a real pincers movement going. The guy has a mind like von Clauswitz.

"Who put this sweetheart package together? You go to them, or they come to you?" I said.

"Little of both. Word gets out there may be an opportunity, and all of a sudden the entrepreneurs start clamoring for a piece of the action. But we're getting ahead of ourselves. First, we have to make way for the new buildings by creating the space. And to do that, well, you know the story," Sharkey said.

It's called gotcha! I didn't know whether to thank Sharkey or to kick him in the balls. But it was easy enough to see that he had a tight grip on mine. He'd just handed me a story he knew I couldn't refuse. And if I ran it, I'd be playing right into his hellszapoppin campaign to sanitize the city, aiding and abetting this unfrocked evangel in the work of what he deemed to be that of the Almighty with a wink that I'd get my reward on the other side. But reporters aren't supposed to look a gift source in the mouth. We're supposed to not care whether we're writing obituaries or verses for valentines. It's all the same crap. Or is it?

Anyway, I shook hands, gave Sharkey a cockeyed half-smile, half-smirk, and pointed my Cole-Hanns toward the door and out of Sharkey's paper-work cocoon. Outside, the air was clear and crisp. A sidewalk vendor was selling hot pretzels. I bought one, salt-free, just for the hell of it, slathered it with mustard, took two bites and slam-dunked the remainder into a municipal receptacle labeled "Trashball."

I am one of the world's great indoorsmen. What I do best I do inside. Over the phone. In journalism, a phone in the right hands is a lethal weapon. Learn how to use one and you'll cover more territory than the best legs in the business. Often I make twenty-five calls to get a single thought into a story, but that's what the chase is all about, for crying out loud. Features writing's the ninny side of the business, for the feint-of-heart who can't sort out information, can't identify the lead. The reading public, what little there is left, doesn't realize it, but what newspapers really do is analyze and process information, tell them what's important, what's not. We stack the information for the reader.

Back in my private little purgatory called *City Press*, the full-mooners were, as usual, in command. The commotion this morning was not over whose story was leading the paper or who would get the day's plush assignment. The fuss was over who would get the one remaining jelly donut from the editor's treat at the weekly staff meeting. I decided to avoid the fray, convinced the donut wouldn't juxtapose very well with the aftertaste of the mustard pretzel I'd sampled, Besides, I might spread donut powder on my jacket.

At my desk, the stern Dutch-uncle wink of the voice mail bead competed for my attention with a plain brown envelope, bulging a bit in the middle. The telephone won. Among the messages the voice mail fed me were: Shelly wanting to know if I'm still alive; my barber advising me that I'd missed my last appointment; Sollie Stein importuning that I call him urgently; Broadway Brown cursing because I never returned his call; the accounting department with questions about my expense account.

Knowing what's important in the news business, I called the accounting department first.

"You know there's a ban on taking sources to lunch," the voice said.

"But sources are where the stories are," I said.

"Still, rules are rules, and what applies to everyone else also applies to you," the voice said.

"We're not talking a lot of money," I said.

"You're ignoring the rules," the voice said.

"Mulligan approved it," I said.

"Mulligan's ignoring the rules, too," the voice said.

"I'll take it up with a higher authority," I said.

"Remember the rules," the voice said.

Next, I dialed Sollie Stein's number and got the answering machine. I thought, oh, shit! another game of tag telephone, my machine talks to his machine. But as soon as I identified myself to leave a message, he picked up the call.

"Sollie, my man, what's happening?" I said.

Sollie Stein said: "What's happening? What the fuck ya think's happening. You know how to ask any other questions? Got the call to serve my country, do my patriotic duty, that's what's happening. Going before the grand jury beginning of next week, the fuckers. Can't figure out what the fuck they want with me. Been out of the business and out of town so many years I forgot what the name of my club was."

"Sollie, relax. They're not after you. If they were, you wouldn't have gotten a subpoena. They have to start somewhere. All they want is some general information so they can begin to sketch a picture of what the hell's going on," I said.

"I don't remember," the sudden convenience of instant amnesia, is the most frequently played refrain before grand juries. The phrase drives prosecutors up the wall and elicits lectures about being sworn to tell the truth. The trick is, stick to the blank slate story and never blink. It was Sollie Stein's lifeline to discover: I was in no position to outline it for him. It's called obstruction of justice, and it'll get you two to five years.

"Easy for you to say since it's not you," Sollie Stein said.

"What day?" I said.

"Tuesday. Grand jury doesn't meet on Monday. That's travel day for the folks from the boondocks," Sollie Stein said.

"Gotta good lawyer?" I said.

"Like I'd go naked. Course I gotta lawyer," Sollie Stein said.

"Then do some rehearsing. And make sure you empty your bladder before you go into the grand jury room. Gotta go. Talk to you before next week," I said.

My heart was about to shut down for maintenance. Something happened. Else why would the great behemoth of justice suddenly start lumbering into motion. I flicked the pages of the little tan book that served as my breast pocket Rolodex, where I record the important private numbers that I refuse to share with the computer list and other reporters who are too lazy or stupid or both to do their own research and cultivate their own sources. Broadway Brown popped up on the second page of B's. I picked up the phone—a dial tone is almost a pitch-perfect tuning fork "A"—and punched off the series of blips. After four rings, as voice rumbled through the receiver that sounded like the roar of a bear whose ass was snagged in a steel trap.

"Yeah," Broadway said.

"Dart returning your call," I said.

"About fucking time," Broadway said.

"What's happening?" I said.

Broadway said: "What's happening is that you got bad fucking manners, not returning calls. My ass is naked in a stiff fucking breeze and you don't return calls like they taught you in etiquette class at that fancy fucking college you probably went to."

"Sorry about that," I said.

"Sorry, shit. You'll be sorrier yet when I tell you that sonofabitch Krall is playing fucking hardball. Totally ignored me and the picture and your big-deal story and all of a sudden I get an invitation, registered letter, to testify before the grand jury, says next week. Now what do I do?" Broadway said.

His syntax was scrambled, his sentences didn't parse, but when the language was decoded, it revealed what clearly was a sharp point.

"First of all, you relax. The subpoenas are flying like confetti on New Year's Eve. It's part of Krall's strategy, get everybody off base, make 'em nervous, throw the goddam things around so that everybody's suspicious of everybody else. Creates an atmosphere of guilt by subpoena. You're the second person in the last fifteen minutes I know who's got one," I said.

"Who's the other guy?" Broadway said.

"You know the rules, Broadway, but I'll tell you this. You got nothing to hide, don't worry about it. You have something to hide, cut a deal, your ass is in trouble, too. So figure out which way it's gonna be. Only you know what you have to hide. My guess is he's trying to scare you off the missing picture, but you're dug in pretty deep on that one," I said.

"Guess I gotta call my lawyer, start the meter ticking and hope for the best," Broadway said.

"Keep me posted. Promise I'll return your calls," I said.

CHAPTER 12

▼

At long last, the grand jury was underway and it appeared that I'd have to go to work in earnest. But first, a little private sleuthing of my own. I let my fingers do the walking through the phone directory's blue pages where government agencies are listed. I cradled the phone receiver in the tuck if my neck and shoulder and clicked off the number of the Motor Vehicles Administration. A woman answered.

"Richard Dart, *City Press*. I wonder if you'd be kind enough to check a couple license numbers, see who the cars are registered to," I said.

"What are the numbers, please," she said.

"Numbers are ZYX 735 and ZYX 736," I said.

"Just a minute, please," she said.

I could hear the slap, slap, slapping of computer keys and the sound of this faceless bureaucrat's steady bellows of breath into the phone. After a few seconds, she came back on the line.

"I'm sorry, sir. I'm going to have to transfer you to the chief public information officer," she said.

I thought, holy shit! What the fuck's going on? After all, automobile registrations are public information, available to any citizen who asks. And now, a department of government that sells computer printouts of license numbers to credit card companies and mail order houses is withholding the names of two car owners. I wondered if the Maryland State Police or the Governor's Mansion were on the Cheese of the Month club mailing list.

A male voice came on the line.

"What can I do for you"?

"My request was for the names of the persons that tag numbers ZYX 735 and ZYX 736 are registered to," I said.

"They're privileged information, sir, kind of like unlisted phone numbers," the voice said.

"Must be important cars, having unlisted owners," I said.

"That's the way it is," the voice said.

"Bullshit. No such thing in this state," I said.

"Is now, at the request of the owners," the voice said.

"We'll see," I said.

End of conversation. The essence of reporting is never accept "no" for an answer, so this meant I'd have to drive to Annapolis for a personal look. But that could wait for another day.

In the reporting game, you reach a certain point in the day when you hate the sound of the human voice—twenty five, maybe fifty, phone calls a day, each one urgent to the person who's calling but none that mean a damn thing to you except the ones you make. I'd had enough of society's warps and wails for one day. I tossed the envelope with the bulge into my briefcase, snapped it shut and headed out of the building.

The air was heavy and pungent with cinnamon and nutmeg from the spice factory across the street on the rim of the harbor. The tease of the strong, sweet aroma of the Indies reminded me that I'd forgotten to eat. Too late for that now, though, the day's almost shot, and besides, why ruin a healthy appetite for dinner. I thought of the perfect mid-afternoon pleaser, non-caloric, low cholesterol, about as non-toxic as food gets. In the food pavilion at Harbor Place, I ordered a fruit shake—a combination of ice, fruit juice and fruit chunks whipped to the consistency of a milk shake, thick enough to eat with a spoon, yet airy enough to sip through a straw, just the right confection to dull the edge of hunger.

Nobody ever said democracy in action comes cheap. Harbor Place did more than put Baltimore on the map and into the tourist business at a time when the gritty factories were shutting down and the city was beginning to show the orange smudges of rust. Harbor Place helped to homogenize a city that was segregated, not only by color but by neighborhood as well. Baltimore was a city where people boasted of never having been downtown or even, for crying out loud, outside of the ethnic wards where they were born, went to school, got married and raised families. Now it's a sign of the times at Harbor Place to gape across a cultural chasm and watch blacks chow down on pizza and whites grazing on ribs. I finished my shake, tossed the cup into a trashcan and burped.

Later, at home, I changed into jeans, a turtleneck sweater and sneakers, the uniform I prefer when nobody's looking. I poured an Absolut over ice with a lemon twist and took a long cold swallow of the silver bullet that set off sparkers in my head. I padded over to my office where the message light was blinking on the answering machine. I punched the play button and the machine said: "This is Shelly. I'll be there with dinner at about six. Have a glass of wine ready....Then two hang-up beeps....This is Colorado Prime. We're a food supply company. I'll call back at another time to speak with Mrs. Dart....Another hang-up beep....Smart hunting dogs know when to turn around and go back home....The machine, having played itself out, clicked off.

Another day, another shit list, I like to say. Goes with the territory. I didn't recognize the electronically enhanced voice issuing from the made-in-Taiwan answering machine. Serves me right for not buying American. One thing I can do something about, the other is often the handiwork of someone else. If this story's going to cause me any physical grief, I might have second thoughts. I'm not a coward, mind you, but deep down I'm a pacifist. I just don't like people touching me, especially with their fists or other lethal objects.

I was pouring a second Absolut when I remembered the envelope with the bulge. I took the envelope out of my briefcase, tore it open, and out slid an audio-cassette. On the label were hand-lettered the words "PLAY ME." Vodka in one hand, cassette in the other, I headed for the den where I'd achieved at least one of my youthful fantasies—to someday have a sound system so powerful that the street lights would dim when I turned it on. I snapped on a couple of switches, punched a button or two and slipped the cassette into the appropriate slot where it was automatically consumed into the tape deck's innards. For a few seconds, there were a series of high-pitched scratches and squawks, like the background noise that used to accompany Rudy Vallee on the old 78s spinning on a wind-up victrola. Then out of the vacuum came a conversation, first in fragments, then in gut-to-gut, bottom-line sermonettes:

First voice: "Hard to control the guy."

Second voice: "Gotta have a soft spot somewhere. Everybody has one."

First voice: "This thing gets outta control, lotta people are gonna be taking dives."

Second voice: "Hear the cops accidentally picked up Little Billy on a wire tap, advising a couple of bar owners how to improve their numbers business by using the State Lottery numbers instead of the treasury receipts. Get seven hours more play every day that way."

First voice: "Christ, Krall gets a hold of that, the shit'll really hit the fan. That gives the screw another twist. He's supposed to have been outta the numbers business for years."

Second voice: "You got nothing on the guy? Shame on you. You got the entire State Police force, and you got nothing to make the guy shut up?"

First voice: "Best thing is probably to go over his head, directly to Washington, let Justice know just what the hell's going on over here. Convince 'em it's just a fishing expedition, maybe they'll back off."

Second voice: "How you gonna do that?"

First voice: "Gimme some time to think about it."

Second voice: "We got a heavy stake in this."

First voice: "Yeah, don't forget, I'm the one who has the most to lose. My ass is on the chopping block...."

In a pellucid moment, like a clear bell on a cold night, my ears cupped by my hands to capture the tone and the timber of the voices through the tinny whine of the tape, I realized that I was listening to a recording of Joe Frank and the governor of Maryland plotting to obstruct justice. Holy shit! I didn't have to check license numbers after all. They visited me in my own home. I'm honored. My brain shot into overdrive for the occasion. This could be a set-up. The person who sent me the tape knew I had it. Trouble was, I didn't know who else had copies. If the tape was already in Krall's hot little hands, I was in possession of evidence. Where was the recording made? Who had the balls to make it? Was it at Eddie Pomeroy's? The trouble with loose ends is that they invariably lead to a knot.

"...My reputation, my job. All you have is a few decaying buildings that are probably under assessed anyway.

Second voice: "Worst thing we can do is start arguing. Gotta stay cool, pool our resources, work together, fight the enemy, not each other.

First voice: "Let me talk to some of my people, come up with a strategy that'll put a damper on this thing before it sucks everybody under."

Second voice: "Somebody's got to shut that reporter up, too."

First voice: "That's your job...."

Now I was in deep dip, like it or not. As I was rewinding the tape, I heard the front door squeak, then slam. After announcing herself at the expense of my door, Shelly made her usual don't-mess-with-me entrance, briefcase in one hand, shopping bag in the other. She bent and kissed me behind the ear, sending all the appropriate hairs to attention.

"Wait'll you hear what I have," I said.

"What is it, Court Basie or Frank Sinatra or, come to think of it, both?" Shelly said.

"Better than that. Joe Frank and Marshall Goodwin singing the blues, all on tape," I said.

"It's been a rough day. First, a little wine while I process that sentence," Shelly said.

"Could get a platinum for this baby," I said.

"Or an artificial knee cap," Shelly said.

Shelly sat down beside me just as I was standing up to go fetch her wine. I returned with a glass and an uncorked bottle, Catoctin Chardonnay Oak, a Maryland vintage that I'd tasted at a recent state wine festival. I poured, she said *salute* and sipped.

"Wait'll you hear this tape," I said.

"Before that, I have some news that's going to find out what we're made of," Shelly said.

"Don't sound so cheerful," I said.

"Got to tell you before it gets too sticky," Shelly said.

"Let it all hang out," I said.

"Remember a while back I told you the firm has a client who's involved in the investigation, but for your sake and mine I wouldn't tell you who," Sherry said.

"That's when the partners questioned you about us," I said.

"You got it. Well, it's show-and-tell time. The Client's none other than Marshall Goodwin," Shelly said.

The blood pressure gauge in my head raced into the danger zone. Holy shit! Goodwin's not only consuming my professional life, now he's invading my house as well. How in the hell could Shelly and I talk, when much of our conversation is about our work. Going to bed would be like sleeping with the enemy. On the other hand, we've survived worse. In fact, because of what we've been through at the White House, we'll probably handle this better than most people would. The thought occurred that I was merely rationalizing a dangerous, career-wrecking situation, that it was much more serious than I pretended. But it was easy to understand why Goodwin would wind up where he did. The firm's senior partner, Shelly's boss, was not only the firm's rainmaker, but also probably the best criminal defense lawyer in town. That Goodwin would turn to him was a signal of concern, if not a suggestion of guilt. I wondered if he was ready to cut a deal.

"Wanna hear my tape?" I said.

"Don't think I'd better," Shelly said.

"Suit yourself. You're probably right," I said.

"Dinner's no big deal, no fussing needed. Gazpacho and Baltimore cheese bread. Ladle the soup, and microwave the bread. Close as you can get to not cooking at all," Shelly said.

"They putting any pressure on you at the firm?" I said.

Instead of answering, Shelly lifted her glass and sipped more wine, which in the body language of relationships means I need more time to think before answering, or I don't want to discuss it, period. From which I inferred that there had been a very stern, boss-to-floss conversation at the office. Shelly looked tense and mournful, assuming that fey look that conveys distance or even an out-of-body experience. I eased toward her, slid my hands on her shoulders and began to knead.

"Don't," Shelly said.

"Sure you don't want to talk about it?" I said.

"Let's eat," Shelly said.

In the kitchen, Shelly ladled, I microwaved. Except for the scraping and clinking of spoons, we ate in silence. This was a helluva way to celebrate what might have been the high point of either of our careers—my jugging the governor, or her helping to save him.

Though it was still early, the sky was beginning to blush, casting the kitchen in a palette of purpley pink and creating a dazzle of fiery sunburst on the windowsill. The early evening laser light show softened Shelly's taut edge and tinted her fair skin the hue of delicate rose-petal rouge. It was painful watching her being ripped apart by what I could only discern were the competing tugs of loyalty at the office and love at home—so to speak. We'd come a long way together, shared a lot, respecting each other's distance, liking as well as loving each other. The limits of our relationship were now being tested. Maybe it's time to settle...ah, ah, ah, don't over-react, especially at a time when emotions are running high. This is no time to pop the question, to get serious and smarmy. Give it a couple of days, let things settle down, see where they lead.

We cleared the table and prepared the dishes for the dishwasher, searching each other's faces for answers rather than talking.

"I think I'd better go home," Shelly said.

Suddenly it struck me: She hadn't changed from her day clothes, was still dressed as if she were at the office and not nesting with me.

"Can't you stay for the night?" I said.

"Better not. We both need a couple of days to think," she said.

"You sure?" I said.

"I'm sure," Shelly said.

I took her in my arms and pressed her close, and I kissed her, not a wet, passionate kiss, but a soft loving kiss that said what had to be said. It said I understand. I walked Shelly to her car and said goodnight.

I was pissed. Back in the house, I went to the John, put on a suede baseball-style jacket and stuffed my prize tape recording into a pocket. I armed the burglar alarm, let myself out and jumped into my car. In the dark, I headed for *City Press*, popping a mint in my mouth to neutralize the camel breath of the garlicky gazpacho. The radio was kicking out Harry Connick Jr...."If they asked me, I could write a book/about the way laugh and look...." I could have done this the easy way, of course. At the computer terminal at home, I could have sat down and written my story and flashed it downtown in a nanosecond to *City Press*. But the easy way has its dangers. The e-mail address is a general file that too many people have access to, and I don't like exposing myself or my stories to rubberneckers and gossips. Christ, I was beginning to sound like a technical writer. Back in the bad old days, the tools of the trade were manual typewriters and telephones. At conventions and in Congress, at riots or demonstrations, at deadline time you simply went to the nearest phone booth and dictated thirty paragraphs off the top of your head or from notes. On the road, Western Union took care of the copy. Nowadays, the young hot shots carry cell phones and lap top computers into battle zones and transmit their stories via satellite. Editors know the body count before the Pentagon.

It's only been the last thirty years since we've had the personal computer, the Cellular phone, the communications satellite, the pocket calculator, Palm Pilot, uplinks, downlinks, the VCR, the Camcorder, the compact disc, the computerized camera, the digital camera and, damn it all, the boom box, that enduring contribution to inner city culture. Pull the plug and society would probably collapse.

My mind wandered back to Shelly. This whole investigation was lunacy on the loose, and now it was even tearing apart the security of my personal life, which I'd vowed would never happen again. My derring-do as a reporter had cost me one wife; now I was determined that I wouldn't lose the love of my life. The issue here was not the pismire politicians involved. They were secondary players in this municipal morality play. So was Krall. The key issue was real estate, two blocks of it, enough to keep developers busy for the next ten years. Really, the Block was more like an archeological dig than a demolition derby. It'd be interesting to see what comes out from behind the bars and from under the rafters—other than mice and lice. Old numbers slips, used condoms, a few errant pasties and G-strings, how many stray business cards left behind by those drunk and in love for the night, and maybe even a stash of cash that Lord Julius Salisbury had left between the boards when he hot-footed it out of town in the middle of the night while Baltimore's finest were sleeping. Most of all, the second floor gaming room where Marshall Goodwin was said to satisfy his passion for galloping dominoes.

Pedal-to-metal, I raced down the Jones Falls Expressway, drenched in the ghostly amber of the overhead mercury arc lights. Funny, how technology has caused us to color people by what they're doing—green glow of the computer screen, amber glow of mercury arc lights, day-glo colors of neon, psychedelic spray of laser lights, purpley pink tint of sunset. Now Connick was through and Sinatra took over the radio with Nelson Riddle laying down the beat behind him: "The summer wind/came blowing in/from across the sea. It lingered there/to touch your hair/and walk with me...." I thought of Shelly. And I thought, hearing Connick and Sinatra back-to-back, how much alike they phrased, though nobody'll ever catch the old saloon singer for breathing and phrasing, sliding and gliding effortlessly over octaves, sneaking little pin holes of air into his tank to push the notes and phrases right on pitch. Near the bottom end of the JFX, I swung off onto South Street and headed straight down to *City Press*. I had no idea of what the hell I was going to do. I just knew I had to be there in case I decided to do something.

CHAPTER 13

▼

I had Sharkey's list of real estate opportunities. I had Russo's tip. I knew that Goodwin had hired a lawyer, but that little snippet of intelligence was privileged information. No way I'd compromise Shelly unless I absolutely had to. I knew that Sollie Stein and Broadway Brown had received subpoenas, probably among dozens of others who were on Bob Krall's greetings list. And I had my newly acquired tape recording of Baltimore's Best, Marshall Goodwin and Joe Frank, which corroborated Russo's tip about going over Krall's head directly to the Justice Department. I also had a very tight sphincter. Not only did I have an audio tape containing highly combustible material about a public official and a political fixer. But the tape had my name on it. And in not a totally friendly way. I thought, reporters' reflexes are curious. Funny how I hadn't reacted to the mention of my name earlier, because my juices had accelerated their flow only over the excitement of having come into possession of new and explosive information. Comes now the headachy part, the reality check, when the invisible band around the head begins to tighten, the stomach gets feathery and the oh, shit, what-do-I-do-now, feeling takes over. I was having a sudden head rush, that lead-heavy crunch that seems as if there's an anvil sitting on your noggin forcing your brains down into your throat.

Interesting that Goodwin understood the limits of his dealings with reporters. He assigned the dirty work to Joe Frank, which was about as dirty as it can get. Based on what he'd already tried—money, women, even his own son—no telling what Frank would introduce next. Still puzzling was who sent the tape and where it was recorded. If, in fact, the meeting between Goodwin and Frank took place, and if, as I suspected, it occurred at Eddie Pomreoy's after they attempted the old dipsy-doodle, then Eddie Pomeroy and his cousin Sollie Stein could have planted the tape recorder. Suddenly, the anvil finally dropped with a terrible swift thud that got my attention. Joe Frank was a celebrated electronic eavesdropper, always ready and eager to get the goods on people, his notion of political security. Could this be a case of Frank attempting to protect himself against a deal that might go sour, someone ratting to the feds to protect his own ass? But why would Frank send the damaging goods to me? Maybe Frank was settling a score, getting even with Goodwin for breaking away from his organization years ago. As it was stated on the tape, Goodwin had a helluva lot more to lose than Frank. But this was big-time lunacy, conspiracy to obstruct justice, get them ten to twenty years at a federal country club every time. Wearing a wire a part of his undergarments was not above Joe Frank. And the unintended consequence was that the tape landed in my lap.

I nosed my mean Swedish machine around the corner of *City Press*, popped the gear lever into reverse and backed into my parking space next to the building. I felt disoriented, kind of unplugged, still not sure of what I was going to do or to whom I was going to do it. On the elevator, I thought running with a story of the taped conversation would be risky until it's double-checked and approved by the lawyers. Even then, the lawyers would probably discourage its use on the grounds that it would expose me (and *City Press*) to charges of withholding criminal evidence. Worse, Bob Krall would get the chance he's been looking for to rough me up, haul me before the grand jury and start asking a lot of questions just to rattle my cage. Where was the only lawyer I trusted when I needed her? This time, the joke's on me. Shelly's representing the man I'm about to nail, and the tape has put me in the same position as the television reporter who has Broadway's picture.

The biorhythms of the *City Press* newsroom are different at night than by day. At night, I was an outsider in my own office. I knew very few of the night-siders, the mechanics who actually dirtied their hands and put out the paper—news editors, copy editors, make-up editors, artists with airbrushes, a couple of police reporters checking the districts for the latest body count. Every body busting their asses for what? The truth is, for anybody who wants to admit it, the guts of any newspaper are neither the news that squeezed in between the ads for Red Dot sales and supermarket come-ons, nor the opinion that's delivered by editorial writers, the fearless folks who come over the hill after the battle and shoot the dead. The real content is the comics, obituaries, horoscopes, grocery store coupons and baseball box scores for fantasy league freaks. They are the newspaper staples that even television doesn't deliver. Anyone in a hurry can stay on top of the major issues of the day simply by reading "Doonsbury," "Kudzu," "The Boondocks" and "Sally Forth." Toss in a couple of cartoons and just about anyone can be well-informed without ever putting on hip boots to wade through those boring news columns and woe-is-me editorial page screeds. Another difference between night and day at *City Press* was the notable absence of Buck Mulligan, a psychic reward that made the newsroom a safer and saner place to work that even the Occupational Safety Hazard Administration would approve.

At my desk, I took out a notebook and began jotting reminders in a hieroglyph that probably only I could decode, a crawl of characters, symbols and words that served as a form of shorthand that I'd developed over the years. They were buzzwords, keywords that would unlock whole paragraphs in my memory circuits when I needed to retrieve the information. I was always careful not to keep detailed notes or any kind of schedule or calendar in the event I was ever subpoenaed. And when I was finished with a notebook, I made certain to destroy it, especially now, just as I was careful to erase messages from my answering machine at home and my voice mail at the office. Sounds paranoid, I know, but that doesn't mean somebody's not after me. If Bob Krall ever hauls me in, he could try to read my notebooks, but he'd never be able to read my mind.

Now I was doodling, stalling for time, thinking about calling Shelly, still not sure of what I was going to write for the next day's editions of *City Press*. I knew I'd have to decide soon, because the paper was being made up and space was getting scarce. News competes with news. One day's banner headline story is the next day's crab wrap. I was dancing around the rim of the dish on the idea of calling Shelly, a push saying do it, a pull saying don't. I decided to stick with the pull. Jack and Jilling is tough work.

A voice behind me said:

"You Dart?"

"That's me. Who're you?" I said.

"Bob Kirby, police reporter," the voice said.

"What can I do for you?" I said.

"Been reading your stuff. Making the rounds of the districts I came across some information you should know," Kirby said.

"Like what," I said.

"Acquaintance of yours is wearing a body bag. He was found dead in bed, apparent suicide, guy the name of Broadway Brown," Kirby said.

"Holy shit! Holy shit! Gimme your notes. Who'd you talk to?" I said.

Kirby surrendered his notes, which contained the basic police-blotter information along with the name and phone number of the desk sergeant at the Central
District, which was police headquarters three blocks from *City Press* and two
blocks from Broadway Brown's establishment. I told the night editor what information I had and how much space I'd need. I stuffed a fresh notebook into my
back pocket and took off for the Block like a car burglar in felony shoes.

My first stop was Pandora's Box. The pandemonium inside the nightclub
resembled that of a whore house being raided—women crying and running for
cover, a few customers stupefied over the mayhem around them, cops trying to
preserve order, and Captain Joseph Nelligan presiding over the commotion with
the finesse of the running of the bulls at Pamplona. The band had stopped playing. The lights were up, full glare, illuminating the sticky bottle-bottom circles
on the bar, the skuzzy worn-out floors and rickety chairs. Here in the home of
perpetual night, the unaccustomed kilowattage peeked through the protective
wrapping of transparent gauze and exposed the dark patches of Velcro and chocolate nipples on lollipop tits. And the miasma of human pores that never fades. I
wondered what in the hell Nelligan was doing here. This was a case for homicide,
not narcotics. I scanned the room. My eyes locked in on Faye and Fern huddled
in a corner. Which answered my question about Nelligan. He'd just lost his
snitch. Now he was here to protect his other merchandise.

Nelligan said: "Nothing's wrong. Nobody here's in trouble. I just want to ask
a few routine questions. As you may or may not know, the owner of this fine
establishment is dead, by his own hand, we think. We'd like to know when you
last saw him, who was the last employee to talk with him, that kind of thing.
Whether he was acting strange, and, most important, whether he said anything
that could hint at why this terrible thing has happened…."

Time to disappear into the outside world, I thought. This could be a case of
my knowing more than the cops, and I wasn't about to share information with
Nelligan. I'd just talked to Broadway Brown earlier today, and could've been the
last one to hear him alive. I'd catch up with Faye and Fern later. I eased out of
Broadway Brown's club and on to police headquarters where I found the duty
officer watching "Homicide" on television. The nameplate on the desk said Sgt.
Roman Palowski.

"'Scuse me, sergeant. I'm Richard Dart, City Press. I wonder if you'd help me
with a few crumbs of information," I said.

"Like what?" Palowski said.

"I need some details on Broadway Brown's death," I said.

"Gave it to Kirby," Palowski said.

"And Kirby gave it to me," I said.

"So you've got it. Watcha need now?" Palowski said.

"Details. Who, what, why, when, where," I said.

"Happened late this afternoon, 'bout four o'clock, the coroner says. When he didn't show up at the bar the usual time, couple of the employees got suspicious, called nine one one. Found dead as a side of beef, no foul play, suspected overdose of sleeping pills. Found an empty bottle and a half glass of water on the nightstand. That's about it," Palowski said.

"Any note?" I said.

"None I know of," Palowski said.

"Know which employee called nine one one?" I said.

"Nope," Palowski said.

"Dressed or undressed?" I said.

"Shirt, pants and socks, a Bible in his hand," Palowski said.

"Which hand?" I said.

"Right," Palowski said.

I could see that the television set commanded more of Palowski's attention than my penetrating questions, which were about as clever as they ever get in police-beat work. He was absorbed by the pixeled cops, of art imitating life. I thanked the sergeant, and made my exit thinking: Broadway Brown was agitated when I talked with him this morning, probably more upset than I understood from the jabs he took at me over my telephone manners. Broadway had two problems. He had been caught between the long arm of the law and the short leash of Joseph Nelligan. And the thought of appearing before a grand jury and risking spilling his guts must have been a powerful image, compelling enough to choose a toe tag instead of a long happy life in a federal hot house for either perjury or obstruction, the two choices available to anyone unwilling to play by the prosecutors' stacked set of rules. Some choice. Poor sonofabith. Now I knew what I was going to write.

The Bible was a nice touch, even God would agree, if there were a moment for humor in all of that heavy business that comes with omniscience. The man who operated one of Baltimore's most celebrated meat markets making peace with himself and his maker, probably recalling the innocence of his childhood by reading the *haf tora* from his Bar Mitzvah. I thought only Catholics relied on deathbed confessions.

I quick-stepped back to *City Press*, composing the story in my head as I scooted across Baltimore Street for one more peek in Pandora's Box. The word must have spread as rapidly as a yeast infection. Along the Block, men and women had gathered outside the other bars, staring in silence at the outside of Broadway's club as if it were some kind of shrine. I wondered what they thought they'd see. After all, this wasn't Fatima or Lourdes, where apparitions occur every once in a while.

Inside Pandora's box, Nelligan was gone, the noisy commotion had settled into a funereal calm. Broadway was not the only thing that was dead. Business was finished for the night, the band had packed up, and all of the girls must have gone home. The bartender with the ham-sized hands and the fuck-you look was the only malingerer, at his usual post by the cash register as if the guy on the slab was just another bozo instead of his boss.

"Hi, again. Wonder if you'd be willing to help me out?" I said.

"The fuck I look like, an information desk?" he said.

"Just a couple routine questions," I said.

"Who called nine one one?" I said.

"Tell you the same thing I told the cops. I did," he said.

"Why?" I said.

"'Cause Broadway didn't show up his usual time this afternoon," he said.

"What time's that?" I said.

"Four, five o'clock," He said.

"When's the last time you talked to him?" I said.

"Last night, closing time, putting together the liquor order. Man sleeps most of the day, doesn't like to be disturbed," he said,

"For the record, what's your name?" I said.

"For the record, time's up. Good night," he said.

Even though I didn't learn the bartender's name, I did better than I thought I would from a normally combative person who didn't like me to begin with. Goes to show what persistence disguised as begging will do. Now I was double-timing it the two blocks back to *City Press*, my heart rhythms accelerating their thumpity-thumps along with the quickening of my footsteps.

Back in the fun house that is the *City Press* newsroom, I alerted the night editor that I was back, settled down in front of my computer and punched in my access code. Lickety-split, with the speed of light, there appeared on the screen a scramble of letters that resembled oozy green alphabet soup. I slugged the story "Brown," and decided to pump a little sunshine up Kirby's ass by sharing the by-line because he came up with the first catch.

By Richard E. Dart
and Robert Kirby

"Broadway Brown, prominent nightclub owner on the Block and a known police informant, was found dead in bed with a Bible in his hand at his East Baltimore home late yesterday in what police described as an apparent suicide.

Brown's body was discovered after he failed to show up at Pandora's Box at his usual time early in the evening. Employees at the popular show bar became suspicious and called 911.

Police were dispatched to Brown's home where they said they found his fully clothed body along with an empty sleeping pill bottle and a half glass of water. Brown was clutching a Bible in his right hand.

Earlier yesterday, Brown was known to have received a subpoena to appear before the special grand jury investigating political corruption on the Block, especially links between political entrepreneur Joseph Frank and his one-time protégé, Gov. Marshall Goodwin.

Brown has also been engaged in a legal standoff with Robert Krall, the special prosecutor who is heading the investigation, over a photograph of Brown and Gov. Goodwin that was confiscated by the federal Strike Force during a raid on Pandora's Box. The framed 8x10 picture, displayed over the cash register in Brown's nightclub, was one of hundreds taken at a fundraiser for Gov. Goodwin and sent out to those who paid the $100 a ticket admission fee.

The picture is now believed to be missing from Krall's safe in the Baltimore courthouse and in the possession of a reporter for television station WACK. Brown had threatened to take Krall to court unless he was able to produce the photo. Illegal possession of criminal evidence carries fines and penalties up to $10,000 and ten years in prison. The standoff had not been resolved at the time of Brown's death.

Brown was also known to have close ties to Capt. Joseph Nelligan, who heads the Baltimore Police Department's narcotics squad. Nelligan, in an unusual move, was conducting the questioning of employees and patrons last night at Brown's nightclub."

Blah, blah, blah, another dozen paragraphs of background. After a run through spell check, I executed the electronic wizardry of sending the story slugged "Brown" to the night editor's terminal at the punch of a button. He read it, pronounced it fine and thanked me for turning in the lead story. I, in turn, thanked Kirby. This little stroke of luck and timing ought to keep Mulligan off my back for a while.

I went to the men's room, whizzed, washed my hands and threw some cold water on my face—in that order. The kid in me still wasn't dead. I could still get a cheap high from a merry chase and a good story, and as I boarded the elevator my heart was still running faster than my electric meter on a subzero day from the unexpected excitement of the night. Outside again, the night air had some teeth in it. I turned the corner and headed for my car. Suddenly, I had a case of the whim whams. A large hulk of a man was resting his buttocks against the fender of my car. As I got closer, I could see that the hulk belonged to Captain Joseph Nelligan. Oh, shit! I thought of why the team of Laurel and Hardy had worked with such success: One was dumb, the other was dumber. In this case, I wondered which was which.

"Been waiting long, captain?" I said.

"Long enough, you little maggot," Nelligan said.

"No need to get shitty," I said.

Nelligan said: "Look, I'm sick and fucking tired of tripping over you every time I turn around. Heard all the lectures about freedom of the press, but your freedom ends when you start fucking with me. I'm not gonna ask you what you wrote tonight, but when I pick up that bird cage liner of yours tomorrow It'd better be right."

"I'll take my chances," I said.

"This is the last warning. I don't like wise asses, especially wise ass reporters."

"Tell you something, too, Nelligan. Remember, you're not fucking with one of your police beat jockeys who likes to play cop."

The way he stiffened told me in body language that was precise and unmistakable that no one had ever talked to Nelligan the way I just did. I decided to seize the moment before he recovered from the sheer shock of my defiance. I walked around to the driver's side of the car, unlocked the door and slid in, making certain that I locked the doors once I was settled in the cockpit. I revved the engine while Nelligan stared his gonna-get-you look through the windshield. Slowly, I slipped out of parking space number seven and headed for the Jones Falls Expressway and home. On second thought, I decided the open expressway was dangerous. Not beneath Nelligan to radio ahead and rig a speeding charge. I pointed toward Charles Street, the city's grand old dowager of a sluice, north through the center of town, bright lights, big city, lots of traffic and traffic lights and no way to speed. I was shaking. I needed a brandy. Heading north through the Charles Street canyon I was wresting with two demons: The headache I was developing worrying about Nelligan, and the heartache I was feeling over the conflict with Shelly. But it was late and right now I could do nothing about either. At home, I poured a man-sized brandy and downed it in two gulps, which sent lightening through my pipes. I was tired. Upstairs, I undressed, brushed my teeth, slipped into my queen-size bed and let the brandy do the rest.

CHAPTER 14

▼

It was an up-and-at-'em day that arrived with the customary splashes. My shoes were shined, my tie was tied, my pants were pressed. Broadway Brown's funeral should be the political reunion of the year and I wanted a back row seat. A check with the city desk told me the funeral was scheduled for two o'clock at Sol Levinson's on Reisterstown Road.

Jews bury their dead within twenty-four hours except on the Sabbath and high holy days, following a public health prescription to this day that was laid down five thousand years ago in the covenants. Accordingly, sometime today the body of Broadway Brown would be placed in a plain pine box. Some hollow words would be said over the coffin by a visiting rabbi about his generosity (he contributed annually to his *shule*) and his good citizenship (he always bought tickets to the policemen's ball.) Then he would be transported to a Jewish cemetery, which was guarded by German police dogs, in God knows what outskirt of town, where he would be lowered into the ground and become the dustbin's property as we are all promised. In a year, on the anniversary date of his death, there would be the unveiling of the headstone. That would be the end of Broadway Brown, except for an occasional visit by the groundskeeper to weed whack the grass. Now only God knows what secrets Brown had taken to the grave with him.

Under a bright lemonade sky, tickled by a whisper of a breeze, I stationed myself, at one thirty in the afternoon, on a pad of concrete, like a sentinel outside the entrance to Levinson's funeral establishment. Through its doors have passed the high, the mighty and those who have stood in the shadows of the great. At the opposite side of the entrance, another man was holding forth, hands jammed into his pants' pockets, eyes wandering no place in particular like a gerbil's. After a moment, I thought, holy shit! I'm not the only one who's interested in the attendance list. The guy was one of the two clones who'd been with Krall at Paisan's. Wherever Brown's soul is, it is not resting in peace.

Among the first to arrive was a quartet of the usual suspects, proving, if nothing else, that car-pooling saves both energy and money—Faye and Fern, my favorite bartender with the catcher's-mitt hands, and Milton Frank. Two by two they walked straight ahead, as taut as totem poles, the ladies in black from head to toe, eyelids drooped down by mascara, the men in their finest mob wear, pretending not to see me. From where I stood, I thought, it would be thick of me to make a media event of such a solemn occasion as the entombing of Broadway Brown.

But bartender big-hands woke up on the wrong side of life. He had second thoughts. He detached himself from the cluster of mourners and lumbered around as slowly as if he were a jukebox on wheels being pushed by a mover. A finger the size of a banana was suddenly in my face. The bartender said:

"You sonabitch, you killed him, you and those fucking stories, gave the guy no choice. Guy was looking for no trouble, tried to be your friend, helped you out a couple a times, and you turn around and kick him in the balls for no good reason. Take a hint. Don't come near the club again or your ass is dead meat, I'll see to it, believe me when I tell you. Don't know what you're here for except to make trouble, 'cause you're not family or friend."

The part of the brain that says don't be an asshole activated just in time to disengage my mouth. I stood speechless as the bartender turned and waddled back to his group, which was by now entering a door to Levinson's. As soon as he was inside, I took out my notebook and jotted down some remembrances. My pen was unsteady. Krall's watchdog, smirking, had observed and no doubt recorded the entire encounter. The phrase "dead meat" stuck in my memory bank. I'd heard it before on my answering machine, and I'd seen it before in the anonymous letter warning me off the story of the Block. Was I behaving like a man who needed a quick fix of Prozac? Of course.

Arrivals picked up as the clock ticked off its inexorable seconds toward funeral time. One by one and two by two they came, men and women, in all sizes, shapes and colors, matches and mismatches, suffering the wrath of the daylight that was invisible by night, their hard edges heightened by feigned grief and their eye sockets puffy and red from rubbing. The men were other club owners, bartenders, friends, and the women who were not wives were hostesses in garish get-ups in a palette of Jell-O colors that boosted the light count on an already bright afternoon. Broadway couldn't have asked for a better day.

In a flick of a lid, my camera-eye brought into focus the remains of the Block's once-great overlord. Shuffling along with his over-ripe wife on his arm came Sollie Stein, looking like a couple of rejects from the local senior citizen's center Mah Jong tournament, he in plaid polyester circa 1975, and she in a beehive hairdo the color of borscht.

"Sollie, baby," I said.

"Stay away, Chrissake. You're the kiss of death." Sollie said.

"Just want to say hello,' I said.

"Yeah, and spot me in front of the world," Sollie said.

"No harm in showing good manners," I said.

"Gotta go pay my respects," Sollie said.

"Too bad Lord Julius couldn't be here," I said.

"In spirit he's here. Broadway was like his brother," Stein said.

"See you in the funny papers," I said.

Sollie Stein was right. My presence within two feet of him was like pointing a finger of suspicion in a circumstance when everybody suspected the other guy of being a songbird. Better to ease away with a minimum of exchange and fuss, which I did, thinking that Stein was more use to me alive than dead.

I'd backed away from Stein just in time to avoid a serious mistake. Joe Frank arrived in a white Cadillac with a couple of his cronies. Once they slid out of the car and unfolded, Frank's hulking frame towered a full head over his companions. Wearing his customary bow tie and gold-rimmed glasses, Frank's face was permanently set in a screw-you smile. As the trio headed for the door of Levinson's, Frank broke rank, brushed by me and said: "Weasel."

Frank was gone in a split second before I had a chance to assess the damage he'd done to my self esteem as well as to wonder how to decode his one-word remark. But feelings aside, I thought: If Frank had seen me within even spitting distance of Sollie Stein, the news would have traveled fast and one or both of us would have been dark alley material for his gorillas.

Things were beginning to happen fast. A black Lincoln limousine with license plates that were stamped "Governor" slid up to the curb and out jumped two burley bodyguards. One opened the rear door while the other surveyed the immediate area for potential threats to the limo's precious cargo. When the coast was pronounced clear, out stepped Marshall Goodwin, looking tanned and gray and thoroughly fit like a well-kept potentate of a prosperous duchy. If luxury had a lap, Goodwin was living in it.

Goodwin was a crowd pleaser, a popular politician when the word popular meant he didn't get booed in public places. After all, Levinson's was home base for Goodwin, who grew up not to far from where he eventually might be eulogized. A small gathering had swarmed around him, supplicants waiting to shake hands, bosslets there to remind Goodwin of how many votes they'd delivered in the last election, friends from the old clubhouse who'd kiss the hem of his garment for a friendly gesture of acknowledgement or, preferably, a more tangible reward for services rendered.

"Governor, remember the time...."

"Marshall, you promised my son...."

"Governor, there's a bill in the legislature...."

"Marsh, don't take any shit from the feds...."

The cops, one on each side of Goodwin, began walking within the circle of bodies, using their elbows like bumper guards to prevent bodily contact between the governor and his constituents. The entire clump moved with them, not giving up an inch of ground. The Krall look-alike with the thick soles and puckered lapels positioned himself like an observation tower with a full view of the fuss around Goodwin, clicking off pictures with his tie clip. When the feds said candid camera, they meant it. I assumed I was already in his gallery of snapshots.

I was about to go inside and join the party when the periphery of my eye caught a familiar but incongruous image. I thought, holy shit! What the hell's Charles Sharkey doing at the funeral of a suicidal bar owner whose main commodities in life were alcohol and flesh? Sharkey had spent his later years trying to do away with people like Brown, and now he's patronizing the enemy's funeral. Sharkey acknowledged me with a nod and a thumbs-up gesture that I interpreted to mean Broadway's departure removed one more impediment to deactivating the Block.

I attached myself to a moving tide of bodies and drifted with them into Sol Levinson's. Inside, the pews were filling up, a respectable turnout for a guy in Broadway's line of work, even if most of the mourners were associates from the Block. I did not sign the guest register.

Levinson's was stark and simple inside, light wood paneling dressed here and there with symbols of the Jewish faith, a pulpit in the sanctuary and a few chairs for those who would be participating in the service. From an aisle seat on the backbench, I had a good view of the mourners, mostly profiles and backs of heads, though many of them were familiar. I saw what I came for. Marshall Goodwin sat on one side of the aisle, Joe Frank on the other. Just as I'd expected, but nonetheless a letdown. As far as I could discern, the two hadn't even made eye contact since they'd arrived.

Stakeout journalism is costly loitering. I wanted to leave but I couldn't let myself do it even though attending funerals is not my favorite form of recreation. I went to a Mormon funeral once, and it was about as uplifting an experience as ordering peanut butter and jelly on Wonder Bread. Real *goyisha* stuff. Jews and other Mediterranean derivatives at least infuse the funerals of their beloved with hot charges of emotion, *kvelling,* wailing, flailing, hurling themselves at coffins and at peak point threatening to join the deceased in the open grave and hitching a ride with the soul to wherever it's heading.

For Jews, like Roman Catholics, suicide is a downer, a *shonda.* Stuffing your gut with a hundred capsules and shutting down your pump carries with it heavy penalties that the living must bear and the dead could care less about. For Jews, the punishment is social ostracism, for whom it is not clear. For Catholics, snuffing out your life gets you buried in unconsecrated ground, without the prayers and sprinkles of holy water and wafts of dust that constitute the symbolism of the burial ceremony, a social embarrassment to the living more than an insult to the dead. No matter how you view it, dead is dead and that's that. And all the world knew that Broadway Brown was as dead as a kippered herring.

The heavy stuff was about to get underway. Several old men, one with a beard, were shuffling toward the chairs on the platform while the family of Broadway Brown was filing out of a waiting room on the side of the sanctuary and into the first two pews that were reserved for them. The brief stirring and rustling gave me an opportunity to pop a mint without the crinkling of cellophane being noticed.

The sounds of coughing and throat clearing are always amplified by the silence of solemn occasions in large spaces. On this particular day in this funereal theater of the absurd, though, the syncopated riffs of hacking and grunting served as trumpet calls announcing the arrival of Captain Joseph Nelligan. I thought, holy shit! Our paths crossed twice in less than twenty-four hours, both times over Broadway's dead body. Nelligan and I have to stop meeting like this, or he'll get the idea that I'm soft on him. Nelligan had had Broadway Brown by the balls in life and he's still squeezing them in death. Nelligan pushed his way into a pew beside Joe Frank, forcing Frank as well as Faye, Fern and Milton Frank to give up air space between them so Nelligan's bulk could be accommodated. Nelligan immediately turned toward Frank and began to whisper. Joe Frank cocked his head forty-five degrees to listen, then nod. Though I'd never know, I wondered what Nelligan was saying. Could they have been words of condolence? Naaahhh, not Nelligan's style. Maybe a kind word about Milton Frank giving Faye a ride? Possibly, but unlikely. Could it be that Nelligan was explaining to Frank that

Broadway brown got his tit caught in a ringer by dint of a subpoena to appear before the grand jury? Bingo! I liked the odds on question number three.

Second thoughts are second nature to me. I was beginning to have one. I needed mobility, flexibility, and room to make choices, so there was no point in staying fastened to a bench in the back of the mortuary. The service would be brief, and besides, no earthquakes would erupt inside if for no other reason than out of respect for the dead. Out in the open, the chances of an encounter were far greater because the flow of mourners would force contact among those who normally would avoid even the slightest brush. Then a heads-up thought occurred to me: There are several people gathered here who dislike each other a lot, but there's one person they collectively despise intensely—me. Such distinctions are among the psychic rewards of being a professional pain-in-the-ass. I wore it like a badge of honor.

As an elder began incantations in an alien language and along scales and cadences antiphonic to the eight-tone scale, I slid out of the mortuary and through the lobby as quietly as a Mamenchantz Mime. Back outside, Krall's pit bull was still at his station. I assumed a neutral position near the curb at about the middle of the broad cement pad outside of Levinson's. I like a sidewalk with a view.

The Krall look-alike said: "Nice turnout."

"Very impressive. Give you a great page in your scrapbook," I said.

"Get on the team, Dart. Be a player," he said.

"I'm a one-man gang, and I like it that way," I said.

"Suit yourself. Do it the hard way," he said.

I began pacing, signaling my annoyance as well as an end to the conversation, at least for my part. He leaned a shoulder against the brick building and folded his arms across his gut. The guy made my skin crawl.

I glanced at my watch. It was two thirty and, by my reckoning, the service for Broadway Brown would be over within a matter of minutes. Times like these try my patience, which I usually assuage by cursing under my breath in public and aloud when I'm alone, blaming my own short fuse on every one from God to somebody's mother. I thought of Shelly and decided I'd call her tonight. I thought of the tape recording of Governor Goodwin and Joe Frank. I thought of Sollie Stein getting the quick shits over his subpoena. And add to my ruminations the collection of sleaze balls I was clocking inside of Sol Levinson's.

At that moment, as if on cue, a door sprang open and the recessional began. Broadway Brown was officially dead. The crowd emerged seeming in lighter spirits, chatty, friendly, the heavy shadow of grief and remorse lifted, now that

Broadway Brown had been properly attended and was being loaded through a side door into a hearse. Sollie Stein and his wife—who was supporting whom was unclear—tottered out into the sunlight. He made no move toward me. I responded in kind, thinking that discretion is the better part of protecting a good source. More bodies, waddling at a funereal pace, flowed onto the sidewalk and gathered into several conversational clusters. In the frame of the doorway I spotted the quartet of bartender ham-hands, Faye and Fern and Milton Frank. Now the ranks were thinning and it occurred to me: Something's wrong with this picture. Where the hell are the Big Cheeses? My mouth was dry and my heart was beating its wings against my rib cage. I surveyed the inside of the building and as far as I could see, a few more stragglers and the chapel would be empty. I was careful not to appear too alarmed for fear of alerting Krall's bulldog to the absence of the very reasons we were both here.

I summoned up my reserve of nonchalance and, as casually as I could, I strolled toward the side of Sol Levinson's, careful not to catch anyone's attention. They don't call me Mister Smoothie because I sell ice cream. There were as many people at the side of he building as there were in front, chatting, gesturing, climbing into cars on the side lot. At the back end of the lot, I spotted a clot of people, three, maybe four. I eased closer, squinted and telescoped the faces into focus. Holy shit! There, in the mid-afternoon honeydew sunlight, next to the fender of a late model car, were Marshall Goodwin, Joe Frank, Charles Sharkey and Captain Joseph Nelligan. Nelligan seemed to be doing most of the talking. If I moved in any closer I'd be spotted and that would be the end of the discussion. I decided to do just that. I felt the aura of something behind me. Krall's goon wasn't as dumb as I thought. He just stood, smirking, knowing he'd get the best of this scene.

"I'd like a print of that shot," I said.

"Bet you would," he said.

I resumed walking at a leisurely pace, nothing hard-charging or threatening. On the outside I was smiling. On the inside I was ready to wet my pants. I wound through a nest of parked cars, still smiling, not knowing what the hell I'd say if they decided to accept the challenge I was setting up. Krall's gumshoe must've decided to stay behind and watch the show. Reporting is not a job for the feint of heart. More often than not, it requires more guts than brains. Being a Christian, I should recognize a lion's den when I see one. And here I was, walking head-on into the pit with four wily beasts, my only weapons a notebook and a disposable ballpoint pen. I thought, what ballsmanship. Then Nelligan spotted me, raised his right arm like a directional arrow, and suddenly I had four pairs of eyes trained on me. I turned up my accelerator and quickened my step. None of the four blinked. Oh, shit! What do I do now? I was no less than ten feet away from the group and I could sense the magnetic field between us sending out hot charges of hostility. On my right, I saw two of Governor Goodwin's janissaries moving toward me, one talking into the palm of his hand, which I assumed contained the microphone for the walkie-talkie that was clipped to his belt. Over my left shoulder I picked up on my radar screen Joe Frank's two muldoons who were leaning against a car just out of earshot of whatever conversation had been taking place until a wet blanket fell over it. My adrenalin pump must have an oversized tank. I was running on high-octane juice now. My heart sounded like a conga drum in my ears. I was just about nose-tip-to-nose-tip with these plug-uglies when my brain shut down and my mouth took over.

"Nice day, nice turnout," I said.

Whaddya want, weasel?" Joe Frank said.

"Like to talk to you and the governor—privately," I said.

Before anyone had a chance to open his mouth, Nelligan, with his customary bluster and his take-charge demeanor, stepped forward to claim the podium.

"Look, you goddam pussy-willow ninny, I'm sick of you bird-dogging me, sick of tripping over you every time I turn around. You and your goddam stories are causing a ruckus over nothing, probably even responsible for Broadway, damn good man, checking out the way he did. Now you come around to a funeral you're not invited, 'cause you're sure not friend of anybody's, and all of a sudden you're hassling the governor and his friends in a private conversation to which you're not a party…."

"Lighten up," Goodwin said.

"….You keep this shit up you're gonna have more goddam trouble than you ever thought, sure as my name's Joe Nelligan."

"Maybe you oughta tell it to the guy over there from Krall's office whose been taking your pictures with his tie clip," I said.

"Same goes for him, following me around as if I'm some goddam criminal," Nelligan said.

"Ease off, Nelligan, the man's doing God's work," Sharkey said.

Joe Frank said: "Tell you what. We're all big boys, able to handle ourselves. I've got no more love for this guy than you do. But why don't the governor and I find out what the scribe wants, see if it's worth all the trouble he's going through. Let's the three of us take a walk and have a chat, get this guy off our backs once and for all."

Goodwin flinched. He understood right away that Frank had made a mistake. Through his years of dealing with the press, Goodwin had learned two fundamental rules of public relations: One, never give out information unless you know what it's going to be used for; and two, a reporter rarely asks a question unless he already knows at least part of the answer. Frank couldn't have known what I know. Goodwin might have an idea. I'd been working this story for weeks, and Goodwin had a network of informants so extensive that he knew whenever a courthouse clerk licked a postage stamp in Towson or Rockville, highsiders who pass on information just to suck up and score points. I also had a tape recording.

Goodwin's nod was barely perceptible, but it caught the eye of one of his bodyguards who nudged the other into action. They eased in around Goodwin like mother tigers and swooped him into a flying wedge, walkie-talkies crackling, toward his official limo before Joe Frank could say as much as bye-bye. Frank stood as rigid as a fence post, slack-jawed, disbelieving the swift preemptive stroke that denied him what he must have considered an inspired act of communications.

"Nice try," I said.

"Always willing to accommodate the fourth estate," Frank said.

"You really didn't think he'd buy into that idea," I said.

"No harm in trying to straighten out misunderstandings," Frank said.

"I appreciate the effort," I said.

There comes a point in every story where nothing else can be done except to pull up a chair and sit back and watch it march by. There were so many pieces in motion that the investigation of the Block had arrived at that point, the source of its own momentum, assuming a life outside the newsroom of *City Press*. I backed away from Joe Frank, Sharkey and Nelligan before the niceties ended and Frank realized I was mimicking his clumsiness and Nelligan started his in-your-face ranting again. The weather should be as predictable as Nelligan.

CHAPTER 15

▼

A magnet inside my head was pulling me toward home instead of downtown to *City Press*, and I was rapidly approaching the divide where I'd either have to veer onto the JFX or continue straight along Northern Parkway and into Roland Park. I opted for home. At Falls Road, Northern Parkway becomes one of the longest hills in Baltimore, so long that at normal speed very few cars make it out of second gear and into drive, a real strain on a car's innards. By the top of the hill, I was only a few blocks from home. I turned right onto Roland Avenue and decided to stop at Eddie's for a take-home dinner, which turned out to be boneless chicken breast cacciatore with *crimini* mushrooms, sesame noodles and Caesar salad.

I was born under the sign of Aries. My horoscope usually says one of two things—either I'm going to have sex or get rich. But today, Sidney Omar had added a tag line: "Focus on travel, communication, publishing." Usually I treat this celestial streaking with the same credulity as I do a politician's promise. But this horoscope had a number of playful possibilities, whatever you read into it: Drive downtown, place a few phone calls, write a story. Get out of town while you can. Call Shelly. Start writing the book, for crying out loud. Considering the range of possibilities, I'd rather have sex or get rich—preferably both.

At home, I stored my sack of food on the countertop and reviewed the day's mail which included: *Time* Magazine, a bedding sale circular from Macy's, VISA bill, an invitation to meet personally with Alan Flusser at his Washington store, a solicitation from my college alumni chapter, an invitation to the annual Gridiron Club dinner, a reminder that I was due for a dental check-up and a notice that I'd been enrolled in the Fish-of-the-Month Club. None of this was very high on the cat burglar's list.

For once there were no messages on the answering machine. I dialed into my voice mailbox at *City Press,* and the first sound I heard was the rumble-strip voice of Buck Mulligan yackety-yacking for less cereal box philosophy and more news copy. Next came Sollie stein, in a voice that rustled like dead leaves on a windy day, saying that Krall's office had told him he'd be in the grand jury witness box tomorrow. Holy shit! Finally, after so many false starts, the show was underway. Maybe that's what my horoscope was all about. An advance story and a court-house stakeout to see whether Sollie Stein walks in the front door under his own steam, or they sneak him in through the garage like a sack of dead-letter mail.

Usually I don't drink until the sun's down over the yardarm. But what the hell. It was late enough in the afternoon, and besides, I'm a big boy. I filled a pewter Jefferson cup with ice, topped it with a twist of lemon peel and poured a generous gurgle of Absolut. The first cold blast hit my throat live a silver bullet. I slipped off my suit jacket and draped it carefully over the back of a chair. Drink in hand, I padded over to the den, and after adjusting the creases and pleats of my trousers, let a deep oversized chair swallow me into its folds. I put my mind in a free-float mode and let it roam over thoughts of kings and cabbages, of the tape recording I'd done nothing about so far, of Sollie Stein's bladder working over-time as he confronts the grand jury, and of Shelly, sweet, ripe Shelly. Love aside, I was feeling horny. I picked up the cordless phone and dialed her office number. Her disembodied voice answered:

"Hello. You've reached the voice mailbox of Shelly Klein. I'm not at my desk right now, but if you'll leave your name, number and a brief message, I'll get back to you as soon as possible."

At the sound of the beep, I said: "My voice mail misses your voice mail, and my voice mail would like to hear from your voice mail. I'm at home. Number's the same. Haven't had to change it lately."

In the kitchen, I poured another Absolut, thinking that I'd eat early and head down to *City Press* to write an overnight story and satisfy Mulligan's prurient interest in news of the Block. I transferred the chicken into a microwave-safe con-tainer and nuked it for four minutes. The sesame noodles I'd eat at room temper-ature along with the Caesar salad. Eating alone is the pits, something I'd done often in a number of countries and states and had never accepted the idea. I remember being alone in San Francisco, alone in San Francisco, for Christ's sake, one of the most romantic cities in the world, and going into the dining room of the St. Francis Hotel. It was filled with people having fun, enjoying themselves, and here I was, stuck in the middle of the jollity with a lap top computer under my arm as a companion. The trouble with journalism is, you meet a lot of people but you make no real friends.

I wolfed down my food to fight off the melancholy of missing Shelly, and I washed it down with the remainder of the vodka. I stashed all of the dishes and cutlery in the dishwasher and wiped the table. Upstairs, I took a leak, washed my hands and face, brushed my teeth and tightened the dimple in my tie. I recalled the very first piece of advice I was given by a legendary reporter the very first time I was aboard Air Force One: "Eat when you can and pee when you can, because you never know when you'll get another chance."

Exiting the house, I slipped my suit jacket off its dining-chair valet, punched the magic four digits on the security system and locked the door. Outside, I hung my jacket on the hanger I carry in the rear seat of the car. Better to be cold than wrinkled. In the cabin of the car, I lit the fire, backed out of the driveway and pointed my compass toward *City Press*. In the rearview mirror, in the lengthening shadows of dusk, I saw another car pull out halfway up the block. I thought, I'm beginning to feel like a dog with tin cans tied to its tail. Tooling along well within the speed limit, car number two kept a respectful distance but was nonetheless still there. I popped a Velamint just in case. I snaked my way through Hampden and onto the Jones Falls Expressway, carefully observing the 50 mph speed limit, feeling as if I had a two-ton caboose on my tail. Now I could see the oversized tires and the little red bubble light on the dashboard, and under the magnesium street lights the triple antennas rendered the car like a pregnant porcupine. Fucking Nelligan. Got his rottweilers after me. I thought they gave up messing with reporters. I popped a second Velamint in case there was to be a confrontation, even though vodka's popularity is that it leaves no afterbreath. I eased off the accelerator ever so gently so I could wind down to a playful 45 mph, safely under the limit. If a traffic violation was what my playmates had in mind, I was being tease. Now off the expressway and onto South Street, I was still the object of someone's affection, being surveilled for a reason that only God knew but I believe I could guess. I executed the appropriate turns and slipped into parking space number seven next to the *City Press* building. As I did, the mystery car kept going. I figured Nelligan's agent was more interested in discovering whether I made contact with anyone than in my driving habits.

In the fluorescent bath of the *City Press* newsroom, the ghosts of newspapers past haunt the corners and crannies the way goblins and noises populate funhouses. In a sense, that's what *City Press* was. I remembered a news editor who died and whose last request was that he be laid out on the pool table in Eddie's tavern, at the corner of the building, where he'd sloshed so many boilermakers. His wish was granted. At the wake I thought, what a flash fire his liver would cause if he were cremated. And I recalled the morning I'd just arrived at the office to see the city editor lurch a couple of times, roll his head and die of a heart attack at his desk. Where was I when John F. Kennedy was assassinated? At my desk, on a Friday afternoon full of nubile promise, waiting for three o'clock and a tryst at my apartment with the best body in the building. At one twenty in the afternoon, Eastern Standard Time, a young copy girl tapped me on the shoulder and said:

"Mr. Dart, the president's been shot."

"Cut the shit, that's not funny," I said.

"It's coming over the wire right now," she said.

I went back to the wire room and sure as hell the UPI teletype machine was chattering out its grim message: "Four shots rang out as President Kennedy's motorcade sped through downtown Dallas."

I yelled, "Buck, holy shit, get back here. The president's been shot."

Within twenty minutes, we had an "Extra" on the street, back in the days when they used headlines so big they were called "railroad tracks." But that was years ago, in the days of manual typewriters and hot type, when I was still moving up the ranks. In journalism, as in politics, it's tough letting go of yesterday.

At my computer, I tapped in the commands that booted up my file. I slugged the story "grand." Before I started writing, however, I saw something I hadn't noticed on any of my previous nocturnal visits to the newsroom: A pretty young thing, a Dart kind of woman, alone in the section of the room that was assigned to features writers, presiding over her computer as if it were a Steinway. I liked what I saw. But first, I had some music of my own to make for tomorrow's paper.

"A federal grand jury was expected to resume its investigation into political corruption and influence on the Block today after a brief delay caused by a dispute over a photograph of Gov. Marshall Goodwin and Broadway Bernie Brown that was thought to be missing from the courthouse safe of Special Prosecutor Joseph Krall.

The first witnesses were to begin appearing before the grand jury this morning, according to sources familiar with the issuance of subpoenas.

The resumption of grand jury activity follows the apparent suicide and funeral of Brown, a colorful block nightclub owner and known police informant, who received a subpoena two days ago. Brown died of an overdose of sleeping pills, according to police.

Funeral services for Brown were held yesterday. They were attended by Gov. Goodwin and political godfather Joseph Frank, two of the persons believed to be at the center of the grand jury investigation, as well as a number of Block bar owners and their employees.

Among those who are thought to have received subpoenas is Sollie Stein, former Block kingpin and spokesman who is now retired and living in Florida. Stein is expected to be among the first witnesses to go before the grand jury."

Etc., etc., etc., for about fifteen more paragraphs of background.

I ran the story through spell check, the electronic dictionary that compensates for reporters who can't spell or type accurately or both, and with the touch of a key dispatched the piece at the speed of light to the night city editor's file for processing. At the command of another key, the computer screen went blank and I shut down bad-ass reporter Richard Dart for another edition, that is, with the night city editor's approval, of course.

With great panache and premeditation, I strolled over to the men's room at the opposite side of the room where on the return trip I hoped to engage they eye of the young lady in the features department. I finished my business, washed my hands and threw some cold water on my face. I tightened the dimple in my tie and drew down my shirt, which had crawled up under my braces. I was satisfied with the look. I worry about things like that. After all, flirting is serious business, if it's done right. Out the door, I stopped by the water fountain and after a long cold drink I began my slow killer-diller approach, oozing charm from every pore, bedroom eyes fastened on the face that, upon close focus, told me suddenly why I was attracted. She was a Shelly look-alike, same soft ripe ready-for-plucking look, the easy free-falling lemony hair and jeans that look as if they were on a Calvin Klein model in the New York *Times* Magazine. Holy shit! I was in trouble.

This was an intense person, though, never let her eyes roll away from the computer screen, sitting upright, touch-typing as if she had graduated *summa cum laude* from the Katie Gibbs secretarial school. I thought, concentration like that ought to produce a helluva powerful piece. But on the features section you never knew. She could be writing a story about diet fads among the upper class Punjabi or offering up the latest study of why ocelots make good house pets. It was my move. I eased, toward her, leaned against a filing cabinet next to her workstation and flashed my best Giaconda.

"Hi, we haven't met. I'm Richard Dart," I said.

She tilted her head upward, shifted her eyes and gave me a buzz-off look that could chill a bottle of Chablis.

"So I've heard," she said.

"Must be a heavy assignment you're into, gives you an edge like that," I said.

"On deadline. Besides, not everybody has the luxury of being Richard Dart," she said.

"What's that?" I said.

"Come and go at your own speed," She said.

"Gotta earn it, gotta go to boot camp," I said.

"That's what I'm trying to do," she said.

"Does that attitude have a name?" I said.

"Anne Taylor. You'll see it tomorrow if you let me get back to work," she said.

"Nice meeting you, too, Anne Taylor. I'll see you tomorrow in the funny papers," I said.

Newsrooms are full of sassy-assed women trying to be one of the guys, tough and cynical in a business that's built on a lot of huffing and puffing and male bonding. But she was play-acting, didn't look the part of a person with a case of heartburn so bad that you could fry and egg on her chest. She didn't wear an attitude very well. In fact, if I had to guess, I'd say she's insecure. But what she was saying made me wake up and smell the cappuccino about how the other reporters were viewing my measure of independence at *City Press*. It's tough being tethered to a life-support system that involves layers of editors who control your motions and movements. But it takes years and years and millions of words to cut the cord. Only way to shuck it is to keep producing stories. My game was shut down, so I withdrew and padded over to the city desk to find out if my story met with the usual high journalistic standards of the *City Press* editors. The night editor was on the phone but he signaled thumbs up, even managed a smile. Up yours, Anne Taylor.

The night was still young and I was feeling as frisky as a tomcat, a good time to visit Paisan's and find out what information the human trumpet, Tony Russo, has picked up. On my way out, Anne Taylor followed me with her eyes and composed a half smile in a way that looked almost apologetic at the same time it appeared questioning. I returned the smile, and filed the moment in the appropriate corner of my cortex.

Baltimore is a city of sights, sounds and smells. At night, the harbor twinkled like strands of diamonds in the sky. Thousands of tiny bulbs outlined the Tinker Toy skeleton of Harbor Place as well as the masts and rigging of the Constellation, that imposter of a ship that bobs in the harbor like a lazy black tub. When the wind is right and McCormick's isn't spicing the neighborhood with Cinnamon and Nutmeg, the night air is heavy and damp with the smell of salt and fish wafting in off the Chesapeake Bay.

By foot, Little Italy is ten minutes from the Inner Harbor. The trip can be negotiated on the sidewalk along Pratt Street or over a series of footbridges that cross the water itself. At night, it's safer to stick with the well-lighted street. These days, it's a safer trip to outer space than it is to walk six city blocks. Along the waterfront route is the World Trade Center, I.M. Pie's eight-sided office tower, the Aquarium and Marine Mammal Pavilion, the latest entry in the government-subsidized real estate, the Christopher Columbus Marine Research Center, the Power Plant, a monster pile of turn-of-the-century pile of bricks that has been converted twice over into an entertainment center, kind of a shopping mall with food and booze. And sitting out on the water's edge is Pier Six, an outdoor concert shell that all summer long plays host to big and little bands, famous and not so famous names, have-been's, would-be's and never-will-be's.

I arrived at the intersection where the big faded red, white and green sign on the side of a brick house says, "Welcome to Little Italy." There are 26 restaurants competing for business in Little Italy, and by far the most successful is Paisan's, mainly by dint of its reputation, size and the hours it keeps. The Little Italy Restaurant Association fought the coming of Harbor Place, claiming the new entry would drive them out of business. The opposite occurred. During the tourist season, visitors by-pass Harbor Place, make the ten-minute walk to Little Italy, and lines spill out of the restaurants onto the sidewalks. Business has never been better.

Paisan's was headachy with the competing sounds of chatter and clatter, the continuous loop tape of Luciano Pavarotti's favorite Italian melodies and the squealing of the waitresses who, in their best Baltimore catarrh, attempt to convert a nasal twang into a language.

Tony Russo was at his usual banquette, his rheumy ball-berring eyes panning the room like one of those swivel cameras that monitor bank transactions, his right hand mopping up tomato sauce with a squeegee of Italian bread.

"Tony, my man, what's up?" I said.

"The hot shot himself. Who you fucking tomorrow?" Russo said.

"That's a surprise. Tell you now you might not buy a paper," I said.

"All the shit that's fit to print," Russo said.

"Hear anything worth sharing?" I said.

"Had a visitor like you said I would. Gave me a piece of paper saying be at the courthouse tomorrow at nine," Russo said.

"Going in the back door or the front," I said.

"Front. Got nothing to hide, nothing to be ashamed of. Fucker's gonna learn not to play with people. I been in more courtrooms than Krall has," Russo said.

"You'll have company. Things are getting serious now, and they're moving fast," I said.

"Gonna get nothing out of me," Russo said.

"Never say never," I said.

"Fucking Nazi's playing with the wrong guy," Russo said.

"What else you hear?" I said.

"Hear Nelligan's chasing your ass all over town, find out who you're talking to," Russo said,

"Now where'd you hear that? Does he have a guy in here watching us talk?" I said.

I needed a break in the conversation to think. I signaled a waitress.

"What'll ya have, hon?" She asked.

"Let my buy you a drink, Tony," I said.

"I drink water," Russo said.

Okay, a bottle of *San Pellegrino* for Tony and an Absolut on the rocks with a twist for me," I said.

"There's a bartender from Broadway Brown's comes in here every night, says Nelligan's pissed and has the heat out for you," Russo said.

"Why's Nelligan pissed?" I said.

"Nelligan doesn't need a reason. Mean sonabitch, busted a lot of people 'cause they got in his way, got half the Block on the hook one way or another. You're smart, you stay outa his way," Russo said.

"In my business, you never know where the trail is going to lead, that's the fun of it. Never thought I'd trip over Nelligan like this, but who the hell knows," I said.

I signaled the waitress again and changed the order from an Absolut to an iced tea. Russo reinforced what I'd experienced earlier and I was in no mood to take a breathalyzer test or worse, being tailed and arrested for drunk driving because some tin-whistle cop was probably sitting here watching me have one drink. Besides, my liver could use the break.

Drinks arrived: "Here ya are, hon," the waitress said.

"*Salute and bono fortuna*," Russo said.

"Same to you, 'cause you're gonna need it tomorrow," I said.

Walking the ten minutes from Little Italy to *City Press* where I'd left my car, I mused that Russo was just the kind of witness Krall wanted, no direct connection with the Block but just enough gossip to help fill in the blanks. The wack-a-do world of loose ends called investigating is really painting strictly by the numbers. Only two blocks away from *City Press*, heading north toward the Jones Falls

Expressway, I noticed the steady beam of headlights ready to crawl up my tailpipe. I made a quick course change and headed across Fayette Street, ironically the backside of police headquarters, toward Calvert Street, an alternate route north. The headlights were still like two cat's eyes in my rearview mirror. With crime and criminals shooting up society just for the hell of it, they're wasting a cop tailing me. Go figure. Gotta play the game, though, lead them on a merry chase. Slowly I crept up Calvert Street, making sure I was a few miles below the 35 mph limit. This way, at least, my accompanist was pacing at a respectful distance behind me. Through Court Square, which used to be the hub of downtown activity until the center of gravity was shifted to Charles Street, then the waterfront, up past the Baltimore *Sun*, the long stretch of grand old row houses, many of which now house law offices and other businesses, North Avenue, Twenty Fifth Street and the drug zone, up past the row houses of Charles Village and finally a left onto University Parkway and the greenswards of *haute* Roland Park. The low beams tracking me never let up until I swung into my driveway behind Shelly's car. A half block up the street the car came to rest facing my house.

Inside, the house was dark except for the den where Shelly was watching television, a glass of white wine on the cocktail table. I slipped up behind her and planted a wet kiss on her ear. She responded with goose bumps, a quiver and an arm gripped around my neck that said more.

"I'm glad my voice mail called your voice mail," I said.

"Sometime voice mail doesn't do the job," Shelly said.

"Always glad to be of service," I said.

"I miss you," Shelly said.

"What about the hang-ups and conflicts?" I said.

"At the partnership meeting tomorrow I'm going to announce that I'm taking a leave of absence," Shelly said.

"You must have thought long and hard about this, but don't do it. You'll blow the chance of a lifetime. Your career could take off like a rocket," I said,

"It's either that or us, and my being here kind of answers that question," Shelly said.

I excused myself, went to the kitchen and poured a man-sized brandy and was back in the den quicker than you can say *Remy Martin*.

"But what'll you tell them, what excuse will you give for taking a leave in the middle of the biggest case in town," I said.

"Well, since they obviously know about us, I'll tell them I'm going to graduate school full time, get a master's degree. They'll like that. When I return to the firm, they can increase my hourly rate," Shelly said.

If I were given a multiple choice test among (1)flattered, (2)stunned, (3)dumbfounded, and (4)thunderstruck, I'd flunk if I failed to check all of the above. We'd been through some scrapes together where we've had to wriggle and writhe to get off the hook, but never a clutch where either of us had to make a choice as daunting as this. Not even the brandy was numbing the dull band I could feel tightening around my head. Holy shit! Now I'm in big trouble. Was it finally time to make an honest woman out of Shelly, give her a legitimate reason for leaving the firm? I mentally cautioned myself against offering up anything rash or emotional in a pressure-cooker situation such as this. But here's Shelly, ready to toss aside a career to save my sorry ass from a pincer's movement that I could see coming from Krall on one side and Marshall Goodwin on the other, while Nelligan was working the middle like a pile driver. Besides, being in love is good enough reason not to get married. My hormones were doing cartwheels. I took Shelly's elbow and guided her upstairs.

We must have made the windows rattle all the way up in Delaware. For sure, the floor trembled, the ice cubes tinkled in their glasses and the crystal chandeliers played like a symphony of wind chimes in a seismic swelling of sound in the grand ballroom of the Omni Hotel, where the Southern Conference of Baptist ministers was debating the metaphysical question of whether the apple Eve proffered Adam was a Macintosh or a Wine Sap, proving that God can make a joke even if Baptists can't. At that precise moment, I made my deposit, and my eyelids exploded into a color burst of fireflies, like a kaleidoscope out of control, spinning, turning, putting on a psychedelic light show of shooting stars and crazy comets, Roman candles and Technicolor spiders. Then it was dark again.

"I read somewhere that during intercourse you can work off a couple hundred calories," I said.

"I feel lighter already," Shelly said.

"Gotta stick to the regime, perform every night," I said.

"My kind of diet, beats the hell out of Atkins," Shelly said.

"Sensible, No muss, no fuss, no reading labels. Just careful preparation," I said.

"I like the preparation part, Shelly said.

"Mmmm. When you get right down to it, sex is as basic as putting tab A into slot B," I said.

"Requires some assembly," Shelly said.

CHAPTER 16

▼

When I woke up the next morning, Shelly was already gone, and my brandied brain felt as alert as a box of rocks. Shit. I wanted to say something smarmy about her Jack and Jilling for me at the law firm, hoping she wouldn't turn in her torts and codicils in a grand gesture to a profession that warms its hands by putting them in other people's pockets. I appreciated the gesture, but didn't think it was necessary this early in the comic opera. Unless Shelly was privy to information that I didn't know, which was entirely possible, given that Goodwin was probably supplying information so his lawyers could discover what could be used against him. If that's the case, then Shelly's probably right.

Flushed, brushed, showered and combed, I crossed the threshold into my dream-world closet, where I've often fantasized that I'm, Fred Astaire—dashing, debonair, elegant, a classic dresser and role model for all of us wishful dandies. There's a problem with the fantasy, though. I'm a lousy dancer. There are two ways of dressing—tonal and contrast. I like contrast. I studied the rack of suits, pairing each one mentally with different shirts and ties, rearranging them in my head as if I were dressing store-window mannequins—a navy double-breasted suit with a medium blue broadcloth shirt, straight-point collar, and a regimental stripe tie with a navy ground, or do I go with a blue-bodied shirt with a white tab collar, a dark gray worsted sharkskin suit with a white broadcloth shirt and a burgundy club tie, woven not printed, or will it be navy chalk-stripe with a white cut-away collar shirt and a maroon grenadine tie—until I had the desired combination, hoping the shirt I'd decided on wasn't in the laundry. If I'd been a plumber, I wouldn't have to worry about things like this. I slipped into the navy chalk-stripe ensemble and touched it off with the appropriate poufs of color. I felt smashing. Panache, thy name is Dart.

I swear, a tall glass of cold, pulpy orange juice is the best drink of the day. It moistens the parched parts that've been dehydrated by the alcohol of the night before, and it's full of all that good stuff that's supposed to ward off colds and keep the heartbeat regulated, imputing the juice the same curative powers as the waters at Lourdes. After that, a half bowl of bite-sized Shredded Wheat and non-fat milk and I felt resuscitated and supercharged.

Heading downtown for the courthouse, I noticed that my playmate was a dutiful two car lengths behind me, only this one a different color car, a government-issue maroon. At some point, they must have changed shifts. One saw Shelly enter my house, another saw her leave. Dirtball pigs are probably keeping book on my sex habits.

By the time I reached the courthouse, there was already a flutter of commotion. A clot of reporters had formed at the bottom of the courthouse steps, many of them holding copies of *City Press*, where my front-page story supported a big black double-decker headline:

Grand Jury Back in Action:
Block Probe Resumes Today

Close up, I could see what the fuss was. In the middle of the muddle, Tony Russo was holding forth like a presidential candidate surrounded by the boys on the bus. So consumed by Russo's dithyrambic diatribe against Krall and the American system of justice were my competitor-scribes that they failed to notice the major attraction of the day, Sollie Stein, slip inconspicuously past the crowd with his lawyer and into the courthouse completely unnoticed. Most reporters wouldn't know Stein from a lamppost anyway. Stein looked the color of fog. His step had long ago lost its spring, and he shuffled along as if his feet were too heavy to lift. As they say, the legs are the first things to go, and Sollie Stein's were well on their way.

Poor sonofabitch, I thought, has to go through something like this at his age and condition. Not pleasant even for somebody half his years. Old Sollie's pacemaker will get a workout today trying to keep his heartbeat steady. I eased over to the perimeter of the human circle around Russo.

"….Fascist oughta be running a concentration camp somewhere, that's what. 'Sposed to be a free country, but they got big shots like Krall running loose, hassling little guys like me for no good reason. I get a subpoena telling me to be here when I done nothing wrong," Russo said.

Then he spotted me.

"There's the hot shot that's causing half the problem. Hey, whaddaya say, Dart. Take a bow, round of applause for the man who's got his name in the paper again today," Russo said.

I obliged and took a bow. Only Russo sent up a short volley of mock applause. My press pals were not amused.

"Thanks, Tony, I needed that little pickup. Great way to start the day," I said.

"How'd ya like to trade places, you go in instead of me, since you seem to know more than anyone else what's going on," Russo said.

"Thanks, but no thanks, Tony. It's you Krall wants, not me. You know he's kinda soft on you," I said.

Before Russo could resume his zesty monologue about Krall, a man with a silver U.S. Marshall's badge attached to the breast pocket of his suit penetrated the crowd, tapped Russo on the shoulder and led him by the arm toward the courthouse door. It was the government's gentle way of saying shut up! In front of a courthouse where freedom of speech has been strenuously upheld and where in the marble carving above the door justice is better stacked than liberty.

Sollie Stein had entered the private world of Robert Krall at 9:10 A.M., an innocent bystander in a high-stakes game of Darwinian politics. He emerged four hours later a sad and confused man, a victim not so much of what he knew as much as a misunderstanding of the grand jury process and a willingness to talk openly as if he were among pals in a friendly poker game. Sollie Stein was old and vulnerable, and Krall took full advantage of every opening in Stein's tortuous testimony, muddling his brain, wearing him down until he was a babble of disjointed information that Krall would force-feed into an exercise of pointillism that twisted the truth but from a distance made sense.

In normal circumstances, prosecutors like to deal up. Nab a petty criminal and squeeze him like an orange until he snitches on a bigger tuna, then plea-bargain a lesser sentence for the songbird. In the case of Sollie Stein, however, there were no crimes to threaten him with, no criminal causes for his malfunction before the grand jury. He'd been assiduously coached by his lawyer, counseled to stick with simple "yes," and "no," and "I don't remember" answers whenever he could. But in the end, Stein was done in by incipient arteriosclerosis that clogged the neural pathways of his aging brain. Stein simply could not react fast enough to engage his brain and his mouth simultaneously and do equal verbal combat with Krall and his assistants. That kind of trouble would follow Sollie Stein around like a swarm of gnats.

It was the middle of the afternoon on a day as clear as three fingers of vodka when Tony Russo squinted into the sunlight after two hours in a windowless room with Krall and two assistant prosecutors doing a good-cop, bad-cop routine. To hear Russo tell it, he and Krall behaved like the Katzenjammer Kids in a comic strip brawl. In the end, Krall chose not to take Russo before the grand jury, unsure of what he might do or say.

"Told the sonabitch send me to jail, my wife would love it 'cause I'd lose weight. Kept telling 'em every five minutes I had prostate trouble and had to piss, and every time one of 'em had to go with me to make sure I didn't talk to anyone. Always used a stall instead of a urinal and kept flushing. What they gonna do, come in with me, climb over the top to make sure I'm draining the dragon? Had a court stenographer in the room made 'em get rid of because this wasn't supposed to be a formal appearance. Finally told 'em they want me to talk let's go before the grand jury and that pissed 'em off. Fuckin' Nazi told me I could leave, that I was still under subpoena 'cause they might wanna talk to me again...."

As a one-man street gang, Tony Russo had accomplished what some of the smartest lawyers in town couldn't. He'd outsmarted Krall and waltzed around the system without paying a dime in legal fees. Not that Krall's IQ is off the charts. But with his power and the way the system's stacked against witnesses, it's tough to dance around a subpoena and avoid a grand jury.

"Good show, Tony, my man," I said.

"Write it. Tell the friggin' world Tony Russo's not afraid of Krall and his friggin' subpoenas and his friggin' tin badge. Write that. You write all the other shit that goes on around here, so tell 'em about Tony Russo and what a set of balls he has," Russo said.

The tape recording purporting to be the voices of Marshall Goodwin and Joseph Frank was still in my briefcase. As I drove the few blocks to *City Press*, I popped the cassette into the maw of the deck and listened to it a couple of times, deciding that I'd write the story, check it with the lawyers, then stash the tape in a safe deposit box that I'd lease in the name of *City Press*. What I should do after that is hop on a plane to Rio de Janeiro.

In the newsroom, the editors were in their glass coop for the early afternoon news meeting, which was really a handholding session where everyone attending was more worried about covering his ass than covering the news. On my desk was a peach. I thought, who was the asshole eating lunch at my desk and forgot dessert. If there's one thing I'm territorial about it's my desk and chair. I've made it clear, often enough, that it's my fucking space and I don't like anyone invading it. The newsroom itself was grungy enough, looking more like a hazardous waste dump than an environmentally safe workplace, and now somebody's drippings are on my peacock perch. Pissed me off.

The peach broke my concentration on the tape and how to play the lead of the story. A few minutes into my snit, I barely noticed that the young features writer with the attitude materialized next to my desk.

"Hi," she said.

"Hi, yourself," I said.

"Somebody told me you like peaches," she said.

"Whaaaaa," I said.

"So, I though it bring you a peach, make up for being a bitch," she said.

A procession of images and metaphors danced through my head, Peach. Peach fuzz. Pubic hair. Pubes. Adam's apple. Eve's peach. Peaches and cream. Orgasm. Peach Melba. Peachy keen. The pits. Was she offering me a piece of fruit, or a piece of herself? J. Alfred Prufrock. "Do I dare eat a peach?" Especially this peach. Or the peach I had in mind. Anyway, got to hand it to her for originality of approach. Beats the hell out of come up and see my etchings.

"That's very thoughtful. Anne, isn't it? Or maybe I'll call you peaches," I said.

"Call me whatever, whenever," she said.

Quicker than a hiccup she was gone, her pink cheeks the color of an overripe tomato, leaving a delicious trail of herbal shampoo, snug behind the features section barrier after executing a pretty gutsy come-on. Christ, I haven't been vamped in so long I've forgotten how to play the mating game. Only a few hours ago, I'd been wrapped around Shelly, and now erection control center was sending down pulses over a woman I'd seen only twice. I got back to business before I needed a cold shower.

I entered my password and the computer gave me permission to write. I slugged the story "tape":

> "Gov. Marshall Goodwin and his one-time political godfather, Joseph Frank, held a secret meeting in an East Baltimore restaurant to discuss ways of obstructing a grand jury investigation into the relationship between organized crime and the Block's randy show bars and pornography shops.
>
> A tape recording of the discussion between Goodwin and Frank was delivered in a plain brown envelope to *City Press* shortly after the meeting took place at Eddie Pomeroy's Roadhouse on Pulaski Highway.
>
> Other sources confirmed that the meeting was scheduled to be held in a private dining room on the restaurant's second floor. On the night of the meeting, an unmarked State Police car was spotted on Eddie Pomeroy's parking lot while a second police car was seen heading toward the restaurant. The

license numbers of the two State Police cars are ZXY 735 and ZXY 736, and the autos are assigned to the governor's security detail in Annapolis.

While the quality of the recording is not state-of-the-art, the voices of Goodwin and Frank are unmistakable and can be heard discussing ways of blunting the grand jury probe, among them searching for embarrassing information in the personal background of Special Prosecutor Robert Krall.

Then Goodwin can be heard saying: 'Best thing is probably to go over his head, directly to Washington, let Justice know what the hell's going on over here. Convince 'em it's a fishing expedition, maybe they'll back off.'

Goodwin then concluded the conversation by telling Frank he needed some time to think about how to approach the Justice Department about the investigation.

The grand jury resumed it's investigation into the Block by hearing four hours of testimony from Sollie Stein, a former Block club owner and spokesman for the cohort of owners who make up the Block who has been retired and living in Florida for a number of years.

Also subpoenaed to appear as a witness before the grand jury was Tony Russo, a colorful gambling figure from Little Italy. However, the special prosecutor decided against taking Russo before the grand jury after a private discussion convinced him that Russo would be an unreliable witness."

On and on for another dozen paragraphs before I punched #, the printer's sign announcing ttttthat's all, folks! I made a printout, then zapped the story to Mulligan's computer. I slouched into his black-lung office with the cassette and the copy a few seconds later after the nuclear power plant at Calvert Cliffs provided the shot of energy to make the electronic transfer. Computers had rendered copy boys (and girls) obsolete. Coughing and gagging on tobacco toxins, I entered the polluted world of Buck Mulligan, thinking enough second-hand smoke to turn the air blue and another nine dollars to decontaminate my suit.

"Watcha got, kid?" Mulligan said.

"Take a look. Story's slugged 'tape'," I said.

Mulligan tapped a few keys, scrolled over the files in his cue then hit the command key and began reading.

"Holy shit! You sure of this stuff," Mulligan said.

"Got the tape right here. You wanna play it?" I said.

"Find a tape recorder," Mulligan said.

I walked out into the newsroom, cock-sure of where I was heading.

"Hi, Peaches. You have a tape recorder I can borrow for a few minutes?" I said.

"My pleasure," Peaches said.

"Gonna be my pleasure," I said.

Back in Mulligan's office I loaded the cassette into the recorder and pressed the play button, making certain the volume was high enough to bring out the tonal distinctions in the two voices. I played the tape once, twice, three times, until I saw the skepticism disappear from Mulligan's face.

"Where'd you get this, kid?" Mulligan said.

"As the story says, plan brown envelope, delivered here," I said.

"You the one bird-dogging the restaurant and the cop cars?" Mulligan said.

"You got that right," I said.

"Whaddya gonna do with the tape?" Mulligan said.

"You want the lawyers to hear it?' I said.

"Screw the lawyers. Up to them we'd never get out the paper 'til they check every story for libel at two hundred fifty dollars an hour. Only two tests a story has to pass—is it true and is it good," Mulligan said.

"What I was thinking is that we stash the tape in a safe deposit box in the paper's name and rely on the First Amendment to do its job," I said.

"Don't put it on an expense account. Make out a cash voucher and I'll sign it. Don't want any records. Anybody else hear this?" Mulligan said.

"Nope," I said.

"Good work, kid. You've still got your legs, and your brain hasn't turned to tapioca after all," Mulligan said.

"Thanks, Buck. Now let me out of this fire trap so I can fumigate myself," I said.

I'd fudged, deliberately not saying that Shelly had declined to listen to the tape, figuring if there's a showdown Mulligan might innocently deal me away. Besides, as long as Shelly's still at the law firm, even after, nobody can touch her because she's been part of the defense team. I slipped the cassette into my pants pocket and eased my way toward Peaches' desk.

"Thanks, Peaches," I said.

"Never had a nickname before. I kind of like it. Makes me feel among friends," Peaches said.

"In this business, you want a friend buy a pet," I said.

"Can't be that bad. You're standing here talking," Peaches said.

"I'm different, like your kindly old uncle from upstate New York, jut a great big baked potato with gobs of melted butter floating around inside," I said.

Peaches said I'm a put-on, but her eyes said she liked being teased. She was smiling a open smile, Windex-blue eyes twinkling, hair loose and manageable, cheeks fresh, no goopy Silly Putty make-up to spoil the natural claret glow of Peaches in full blush. I thought, Christ, Dart, keep it in your pocket, the kid's about half your age. Besides, you have a cuddle at home who loves you more than you can shake a stick at.

CHAPTER 17

▼

The first streaks of evening were spreading across the marmalade sky and the Block was glowing like a radioactive rainbow, enough Technicolor neon to light Las Vegas. I remembered Charles Sharkey's list of developers and thought: Two solid blocks of prime downtown real estate, three, maybe four acres that could accommodate as many as four of those Erector Set skyscrapers, each eight hundred thousand square feet, built at a cost of one hundred fifty dollars a square foot, plus tenant improvements, leased as class A space for as much as thirty dollars a square foot. Each building would have a thousand parking spaces—built for fifteen thousand dollars a space with one hundred percent interest-free city loans—going at seven dollars an hour during business hours, flat rate of six dollars for the evening. Build in ground level commercial space rented at seventy-five dollars a square foot—fancy boutiques, restaurants and bars, Federal Express, a copy center, newsstand and flower shop, public meeting rooms, maybe even an electronic conference center. Christ, no wonder the bricks-and-mortar guys were peeing their pants and supporting Charles Sharkey's born-again bullshit every year. Nothing comes between good friends like good money.

There were no public records, but it was common knowledge that about three thousand board room sharks and pin-striped Piranhas shelled out thirty bucks each for revivalist scrambled eggs and coffee, hoping to be smitten like Paul of Taurus on the road to Damascus, but more than likely to get on Charles Sharkey's redemption list of buying futures in salvation and a chunk of very desirable downtown real estate. In one of those charming civic roundelays, proceeds from the sunrise shakedown were paying for the crusade to make a demolition derby of the Block and resurrect the evil ground into temples of capitalism, all with God's blessing, as Sharkey would put it. Redemption city.

But as an attention getter, Sharkey had met his match. Betty Boobs was a natural leader, always out front, so to speak. When word circulated about Sharkey's thirty dollar a plate celestial suck-up and his plans to dismember the Block, Betty Boobs took it upon herself to organize Block workers into an activist organization, kind of a parliament of prostitutes. By eliminating the Block, Sharkey argued, Baltimore was merely ridding itself of embarrassments and eyesores as had other cities such as Washington, Detroit, Philadelphia and Dallas. To the contrary, Betty Boobs said. The Block not only provides a source of entertainment for big boys but a base of employment as well. To those who work there, the Block is a life as well as a livelihood. The women have children to support, rent to pay, food to buy. So being a woman of action as well as of her word, Betty Boobs applied for a parade permit (granted) and organized a lunch-hour demonstration (approved.)

It was a showstopper. At high noon, on a sunny-side-up day, the Block was sealed off to motorized traffic as if the circus were arriving for its annual elephant walk through the midsection of Baltimore. The office towers emptied, the courthouse virtually shutdown, the briefcase brigade lined the sidewalks six deep as a show of support. Many of the young professionals had had their bachelor parties on the Block and some had left their virginities behind. Mounted policemen patrolled the Block's perimeter and foot patrolmen shoehorned through the crowd under the color of keeping order but enjoying the show just the same.

It was Baltimore's first X-rated parade. Betty Boobs, wearing a D-cup halter with large polka dots under considerable pressure exactly where you dream of them, and white shorts so tight they revealed the outlines of what she'd had for lunch, stepped off to the musical accompaniment of applause, whistles, cheers and a three-piece combo playing an upbeat version of "Lady Be Good." She carried a sign" "Red My Tits. Keep the Block." Behind Betty Boobs followed a comic opera procession of *Grand Guignol* mutants—women in too-tight tank tops and sequined G-strings just big enough to cover both cheeks so as to conform to the obscenity laws; women in spandex, their body parts straining to get out; women carrying babies; one woman dressed as the flying nun, another tossing color-wrapped condoms to the crowd like calling cards. Betty Boobs knew a thing or two about grass roots organizing, too. When the parade was over—it was only a block long—the participants fanned out through the crowd with clipboards and ballpoint pens, asking the viewers to sign petitions to keep the Block in business. After all, adults need entertainment, too. All in all, it had been one of the most festive downtown lunch hours in a long while, at least since the bar fight at the Gayety Theater, which drew a squad of cops, forcing several patrons to dash out with their pants around their knees. But that's neither here nor there, just an amusing anecdote about the Block.

No pain, no gain. I decided to wear out the unwelcome mat. Normalcy had returned to the dim, dank world of Broadway Brown's club, no wreaths, no black crepe, no more indication that he was missing in action than let alone the man had slipped on a banana peel and landed in a hole under six feet of worm-turned earth. Krall was happy now. So, too, was the television reporter who had misappropriated Broadway's picture.

The place looked as if it had died along with Broadway, grungier than usual, lights down low to create an artificial Phantom of the Opera mask of darkness to disguise the pathetic reality of the people and the place. Tough night for the girls doing bottles and lap dances. There were only two men at the bar, and they resembled street people, each drinking beer from the bottle, one a Bud, the other a Miller Lite. Doing bottles, as they say on the Block, is how the girls supplement their incomes. They hustle customers to buy bottles of champagne at a price set by the bartender—usually $110 to $150—and they get to keep anywhere from twenty to thirty percent of the cost. Bottles, like blow jobs, are tax-free. If they're lucky, the girls don't get bopped over the head with the empty when the victim finds out how much he's being charged. Lap dances explain themselves.

But even on the Block, business sometimes gets too entrepreneurial. On one occasion, an organization as American as American Express almost gave its coveted gold card a bad name. American Express took one cardholder to court for, literally, abiding by the AmEx decal on the door of a Block establishment. Turned out during testimony that he'd fallen in love with a hooker and had been having steady sex on the Block at prices ranging from $100 to $200 a throw, charging the frequent encounters to his gold card. The bartender was running the receipts through the club's cash register and paying off the hooker in cash. And for acting as pimp and paymaster, the bartender got ten percent of the action. The state's consumer protection agency was drawn into the case on the side of the plaintiff, arguing that as long as the AmEx decal was on the door, its presence implied acceptance of the card no matter what the product or purchase was. American Express eventually dropped the case and agreed to remove the ubiquitous decals from such establishments.

It was show time. My favorite bartender, right foot propped on a bar shelf and drill-bit eyes cocked on the television set suspended from the ceiling, finally saw me. He reacted like a man with a bad case of jock itch.

"Thought I told you to stay outa here," he said.

"Looking for Faye," I said.

"Faye's not here. Now get the fuck out," he said.

"Your doorman outside says she came in about an hour ago," I said.

"For you she's not here," he said.

"Mind if I look in the back?" I said.

"You do, and you're gonna come out needing plastic surgery," he said.

As he swung, I ducked through the archway to the back room and his hand slammed the frame like Mohamed Ali landing leather dead center on a punching bag. The bartender screamed "mudfuck," then lunged at me with the good hand as I pushed a table between us. Suddenly he grabbed the wrist of the hand that had withered against the doorframe. It took a few seconds for the crunch of bones to reach the bartender's pain center, and from the pleats on his face it was clear that he was hurting. He went back behind the bar and plunged his right hand into the ice chest. I decided to get the hell out of here fast, and as I spun around to leave the back room I saw what the bartender was trying to protect. In a shadowy corner of the room, near the runway and the stage with the fuck pole, Faye sat at a table shooting up with a chemical substance while Captain Joseph Nelligan, of the narcotics squad, held her arm. I was sure Faye was not diabetic, and just as sure that the fluid squirting into Faye's arm was not insulin.

Nelligan heard the commotion and jumped up, still holding Faye's arm pinned to the table to protect the accepting vein. It was an electric moment of accelerated heartbeats and nanosecond reflexes. The bartender was icing his hand. Nelligan couldn't let go of Faye's arm. And the compass in my head pointed straight to the door. I shot through the bar area. The bartender used his good arm to hurl a bottle at me that crashed on the wall a foot from my head. I never did like bourbon. A second bottle looped off the door just as I opened it, a very near miss. The bartender shouted to the doorman, but by the time he decoded the message I was halfway down Baltimore Street, picking up speed as I sprinted toward *City Press*. By the time I reached my car in slot number seven at the side of the building I was winded, chest heaving in quick shallow breaths, heart-thumping protests in double-time against my rib cage. I fished out my car keys and in one fluid motion opened the door, fired up the engine, slid the car into drive and slipped into the night.

As I turned left onto the one-way street, the hood of my car resembled a rifle sight as the headlights framed the body of Nelligan standing defiantly, arms crossed, dead center in my pathway. I thought, holy shit! If this were a drunk or anyone else menacing, I'd just sideswipe him and plead self-defense. With *City*

Press's parking spaces taking up half the street, there wasn't enough room to get around Nelligan without jumping the curb and messing up the wheel alignment or worse, ripping off the underbelly of the car. I thought of slamming the car into reverse and backing out onto Pratt Street, but there was already a set of headlights staring into my rearview mirror. I had no choice but to slide back into my parking space. As I did, I punched the electric switch and snapped the door locks. The car stopped, rear to curb, and Nelligan lunged for the door handle. I put the heat to the engine, peeling rubber like Mario Andretti at the Indy 500, leaving Nelligan curbside flat on his ass.

I needed a drink, badly, and I hadn't eaten all day. Nelligan had probably figured I'd be heading for home and cut right to the chase. But right now, the safest place to be was in the newsroom at *City Press.* I swung around the block and parked my car at a meter a block up the street. I slipped back into the building and up to the third floor faster than a runner doing a nine second hundred-yard dash.

Fear heightens bladder activity. The first thing I did was pee. I tried to settle down by splashing cold water on my face and taking deep breaths, sucking and blowing as if I were partnering in a Lamaze class. When I finally decompressed, I went to what passed for a cafeteria, changed two one dollar bills, for silver, and from the vending machine I bought a cup of coffee and a tuna salad sandwich. A gourmet dinner at my desk. For dessert, I'd probably need a tetanus shot.

Next, I dialed my home number and heard my voice telling me that I couldn't come to the phone. I told the answering machine:

"Shelly, if you're there, or if you come by later, leave right away and go to your place. And don't forget to re-set the alarm. I'm at the paper. I'll explain later."

I also told Shelly's machine essentially the same message—stay away from my house.

I knew I was in deep shit. Nelligan'll nail me now just for exercise. The trouble with my line of work is that it's impossible to make friends but easy as hell to collect enemies. Big ones. Nelligan's a tough sonofabitch who once faced down the Mafia and doesn't take crap from anyone, especially piss-ant reporters. I decided to write a file memo outlining what happened tonight, keep a copy in the computer and stash a printout in the safe deposit box along with the tape recording of Goodwin and Frank. I told the story straight ahead, no embellishment or hyperbole, and when it was finished I re-read it once and made a printout, which I folded and slipped into the inside breast pocket of my jacket. I hit the save button and sent it to the computer's memory bank.

As I did, Peaches tiptoed up to my desk as softly as if she were wearing ballet slippers.

"Thought you left for the night," she said.

"I thought so, too, but I'm in a bit of a pickle and I need a place to hide," I said.

"What kind of trouble?" she said.

"Reporter kind of trouble, basically getting in the way," I said.

"Anybody I know?" she said.

"Christ, I hope not," I said.

"About a place to hide. Are you staying here for the night?" she said.

"Can't go home, too risky right now," I said.

"I know a cozy little hideout with a well-stocked liquor cabinet not to far from here," she said.

I was being propositioned, an old horn-ball like me, by a kid probably not long out of one of those fancy New England colleges or maybe fresh out of graduate school with a master's degree in journalism. You know the type. They always go for features writing instead of news. Peaches said she had an apartment in the Mount Vernon area on one of those leafy side streets that runs east-west between Charles Street and Maryland Avenue, nice but not the safest neighborhood in town. But these days, what is? Tempting. Something strange for a change, maybe a couple of new tricks. I could taste those little rosebud lips sucking on mine, our tongues tickling each other's tonsils. And those taut little Wonder Bra titties, I could feel them stabbing into my rib cage. But a reality check told me that come-ons are terrific for the ego, but right now my Id wasn't interested. Any encounter tonight would probably be like putting oysters in a slot machine. My mind just wasn't into it. Not right now. And with sex, it's important not to disappoint the first time.

"Best offer I've had all day," I said.

"Is that a yes?" Peaches said.

"Love to. But better not. I don't want to get you mixed up in the mess I'm in. But I'll definitely keep it high on my future's list," I said.

"I'll keep the vodka chilled. Sleep well, wherever it is," Peaches said.

"You, too," I said.

In a few hours, the paper would hit the streets and my name would be double dirt all over town. The responsive twitch is more predictable than Baltimore's weather—phone calls to lawyers humming along underground fiber-optic, the competition scrambling for reaction and comment, hastily arranged news conferences in Baltimore and Annapolis, Krall sucking wind because he came up on the short end again, looking for ways to scoot around the babble of the law and stick it directly to me. This was no ordinary case as clear-cut as a speeding ticket, messing as it did with the anti-wire tap laws, the Constitution, possible criminal evidence and the state's shield law that protects reporters from revealing sources or information. Wham! When I make a statement, it's as big and bold as if I'd rented a billboard.

The background noise of a newsroom is a constant low percussive buzz, a coming together of thousands of clicks, clumps, rumbles, slams, rings, voices, dings and whirrs into a harmonic convergence of sympathetic vibrations. One trick to success in the news business is learning to tune out the ambient sounds, like switching off a radio, and letting the inner ear do the work of processing the rhythms and cadences of all of that deathless prose. It's like a metronome somewhere way down in there making certain the words have the right number of syllables and attention-getting tricks so there are no bumps or truncations to jar the reader. Most people don't realize it, but they read with their ears as much as their eyes. Tonight my sound switch was on the blink and the jumble of noise around me was a clash of annoyance. I had a fucking headache, a four alarm head-banger as big as the Goodyear blimp. I ambled to the conference room and was grateful that it was empty. I slouched on a sofa that looked as if it had decorated an airport waiting room in the Fifties. It was so hard and stiff that it seemed to be made of linoleum. I loosened my tie, tilted my head on the sofa's back and snuffed out into a trail of zzzzzzzzzzzzzzzzzzz.

An hour later, I woke up and scraped my tongue off the roof of my mouth, the headache gone. Luckily, for occasions such as this, I keep a toothbrush and tooth paste, along with a fresh white shirt and a pair of socks, under lock and key in my bottom desk drawer. The taste of the toothpaste was refreshing, as cool and clean as mint chocolate chip ice cream. To complete the wake-up call, I splashed cold water on my face and pronounced myself restored to my usual robust clear-eyed health and vigor.

I remembered my car, on a downtown street after nightfall, naked and vulnerable to hubcap dealers and radio sneak-thieves and after dawn to the tow truck brigade. That is, unless Nelligan hadn't already been alerted to its location. Not wanting to expose anyone else to the danger of being Richard Dart, I still hadn't decided what I'd do or where I'd do it. Except for this: I'd stay away from my house tonight, not knowing who might be lurking in the bushes capable of being the probable cause of serious bodily harm if not a permanent alteration of my features. Fear of pain and disfigurement aside, I still had to move my car to a safety zone and when the banks open stash my best-selling audio cassette in a safe deposit box along with the file memo I'd prepared detailing my accidental encounter with Nelligan.

I dialed Shelly's number again, still nobody home except the answering machine, which I told:

"Second call, nine fifteen. Stay out of the line of fire. Don't call me, I'll call you. Love and lust."

Next, I dialed my own number, punched the activating code number and after two hang-up beeps, the machine said:

"....This is an electronic survey being conducted by National Marketing Associates. We appreciate your cooperation. At the sound of the tone, we will ask a series of questions and request that you register your answers. If you have a touch tone phone and own the house you live in, press one. If you rent a house or an apartment, press two. If you own a condominium, press three. If you'd like information on a special condominium insurance policy being offered for the first time, press four and stay on the line. Thank you....Another hang-up beep....This is the Alan Flusser shop calling Richard Dart. We have a new selection of custom fabrics we'd like to show you whenever you get a chance to stop by. Looking forward to seeing you soon...Dart, you can't hide in that newspaper office the rest of your life. Sooner or later you gotta come out. And when you do, I'll be waiting...." Another hang-up beep and the machine clicked off.

Fucking Nelligan, about as subtle as a runaway dump truck, though his point was not missed. Hot acid began to bubble up in my throat, and I had the kind of sudden head rush that usually accompanies the fight-or-flight decision. Now I understood the fear of the first man who looked a saber-toothed tiger squarely in the eye. I admit I'm basically a pacifist when it comes to physical danger, liking my nose where it is and enjoying the friendship of a full set of teeth. Nelligan apparently knew where I was. The safest thing I could think of was to try and get my car back into its berth next to *City Press* and bivouac in the office for the night.

On the way out of the building, I told the night watchman where I was going and how long it should take. I added: If I'm not back within twenty minutes, please notify the night editor. End-running editors is a full-time job, but I wasn't ready to answer any questions just yet.

The one thing about Baltimore air is that you know what you're breathing because most of the time you can see it. Tonight the smell of the harbor's brine competed for olfactory attention with the sulfurous sting of diesel fumes from the eighteen-wheelers rumbling across Pratt Street toward the loading docks and shipping hubs along the eastside of the port. The diesel fumes won. A necklace of stars glittered across the sky and the moon was pasted in place like a giant vanilla wafer. I shifted my Cole-Hanns into high gear, accelerating my pace with each step until I achieved a speed of aerobic benefit, my heart banging a call for mercy against my chest. I was scared. And not only of Nelligan. There's a new urban sport in Baltimore called trunknapping. Gangs of thugs, usually three or four, roam the streets looking for high rollers in slick suits getting into fancy cars. They hold you up, take your wallet, lock you in the trunk. Then, while you're screaming your ass off for help, they drive around town and have a helluva good time on your credit cards. When they're through, they just park the car somewhere and forget all about you. I keep a screwdriver and a flashlight in the trunk of my car in case I'm ever napped.

My car appeared intact, hubcaps, radio and tape deck all fastened where they belong. I'm suspicious as well as cautious. I also watch too many good-guy, bad-guy movies. So being that way, before I unlocked the car I peeked into the back seat to make sure there were no unwanted passengers crouched in the foot well. The coast was clear. I jumped in the car, lit the fire and varoooooom-mmmed around the block, made two green lights, and slipped into my berth next to *City Press*.

There are times when reporting is like performing a high-wire act without a net. I realized this was such an occasion when two men stepped out of the shadows and flashed badges that sent out shards of refracted light when they caught the streetlights at just the right angle. The taller of the two asked if they could search my car. My heart did a dipsy-doodle. This was Nelligan's way of saying "gotcha!" If I said no, they'd get a search warrant. If I said yes, I'd be incriminating myself. So I shot a quick smirk, spun around and walked away, figuring they'd already planted the drugs anyway and would make a case later.

Before I took three steps, the big guy pried off the left rear hubcap and held up three plastic bags the size of Sweet and Low packets. I was not surprised, figuring the evidence was cupped in the palm of his hand all the while. The cop who seemed to be in charge told me I was under arrest for possession of narcotics. I bit back the urge to say fuck you. Instead, I was the model of cooperation, having learned enough to know that cops don't like smart-asses, especially when they appear to have you by the balls. And they always travel in pairs so they can lie for each other. The word had been around for years that phony busts were among Nelligan's favorite tricks. Mess with him, get busted for possession, ounce of pot or whatever. I must have been a big-time trophy, going for three bags of blow. I could feel my sphincters tighten, and the helium-headed feeling returned as if I were Mylar balloon being gassed up for a birthday party.

The big plug-ugly replaced the hubcap and read me my rights, which I took literally and kept quiet. He cuffed me (unnecessarily) and asked me to walk with them the two blocks to police headquarters. To humiliate me further, they paraded me down the Block as if I were being led to a public hanging. Being on display has its advantages, but not when it means wearing bracelets in the company of two narcs. A couple of barkers recognized me as we passed Pandora's Box. One gave me the finger, the other hissed "shithead."

At police headquarters, I was taken directly to Nelligan's office, a departure from the normal process that I found both curious and terrifying. I was so scared that even my teeth were sweating. The two officers who did the dirty work left. Except for the furniture, Nelligan and I were alone. Nelligan got up, closed the door and drew the low-bid municipal mini-blinds shut. My heart was fluttering father than a hummingbird's wings. I stood in the middle of the room, facing Nelligan's desk, waiting for some words of instruction. I was still in cuffs. Why is it that whenever your hands are inaccessible you always get an itch on your nose, like when the dentist begins drilling you've got to scratch. Nelligan still said nothing. He eased around in front of me. I remembered that cops were experts at what lawyers call soft tissue damage, strictly under-the-skin stuff that leaves no marks. Now we were staring at each other, like two kids playing a classic game of chicken, waiting to see who'd blink first. Nelligan leaned his buttocks against the edge of his desk and finally said:

"Sit down, asshole."

I said nothing. I preferred standing, but I figured I'd better accept Nelligan's offer. Besides, it wouldn't be very comfortable to sit, because my host still hadn't removed the handcuffs. Now I know what's meant by the saying, sitting on your hands.

"....You're in deep shit, now, smartass. Wouldn't back off while you stall had a chance. Fucking with the law's a serious offense on my territory. Three bags of coke'll get you ten, maybe twenty years. You like your name in the paper so fucking much, this'll get you all the attention you want."

"Phone call. I'm entitled to one phone call," I said.

Nelligan said: "Stop whining, you fucking ninny. Around here the only entitlement you get is what I give you. You keep your fucking mouth shut unless I ask you a question. You got that? 'Cause from now on it's my show. I've got evidence, two witnesses who'll swear to God Almighty that you were packing the stuff in your car like a common fucking junkie, you and your girl friend, the lawyer, doing nose candy at your house every night. That's why we had you under surveillance, on a hunch you and the pretty lady were snorting. Only thing we haven't figured is who your connection is. We'll find that out, too. Lotta low-life's out there selling the stuff, happy to testify they're supplying you instead of being busted."

My stomach was doing a low boil and I was beginning to get the flutters. The air in Nelligan's office must have been a month old, recycled through miles of ancient duct work and filters that were never changed, carrying with it an invisible trail of heavy duty disinfectant masking other odors. I remembered, too, that police headquarters had recently been declared a health hazard because it was stuffed with asbestos. I was gagging on municipal toxins. Even though I was beginning to feel sorry for myself, I wondered just what the hell Nelligan thought he'd accomplish by trumping up chargers to get me out of the way. There are a dozen—well, maybe one or two—reporters at *City Press* who could pick up the pieces and run with the story if I disappeared. I know everybody's supposed to have a Rosebud somewhere, but apparently Nelligan couldn't find mine so he invented one. I now knew his, although no mention was made of what I'd witnessed this afternoon in the dim shadows of the back room at Pandora's box. An alarm button clicked on in my memory circuits reminding me that *City Press* would hit the streets soon, and if I were still in Nelligan's custody he might throw me into a cell with a six-foot dude named Jahmal.

"About the phone call," I said.

"Forget the phone call. In this room I'm the law," Nelligan said.

Luck is an occasion when preparation meets opportunity. The phone on Nelligan's desk rang once, twice, three times before he picked it up.

"Nelligan here (pause)....No shit (pause)....No shit (laughter)....Tell 'em he can have the little prick when I'm finished with him (hang up)...That was the duty sergeant saying your editor's reporting you missing. Like you're some kind of hot-shit valuable property or something. Tell you what. Now that you're acquainted with Nelligan's justice, let's make peace, make a deal," Nelligan said.

"What kind of deal," I said.

"Simple deal. You back off. I back off. Simple as that," Nelligan said.

To punctuate his offer, Nelligan came around to the back of my chair, stretched down behind me and uncuffed my wrists. At least now I could rest my back against the chair. I rubbed my wrists and tried to look thoughtful.

"You've got a boss, and I've got a boss. Reporting isn't as simple as shaving points or tossing a game," I said.

Nelligan said: "This time I'm going to let you walk out of here, give you time to think about it. Next time, I'm gonna bust you, throw you into the detox tank and try your ass not only for possession but also as a distributor. You know the way out of here. And don't try any funny stuff or I'll blast you out of your undershorts. Remember, I have witnesses who see things the way I want them to. And I have eyes on you twenty four hours a day."

I felt as drained as an empty tequila bottle after an all-night binge, but I decided it was safe to go home, at least for tonight. The drive was uneventful. No headlights were climbing up my tailpipe or blazing into my rearview mirror. At home, I ate a small container of lemon yogurt (low fat) and chased it down with two fingers of brandy. After what I'd been through, the shower felt like a delousing. I hit the pillow sleeping, thanking my guardian angel that I was safe in my own bed instead of in a municipal cell slow dancing with Jahmal.

CHAPTER 18

▼

It was crack-of-dawn time when the trembling phone shook loose the sleep. I felt like a patient coming out of anesthesia. The digital clock read 7:30 A.M. The voice was the unmistakable rasp of Mulligan's butt kit:

"Wake you up, kid?"

"Yeah. Christ, what a night," I said.

"Better get your ass down here fast, I mean double-time," Mulligan said.

"What's up," I said.

"The price on your head," Mulligan said.

"In that case, I'll make sure I'm worth every penny," I said.

"Fast," Mulligan said.

Mulligan sounded like a man who hadn't had his bran muffin this morning. Shaving, I wondered just what, for crying out loud, was going on in the hoary head of Buck Mulligan. More accurately, I wondered who—Nelligan? Nah, we'd had our little showdown and we'd wait to see who blinked next. Krall? Good possibility, judging by past performances. Frank? Goodwin? Three blue chips down on Goodwin, being pressured to call a news conference to explain his voice on tape with the political boss he's supposed to have forsaken. Sharkey? Whoa! It'd be just like that weasel to grab the action when he sees it marching by, a splendid opportunity to say I-told-you-so.

If I felt like singing in the shower, it would be the executioner's song, a twisted tale of a jolly chopper under a morbid black hood, chuckling and saying, nothing personal, everybody has a job to do, having a beer while he lowered the axe. Instead, I stood under the waterfall, enjoying a good soaking, wondering what to wear to my own funeral. Not many people get to make that choice. I rub-a-dub-dubbed myself dry, finished my morning ablutions and went to the closet.

A muted glen plaid seemed appropriate since everyone else is buried in navy or gray, this one with a blue windowpane pattern. I paired it with a solid blue end-on-end shirt and an ancient madder tie with blue sperms swimming on a red grounding that picked up the tones of the shirt and suit and corresponded nicely to the proportions of the plaid. I added precision to the ensemble by tightening up the look with a silver collar pin. If they laid me out now I'd look as if I'd stepped out of Alan Flusser's window. Mulligan had said fast, but I was in no hurry. I dawdled over orange juice and after it bite-sized Shredded Wheat with non-fat milk, my standard morning fare, only 170 calories and six grams of dietary fiber.

I stacked my car in its usual slot, not forgetting that only a few hours ago there was a surprise waiting for me at curbside, the two bozos who make a living playing follow the baggie. I get the bends every time I think about it, coming as close as I did to getting lost deep in the system of justice.

Slouching toward the *City Press* entrance, I stopped at a news box and came face-to-face with a headline writer's playful handiwork:

Gov. To Frank:
Block That Probe

Headline writers are the scourges of the newspaper business, working as they do within limitations of space, time and often the collective IQ of a speed bump. Readers complain more about headlines than stories, especially on those occasions when they're such a mis-match that the story could sue the headline for non-support. Except that this headline worked. Not only was it accurate, but it was also a nice play on words. For once, someone got it right.

Pissing off people goes with the territory, kind of like a reporter's birthright, and judging by the smirk on Mulligan's face when I entered his office I was getting pretty good at it. So far this morning, Mulligan said, he'd had calls from Governor Goodwin saying he was going to sue the ass off *City Press* for violating the state's wire tap law, from Bob Krall demanding the tape as evidence pertinent to his investigation, and from Charles Sharkey saying the recording only validated his case and he'd like a copy of the tape to make radio commercials advancing his cause of tearing down the Block and sanitizing the city.

"That's smoking 'em out kid. Good job," Mulligan said.

"Glad you're getting a charge out of my neck being on the chopping block," I said.

"What I'm paying you for, kid. Want a sissy's job, take up ballet," Mulligan said.

"What's with getting me out of bed in the middle of the night?" I said.

"Thought you'd wanna know what's going on. You're a celebrity, everybody's after your ass," Mulligan said.

"With all the yelling over the tape, I'd better get to the bank right away. Tell you a story when I get back," I said.

The audiocassette was in my pants pocket. I made another printout of my file memo on Nelligan and Faye, making like a diabetic, and sealed it in an envelope, which I tucked in the inside breast pocket of my jacket. On the way out of the building I came within inches of colliding with Peaches, looking for all the world to see like a sorority pledge during rush week—nubile, eager, teeth braces-straight and eyes sky-blue dancing behind the faint glint of contact lenses.

"Hello, Peaches," I said.

"Hi! Where'd you end up sleeping last night," Peaches said.

"Several places, none of them much fun," I said.

"We have to put a stop to that," Peaches said.

"Don't start anything you don't intend to finish," I said.

Peaches smiled and turned the color of Beaujolais. My mind was dirty-dancing, but I realized I was playing a tease, something I didn't like very much in other people. Sooner or later, working side-by-side as we did in the newsroom, this little dance-around-the-rim-of-the-dish that we were engaged in would have to play itself out. Either that or end it.

I smiled and mumbled an excuse, leaving Peaches behind in a trail of puzzlement. I worked my way up the street, across the intersection and halfway up the next block to the stately old bank with the marble front and the big brass doors, the way they used to build banks—rock-solid to convey integrity and security. These days, it's tough to tell a bank from a pizza shop. Inside, the old bank was a cool cavern of marble and brass, Tiffany skylights and a huge solid brass door full of cranks, clocks, handles and levers. Inside the vault, my treasures, a memo and a tape, would repose like the family jewels in safe deposit box No.8572, according to the form I'd filled out and the key I was given—only one of two keys in existence, which I planned to hide from even myself. The bank had the other, and it wouldn't work without mine. If Krall wanted the tape, let his fucking coppers on the Strike Force drill the box open, then I'd have a helluva story about invasion of privacy and seizure of information.

By the time I got back to the office—not more than a half an hour—there was an announcement on the wire of a news conference in Annapolis and a subpoena from Krall for me to appear before the grand jury the next day. I decided, what the hell, to drive to Annapolis. Even governors are allowed the right to confront their accusers. But first I checked with Mulligan about the pain-in-the-ass subpoena. He told me, as I would have guessed, to call the company lawyer for guidance. Which I did, and was told to sit tight, he'd try to arrange a meeting with Krall to see if the stand-off could be resolved in a reasonable way, without the law going full blast into a firestorm of charges and counter-charges, as they say.

In all the bungling, botching commotion of the past eighteen hours, I suddenly remembered, like a jolt, that I still hadn't caught up with Shelly. I wanted to know how she resolved her decision with the law firm about taking a leave and returning to school; and I wanted to tell her about my own hair-raising (don't I wish) misadventures. I dialed her direct number and she picked up on the third ring.

"Where you been, lover, tried to reach you last night," I said.

"I got your messages and followed your instructions not to call you," Shelly said.

"Long story," I said.

"Speaking of stories, I see you've been at it again," Shelly said.

"Krall sent me an invitation to visit him tomorrow," I said.

"You'll be the life of the party," Shelly said.

I told Shelly an abbreviated version of what had happened to me since yesterday afternoon, how I'd flounced into Broadway Brown's club and caught Faye shooting up while Nelligan held her arm to the table. And how I'd been accosted and framed by two of Nelligan's rottweilers and hauled off to the jug like a common criminal and offered a deal in exchange for my backing off the story of the Block. And how today's story had me on every shit list from here to Tierra del Fuego. I told Shelly my plans for today, facing Goodwin and later meeting with lawyers, and said I'd call when it was over so we could get together for dinner.

"We've got to talk about where were headed," I said.

"You bet we do," Shelly said.

"Meaning what?" I said.

"At dinner," Shelly said.

There's a Maryland story of apocryphal origin that goes like this: An Eastern Shore father took his young son down to the water's edge of the Chesapeake Bay. Son, the father said, there are only two ways to make a decent living in Maryland. One is here, the father said, pointing down to the Bay water and what H.L. Mencken called "the world's largest protein factory." And lifting his arm, the father said the other is over there, pointing across the water to the State House in Annapolis.

It was in this very same State House, surrounded by history's ghosts and goblins, where every corner and cranny had a story to tell of high and low-jinks, where the House and Senate chambers serve as caves of wind echoing with the dithyrambic diatribes and debate—it was in this hallowed sanctum that Marshall Goodwin would step forth in pin stripes and pomp to declaim his innocence in the very same reception room where Spiro T. Agnew's portrait was banished from the gallery of governors after he was caught with his fingers in the tambourine.

The State House reception room was packed, the bloodhounds had picked up the scent, the atmosphere crackled with the electricity of the satellite messages. Goodwin's ass was on the line. The corps of State House reporters usually numbered about thirty-five. Today, the head-count was about seventy-five, including cameras from the Washington stations as well as the networks. All because of me. I felt smug as I staked out my patch of oriental carpet, standing behind an amphitheater of four rows of folding chairs that were already filled. Except for a few gray heads and bald spots, the State House press corps was composed of a bunch of kids, some of whom probably wouldn't know how to dig for fishing bait let alone forage for a story. I knew virtually no one in this crowd, except for a couple of the network cameramen whom I'd known in Washington. But I could see heads cocking and eyes boring holes in me like lasers. My curator's eye was scanning the reception room artwork, most of it historically symbolic but artistically drab, when the set of double glass doors swung open. Two state policemen in plain clothes preceded Goodwin and a man that I assumed was his press secretary, who said the governor would read from a prepared statement before taking any questions. Goodwin mounted the podium and began in his tin-whistle voice:

"….Shocked and dismayed by this total disregard for an individual's right to privacy as well as this high-handed violation of the laws of this state. One zealous prosecutor has seen fit to turn a fishing expedition into a comedy of errors. And one reckless reporter has made a mockery of our system of justice. I have asked the attorneys on my staff as well as the attorney general's office to determine what state laws have been violated and to recommend an appropriate course of action. And I have instructed them further to prepare a communication to the attorney general of the United States protesting the unlicensed behavior and abusive conduct of the Special Federal Strike Force assigned to Baltimore. And I want you to know and to convey to the public that I welcome this investigation. In the end, it will prove fruitless and a waste of taxpayers' money as well as an abuse of government resources."

I'd decided not to ask the first question because it would put me in a position of questioning the credibility of my own story. Letting someone else ask the question for me was risky, but it was too obvious to miss. As soon as Goodwin's voice dropped off to a period (.), signaling an end to his prepared statement, a Greek chorus of reporters, as if on cue, shouted "Governor" in unison, commencing of the few remaining blood sports in the Western world: The news conference.

Goodwin: "One at a time. We'll get to everybody."

Reporter: "Governor, as you've indicated in your opening statement, you are aware of the story in today's *City Press*. Did you have such a conversation with Joe Frank, and are they your voices on the tape?"

Goodwin: "As you know, Joe Frank and I are old friends even though we've had some political differences. I've heard no such tape recording, so I can't testify to either the conversation or its authenticity.

Second reporter: "Why, then, are you saying that you might take legal action, that some laws might have been violated?"

Goodwin: "I'm simply saying that I'm asking my staff lawyers and the attorney general to decide whether any laws have been broken."

Third reporter: "How can you suggest, as you did in your statement, that your right to privacy was invaded at the same time you're saying you haven't heard the tape recording?"

Goodwin: "What I'm saying is that somebody's right to privacy, if not mine, was invaded because a conversation was illegally recorded."

Fourth reporter: "If, as you claim, you know nothing of the tape, how do you know it's illegal?"

Goodwin: "All I know is that somebody's playing games and trying to set me up. And it's all in keeping with what's been going on since the Strike Force was set up. It's a blatant attempt by the Justice Department to entrap and embarrass elected officials around the country. And believe me, if you want to do some checking, some real journalism, you can find out and print the truth instead of all the leaks that have been filling the papers."

Metaphysics and journalism have one thing in common. News conferences, like philosophy, proceed from the question and not the answer. I'd often joked that if I ever teach journalism, it'll be a course on how to ask questions. It was time, I decided, to add my voice to the hootenanny, since the dissembling over the tape was bogging down progress toward the central question of the investigation.

Dart: "Governor, do you have any formal or informal relationship, or any business arrangements at all, with any establishment or individual on the Block?"

Goodwin: "I have no ties with the Block whatsoever, formal or informal, never have, never will."

Dart: "Governor, why, then, did you say on the tape that you'd figure a way to try and thwart the investigation if you have nothing to hide?"

Goodwin: "So far, you're the only person in this room or anywhere else, for all I know, who's heard the tape you describe. Why didn't you bring it along and play it for us so we could all decide together who's who on the tape you claim to have heard. So how can I answer a question like the one you ask? I've told you, and I'll repeat it, I have no interests in the Block at whatsoever."

Playing games, the slick sonofabitch. I show up with the tape and he's got me, his voice or not. He hears his own voice and he's got me even better, invasion of privacy, violation of wire tap laws, recording a conversation without permission.

Dart: "Maybe I'll do that next time. But 'til then, could you tell us whether you've heard from the grand jury, whether you've received a subpoena of any kind, personal or for your records?"

Goodwin: "I haven't heard a word from anyone remotely connected with the grand jury. Only thing I know is what I read in your newspaper, and you seem to know more about the investigation than anyone else. Maybe your imagination's working overtime. Or maybe you're getting information in a way that violates the secrecy of the grand jury system."

And on, and on, and on. Blah, blah, blah, blah blah. Ninety percent air and ten percent foam. Asking this guy questions was like trying to lasso a lightening bolt. But sooner or later the truth, like pregnancy, will out. And I hope I'm the one who injects the magic fluid. After about ten more minutes of misfired questions and misdirected answers about such arcane topics as budget cuts, funds for battered spouses, the condition of the state yacht, the gypsy moth spraying program and the possibility that Goodwin might run for the U.S. Senate, the senior reporter, a bourbon-breathed radio man who looked like a gunny sack full of old galoshes, mercifully, put an exclamation point on the news conference by bellowing, "Thank you, governor."

The reporters all stood up as if they were brought to attention by the words that boomed over the chatter. Goodwin stepped off his elevated podium. The reporters formed a clump around him. But Goodwin, in high dudgeon and low boil, made his way to the double glass doors encapsulated in a flying wedge of Ton-Tons. As the reporters straggled away, some of them gathering in a small knot to compare notes, there was a tap on my shoulder and a whisper in my ear. The man I assumed to be the press secretary asked in a voice as soft as a wheeze if

I could stick around for a minute, the governor would like to talk with me. I said: "You bet your ass I can."

The reception room finally cleared, the press secretary emerged, nodded to the trooper at the desk by the entrance and a buzzer clicked open the double glass doors. I was escorted through a long room that was populated by half dozen secretaries and their desks, a water cooler, a Mr. Coffee, a bookcase and more dubious artwork depicting Marylandia. Finally, into the sanctum of sanctums, the governor's own office, a large warm room dominated by a marble fireplace and a huge gilded mirror framed by hurricane lamps, an oversized oriental carpet, heavy gold drapes drawn and blocking the outside world and desk, bookcase, media center and a credenza—all in heavy burnished wood. The desk was surrounded by a semi-circle of a half dozen chairs upholstered in black leather, taut and tacked to the wooden frames by brass studs—the forceful look of a manly office as well as an emblem of authority. More artwork of mustachioed men in Errol Flynn swashbuckler's clothes and women in high stiff collars and petticoated swells of lapidary fabric—the founding fathers and mothers enshrined by ancient court painters more intent on flattering their subjects than in producing decent art. The office looked like the library of a British men's club.

I'd spent much of my life in the shadows of the great and the near great, and if I were tethered to a polygraph right now, watching the flicking needle measure my character in jagged lines, I'd confess to the machine that this was not one of the inspirational high points of my life. There was no aura of a compelling presence radiating a magnetic field of heavy vibrations urging me to bend and kiss the hem of Goodwin's garment. Good thing. I'm not Catholic. I'd known Goodwin in the early lean years, and the only thing that's changed about him now is that he exuded the sweet smell of success. The cunning, screw-you attitude was now draped in expensive well-cut cloth that wore the mark of a man with a tailor on someone else's payroll.

I was offered a chair and coffee, as if they were paired together, pre-packaged in plastic blisters. The chair I accepted, the coffee I declined. Goodwin asked his press secretary to leave the room, an unusual departure, I thought, because most public officials want witnesses to their discussions with reporters. But, I ruminated, maybe Goodwin was protecting his press secretary from the burden of knowing something he might be forced to regurgitate to the wrong people. Or maybe he was going to say off the record, between us, out of bounds for the spokesman as well as the public, my word against his, a tack I'd resist. Or maybe, maybe he didn't trust his press secretary. The rules say always protect the deniability of the executive. My receptors flashed, Uh-oh.

When we'd both wiggled our heinies into place—me to protect the integrity of my creases and wrinkle-free jacket, Goodwin not caring one way or the other about the condition of the king's new clothes, slumping into position like a rag doll in distress—Goodwin cut right to the chase:

"I wanted to have a private talk with you, find out what's bothering you, why you've got some kind of bug up your butt. Thought maybe we could get this thing straightened out.

"Not a bother in the world. Got an assignment, just doing my job," I said.

"I don't know who your sources are, but all these leaks can only be coming from one place and that's the Strike Force. The Justice Department's going after elected officials all over the country and they're manipulating the press into being part of the scheme, a leak here, a crumb there, and they've got you on the hook like a junkie," Goodwin said.

"Governor, you know better than that, because you know the reporter you're talking to. Maybe that's true of police and sports reporters, but that's not the way I operate," I said.

"Look, we've both been around, both know how the game is played. You're enjoying this too much to call it just a job. What the hell do you think you're gonna find? Do you think I'm stupid or something?" Goodwin said.

"The last thing I think is that you're stupid. That's what surprises me, getting yourself involved with that crowd of thugs. You're supposed to be finished with Joe Frank, no more of his payola politics, remember? I'm not telling you who to associate with, but the public deserves better. Christ, you're governor now, and you still haven't risen above representing the pimps and the whores on the Block. And you talk about a bug up my butt? Gimme a break," I said.

"You don't back off, I'll give you a break. I've got sixteen hundred State Policemen. I'll have them on your tail, you so much as spit on the sidewalk your ass is in the slammer," Goodwin said.

"I take it back, you are stupid, talking Gestapo crap like that. Your State Police are so inept they can't even cover their own asses let alone yours, like the night you met Joe Frank at Eddie Pomeroy's, one unmarked car a decoy, the other hauling you a mile behind. I have their license numbers, and both cars are sitting on the mansion parking lot right now. So let's talk stupid," I said.

I'd stunned Goodwin with that little droplet of information I'd checked out while walking past the mansion to the State House. He was squirming like a slug dodging salt, white knuckles clenched around a Styrofoam cup, inhaling a long sip of coffee, giving him time to think of what to say next. Funny how when they're cornered so many politicians resort to thinking like Latin American dicta-

tors, ordering the troops to protect the sovereign and the palace, threatening people with police reprisals, all of that commander in-chief crap on a power trip
straight to their noggins, jerking their egos off by surrounding themselves with
uniformed strutting apes who probably couldn't hit the side a barn with a bag of
rice. But I wasn't anxious to test my theory. Goodwin finally snapped back to life
on a surge of caffeine.

"You're right. Stupid is stupid, I'm the first to admit. Now whether I met with
Joe Frank, and I'm not saying I did, is not the issue. What I'm concerned about is
fairness, all these unfounded rumors and wild stories without a fact or foundation
ruining lives and wrecking reputations. If there's something legitimate to write
about, or some basis for an investigation, then fine, I welcome it. But until then,
this character assassination has got to stop. That's all I'm asking," Goodwin said.

"Governor, the investigation is your problem to deal with. You're the only one
who knows what they've got or what they can get. My job is to report what
they're doing. Simple as that," I said.

"Just don't lie," Goodwin said.

"Don't worry governor, the truth is probably bad enough," I said.

Goodwin had it all wrong. The trouble with politicians is that they begin
thinking the rest of the world operates like politics, especially the lawyers, which
in a sense it does. Because whenever two or more people meet, whether it's in a
supermarket or a Roman Catholic Church, they're sizing each other up, signifying, politicking the hell out of each other, body language and all. Popes get to be
popes the same way governors get to be governors. But the difference is that when
politicians are trapped, they begin seeing conspiracies, wheels-within-wheels,
reporters ganging up on them with the help of the law. And I've never met a
guilty one yet who didn't say, "I welcome this investigation." My other favorite
is, "I've done nothing illegal." Right or wrong, moral or immoral, never enters
the equation. Trouble is, Goodwin and his kind don't recognize that reporting is
all form-follows-function and a lot of dull-ass fundamentals such as phone books,
records, crisscross directories, sitting and waiting, and miles of legwork, although
in this case I must confess that I've been lucky. Where would I be without Sollie
Stein, the anonymous tips on my voice mail and the great American who
dumped the audiocassette into my lap? In journalism, as in life, you make your
luck.

I was smoking along at a law-breaking 65 mph, sucking the doors off everything I passed, streaking toward Baltimore and a late afternoon date with the *City
Press* lawyers. I needed a bathroom, but I calculated that my bladder could con-

tain itself until I reached the newsroom, about 30 minutes away. I flashed back to my confrontation with Goodwin, but I put the thought on call-waiting while I took the incoming thought about my meeting with the lawyers. The part of my brain that does the reasoning told me that this was no fucking joke, don't treat it lightly. Truth is, I viewed the encounter as an aggravation that was likely to cause me some grief.

About ten minutes outside the city, I decided to stop at a gas station phone booth and call in for my messages. The phone booth smelled like a urinal. I slipped a quarter into the slot and punched off the seven digits of my voice mail. The machine activated and spoke: "....This is Cy. Just a reminder that you're due for a haircut on Friday. See you then....This is the New York *Times* Washington Bureau calling. We'd like to ask a couple of questions about your tape recording story in today's paper involving Governor Goodwin. Please give us a call. You have the number....Dart, you weasel, you keep fucking over the wrong people you're gonna end up with your lungs cut out so you sink to the bottom of the harbor and stay there. Do I make myself clear....Ocean City time-shares calling Richard Dart. If you're interested in a great vacation package deal at Maryland's premier resort, give us a call at one eight hundred T-I-M-E-S-H A-R-E-S.... This is John Doyle, attorney for *City Press* and your lawyer by default. It's two fifteen. If you receive this message before you arrive at the paper, forget about *City Press* and come directly to my office. Things are getting touchy....Two hang-up beeps and the machine clicked off.

The menacing voice on the machine was unfamiliar but no less a threat. They're called "scaggers," specialists who kill then rip out the lungs so a body will sink like a boulder and never resurface. Bloody business, messing with lungs. Now even scaggers have to wear rubber gloves or worry about contracting AIDS. I was beginning to wonder whether I was worth all the trouble people were going to just to shut me up, the threats and all the fuming and fussing. What's scary is that the level of threats is beginning to heighten, getting really ugly and serious. There's a "Rosebud" out there somewhere, and by the luck of the draw it's my job to find it. And the payoff might be to end up as fish food.

Back in the car, I pointed toward the glass-and-steel tower where my newly acquired lawyer was waiting to meet his newly assigned client. Within minutes, I was screeching down a ramp into an underground garage where I took a ticket and began the endless circling through aisles and around ramps until I finally found a slot in what must have been the bottom circle of hell. I had trouble finding the elevator, but I finally located it next to a wall of hissing steam pipes.

My ears popped as I shot up the shaft at warp speed to the twenty fourth floor, probably the closest I'd ever get to power-lunching with God. I stepped off the elevator onto endless chevrons of inlaid high-gloss wood. I pointed my Cole-Hann's toward the hyphenated law firm with the nameplate on the double glass door that said: Swindle-Duff-Dander-Ducket and Doyle. Old Baltimore, *haute* Republican, decidedly WASP, the best First Amendment law firm in town, lots of banks and business clients in addition to *City Press.*

The lobby was a monument to trickle-down economics, offering all of the comforts of gentility, inherited, earned or affected—oriental carpets beaten to the proper degree of thread-bareness, antique hutches and sideboards, chairs and sofas covered in Schumacher's Williamsburg fabrics and a gallery of prints and lithographs featuring dogs, ducks, geese and hunters. The first lesson in life for a proper Baltimore WASP male is learning to be a gunner who shoots defenseless waterfowl. But, I'm told, it's the bonding that counts, standing up to your ass in marsh water at five o'clock in the morning, drinking bourbon for breakfast with good old dad and his buddies, stringing out decoys, making honking sounds to lure the dumbest bird on the planet into the hairpin sights of a .12 gauge shotgun. And by your side in the duck blind is the family Labrador retriever, preferably black, ready to swim and fetch. In Maryland, such behavior is a right of passage, a validation of manhood more meaningful than confirmation or *bar mitzvah* or even a first piece of nookie in a culture who's blood has run thin from inter-marrying with cousins. The only badge of honor more worthy is being arrested by a game warden for shooting over a baited blind.

On hearing my name and the purpose of my visit, the receptionist reflexively pushed a button and echoed it into the receiver. Within seconds, I was shaking hands with John Doyle and being steered back to his office. We'd met once before, Doyle and I, on the occasion when Krall was threatening me over the story of the picture he'd confiscated from Broadway Brown and slipped to the television reporter. Doyle's deceptive. Behind the pomp and panoply of the upperdog law firm, the slick suits and the thick cloud of gray hair, Doyle's a street fighter who's known for battling for his clients. I hope he lives up to his reputation.

The second law of thermodynamics translates roughly to this: Sooner or later everything turns to shit. Doyle began explaining my predicament and outlining my options. Krall, he said, was prepared to take me before the grand jury but would prefer to have an informal chat in his office if I'd cooperate and supply the information he wanted. If I agree, he's waiting for a phone call and would like to meet as soon as possible.

"Do I have any choices?" I said.

Doyle said: "Well, you have the obvious choices, meet with Krall or go before the grand jury. What I'd like to do is go before the presiding judge and try to have the subpoena quashed, arguing that whatever information you uncover in the pursuit of a story is protected by the shield law."

"What if the judge doesn't go along?" I said.

Doyle said: "That's the chance we'll have to take. The last thing we want to do is let it go before the grand jury, have them start wondering why reporters have privileges they don't. Pisses them off. And make no mistake. Krall's a bulldog. And before a grand jury he's boss. He might appear thick and slow, but he's tenacious as hell and he won't let go until he wears you down and gets what he wants. Might take all day, but that's the way he operates. In that room, it's you against Krall and twenty-one citizens he owns. That's the good news. The bad news is that you could end up in jail for contempt."

"Sounds like a level playing field," I said.

"Doyle said: "I don't want to sound grim, but I also don't want you to laugh it off as if it's a game of peek-a-boo."

"I know, I know. I've been giving the same advice to some of Krall's other customers who think a subpoena's a joke," I said.

Doyle said: "I'm glad we understand each other."

Doyle said: "Let me get on the phone, see if we can wrap this sucker up this afternoon."

"Where's the bathroom. I'm about to become a puddle." I said.

Refreshed and back in the reception room, I stared through smoke-colored glass across the skyscape and the outline of the harbor plastered against an oncoming watercolor sunset. There were the twin pavilions of Harbor Place, the Aquarium, the Power Plant shopping and restaurant complex and beyond it Pier Six and the latest installment payment of government largesse, the Christopher Columbus Marine Research Center, which bombed and went bust. On the opposite side, at the foot of Federal Hill, were the Maryland Science Center, the Rusty Scupper and the rising stack of apartments at Harbor View, another of those waterside colonies of condos and marinas. Dominating the entire tableau at the harbor's mouth was one of Baltimore's most identifiable monuments, a one-of-a-kind architectural triumph that rivals any eye-boggling entryway into any of the world's great ports, Baltimore's Lady Liberty, her landmark rising a hundred stories into the sky, lighting the way for ships in the night, a lodestar by which to steer a straight course: The Domino Sugar factory with its curly-cue neon sign. Doyle interrupted my reverie.

"Let's go," he said.

CHAPTER 19

▼

At the courthouse, the story bounced to life like a celebrity roast. Krall had his shorts in a knot because I'd been temporarily (at least) snatched from his clutches. The judge had agreed to meet informally with us in his chambers, denying Krall what must be the same kind of sadistic thrill that little boys derive from impaling flies on straight pins. Doyle headed for the judge's chambers while I detoured to a lounge that doubled as a waiting room. I opened the door with the frosted glass and my head swiveled over the lifescape as if I were at Wimbledon watching a tennis match. Seated on government-issue chairs, in a room that had probably been decorated by a G-14 accountant, were Faye and Fern, Joe Nelligan, Milton Frank, Charles Sharkey and several suits with briefcases that I assumed were lawyers. It's an old prosecutor's trick. Stack the witnesses so they see each other and begin to sweat and become suspicious over who's saying what. I was about as welcome as root canal surgery.

The lottery should be as predictable as Joe Nelligan.

"Shoulda put you away when I had the chance, ya little shit," Nelligan said.

"Careful, captain, we're in a court of law and anything you say might be used against you," I said.

"You're fuckin' with something bigger than you, and my advice is let go before it's your ass they're dragging around in a body bag," Nelligan said.

"Ladies, you're looking lovely today," I said.

Nothing pisses Nelligan off like short-circuiting his ego, something I do habitually even though it's not in my best interest.

"Look me in the eye, you little shit. When this is over, you're gonna regret the day you ever heard the name Joe Nelligan. You shoulda stayed in Washington with your dandy-assed friends and all the other faggots who work over there sucking the public tit. Baltimore's a people town, not a Chablis-and-cheese party town, and over here we do people things. And all of a sudden a dick-head like you comes over here and turns the goddam place upside down for no reason at all except to make trouble," Nelligan said.

"Joe, calm down," Faye said.

"I'll calm down when this pimple on the ass of humanity is out of here for good," Nelligan said.

Nelligan was right on course, brittle and mean. Just as I was about to abandon my customary self-restraint and make an ass of myself, Doyle stepped into the room and saved me. He shuffled me out so fast that I didn't have time to wish the witnesses good luck. We clip-clopped down the corridor on government regulation black-and-white Harlequin diamonds of marble, Nelligan's rumbling still ricocheting in my head, Doyle at my side instructing me on protocol and the nuances of style and substance of being (temporarily) government property.

"....doesn't like to waste time. And the closer it gets to five o'clock, the better for us. The judge's newly re-married and at quitting time he wants to be home having a drink and screwing. It's four fifteen now, so he'll give Krall the bum's rush. Be polite, yes sir, no sir, no smart aleck stuff. Give simple answers, yes or no, whenever you can. Don't try to explain or volunteer information. And don't lie but feel free to fudge if there's enough wiggle room."

"What kind of mood's the guy in?" I said.

"At four fifteen, horny and anxious," Doyle said.

"My kind of judge," I said.

You've seen it, if not in real life then in the movies and on television, the drab sameness, the contrived juxtaposition of intelligence and authority. The judge's chambers looked as if they had been stamped out by a giant cookie cutter and assembled like a pre-cast module—the oversized mahogany desk, the flags of nation and state flanking on each side, the rows of law books, the portraits of the incumbent president and attorney general, college and law school diplomas and the judge himself, robed and avuncular in the swallows of a worn leather chair. The judge signaled Doyle and me to two chairs opposite Krall and two of his assistants. Judge Michael Falcone looked at his watch and said:

"Mr. Krall, it's my understanding that you want certain information, material, that you consider evidence you believe might be in the possession of Mr. Richard Dart."

"That's correct, your honor," Krall said.

"Would you identify the material," Judge Falcone said.

"It's a tape recording that purports to be a conversation between Governor Goodwin and Joseph Frank that may have been legally or illegally recorded but that we believe has a substantial bearing on the grand jury investigation into the Block," Krall said.

"Objection, your honor," Doyle said.

"What's your point?" Judge Falcone said.

"My point is, that whatever information my client obtains in the course of his investigative duties as a reporter, whether it's the material in question or anything else, is privileged information and therefore protected by the state's shield law," Doyle said.

"Does your client have a court order to record private conversations? Seems to me there's a larger issue of criminal violation that supersedes the question of privilege. Besides, this is a federal matter that overrides state law," Judge Falcone said.

"Your honor, my client, Richard Dart, in no way violated anyone's rights by invading their privacy," Doyle said.

"Then where'd he get the information that was the basis for his story?" Judge Falcone said.

As I thought Uh, Oh, I could almost lip-synch Doyle's response and the judge's next question.

"I'd like a brief break so that I can confer with my client, your honor," Doyle said.

"No need for a break. It's getting late. Mr. Dart, do you have in your possession any tape recording that might be relevant to Mr. Krall's investigation?" Judge Falcone said.

I thought for a nanosecond about what Doyle had said about wiggle room, and said:

"I do not, your honor."

Judge Falcone said: "All right, I'll take your word for it for now. But if any further information appears indicating that you have access to any highly irregular information, I'm going to issue a contempt citation. So you'll be operating under the threat of contempt of this court. Furthermore, I'm placing all parties involved in this investigation under a strict gag order. And if any more leaks occur, I'll issue a show-cause order holding any party guilty unless they can prove otherwise. That ought to put a lid on this whole argument over who's talking and who's not. Do I make my point, Mr. Krall?"

"Your honor, I'd still like the court's permission to take Mr. Dart before the grand jury and place him under oath," Krall said.

"He was, in effect, under oath in this chamber, in case you hadn't noticed, because if I find out that he lied or withheld information, he'll be cited not only for contempt but for perjury as well," Judge Falcone said.

"I'd still like to question him," Krall said.

"That's not up to you to decide. Session's over, Mr. Krall," Judge Falcone said.

I checked my watch as Judge Falcone stepped out of his robe. It was two minutes 'til five. Doyle should have been a stand-up comic. His timing was exquisite. With a geezer Falcone's age, you'd think he'd be pissless let alone upright. I resumed my thought about wiggle room and smirked, pleased with myself. After all, the judge had asked if I "had in my possession" a tape recording and I answered honestly. It was in a bank vault.

Five of us arrived at the doorway simultaneously. Doyle shifted aside and motioned me through. I demurred and smiled my up-yours smile, bowed slightly and waved Krall through with the grand gesture of a policeman directing traffic. He stared me down with those milky squid eyes of his, the flat plane of his face taking on a second dimension of a don't-fuck-with-me scowl as he accepted my hospitality. The smirk and the scowl were our rules of engagement. I did, however, keep my index finger in my pocket.

Krall must have been doubly pissed. He'd lost not only round one in the judge's chambers. But it was now too late to resume testimony before the grand jury. Jurors get hungry and irritable around happy hour time. The five witnesses would have to return tomorrow. But Krall had made a point of sorts. The witnesses would be suspicious of each other, heightening the tension among all those involved, wondering who said what.

Out in the diamond-lined hallway, Doyle said he was pleased for my sake that we were able to sidestep Krall (for the moment, at least.) Except that Doyle expressed bafflement over Falcone's high-handed treatment of Krall, almost as if he were trying to stifle the grand jury investigation by fettering the prosecutor in charge.

"You noticed that, too," I said.

"Strange behavior for the presiding judge. Usually they give the government the benefit of the doubt," Doyle said.

"Helluva story," I said.

"You're not thinking of writing this after what Falcone said about gag orders," Doyle said.

"The gag was for Krall, the contempt was for me," I said.

"What a set of balls," Doyle said.

"They'll be on display on the newsroom bulletin board if I don't write it and Mulligan finds out," I said.

"At the rate you're going, I'll be seeing you again real soon," Doyle said.

"Looking forward to it. Thanks for your help today, especially the advice about wiggle room," I said.

With that exclamation point, I peeled off from Doyle, leaving him to ponder what I meant, and double-timed my Cole-Hann's the three blocks toward *City Press*. The pink and violet splotches of evening hung behind the Baltimore skyline like velvet drapes. Along the canyons of Baltimore's business district, millions of candlepower of fluorescent tubes flickered on almost at once as if they were fired up by a master switch at the main generating plant of the Baltimore Gas & Electric Company.

At the *City Press* entrance, I flashed my ID card to the guard on duty. He nodded me toward the elevator like a uniformed robot who performed the same function with metronomic monotony hundreds of times, day and night. The elevator door opened and revealed Peaches on her way out, arousing once again the tortuous battle in the libido of my conscience between Good Richard and Bad Richard. Bad Richard was gaining. Peaches stepped off the elevator and into the lobby looking as if she had shoehorned herself into her jeans and silk blouse. Her hair was loose and jiggly and she had on her best fifty thousand kilowatt smile. Little Miss cuddle-cock would fit right in with the best of them in the Victoria's Secret catalogue.

"Evening, Miss Peaches," I said.

"Hi, how are you?" Peaches said.

"Pretty good. You ought to try me sometime," I said.

"Coming or going?" Peaches said.

"I'd like to be doing both," I said.

"Anybody ever get a straight answer out of you?" Peaches said.

"I've spent a lot of time covering politics," I said.

"Well, are we going to keep standing here, or are you going to ask me to dance?" Peaches said.

"I have a story to write," I said.

"Excuses, excuses, excuses," Peaches said.

"Business before pleasure, and I assure you the pleasure would be all mine," I said.

"Why do you keep me standing on my tip-toes if you're not going to kiss me?" Peaches said.

"Catch you later. Got work to do," I said.

On the elevator, Bad Richard reared his ugly head again. I fantasized that Peaches unfurled was a very powerful image, so powerful that....Then suddenly I was hit by a reality check. I'd promised to catch up with Shelly after my day was done and try and sort out our tangled lives.

Once in the newsroom, I was in no mood to screw around. Having gone to the composing room and poured a cup of coffee, black and strong like my heart, I removed my jacket and sat down at my computer and booted up my file. I slugged the story "gag" and took off as if I were Leon Fleischer at a Steinway grand piano playing a Beethoven piano concerto. Having lived the story, I finished in record time. I re-read the story a couple of times to check for bumps in the rhythm. I'm a stickler for rhythm. I once had a helluva fight with Mulligan who changed a single word in one of my leads. I said:

"Mulligan, next time you change a word in my copy make damn sure you put back the same number of syllables you took out. You fucked up the rhythm of that sentence."

I called Shelly's law office. Whoever answered the phone said she'd left an hour ago. Playing tag telephone was not my favorite sport. Nor was talking to machines.

I had to pee. I slouched across the newsroom and into the men's room and made my deposit. Some days I feel like a hamster in a wheel, I thought, as I splashed cold water on my face. Started off with a bang, all right, putting Goodwin in the soup with Joe Frank. Then confronting Goodwin at the news conference and later in his office. And the codicil to the day was being hauled before Judge Falcone as if I'm part of the scenery in Krall's investigation. Who says reporting beats working?

I slid into my jacket and headed out of the building into the clammy night. The tastemeisters must have been working overtime at the spice factory at the harbor's edge. The air was perfumed with the heavy sweet scent of nutmeg and the whole downtown smelled like grandmother's pumpkin pie. It was still and quiet except for the rumble of an occasional eighteen-wheeler. Gulls could be heard squawking over the harbor, as could the steady creaking of the Constellation tugging at its moorings as it heaved and swayed in the shifting tide.

I'd made my way around the *City Press* building to the parking area without a pause. Nobody in sight. Then suddenly I remembered. Holy shit! I'd parked my car in Doyle's building, six blocks away. Pain in the ass at this time of night. I did an abrupt about face and stepped off, double-time.

Except for a few brain-dead tourists scattered around the harbor and happy hour couples in the business district pubs, downtown Baltimore is deserted after dark. The city has become one of the nation's murder capitals, drug deals gone sour, kids caught in the crossfire, cops now shot in the head because everyone knows they wear body armor. It's almost as if crime and criminals are stalking the lifescape like a menacing plague, shooting up society as if it's the new urban sport. Christ, hereabouts they'll gun you down if you don't give them your wallet or jacket fast enough. The sidewalks are littered with panhandlers, some of them real nut cakes. Nobody objects to parting with a coin or two, mind you, but a person has to be crazy as hell to reach into his pocket, let alone show any kind of money. The sensible thing is to hunker down and charge ahead like a fullback. Which I did, and by the time I'd reached Doyle's building I was winded even though I'd given up smoking twenty years ago.

Instead of the lobby and the elevator, I entered the tunnel and hot-footed it down the ramp and into the garage, then around and down another level where I began my search for the hissing steam pipes and my car. I was becoming thirsty, hungry and cranky—in that order. It had been a long time since I'd had any solid food. And I thought about seeing Shelly and maybe getting together for dinner or even ordering Chinese or pizza. For the most part, the garage was empty and my footsteps echoed in the underground cavern. I heard the hissing, turned another corner and spotted my car. In what was becoming a habit, I checked the tires and peeked inside before I slipped the key into the lock. And once inside, I popped the locks again.

I lit the fire and let the engine idle a minute before I screeched out of my slot and wound around two ramps to the cashier's booth. I handed the attendant a ten-dollar bill and asked for a receipt. The fucking bandits, I got two dollars change.

CHAPTER 20

▼

I was in my house, looking forward to having dinner with Shelly. First things first, though. I removed my jacket and draped it over the finial on the banister leading upstairs. In the kitchen, I poured three fingers of Absolut over a glacier of ice and a twist of lemon. The first blast shot a cryogenic ache to my brain stem which, when you get right down to it, is only forty centimeters away from the wisdom teeth. Vodka in hand, I slouched over to the den and punched the play button on the answering machine....(beep) "This is First Union Bank of Wyoming calling to offer Richard Dart the lowest interest rate credit card in America. Our automatic calling service tells us you're not at home now. So we'll get back to you later....(beep) Ace home remodeling service calling Richard Dart to offer a fantastic deal on a new deck. Please call us at ONE EIGHT HUNDRED NEW DECK....(beep)....(beep) Dart, your ass is grass unless you back off. You know what I'm talking about. So wise up or you're dead meat....(beep) Richard, this is Shelly. I know you're planning on dinner, but there was a long meeting at the office today, and I think it's best for both of us that I get out of town for a few days. Don't call, and don't worry. I'll call you tomorrow. Love you madly....(beep)....(beep)....click.

Holy shit! First the story of the Block invades my nightmares, now it's between the sheets mud-wrestling Shelly and me apart. I punched the automatic dial button assigned to Shelly as fast as the answering machine clicked off. Shelly's machine responded...."Hi, Richard. I know I must seem like a bitch, but let's do this my way and everything will turn out for the best. Trust me. I'll call you tomorrow...." Being a crybaby is not my style, but all of a sudden everything was turning to shit in a hot hurry. I have a city editor nagging me and a posse of cops, thugs, lawyers, barkers, bartenders and an assortment of assholes from government officialdom chasing my ass all over town as if I'm the guest fox at the annual hounds' hunt. Now the business of Shelly taking off in the middle of the night for who knows where—friends in Washington, family in New Jersey, or her sister in Connecticut? I sucked down the last finger of vodka and headed to the kitchen to reload.

Thus armed, I meandered to the sitting room and allowed my favorite chair to encapsulate me in its huggy folds and swallows. This is the room where I sit and stare to downshift my brain and my metabolism into low gear. This is the room where I entertain the occasional luxury of feeling sorry for myself. I was already bluesy-woozy and lonely without my squeeze, wondering when the hell I'd see Shelly again. And to add to the blue funk, I got up long enough to slip a Sinatra disc into the player:

> "Each place I go/Only the lonely go/
> Some little small café/
> The songs I know/Only the lonely know…."

I laid my head back on the soft folds of the chair and within a course of seconds the vodka and the music performed the therapeutic magic of a thousand darting fingers massaging me into a boozy haze of sleep. When I woke up an hour later, my head felt as dull as an Adam Sandler film and my tongue seemed as thick as a New York strip steak. I rattled my head to shake off the sleep, and I drained the remaining puddle of Absolut. I remembered I hadn't eaten when all of a sudden a wicked thought crossed my mind and subsumed the twinges of hunger. Bad Richard was on the loose. I was feeling horny. On impulse, I picked up the cordless phone and punched the auto dial for *City Press*. On the third ring, the operator clicked on and released a string of diphthongs around her adenoids that sounded like: "Titty Pwess. Goob evenin', my ah helb yew."

"Yes. This is Richard Dart. Could you give me the home number for Anne Taylor? I have to discuss an assignment with her."

"Shur, hon, hode on a minnid," the operator said, and within a second or two, she came up with the number and I had the seven digits locked in my mental Rolodex—752-3545.

I wasted no time dialing, Peaches wasted no time answering.

"Peaches, Richard Dart here. How are you?"

"To what do I owe the honor?" Peaches said.

"Rain check time," I said.

"How so?" Peaches said.

"You offered. I took a rain check. How about a late dessert? My treat," I said.

"You're a generous date," Peaches said.

"See you in an hour," I said.

Bad Richard is badass when he takes over. Good Richard's a pretty straight arrow. But Bad Richard would fuck a keyhole if he could. I poured another dram of vodka and headed upstairs for the shower. And in one of those emotional dipsy-doodles, I was feeling guilty about not feeling guilty about what I'd just done. Christ, Shelly had just put her neck on the chopping block and her career on the line so I could play Clark Kent without her getting in the way like Lois Lane always does. I undressed, peed, showered and re-dressed in record time, the uniform of the night being my cock-o-the-walk, Banana Republic studley look of jeans, denim shirt, sneakers and a suede jacket. A Bad Richard look. After all the years of monotonous monogamy with Shelly, I was eager not only to test myself, but also to find out if I still knew how to play the game. In my prime, I was Mister Make-Out. With Shelly, I had no need for condoms. I wondered if Peaches stored them.

Out of the house and in the car, I wound through the side streets of Roland Park, a nip here, a tuck there, an occasional zig and a zag, to the point where Old Roland Park and its haphazard of idiosyncratic day-glo colored houses co-exist with the rigid rows of Hampden's austere cookie-cutter two-story brick dwellings. The two worlds never meet except at the Rotunda, a shopping mall of boutiques and a supermarket in a re-cycled insurance company office building, where the aging matrons of Hampden and the uppity young professionals who wear Rolexes and drive Beamers eye each other warily over the foodstuff. The younger generation patrols the supermarket for faddish food such as heart healthy, radicchio, three-color pasta and tofu, while the wives and mothers of Hampden still buy sticky buns, Mallomars, cigarettes, stew beef and soup bones. Enough cholesterol to give a Big Mac clogged arteries.

I wove through the aisles, dodging push-baskets and sourpuss people who resent having to shop, to the produce section where I studied the artful pyramids of fruit. Two large blushing peaches passed the visual and tactile tests and I glided them in to a plastic bag, careful not to bruise them. From there, I navigated to the refrigerated cases and removed two one-pint containers of Haagen Daazs vanilla ice cream. At the express lane, I was about sixth in line, which was enough time to explore the rack of tabloids: "Oprah Dumps Stedman"; "Liz You Is, or

Liz You Ain't His Baby"; "Child Born With Two Heads"; "The truth About Burt"; "Oprah's Secret Diet"; and the perennial favorite, "Wolves Raise Boy."

Time's up, so's the front-page entertainment. I paid the bill, moseyed out to the car and pointed my machine down Forty-First Street, hung a left onto Falls Road through Hampden to the Jones Falls Expressway. The news tonight was the usual mosaic of the urban lifescape.... "A mother was shot twice in the face as she swirled to protect the two-year-old child she was holding in her arms. She was rushed to near-by Johns Hopkins Hospital where she is listed in critical but stable condition. The incident occurred on an East Baltimore street corner and is the latest in an epidemic of drive-by shootings....There were five ATM robberies overnight, and police believe they were all the work of the same gang-of-three. Their method is to kidnap a victim, put a hood over the victim's head and drive to an ATM. The victims were all released unharmed after they removed money from the ATMs and turned the cash over to the kidnappers...."

Who needs this shit. I ordered format relief. Punch the FM button and it all goes away as if it never existed, and suddenly you enter a recording studio where one hundred and two musicians are halfway through Mozart's Jupiter Symphony. The abrupt distraction almost caused me to miss my exit at Maryland Avenue, between the Lyric Theater and the rear end of the University of Baltimore. Cross over Mount Royal Avenue and the avenue becomes slightly smudged, but the look picks up again as Mount Vernon Place rolls into view along with the cross streets before it. Peaches lives on Read Street, number eleven, and lucky for me there was a parking place on the corner where Maryland Avenue and Read Street intersect. I backed in, got out, locked up and instinctively looked over my shoulder, checked all four corners and was satisfied that I hadn't been followed. Being an optimist, I'd have to remember that the sign said no parking between seven and nine o'clock in the morning. Swinging the plastic tote of peaches and ice cream, Bad Richard smiled a Lothario's leer and stepped off a jaunty swagger toward number eleven. As the sign carried by the bearded guy in the cartoon says, prepare to meet thy maker.

I came face-to-face with a grand old townhouse, literally a hundred years ago a merchant prince's mansion, that had a well-cared-for façade and a patina of mon-eyed gentility, even a little garden behind a grated wrought iron fence, unusual for the middle of the city. At the door, I was buzzed in by Peaches, and told sec-ond floor front. The entry was heavy with old money and polished wood, lots of carved wainscoting by a long-gone craftsman, a winding staircase that spiraled up four stories and wrapped around a Tiffany chandelier under a stained glass sky-light. It was easy to see why Peaches had chosen this architectural dazzle over an elevator building with two hundred fifty boxes that are called apartments. I took the stairs two at a time and arrived at second floor front where Peaches was waiting, framed in the doorway. She was wearing her signature jeans and white silk shirt, and her nipples strained against the gossamer fabric like two Hershey's Kisses. Anyone who saw the way I looked at her knew that every home pregnancy test kit within fifty miles automatically came out positive.

Inside, the apartment was right out of Laura Ashley, twelve foot ceilings, real plaster walls, floor-to-ceiling windows with four decks of miniature shutters, all prints and chintz, fabric and ceiling boarders matching, several dhurrie throw rugs on polished hardwood floors, sofas, loves seats, Billy Baldwin chairs, antique chairs with striped fabric seats, heavy wood hutch, dining room continuing the theme, done in light wood and florals. I couldn't wait to see the bedroom.

"Nice place you've got here," I said.

Thanks. I like it a lot," Peaches said.

"As promised, here's dessert. Better put the ice cream in the freezer," I said.

When Miss Anne Taylor saw the peaches, she turned as red as the blush on their skin.

"What's this? She said.

"Returning the compliment. Somebody told me you like peaches," I said.

When Peaches disappeared into the kitchen, I thought, no kid just out of college, working as a features writer at the bottom of the wage scale, could afford to put together digs like this. Mommie and daddy must have hired a decorator, signed a blank check and said make it warm and feminine. Which the decorator, without question, had done. Peaches had said that she lived outside of New York City, probably around Larchmont or Tarrytown. Has the look of Wellesley or Smith, maybe did some graduate work in journalism at Columbia. Dad's probably a dermatologist, practice in Manhattan, treating rich kids with raspberries on their faces that only time will cure. The beauty of dermatology is that the kids don't know that, and the parents don't mind paying to keep the kids happy. A dermatologist's hours are regular, too. There's no such thing as an acute attack of acne. Mother, let's see, mother runs a small gallery in the East Fifties, specializing in oriental art and artifacts. They belong to a country club, dinner there most Saturday nights, working off the monthly minimum. And no doubt Episcopalian. I wandered to the kitchen, which turned out to be a full-sized, fully equipped, eat-in kitchen, surprising because many converted houses have all-in-one modular units instead of individual appliances.

"I haven't had dinner, mind if we eat now?" I said.

"Your treat," Peaches said.

"I'll peel the peaches, you scoop the ice cream when we're ready. Why don't you chill a couple of dessert dishes in the freezer?" I said.

"You've got a deal," Peaches said.

"How'd you wind up in Baltimore?" I said.

"I wanted to write, and this was the best offer I had," Peaches said.

"What kind of writing?" I said.

"Eventually magazines, long pieces," Peaches said.

"Hell, this is no place to be. Why didn't you tough it out in New York? By the looks of your apartment, you could have survived on subsidies," I said.

"That's part of it. I wanted to get away from home, make it on my own. The real problem, though, is everybody wants experience but nobody's willing to let you get it," Peaches said.

"Well, writing that fluffy crap for the features section is no way to earn your stripes," I said.

Christ, these kids slay me. They all want to make it on their own, but it's daddy's checkbook that creates the opportunity. That's what parents are for, I guess. I'd just finished removing a long curl of skin from one peach when I felt Peaches' Hershey's Kisses nipples drill into my back and her hands rubbing the insides of my thighs. She licked the back of my neck. I turned, peach in one hand, peeler in the other, and slipped her a length of tongue as she pressed her groin against my awakened Johnson. Then I went limp and resumed the peeling. Good Richard had tapped me on the shoulder and whispered in my ear.

"Let's take it easy and eat," I said.

"Christ, can anybody ever pin you down?" Peaches said.

Peaches retrieved the frosted crystal dessert goblets from the freezer and began ladling ice cream, nearly a pint in each one. I built a lattice of peaches over the mounds of ice cream and pronounced them ready to eat.

"Wait a minute. Let's add some zest," Peaches said.

She stepped out of the kitchen for a blink of the eye and returned with a bottle of Grand Marnier. She drowned the desserts with generous splashes of the orange-brandy liqueur and said:

"Now we're ready to eat."

Each carrying his/her own ladled and fortified waist-thickener, one by one we tiptoed over the dhurries and into the dining room where Peaches produced two placemats and spoons. She motioned me to sit while she strutted her stuff over to the sound system in the next room. Peaches fiddled and fumbled with toggles, flipped and filed through discs until she apparently found the right one, watched as it was swallowed into the compact disc player's maw and suddenly came alive—guitars picking, rhythm section kicking, Ziljans cymbaling, Yamaha key-board keyboarding, a voice almost falsettoing suddenly penetrated the electronic commotion at the end of the eight-bar introduction. Recognizing neither the music nor the singer, I felt totally disconnected from the Pepsi generation.

Now both sitting, we shoveled into the whorls of the boozy ice cream peach orchard, sweet, tart and cold, filling while it offered the same medicinal stomach coating as a shot glass of Pepto Bismal, only much more to my taste.

"Who's singing?" I said.

"Jimmy Buffet," Peaches said.

"Is that the kind of music you like?" I said.

"Went through college listening to him. Besides, he's a sellout everywhere he appears," Peaches said.

"Hey, wait a minute. He's the one with the restaurants, Margaritaville, I believe, and his followers are called 'Parrotheads'," I said.

"Welcome to the new age," Peaches said.

"Big on tequila sunrises, too," I said.

"You show promise," Peaches said.

"Also a writer, isn't he? Real Renaissance man," I said.

"Send this man to the head of the pop chart," Peaches said.

The sump of the dessert dish cupped a reservoir of light orangey cream like a puddle of liquid marmalade, the runoff from the sweet mountain lattice we had built, and I spooned it slowly, almost inhaling it as if it were a curative nectar imparting a healing vapor. Buffet, kind of a Cajun troubadour, was still belting 'em out in his laconic but humorous way, segueing from song to song on a bridge of applause and good cheer from the audience and some amusing smart-ass patter of his own in between. I might get to like this guy. The band played on:

> "I really do appreciate the fact that you're sitting here/
> Your voice sounds so wonderful, but your face don't look too clear/
> So barmaid, bring a pitcher, another round of brew/
> Honey, why don't we get drunk and screw."

Holy shit! I'm not all that hip on the library of contemporary pop/rock lyrics. But it was clear why Peaches had spent so much time sorting through the discs to find the appropriate soft porn background music to tart up the mood for what she had on her dirty little mind. She was propositioning me through a balladeer's raunch, using a Cajun country singer for a pimp, saying so much without saying a word. Her underpants must be wringing wet. Peaches sat there smiling like an impish mischief-maker, elbows on the table, her chin resting on laced hands, waiting for a reaction. Christ, with the younger generation, there's no subtlety, no nuance, no dancing around the rim of the dish before moving in for the kill. No foreplay at all. It's simply, "Wanna fuck?"

Without a word, I carried my dish to the kitchen where I placed it in the sink and ran a warm waterfall over it. Peaches did a ditto. Now both at the sink, where it all began, I slipped my arm around her waist and pulled her body frontally against mine, feeling the heat in my jeans rise like a vagrant gland. I kissed her full on the lips with just enough tongue to tease her before the next full whammy, our orange-liquored breath creating an explosion of citrus saliva. She backed me against the sink, her firm kumquat nipples poking into my chest while she wiggled her crotch into my manly staff. I stared into her eyes like a laser, and she responded with another open-mouthed kiss wet enough to produce piddle of drool. I thought about Shelly while all the dire societal warnings about mixing business with pleasure ran through my mind like thousands of winking bulbs on one of those moving-light marquees that flash out messages: Don't dip your pen in the company inkwell; Don't buy your bread and meat at the same store. Don't sleep where you work.

To create an air space between us, I eased up on the pretzel-lock we were in but didn't let go of Peaches' taut body, which was producing BTU's like a wood-fired brick pizza oven. Gently I steered the two of us into the living room and began boogying among the coffee table and chairs to the music of the troubadour who had originally invited me to boink Peaches. Bad Richard was really badass tonight.

As the last wails of music petered out, so, too, did Peaches pretend to be weary and winded. She collapsed on the sofa like a rag doll, feigning deep-breathing exercises, which must have put considerable strain on her Maidenform, pulling me down with her for a perfect three-point landing that touched all bases like a grand-slam home run. All that separated us now were two zippers. We smeared each other with kisses, Peaches now heaving in a steady rhythm to her own accompaniment of low moans and an occasional bass-drum swallow. I rolled off Peaches and onto my side. As I did, I slipped my hand under her panties and into her jeans, and when it arrived at the magic button in the lips of her loins, I let my fingers do the walking. Peaches responded by fumbling with my zipper. Suddenly, as if guided by the compass of my conscience, I apprehended the offending hand.

"Don't, I said.

"What do you mean, don't?" Peaches said.

"Just don't. Not now," I said.

"Nobody's ever gone this far and rejected me, you bastard. What is it with you, anyway? Remember, you called me. I didn't call you," Peaches said.

They say that a stiff wand has no conscience, but all of a sudden I was on a one-way guilt trip out of here. It may be an old fashioned notion, but the idea of cheating on Shelly while she's virtually in mourning for me lit the candle of my conscience, at least what little there was left of it. I retrieved my hand from Peaches' saltlick and asked directions to the bathroom. Still puzzled, Peaches pointed and I followed the signpost of her outstretched arm. I waited for my wick to unstarch, then I drilled my pee into the toilet bowl like a racehorse. I washed my hands, dashed my face with cold water and used one of the floral paper guest towels to dry. I returned to the living room, prepared to do some explaining.

One of the fine points of life I've learned is that women generally like men who are considerate of other women. I switched on the bullshit machine and went to work. I told Peaches in reassuring words that my abrupt withdrawal of consent had nothing to do with her, that, frankly, I wanted to get into her pants in the worst way. I explained my relationship with Shelly and how the story I was imported to Baltimore to crack had become a conflict of interest, an unintended consequence, as well as a major pain in the ass. I repeated that I still wanted to see the color of her underpants as they were drawn down her legs into a pool of silk on the bedroom floor. But not tonight.

"You're a strange dude, Mr. Dart," Peaches said.

"Maybe so, but at least you'll respect me in the morning," I said.

"Not if I'm going to bed all horned up and alone," Peaches said.

"Sorry about that, but you understand," I said.

"Take your chances," Peaches said.

Feeling a little—a little? a lot—like a jerk, I slouched over to the door with Peaches pitter-patting behind me. I turned around a gave her a kiss, more of a friendly smooch that the steam heat of our earlier lip-locks, and she stood there as limp as overcooked pasta, sending me a message in very emphatic body language that said: If there's ever another encounter, I'd better finish what I start. I never did get to see the bedroom.

CHAPTER 21

▼

By the time Mulligan woke me with a phone call in the morning, the police had already found Faye's body, bruised, broken and splayed in the alley behind the East Baltimore row house where she lived with her pet poodle when she wasn't jiving guys at Broadway Brown's or shooting up under Joe Nelligan's protective eyes. One way or another, Faye's habit had gotten the best of her.

"Getting interesting now, kid," Mulligan said.

"When and how did it happen?" I said.

"How about you high-tail it over there and find out. I'll have a photographer meet you there," Mulligan said.

"Give me an hour," I said.

"Hour my ass. You'd better be out of the house in five minutes," Mulligan said.

"Have it your way," I said.

"Incidentally, where am I going?" I said.

"Row house in Patterson Park. Thirty five seventeen East Baltimore Street," Mulligan said.

"Oh, the classy side of town," I said.

I headed for the bathroom to brush my teeth and splash my face, thinking that I'd done the smart thing by coming home last night even if it meant giving up a slice of Peaches. Mulligan would've gone off like a bazooka if he'd been unable to find me. Saving time, I put on the same jeans, shirt and jacket I'd just taken off a few hours ago. Downstairs, I gulped some orange juice straight from the carton and headed for my car. I vaaarrrrooooooommmmed out of the driveway and switched on the news.

Baltimore Street dead-ends at Patterson Park, which is about where I was when I spotted several police cars with their bubble-gum-machine lights blinking menacing warnings like a blue light special at a K-Mart midnight madness sale. I parked half a block away and marched myself toward the circle of uniforms and suits that surrounded what I assumed to be Faye's body, notebook in hand. At the rim of the circle, I settled on a man in civilian clothes, a tough-as-nails type, probably a sergeant, lieutenant tops, who seemed to be in charge.

"Richard Dart, *City Press*," I said.

"Well, I'll be damned. They're sending celebrity reporters to cover homicides now. I'm Pete Gallazio, lieutenant," the detective said.

"How about that," I said.

"Been reading you stuff about the Block. Joe Nelligan must love you already. He'll be absolutely ecstatic when he hears you're on this story," the detective said.

"How do you know about Nelligan and her?" I said.

"Wake up, hot shot. Everybody in the police department knows about her and Nelligan," the detective said.

"How'd it happen?" I said.

"Swan dive off the roof," the detective said.

"Pushed or fell?" I said.

"Looks as if she either jumped or fell. Nobody else was on the roof that we can find," the detective said.

"What time did it happen?" I said.

"Just as the sun was coming up, about an hour ago," the detective said.

"Anything suspicious?" I said.

"Arm's got more holes than a strainer. Could have been flying higher than Air Force One and lost her balance up there. Autopsy will tell us how much stuff was in her," the detective said.

"Been through her apartment yet?" I said.

"Couple of the guys are checking it out now," the detective said.

"Mind if I stick around, see what the search shows?" I said.

"Suit yourself," the detective said.

I looked down at Faye, limp and serene, hoping as was the case with many jumpers, that she had died of shock before she hit the ground. She was as dead as meat. The detective was right. Her arms had more perforations than a colander. The wonder always is what drives women like Faye—why they turn to the Block and drugs, why they end up alone and dead in some alley. The headlines demonstrate that it's not as uncommon as it appears—Block dancer strangled by irate customer; Block dancer commits suicide in jail cell; Block dancer dies smoking crack cocaine; Block dancer stabbed to death by jealous boyfriend. What I'd learned while working this story is that many of them come from small towns, broken homes where they have no respect for their parents or themselves. They drift to the big cities and end up on the Block where they get caught up in a life full of false promises. Their bodies surgically enhanced, and their brains fried on booze and drugs, they take a beating every night, humping the furry pole and being slapped around by drunks who treat them like possessions. The smart ones save their money and get out early, or could end up owning a bar as others have done, and move on to respectable lives. But with many, eventually self-pity and self-doubt torture their drug-numbed minds—the breasts begin to sag, the pleats begin to show, the thighs begin to thicken. To themselves, they're no longer pretty inside or out. The drinking gets heavier, the habit more expensive. Finally, the black hole of depression and the plunge into some garbage-strewn alley a thousand miles from home in Pallookaville, U.S.A. And peace, finally peace. No more fur G-strings. No more pasties. No more bumping and grinding at the stripper pole. No more doing bottles or lap dances. The best, though, no more Nelligan.

The prick alert in my head shot into the danger zone. A blue government issue Ford screeched to the curb and out sprang Captain Joseph Nelligan like a Jack-in-the-box. He shoved his expansive frame into the center of things, stared down at Faye without a twitch of emotion, and in his bully-boy manner immediately caused a ruckus with the detective and a couple of other suits. In voices that would have drowned out the brass section of the U.S. Navy Band, a turf battle was developing, with homicide claiming territorial rights over Faye's stiffening corpse and Nelligan pushing around the weight of his captain's badge like a bulldozer in a crystal factory. It was a close call. The case was a homicide, all right, but it could be argued that it was narcotics as well because of all of the holes in Faye's body that God hadn't put there. If the detective's observation was true that the entire police department knew about Faye and Nelligan, then Nelligan had reason to assert jurisdiction and attempt to divert the investigation. Otherwise, his ass would soon be in a sling. He could be accused of aiding and abetting an addict. And from what I'd seen, also supplying.

An ambulance arrived, its red lights spinning, its siren silent. There was no sense of urgency. A medic checked Faye's pulse and stethoscoped her chest just to make certain the stuffing was gone out of her, then two of them straightened Faye's body and slid a black bag up and over her and zippered her in. Soon she'd be on a stainless steel table in the coroner's workshop wearing nothing but a toe tag. Come to think of it, there were times in her line of work when she wore little more.

Discretion being the better part of staying alive, I decided to get out of Nelligan's line of vision. I crossed the street to a phone booth on the corner and deposited a quarter, which got me a dial tone and eventually Mulligan's chain-saw voice. I reported what information I had so far and learned that the photographer was already back at *City Press* processing his film.

"What's it look like, kid?" Mulligan said.

"They're calling it a suicide for now,' I said.

"Any witnesses?" Mulligan said.

"Not that they've come up with. Couple of cops are going through Faye's apartment. Funny thing, too. Nelligan's shouting it out with homicide over who has jurisdiction and I think I know why," I said.

"Don't keep me in the dark, kid," Mulligan said.

"Later. Something interesting's just come up," I said.

No matter how famous a reporter becomes, a good digger never forgets the fundamentals. He just keeps getting better at them. Putting my birddog nose to work on the unexpected detour of Faye's sudden fade-out called up the old rule book about the rudiments of police-beat reporting. This was Mulligan's kind of story—sex, drugs, intrigue, lots of cops and even more unanswered questions. He'll play it like a Stradivarius for a week. I thought of asking Mulligan to assign me a police reporter as a helper, but decided to do the leg work myself to see where it leads. My instincts were as sure as a compass needle.

The reason I'd cut mulligan short was the curbside arrival of yet another government-issue car with a trunk-lid full of antennas that gave it the appearance of a satellite tracking station. Holy shit! I thought, this story has more hairpin turns than the Indy 500 and even less braking distance. Ruining my morning was one thing, but this breakfast-hour showdown was going to make fireworks history or my name isn't Richard Dart. My system was churning more cholesterol than an Egg McMuffin. Out of the car and into the semicircular fray stepped Robert Krall, special prosecutor, flashing a Justice Department cereal-box badge and leading with his dimpled chin into a certain scuffle with local law enforcement officials who had no stomach for dandy-assed feds in the first place. Krall did a modified limbo under the yellow police-line tape that cordoned off the immediate area of Faye's landing pad. Her body was now a chalk outline on an asphalt blackboard. Seeing Krall, Nelligan turned the color of Zinfandel. Small wonder, another body-snatcher on the scene, all of which suited me fine because while dealing with Krall and the detective from homicide, Nellgian would hardly notice a harmless pipsqueak like me. Emboldened by the modest thought, I left the relative safety of the phone booth and retraced my steps across the street to see what I could pick up on my radar screen. They were behaving like buzzards around road kill.

Krall: "….want a copy of the full report and a copy of the autopsy soon as they're ready."

Nelligan: "This is strictly a local matter and what we have here is a possible narcotics case."

Homicide detective: "It's homicide and it stays with me."

Krall: "This woman was under subpoena to appear as a witness before the special grand jury. I might have dibs because it could wind up being a federal case."

Nelligan: "Buzz off, for Chrissake. What's a federal case about a stripper full of horse falling off a roof because she's high enough to think she can fly?"

Krall: "When the stripper's name is Faye, and Faye is a friend of a certain narcotics captain and the narcotics captain is a reluctant witness in a federal investigation into the Block, then I think I can make it a federal case. Especially since her untimely and unfortunate departure occurred only a few hours after she was with you in my waiting room."

At that, the homicide detective stepped aside and smirked, and Nelligan's skin darkened from Cabernet Sauvignon to a deep purply Syrah.

Nelligan: "…. the fuck's that supposed to mean. You suggesting I'm involved in some kind of illegal hanky-panky."

Krall: "….not suggesting anything for the moment, captain, just saying this could wind up in my filing cabinet."

I felt like a canary in a coal mine. It was kind of depressing hearing three cops of various levels of law enforcement importance arguing over Faye's cadaver as if she were nothing more than a side of beef in a meat locker. Just a few hours ago, after all, Nelligan would get all wet just talking about her. Now the hard-nosed bastard's behaving as if he barely knew her at all. Which I discerned was all part of a deliberate effort to deflect attention from their relationship, or whatever they called it, treating her like an ordinary addict when the immediate universe knew that he was her source. It could, in fact, be argued that Nelligan actually killed Faye.

Playing the percentages is one way of staying ahead of the game. Since I'd been virtually unnoticed during the policeman's brawl, I decided it was a good time to withdraw from the scene and head back to *City Press*. As I pulled out, two television trucks rolled up, ready from the get-go to videotape a couple of talking-head cops and the chalk-mark profile of Faye on the garbage-heaped street—

the only visuals that were left for the camera's eye since the ambulance carrying the body bag had long since departed. I squeezed the brakes and slipped the gear lever into park. A toothsome moment was about to happen and I wanted to see which of the three cops would act as the official spokesman for the death in the alley.

It was tough reading lips from a distance, so I interpreted the body language instead. Homicide appeared to defer to narcotics, but narcotics apparently pulled rank and told homicide to do the talking. So into the middle of the muddle stepped Robert Krall, offering a rendering that went something like this:

"….important link to the federal strike force investigation into connections between the Block and local political figures….ask the Justice Department to give me full jurisdiction over this tragic death and hope that local law enforcement agencies will cooperate fully with my request and investigation…."

Homicide sniggered a cynical sneer of amusement and narcotics looked as if he'd just messed his pants. Nelligan had tried to cut a deal whereby he'd have private dominion over Faye's death but no public connection with her life. In short, a cover-up. But Krall beat him to the best of both worlds: He not only went public with the case, but he snatched it away from Nelligan in swift gotcha! Krall usually comes through in one dimension. He had just added a second. Nelligan stood as rigid as if someone had sneaked up behind him and yanked up his undershorts and gave him a wedgie.

By the time I resumed driving, I was beginning to hear the growls of an angry stomach. On the radio, a talk show host was soapboxing an entropic wail about the impending apocalypse, a broad indictment that included, but was not limited to: The liberal welfare pimps in Congress; the welfare queens on the streets; the virtual disappearance of values of any kind; the butt-fucking hip-swishers who march on Washington demanding protection against discrimination and insisting on marriage licenses; drug runners; teenage pregnancy among blacks; the billions of dollars that are flushed down the sinkhole of public education; the decline and fall of America's cities; the ultimate takeover of the country by the colorful palette of minorities; the muddle-headed liberals who are trying to disarm Americans with unworkable gun control laws. It could be argued, he was saying, that we owe blacks something because we were too lazy to do our own work and we forced them into slavery. But what, he asked, do we owe Mexicans, Haitians, or for that matter, El Salvadorians? Trouble is, he concluded, as long as we keep passing out welfare checks they'll keep coming. Too lazy to work. They want role models, they ought to take a look at Asians. They work eighteen hours a day, seven days a week, and never ask for a penny. In search of format relief, I flipped to the FM side of the dial where I beamed in on Miles Davis' rendition of "Bye-Bye Blackbird."

Bumpity-bumping west on Lombard Street, my mind floated free form to Faye, a looker, all right, with that crop of taffy-apple hair and wide aperture baby-blue button eyes. I began composing the story in my head so that by the time I reached *City Press* I'd be ready to sit down and write, get it over with and get the hell out of there. The facts unscrambled and raced through my mind, arranging themselves in neat top-to-bottom order in much the same way that Mozart wrote music. Every snippet was falling into place the way God intended it to be. The backside of *City Press* was looming into view. I circled the building and suddenly I was pissed. Somebody was in my reserved parking space, number seven, and I had the parking pass to prove it. Screw it, I'll just take somebody else's and wait for the fur to fly.

Inside, I flashed my pass to the guard and explained that I'd borrowed another space because mine was taken and I'm up against a deadline. He'd call, he said, if there's a fuss. The elevator swooshed up to the fourth floor where I fetched a cup of coffee from the composing room and walked down a flight of stairs to the news room where my immediate life was spread out before me—Mulligan sitting in his glass box like a benign Buddha enveloped in a gray beard of smoke, and Peaches touch-typing daintily like a secretarial school graduate on her computer keyboard.

If second-hand smoke's the killer they say it is, anyone who gets within fifty feet of Mulligan ought to drop dead within minutes. I stood in the doorframe of his office, my body positioned so that I could turn my head occasionally for a breath of uncontaminated air.

I said: "Your kind of story, Buck. You always say you like dancing girls in the lead, and this time you're going to get them, literally."

"Whatcha got, kid?" Mulligan said.

"I can write it faster than I can tell it, so get ready to clear page one," I said.

I spun away from Mulligan's office before he could argue, and on the way to my workstation I gave Peaches a sly little wink. It must have sent a hot charge up her thighs, because she squirmed and turned the color of an American Beauty rose. At my desk, I slouched out of my suede jacket and draped it over the back of my chair. I was ready for work. I clickety-click-clicked on the keyboard, logging in and entering the password that would boot up my file. I was ready to play this sucker like a Yamaha concert grand.

"The bruised and broken body of a well-known exotic dancer on Baltimore's notorious Block was found in a garbage-strewn alley behind her Patterson Park apartment early today in what police believe was an accidental plunge to her death caused by an overdoes of heroin.

Shortly after the body of Faye Madison—who danced and hustled drinks at Broadway Brown's Pandora's box under the name of Fabulous Faye—was discovered, a jurisdictional dispute erupted among local homicide and narcotics officers and federal law enforcement officials over who would have custody of the investigation.

At the scene of the fatal fall were Captain Joseph Nelligan of the narcotics squad; Robert Krall, head of the Special Federal Strike Force that's investigating the Block; Lieutenant Peter Gallazio, of the homicide squad; and several other unidentified homicide detectives.

Following a lengthy and at times intensely personal argument, Krall said he would ask his superiors at the Justice Department to give him full jurisdiction over the case. He also asked local law enforcement agencies to cooperate with his request.

Ms. Madison is believed to be personally involved with Nelligan. Just yesterday, the two were among several witnesses who appeared at the federal courthouse under subpoena to testify before the grand jury investigating connections between the Block and major political figures.

At the scene of Ms. Madison's death, Krall implied that the relationship between the two was the main reason that he is seeking jurisdiction over the case.

Ms. Madison was a known heroin addict, and her friendship with Nelligan raises questions about whether he was covering up her addiction. Moreover, there is also the question of why a narcotics squad captain would befriend a known drug addict.

One homicide detective at the scene said that the 'relationship' between Nelligan and Ms. Madison was common knowledge within the police department. Ms. Madison was known to be Nelligan's eyes and ears on the Block. Police at the scene took note of perforations on both of her arms.

Ms. Madison is the second person associated with Broadway Brown's nightclub to die under mysterious circumstances in recent months. Earlier, the owner of the popular Block nightspot committed suicide by swallowing sleeping pills shortly after he received a subpoena to appear before the special grand jury.

He had been a target of the strike force ever since his bar was raided and federal officials confiscated an 8x10 photo of him and Gov. Marshall Goodwin. The photo was later leaked to a television reporter in an apparent attempt to embarrass the governor. Goodwin and his one-time political mentor, Joseph Frank, are believed to be targets of the investigation.

Homicide detectives said they are withholding the official cause of Ms. Madison's death until they receive the coroner's report and complete a thorough search of her apartment, where her toy poodle was heard yelping at the time her body was discovered."

I tapped out several more paragraphs of background, smoothed out the bumps and transitions and through the magic of electronics shot the story to Mulligan's computer screen at the speed of light. Within minutes, I was summoned to the smokehouse Mulligan called an office.

"This is serious stuff, kid. You sure of what you've got?" Mulligan said.

"What stuff are you talking about?" I said.

"The business about Nelligan and the hooker and the drugs," Mulligan said.

"Remember the cassette we stashed in the safety deposit box? I also put a memo in there with it to document the fact that I saw Faye shooting up in the back room of Broadway Brown's while Nelligan was holding her arm," I said.

"Why the fuck didn't you tell me at the time?" Mulligan said.

"Because I was waiting for it to fit in somewhere. See how nicely it works here," I said.

"That's what I'm afraid of," Mulligan said.

"If you can't trust me, Buck, who can you trust?" I said.

An hour later I saw living proof, in ninety-point gothic, that Mulligan did indeed trust me. The second edition appeared with a headline that guaranteed an immediate bubble in street sales:

STRIPPER HIGH ON HEROIN PLUNGES TO DEATH IN ALLEY

Block Dancer Linked to Narcotics Squad Captain

I heard the sound of whippoorwills calling. Without another word or gesture of felicity to anyone, I headed out of the building and up to the Block and Pandora's Box. It was a sunny-side-up kind of day, and there in the middle of the morning was the urban hum of commerce on the Block—honks and toots, beer trucks, whiskey wagons, courthouse lawyers hauling Naugahyde briefcases, hung-over winos sleeping off cheap booze in doorways and a grungy advertisement for a tattoo parlor hosing down the sidewalk, playing dodge the squirt with pedestrians—business as usual at Broadway Brown's. Inside, the bar was dark and dank, the human mildew of contaminants that the room exuded like the fenny odor of an overused gym sock. I sensed no danger lurking. Bartender big hands was not at his usual station behind the bar. I continued toward the arch that led to the back-room theater where I'd seen Faye jagging her veins, and in the center of the room at a large round table was a circle of Faye's sorority sisters smoking, drinking coffee from Styrofoam cups and sniffing back tears.

"....Could have gone to the top if she hadn't hooked up with that Irish prick," one said.

"....He's the one that killed her, pumping her body full of that shit," another said.

"....Keeping her stoned all the time, making sure he'd get his weekly blow job," another said.

"....Yeah, and the way he forced her to squeal on who's doing tricks with her and the rest of us," another said.

"....Scared the shit out of everybody, threatening to plant stuff on them then bust 'em," another said.

"....Like to see the sonofabitch get his the way Faye got hers, in a dark alley full of garbage with nobody there to give a shit," another said.

The circle had just about completed its mournful lament when I punctuated the air with a friendly "good morning."

"Fern around?" I said.

"You're another one of the bastards who helped kill Faye," a pneumatic blonde in tiger-striped Spandex said.

"You and your goddam newspaper making a fuss over nothing," a skinny red-head with a poodle warming her crotch said.

"Fucking over people who're trying to make a living's no way to make friends with us," a brunette with a sequined chest out to here said.

"I'm looking for Fern. She around?" I said.

"She's up at police headquarters filling in the blanks for the cops. She was Faye's best friend," the tiger-titted blonde said.

"Thanks. I'll find her." I said.

"Better you get lost trying," the chest said.

I was a step ahead of myself. Danger was lurking. Just as I opened the door and stepped out onto the duck-puddle sidewalk, I saw the bartender big hands was within punching range. His eyes flared, mine flashed my best scared-shitless look. He lunged. I bobbed and weaved and ran like hell, dodging people, ducking cars. Bartender big hands huffed and puffed behind me, hauling the weight of too much beer and too little exercise, no match for my lean, low cholesterol, high fiber running machine. The guy was slower than evolution.

In breathless bursts, he flailed and shouted, turning the air blue with a stream of dark curses and menacing threats:

"....Warned you before—puff—stay the fuck away—puff—or your ass has had it—puff—two good people—puff—dead because of you—puff—you don't back off—puff—you're in deep shit—puff...."

When bartender big hands finally gave up the chase, I was across the street dashing toward the safety of *City Press* and my car. Over my shoulder I could see him standing on the corner of Baltimore and South Streets, waving a fist and mouthing words that I assumed would embarrass even one of his customers. Moisture was building on my forehead as well as under my arms, so I downshifted to a fast walk, though I wasn't even breathing heavily. Right now I needed a shower, a change of clothes and an expense account lunch and I was determined to get all three. Arriving at my destination, there was a note tucked under the windshield wiper of my car: "The next time you park in my space you'll be paying a towing bill." Fuck you, I thought. No name, no need to explain. Underway in the car, I punched the AM band for the news.

I damned near drove off the road when the commercial caught me by surprise and interrupted my newly restored equanimity. Listening to radio requires no effort or concentration at all. It's environmental. It's there, a great big ambient surround, a bubble of sound in a Volvo studio. In fact, listening is the wrong word. Radio is heard, not listened to. You hear what you want to hear and the rest just sort of drifts by in a drone of foghorn words from out of the mouths of announcers who're trying to sound as if they ought to be singing baritone in the Mormon Tabernacle Choir. And that's the way it happened. The news marches by in studied cadences, with numbing familiarity—rape, murder, robbery, pederasty and an appropriate period of mourning for a deceased mammal. Then all of a sudden, WHAM!—a compelling item jumps out of the speaker and grabs you by the earlobes and shouts, LISTEN UP, CHUMP!

"By now you've heard that Faye Madison plunged to her death. She was an exotic dancer, a stripper using her body not as a temple but in lewd ways. And she died not because of the heroin in her veins but because of the Block where she worked. The Block killed her the way it's killing Baltimore. Think about it. A whole city dying because of a single Block. There's still time to take back our city before it perishes the way Faye Madison did. Let's do it. Let's all support Question Six on the ballot and get rid of the Block once and for all. This commercial was paid for by Citizens for a Christian Baltimore."

That fucking Charles Sharkey, as slick as a ski slope. He had a commercial on the air only hours after Faye's body had been discovered, taking advantage of the poison in the environment by plugging right into today's headline and tomorrow's gossip. I remembered Marshal McLuhan's observation that "instant reaction creates instant involvement." That's exactly what Sharkey's done: Seized the issue and harnessed the workforce of listeners as part of his cockamamie crusade to eradicate the Block. Got to hand it to Sharkey, or whoever's advising him. Doing God's work may have its own rewards, all right, but it often has a punch line of amusing sidelights.

One of the quality factors of life in Baltimore is that rush hour lasts about fifteen minutes. After that (except when it rains), there's little traffic at all. I'd made it home in record time. First things first. I had to pee, so I headed straight to the powder room, where I drilled a forceful stream into the toilet bowl. Every man's dream is to be able to arc his stream over the fence throughout the aging process. I was still in business. Relieved, I washed my hands and proceeded to step two. I needed some nourishment to get me through 'til lunch, so I retrieved the carton of orange juice from the refrigerator and poured a water glass full. Then I popped a bagel into the toaster oven and watched it go from doughy off-white to crunchy burnt-brown. I waddled over to my office to check my answering machine, snapping bites of bagel and irrigating them with great washes of ice-cold pulpy juice.

"....This is Federated Financial calling Richard Dart about our new low interest credit cards, the lowest rate you'll find anywhere. If you're interested, please give us a call at one-eight-hundred-Low-Rate....This is All-State chimney cleaning service calling Richard Dart. We'll be working in your neighborhood for the next several days, and we'd like to know if you're interested in having your chimney cleaned and ready for winter. Please give us a call at one-eight-hundred-Clean-Sweep...It's Shelly, Richard. It's eleven o'clock in the morning and I still don't know where you are. But you'd better be behaving yourself. Don't worry. I'm fine. I'll find you sooner or later....Two more hang-ups and the machine clicked off.

CHAPTER 22

▼

At least Shelly hadn't lost her sense of humor even if she had temporarily given up her life. I'd come as close as an unzipped zipper from misbehaving in a major way and I still felt no tug of moral traction holding me back. I've always been convinced that the male sex drive proceeds more from the ego than the id. I'd still like to diddle Peaches, if for no other reason than the challenge of saddling up on a strange set of bones. Not a very good reason, I admit, but a powerful image nonetheless—Shakespeare's "beast with two backs." I put the thought on hold. Wondering where Shelly had re-potted for the indefinite future, I replayed the tape to determine whether I could get a sense of distance from the sound of her voice. No luck. Fiber optics and satellites have eliminated space from sound. Voices no longer sounded as if they were echoing up from the bottom of a barrel. Nor did people feel that they had to shout to close the three thousand mile vacuum between a voice in San Francisco and an ear in Baltimore. For all I could tell from the tape, Shelly could be sitting across the street, as cool as a burpless cucumber, sipping an iced cappuccino. Which would be just like her, the little dickens. Maybe that's the moral imperative, this unencoded synapse we have, that tapped me on the shoulder at Peaches' last night and said, bug out of here, hornball, before you drizzle on your own parade.

I rinsed the juice glass, stacked it in the dishwasher and drifted upstairs. I peeled off the clothes I'd recycled from last night and stepped into my haberdashery store of a closet. Military-straight, two inches between each, hung forty suits in different hues and patterns—stripes in pins and chalks, blues and grays, plain flannel suits in navy and charcoal, glen plaid suits, gabardine suits, nailheads, worsteds, even a tweed herringbone number to give weekends a zip of country flair. And at the end of the suits were two navy blazers, one a single breasted, the other a double. And ties. Talk about ties. The kaleidoscope rack held a hundred, but I doubled up on many of the hooks. There were Mackelsfields in a dozen tiny geometric designs, solids in twill and grenadine, rows of regimental stripes in different tones and widths, a half dozen clubs of dubious heraldry, polka dots, Italian madder, English foulards, wool challis and several small-patterned woven silks. Shoes came in two flavors—black lace-ups and tassel loafers and several shades of brown suede, even burnished bourbon leather. Shirts are another matter, my favorite article. Name it, I have it, especially if it's blue—in broadcloth, end-on-end and pin oxford. Chalk stripes, pencil stripes, windowpanes and just plains, miniature check, pin check, tattersal, candy stripe, long staple, four bar stripe, mille raie stripe, gingham check and fancy check, hairline broadcloth and double-bar stripe, all in an equal assortment of French and barrel cuffs. And add to the collection several blue-bodied shirts with white collars, in tabs and three-inch straight points. Decisions, decisions. Being properly harberdashed may be a luxury to others, but with me it's a compulsion.

I showered, flossed, brushed, combed and peed again before stepping into a navy herringbone suit with hand stitched lapels, softened by a medium blue broadcloth shirt and a striped tie of blue tone-on-tone with a fine red line that was topped off by a white linen pocket square and Ferregamo lace-up wing-tips. As composed as a Mozart sonata, I was once again feeling just loose change short of a million bucks.

My mood swing took just a hiccup of a second when the ding-dong of the door chime set off ripples of cataclysm. I did a quick shift from a Bermuda High to a Mississippi Low while I played a guessing game kind of like "Wheel of Fortune" where the wheel spins and instead of numbers there are names. The Avon Lady no longer makes random house calls. And I wasn't expecting anything from Federal Express or UPS. It was too early in the day for mail. And surely it couldn't be Ed McMahon coming personally to tell me that I'd won ten million dollars in the Publisher's Clearinghouse Sweepstakes. When the wheel stopped at a blank, the audience Oooooooohhhed! I should have known better than to make plans for lunch.

Filling the frame in the doorway was the heaving mass of protoplasm of another kind of game show host—this one more like "Let's Make a Deal"—Joe Frank. And with him was what passes as his *consigliore*, his son Milton, kind of a manqué Sonny Corleone, always traveling in pairs to cover each other's asses. Frank's face had the pained look of a man who needed a double shot of Milk of Magnesia.

"Well, I'll be damned, if it isn't the insurance man. Things so tough you have to go selling door to door?" I said.

"Not a bad way to go. Lotta money to be made that way," Frank said.

"You didn't come here to sell me a policy. So what's on your mind?" I said.

"We come in for a minute," Frank said.

"I was just on my way out, but I see I have little choice," I said.

I slammed the door with a thud of authority that displays irritation and guided my uninvited guests to the den. Before I sat down, I removed my jacket to avoid wrinkles. Frank and Frank slumped into the folds of the sofa as carelessly as if they were wearing burlap, surprising because Milton Frank had the reputation of being a dandy and Joe Frank was no sartorial slouch, either. Some people just don't care, I guess. To show my contempt for the intrusion, I made no gesture of courtesy or accommodation, not even the offer of a glass of water, let alone coffee. If body language could kill, I'd be guilty of murder one.

Big Frank spoke first and wasted no time getting to the point: "Stories you've been writing are hurting a lot of people, solid businessmen, people who work on the Block, got no axes to grind with anyone. When are you gonna back off, give 'em a break, lighten up on this whole thing?"

I said: "It shouldn't be long now. The investigation is either going to dry up or produce results. Christ, already two people are dead because of what's going on. And that asshole Sharkey's running around like a manic Jerry Falwell. So why come to me? I'm not causing the trouble. I'm just covering it. I'm a mirror, not a microscope."

Frank said: "You're the one who's stoking it up and keeping it going. You seem to know more than the prosecutors, and what you're writing is feeding them enough information to raise their eyebrows."

I said: "Prosecutors are assholes. They don't understand the system or the process or how business gets done. And worse, they don't know the players. Besides, I keep my eyes and ears open. Prosecutors talk mainly to each other."

Frank said: "I can see you like to live well and newspaper salaries aren't all that great. I could put a decent suit of clothes on your back. Fella like you could make a lot of money just by keeping quiet. You ought to think it over."

I was certain it wasn't a bad connection, but I could swear I heard Joe Frank bribing me all over again, forgetting that he'd tried the same trick by the potted palm many years ago. Except this time he really pissed me off.

I said: "Everyone who knows me understands that the last thing I need are clothes. They also know that every suit I own is decent. So, Mr. Frank, it burns my ass that you come into my house and think you can buy me off. Not only that, you also insult me. Well, sir, I'll see you in the funny papers. Now get the fuck out of here before I call the paper and dictate a story that you tried to bribe a reporter." Talk about your flashbacks.

Milton Frank shook his corrugated Bassett-hound face and put in his two coins worth: "Dad, I told you it was a waste of time trying to make sense with this guy. Let's get out of here. And be advised, hotshot, that if this ever comes up we'll both deny it."

Great legal advice, I thought. He must have gotten his law degree through the correspondence course that's chartered in Grenada. I led the way to the door and slammed it shut as their ample backsides passed through, hoping the doorknob hit one of them squarely on the tailbone to give them something to remember me by.

The expense account lunch I'd promised myself was waiting to be ordered. When I plunged into the lunchtime crowd at Paisan's, I was greeted, as usual, by the thunderclap voice of Tony Russo who was seated at his wide-angle banquette ladling chicken broth with *pastina* into his busy mouth—the kind of food infants and grown men with ulcers eat.

"Hey, whaddya know, it's the killer. Everybody you write about ends up dead. Stay the hell away from me," Russo said.

"Don't worry, Tony baby, you crap out I'll see that you get the greatest obituary since the Pope died. I'll even write it myself," I said.

"Too bad about the broad. Nelligan stuck it in her every way he could—in her arm, in her mouth, in her groin. Worm shoulda died with her," Russo said.

"Yeah, another whore with a heart of gold story. What I can't figure is that it seems as if everybody in town knows about Nelligan, so why isn't somebody doing something about it?" I said.

"Everybody's afraid. Rumor is he's got a lotta shit on a lotta people. Big shit. That's how he keeps 'em in line," Russo said.

"Like what," I said.

"Like use your imagination," Russo said.

Russo resumed shushing his soup with bellows of breath to cool it down a few degrees Fahrenheit before slurping it in, a gesture that I assumed was meant to put a final punctuation mark on the conversation.

"Hear about anything coming down?" I said.

"If I was you, and I'm glad I'm not, I'd keep an eye on the other trick. She was the dead lady's best friend and the word is they're gonna turn up the heat on her 'til she says cockadoodle-do," Russo said.

"Hell, you oughta be me. You're pretty good. Have a good lunch," I said.

Seated and presented with the customary basket of bread and glass of water, I ordered a Campari and soda with a slice of lime to keep the waitress occupied while I scanned the menu. Why I bother I don't know. I usually order the same dish every time—homemade thin spaghetti tossed in a garlicy tomato cream sauce with mussels, clams, shrimp and calamari. This time I decided to switch the fare just to convince myself that I'm not an old coot in a bottomless rut. I ordered grilled grouper with capers and tomatoes, giving my salivary glands reason for increasing their output.

In my wildest wooley-eyed fantasy, I would never have believed that a glass of Campari could double as a crystal ball. But as I sipped and stared over the rim of the glass, the part of my brain circuitry that processes instant photographs thought it was being deceived by my eyes. There in the hub-bub of human chatter, the tinkling of silver and the slinging of dishes sat Judge Michael Falcone with a steroidian pile of a man three times his size and twice as ugly, an unfamiliar face with an unforgettable mole that I'd never seen before either in Paisan's or on the Block. The mole on his left cheek resembled and over-ripe berry that was ready for the jelly jar. Beyond that, he was as thick as a refrigerator and appeared solid enough to fuck a grizzly bear and walk away without a scratch. The comparison was stark. Beside the mountain man, Judge Falcone looked plump and wizen like a Corn Flake, no judicial robe to camouflage the paunch or the sloping shoulders that made him appear almost like an inverted ice cream cone. And odd couple if there ever was one, which is why I was hoping that Tony Russo would be at his customary observation post when I'd finished lunch.

As I watched for any clue of body language or lip movement that might signal the subject that was under discussion, a steaming platter was slipped under my nose. It sent up tantalizing vapors of capers, garlic, oregano and just a hint of fish, altogether a bouquet that induced me to hit the remote control button and turn off for the moment the image of Judge Falcone and his mystery guest. That a twenty-five pound Grouper (a.k.a. Jewfish) gave up its life so that I could enjoy a slab of its side the size of a thick New York strip steak was one of life's great inequities. But that's the way God (and some anonymous fisherman) intended it to be. At times like this, the senses go to work as a tag team. Most people think they taste food when it hits the tongue, but actually they smell it. The old schnozzola, with a little help from the eyes, does most of the hard labor because the taste buds are dumb little flakes that can't tell the difference between hamburger and sushi. Sensing and smelling food tells the tongue what's it's raving about because a good meal always tastes better when somebody else is paying for it.

I chopped and forked, keeping one eye on my platter to make certain that I didn't splash my tie and the other on Judge Falcone and his oversized companion. About halfway through my capered fish, the two of them shook hands, scraped their chairs backwards and got up to leave. Unfolded, the jolly giant was even larger than he appeared in a seated position, his left armpit swollen by a piece of artillery the size of a rocket launcher. He deferred to the judge and let Falcone lead the way out and to who knows what or where else. I finished the fish and mopped up the remaining sauce with sponges of soft bread, not very mannerly, perhaps, but nonetheless a toothsome finish to a tasty meal. I signaled for the check and with great pleasure presented a piece of fantastic plastic, whose receipt I would submit to Mulligan as reparation for waking me up so early this morning. I rattled a couple of Tic Tacs into my mouth to mask my sour-breath lunch.

As I'd hoped, I found Tony Russo still stuck to his perch, reading the racing form. I pulled up a chair across from him so we'd be dealing with each other at eye level.

"Question, Tony. Who's the gorilla with Judge Falcone?" I said.

"Never seen the guy before, but he looks like he's bad ass," Russo said.

"You see the size of the piece in his armpit?" I said.

"Sucker's big enough to pack an Uzi in there," Russo said.

"What the hell's Judge Falcone doing in public with an obvious thug like that?" I said.

"He's supposed to have out-of-town connections with people whose names end in vowels like his and mine," Russo said.

"Holy shit! You telling me out-of-town mobsters are connected with a Baltimore judge?" I said.

"You're the reporter. Go find out. But it isn't worth getting you ass shot off trying" Russo said.

"Thanks for the encouragement. Maybe I'll put in for hazardous duty pay," I said.

"Remember I told ya," Russo said.

"Thanks. And good luck with the ponies," I said.

"I don't play 'em. I just book 'em," Russo said.

"*Ciao*," I said.

It was a eureka moment. I hotfooted it out of Paisan's thinking I was on to something. Finding pegs and holes that match is the foreplay of the news business. If Russo was right, it would explain why Falcone came crashing down so hard on Krall, forcing him to pull back as he did by denying him one of the most compelling weapons in a prosecutor's gun rack—the leak. But there had to be more to the dry-hanging than that. Most of the stories about the Block and the investigation were my handiwork and I sure as hell wasn't getting my information from Krall. The thought zigzagged across the neural network of my mind that as the judge who was presiding over the grand jury, Falcone had access to the investigation's progress as well as its direction and content. Was this his way of feeding information to someone who might be sent crashing through the windshield if Krall were allowed to stomp on the brakes? Or was somebody about to have his brains scrambled by a well-placed projectile of lethal caliber? I tucked the thoughts away on a prominent shelf in my memory bank so that they could be located quickly when needed.

Faye got a grand sendoff before her body was shipped for burial in her hometown of Aliquippa, in the heart of Pennsylvania's Anthracite region, where her father had contracted black lung disease from working a lifetime in the mines and her mother stitched away her years in a dress factory. On the afternoon of her last trip home, Faye's remains were driven around the original route that legend says gave the Block its name. In the old days, a pair of limousines was kept at the ready along Baltimore Street, and for a few bucks a man could rent one for five minutes. The driver took his time so the customer could get his money's worth from the woman he'd booked for the ride. And the route was always the same: South on Front to Lombard Street, east on Lombard to the Fallsway, north on the Fallsway to Baltimore Street and back to the nightclub. It was called "taking a ride around the block."

On this appropriately funeral gunmetal-gray day, a Cadillac hearse, led by a police motorcycle escort (courtesy of Captain Joseph Nelligan) did a once-around the original Block for old times sake as a last tribute to Faye. And as the petty-paced one-car funeral approached the bunker of neon rumps and pinwheel tassels that explode along the Block like an ordinance testing range, the motorcycle policeman let his siren wail the arrival of Faye. As he did, the doors of every nightclub on the Block swung open and dozens of girls, still in their work-a-day stripping attire, poured onto the street and lined the curb, crying and waving their handkerchiefs as the hearse crawled by before it headed north for the coal towns of Pennsylvania and Faye's last dance.

The coroner's report said that Faye could have died of shock before she hit the ground, say by the time she reached the second floor on the way down without the benefit of an elevator. And as if that weren't enough, the report added dryly that Faye's nose-dive resulted in a fractured skull, multiple bone-breaks and rib-cracks, internal bleeding and several snapped teeth. The report noted that there were no signs of violence except that which Faye had caused to her own body by injecting it with damaging substances. Enough heroin was found in her system to keep a detox team busy for a week. And yes, the coroner appended in one of those random oh-by-the-way afterthoughts, Faye tested HIV positive.

Ah, sweet mystery of life. A wack-a-do thought rumbled through my head. Faye was a controlled user. She knew just how many molecules of the white powder were required to adjust her body chemistry to an acceptable level of comfort, and not a smithereen more, not intentionally anyway. Yet the coroner reported that there was enough of the Columbian marching powder in her bloodstream to give a horse a kick, leading to the tentative conclusion that this dosage might have caused enough disorientation to result in an accidental fall. And pardon the smirk, but the notion of Joe Nelligan's body playing human host to an HIV bug swimming around in his arteries like a runaway tadpole had the impact of a raunchy punch line in a raucous comedy club. The two snippets of information seem somehow connected. I put the thought(s) on call waiting.

Back at *City Press*, I took care of first things first. I filled out an expense account sheet, fiction writing we called it, and slipped it into Mulligan's in-box. Next, I meandered back to the library and pulled the clips on Judge Falcone, a reporter's way of playing getting-to-know-you. The official biography was routine stuff—Loyola Blakefield High School, Loyola College (day-hop), University of Baltimore Law School (nights), assistant state's attorney, then on to the bench and finally up the ranks to a federal judgeship—a typical up-from-working-class climb to the security and respectability of the courts, hardly your Oliver Wendell Holmes or Louis Brandeis. Riffling through the old clippings that over the years had become as brittle as dry leaves, I learned that as a bright young city prosecutor, Falcone had been attached to the organized crime unit and that he'd once threatened to put the Block out of business. When it came time for his move to the bench, however, Falcone was locked in a bitter three-way battle with two other lawyers for the single judgeship—typical bar association fudge-factory stuff to populate the bench with Ivy Leaguers from within the old-boy network of silk stocking law firms instead of street-savvy night-school ethnics. It was only the intervention and patronage of Joe Frank and his political organization that was able to save the day for Falcone and hustle him off to the tailor to be measured for a robe. Holy shit! Payback time.

I'd just finished reading and replacing the clips when an intern appeared to tell me that Krall had scheduled a news conference that Mulligan wanted me to cover. It was to begin in twenty minutes. I made a quick stop in the men's room, then scrambled up to the courthouse where I'd stand with the scrum of other reporters waiting for a man who operated on lawyer's time.

Bob Krall had decided to torque up the action a notch. At this point in his probe, Krall knew that he could attract a platoon of reporters even if he stood on the court house steps and recited the dietary information on the back of a box of Fruit Loops. Twenty minutes after the appointed time, Krall waddled out of the courthouse's vault of brass doors and up to the thicket of microphones.

"....asked you to come here because I have an announcement that I think will interest you. I want you to know that certified letters have been delivered and accepted by attorneys for Governor Marshall Goodwin and Joseph Frank notifying their clients that they are now formally targets of the investigation into the Block. As you know, we had subpoenaed certain information from the governor and Mr. Frank. We have completed our review of that information. And now the letters are inviting Governor Goodwin and Mr. Frank to appear voluntarily before the grand jury if they so choose...."

"Does this mean there'll be indictments soon?" a reporter said.

"What it means is they're targets and we'd like their voluntary cooperation in the investigation," Krall said.

"Do you expect to get it?" I asked.

"That's up to them," Krall said.

"If they're targets, why would they want to go before a grand jury and risk incriminating themselves?" I said.

"We're giving them an opportunity to explain some things," Krall said.

In a pig's ass, I thought. A target letter meant that the jig's up, please stand by while we arrange a form of public transportation known as the paddy wagon. Sphincters must be tightening in Annapolis and down on Redwood Street. Krall was on to something or he wouldn't be playing the role of risk-taker in public. Simply put, a target letter meant "gotcha." Krall had just added the tweak factor. At the intersection of destiny and doubt, every reporter wonders what he overlooked, which rug something was swept under whose corner he neglected to turn over, who was waiting around the bend to yell SUCKER! and laugh in his face. What did Krall know that I didn't?

Krall was saying, "....the investigation's continuing, although the pace may accelerate. I want to get this matter wrapped up so I can do my Christmas shopping."

"What's the timetable?" I said.

"Events determine the timetable, not the calendar. Events and witnesses," Krall said.

"Why'd you decide to go public in such a big way?" I said.

"To keep you busy. Busy and honest," Krall said.

I was feeling as if someone had pasted a "kick me" sign on my back. Krall was being a tease. Here's a man, as thick as a law book, whom I'd faced down in front of a judge only a day ago now being as sweet as honeysuckle. Something's slipped by me, and Krall's tucking it to me pretty good as well as to Goodwin and Frank. He must know that he's got the two of them by the balls, and now he's going to play the game of death by a thousand cuts. A nick here, a gash there, and pretty soon they're so bloodied up from the steady stab of publicity that nobody would trust them enough to give them change for a dollar so they could use a pay toilet. As for me, Krall intended to drive me bonkers by holding out whatever he had, knowing that I or any other reporter, for that matter, would be unable to prowl the dark corners and crawl spaces of another person's private life without the intrusive power of a subpoena. Legalized voyeurism has its rewards. Though Krall's announcement was a legitimate public relations maneuver designed to heighten the drama, I wondered how the news would square with Judge Falcone's gag order. Then again, this was an announcement, not a leak. But more to the point was whether the Justice Department had given Krall a wink and a nod to proceed as if Judge Falcone was just a crotchety pain-in-the-ass to be ignored. Turf battles such as this are sometimes resolved by disregarding orders. After all, without the word "Huh?" there'd be no such study as metaphysics.

By the time I returned to *City Press*, the governor's press office in Annapolis had issued the following statement over the Associated Press wire: "Once again the Special Prosecutor's office has demonstrated the highhanded and abusive power of the Justice Department in a manner that is totally un-American and contrary to our system of justice. In this country, a person is supposed to be innocent until proven guilty. To the Special Prosecutor, and the Justice Department that is sanctioning this fishing expedition, the opposite appears to be true. The steady drumbeat of leaks and publicity is nothing more than lynch-mob democracy and trial by newspaper. I said at the outset that I have nothing to hide and that I welcome this investigation. I stand by that statement with full confidence that in the end I will have been an innocent victim of a pointless witch hunt."

It was a case of the old ju-jitsu. Krall farted, Goodwin farted back. All of which meant that I had to grind out a quick six hundred-word overnighter. Goodwin was in the grip of a no-win pincers movement. Normally a guy who's getting the linty end of the lollypop keeps his mouth zippered up. The last people to realize that other people don't have to talk to reporters are reporters. But Goodwin's a public official. And his constituents could construe his silence for legal reasons as a faint signal of guilt. He had no choice but to squirm and to issue a parade of clichés declaiming his innocence and protesting the abuse of power by his hangman. I'd known Goodwin before he was a virgin.

I assembled my notes along with the wire copy of Goodwin's statement and issued the appropriate commands to the computer's nerve center in a large air-conditioned room one floor above me. As quick as the flick of a light switch, the blank screen came to life in little green squiggles that told me to go for it and get the hell out of here.

It was a straight-ahead confirm-and-deny lead paragraph, no jazz, no razzmatazz, no verbal summersaults, just the facts please, the way journalism schools teach the five w's—who, what, why, when, where. In other words, a good story is supposed to tell itself without the help of additional spices from the *sous* chef. That's fine with me, because stories like this one also write themselves. I clickety-clacked the down-and-dirty six hundred words in just under fifteen minutes, and after a quick fine-tuning I beamed the story to the night city editor's file. He acknowledged the story's arrival with a thumbs-up sign that was also my signal to evaporate.

But I could feel an aura encapsulate me that conveyed an airborne message that translated roughly, not so fast, chum. The aura also had a delicious fragrance. And the fragrance was the unmistakable scent of Peaches all starched and laundered. Bad Richard began thinking X-rated thoughts. I wished to hell Shelly would high-tail it back here.

"Writing about hookers again?" Peaches said.

"Whores of a different kind," I said.

"I'm still upset with you," Peaches said.

"Good thing it worked out that way. I got a wake-up call bright and early from Mulligan. If he hadn't been able to find me he'd have sounded like a seal barking," I said.

"Excuses, excuses," Peaches said.

"When I go with my gut, I'm right ninety nine percent of the time," I said.

"What's your gut got to do with this?" Peaches said.

"Being in the right place at the right time," I said.

"Spending the morning with a dead hooker is better than waking up with me?" Peaches said.

Acting as haughty as if she'd just won a round of Double Jeopardy, Peaches fluttered away on a pregnant pause to let me ponder the thought. Which I did for a second or two as her sculpted bottom jiggled away from me as deliberately as a Jell-O mold in a Bill Cosby commercial. She was ripe and ready, and as God and his celestial sperm bank knows, certainly a desirable little nooky. But there was something of a turn-off about Peaches that I suddenly began to discern. She was overeager, probably more enchanted with the notion of sex as a naughty experience rather than the thrill of it as an act of lust. Because when it's done right, sex is definitely dirty. I watched Peaches hip and hug through a pathway of file cabinets until she finally reached her desk. As she sat down, she turned and shot me a quick wink. I'd probably have more fun fishing in my pocket for my keys. For the moment, at least, I'd consign Peaches to the what-the-hell-was-I-thinking file in my mental circuits.

It was the suicide hour—too early to drink, too late to undertake any heavy lifting. I slouched back to the morgue to engage in some random rummaging through rust-colored clips on the Block. The first was a doozey.

Item: Blaze Starr, who's undressed before more men than the entire chorus line of the Ziegfeld Follies, was once arrested for lowering her G-string and revealing her Velcro. Concerned that the authorities might close down her Tick Tock club, she retained a young attorney to defend her if it became necessary. On the day of the hearing, the two walked the few blocks to the courthouse. Upon entering the courtroom, she turned to her lawyer and said, "you can go home now, everything's going to be fine." And it was. Judge Michael Falcone was seated on the bench that day. Case dismissed.

Item: Back in the mid-Fifties, there was a toothsome young lady who spent her afternoons gigging on the Block and her nights hustling at the bar of the gingerbread Marlboro Apartments, when it was fashionable, on a leafy boulevard on the west side of town. The bar was a favorite meat market for several New York Yankees when they were in town to play the Orioles. Three Yankees' stars befriended the woman and enjoyed her services (for a fee) whenever they were in Baltimore. As it turned out, the woman had been under surveillance by the vice squad for solicitation. So when the pussy posse swooped down to arrest the woman in the act, she produced testimony that she was not partial to baseball players. She'd serviced most of the police department's top brass as well. The Yankees went back to New York, and the crotch cops went home red-faced and empty handed.

Item: Upon the beating and hospitalization of one of their co-workers, the strippers and hookers on the Block organized and joined the bartenders' union. They were demanding health insurance to cover the risks of their business. When the Block show bar owners resisted, the ladies refused to undress in public or "do bottles," thereby cutting into profits considerably. After a two-week standoff, the club owners relented and agreed to pay eighty percent of the ladies' medical care benefits as was agreed upon in the bartenders' union contract.

Item: On one of his very infrequent personal visits to Baltimore and the Block, Gaetano Terrachio, territorial mob patriarch of Philadelphia and much of New Jersey, was given if not the red carpet treatment then a high-priced linoleum reception. The notorious Terrachio was taken on a brass-band tour of the city's police headquarters, its cell blocks, all of its electronic gadgetry and its command-post suite of offices where ranking officials pretend they're fighting crime when actually they know there's little they can do to stop the mayhem. The police commissioner of the hour was a harmless nincompoop by the name of George Forrester who hadn't a cretin's notion of whom he was entertaining. He was, he said, simply honoring a request by his good friend, Michael Falcone.

Holy shit! For all the whooping and hollering and posturing and other rackety commotion that Falcone was putting out, he was, it turns out, as much of a link to the Block as Nelligan, Joe Frank, Marshall Goodwin, Charles Sharkey and all of the other weasels and crumb-buns who were on the front burner with the heat on high. All of which suggests that under Falcone's gown beats the heart of a judge whoop-de-doing it on payola. The story had been written years earlier, in the innocent facts-only style of the era, and had been resting comfortably ever since in its quiet burial place in the *City Press* morgue, land of the thief and home of the knave. Now, with the flashlight of context limning it, Falcone suddenly became—Bingo!—another peg that's been accepted by an accommodating hole.

Christ, it's been a long day. Careful not to crack them, I folded the toast-brown clippings at the original hinges and tucked them in their envelope, knowing I'd be back for them when the final chapter of the investigation into the Block would be written. Soon, I hope. I padded from the library to the elevator and made an undetected getaway.

CHAPTER 23

▼

In the car, I punched on the radio. I flicked the switch to the FM band and crashed in on Mahler's Ninth Symphony. This was soar-with-the-eagles stuff, the kind of music God would write if he had the talent, proving once again that the human race can't be all bad if one of its own can produce a wall of sound like the Ninth. For every mugger there's a Michelangelo, for every burglar there's a Beethoven, for every porno dealer there's a Walt Disney, for every butcher there's a Bach, for every rapist there's a Raphael and for every drug kingpin there's a Dostoyevski.

Calvert Street is not exactly Howdy Doodyville. I was smoking up the battered and smudged avenue between rows of boarded up townhouses and enough debris on the sidewalks to supply a modest landfill. Here and there a cosmetic alteration put a quick smile on the street—the Baltimore *Sun*, Center Stage, the Waterloo Apartment complex, Government House—but by and large Calvert Street had gone to seed, shoddy and shabby and crime-ridden and definitely a candidate for either the wrecking ball or a very large federal resuscitation grant.

Soon I was back on home territory in Roland Park, heading for Eddie's and a hurry-up take-home dinner. I selected and pointed, and watched the aproned lady ladle penne with grilled chicken into one container and a Caesar salad into another. Amusing. A checkout line with no shrieking tabloids. But that's ditzy old Eddie's, catering to the Volvo station wagon and SUV trade and the blue-haired WASPs in Talbot wrap-around skirts and quilted coats in hues of pink and lime. Back in the car, I made a U-turn at the break in the median strip, executed a couple of quick turns and before I was out of second gear I was home and in the house.

I stashed the pasta and the salad on the counter near the microwave, slid out of my suit jacket and draped it over the knob on the banister. And in a seamless motion, I packed a pewter Jefferson Cup with ice cubes and with the precision of a plastic surgeon I carved a strip of skin from the face of a lemon and twisted and smeared its zest onto the ice. I poured three fingers of Absolut. *Salute*! The first blast of iced vodka always makes me feel as if I'm getting and ice cream headache, which compared to a paper cut is almost lethal.

In my office, the red eye on the answering machine was sending out winks of urgency. But before I could check for messages, the phone rang.

"Richard, where have you been?" Shelly said.

"Well, I certainly haven't been to London to see the queen," I said.

"I've been worried," Shelly said.

"Not to worry, pretty lady," I said.

I recounted the details of Faye's pathetic story and the fact that Krall had finally confirmed that Goodwin and Frank were the objects of his affection. And, as a raconteur would, I added for entertainment value what I'd been picking up on Falcone.

"Sounds as if you've been a busy little digger," Shelly said.

"All in a day's work. Now that we've had the warm-up before Sinatra, tell me what you're up to," I said.

"I'm fine, but I think it'd be a mistake at this point, especially on the phone, I'm going to keep my distance for a few more days, then I'll probably be back," Shelly said.

"You lawyers. Christ, it never occurred to me that my phone might be radioactive. But, then, I wouldn't put anything past Krall, although I don't think he'd risk bugging a reporter's phone," I said.

"You can never be too careful. I miss you, Richard," Shelly said.

"You don't know how much I miss you, dewdrop thighs. Get back here soon before I explode." I said.

"Behave yourself and take a cold shower. Goodbye. I'll call soon," Shelly said.

"Bye," I said.

I pressed the play button on the answering machine and the red light froze in its socket:

"Beep....beep....This is Paul Stuart's calling Richard Dart to let you know that our new fall line of suits is in and we're having a special showing for our preferred customers. You'll be getting a card in the mail this week letting you know the date and time. Thank you....beep....This is AT&T calling to introduce you to our new money-saving plan that gives you a twenty five percent discount on calls placed to one frequently called area code. We know you're not home, so we'll get back to you later....beep....I'm not calling to leave my name and number at the sound of the beep. I'm calling to let you know that you'll be getting something very interesting in the overnight mail at your home address. It's safe that way...."

Two more hang-ups and the machine clicked off. What a depersonalized world we're living in. Machines talking to machines without human intercourse. However, the staticky human voice on the machine was very definitely husky male, but also indistinguishable because of the background noise of honking and revving and the deep belching of diesel engines on buses. I replayed the tape twice but no luck. I couldn't connect the voice with a face, but I did discern the chipped edge of Baltimorese in the way he pronounced certain words—inneres-tin (interesting), ADDress (address). But wait a minute. Listening for a third time and tuning my ear away from the voice, through the ambient sounds of the city, I heard in the deep background a metallic squawk rising up from the sidewalk, saying, "Hey, buddy, we got whatever you want." Sonofabitch. It was a Block barker's call in the night to some luckless passerby, offering up an expensive menu from the city's central meat market. The call came from a phone booth on the Block and the disembodied voice could have belonged to any one of a dozen anonymous bodies.

Nothing I could do but wait 'til morning.

I sucked down the remaining vodka and returned to the kitchen where I poured a second, and a third, before I spooned dinner from the plastic containers. The penne and grilled chicken had a tasty, smoky edge, but the Caesar salad was intended for the timid—not enough garlic. I scarfed down dinner faster than a Weight Watcher's dieter, rinsed the dishes and stashed them in the dishwasher. After a dog's day like today, it was a pleasure having nothing to do but lounge around and wait for the overnight mail delivery in the morning, curious as hell to know what the postman would have in his pouch and why all the mystery of anonymous phone calls and accelerated delivery to get it into my hands.

Upstairs, I undressed, shook my jacket and trousers to snap the fibers into place and encourage the wrinkles hang out, then I made certain that all the articles of clothing were in their proper places before stepping into the shower. The steady needles of water were relaxing. I thought of the times Shelly and I had showered together, moving the soap around in slow gentle circles, knowing that eventually it would end up directly in the cabbage patch. And here I was, alone and lonely, lathering my own loins, in a house as big as a Zeppelin hanger, all because of a couple of two-bit politicians who couldn't keep their sticky fingers out of the tambourine. I missed Shelly. The earth hadn't moved lately.

Dried and decontaminated, I wrapped myself in an oversized terrycloth robe and headed downstairs for the brandy bottle and my favorite huggy chair. The brandy crawled down my esophagus on warm cat's paws and reached the entry-way to my stomach with a great MEOW! Now moderately sedated, I pushed the TV clicker and began channel surfing, finally settling on the umpteenth thou-sandth re-run of "Citizen Kane." A sweet little irony that reminded me that I was still out there searching for somebody's Rosebud. I took a couple more long pulls on the brandy and began to get drowsy. I must have dozed off, because when I woke up two hours later the sled was burning in the fireplace, revealing the secret of Rosebud once again, and the movie was over. Television and brandy are a deadly mixture.

After making certain everything that was connected to a public utility was off but the security system, I wobbled upstairs, peed about a pint of processed vodka and brandy, washed my hands and brushed my teeth, and hit the pillow snoring. In seconds I was, as they say, dead to the world, hoping that it was no more than just a figure of speech.

It was an up-and-at-'em morning and I was in a kick-ass mood. I'd slept later than my usual get-up-and-crow time, but what the hell, I was entitled, seeing as how reporting is no nine-to-five business. Work when there's work to be done and screw off when there isn't. I rushed through my morning functions and headed for the closet. The weather report said mild, so I took the radio forecaster at his word. Clothes jump-start my day. I assembled a dashing medley of a tan gabardine suit, a striped broadcloth shirt in a supporting tone of the suit and a blue-and-white polka dot tie that provided contrast to the subtle blue striping in the shirt. Completing the ensemble were brown suede wingtip shoes and a pouf of white pocket square to continue the theme of the white dots in the tie. Get ready, Baltimore, here I come, a lean, mean reporting machine all dressed up and ready to go. But not before the overnight delivery arrives.

Downstairs, I poured a large glass of orange juice and unfolded the newspaper I'd just retrieved from the front porch. I turned to the comics pages to check my horoscope—I'm an Aries—which on any given day usually assured me that I was going to get rich, or laid, or both.

"Spotlight on you—you're a hot ticket, main event. You gain allies, you'll be supported in fulfilling desires. Cycle excellent for finance and romance. Gemini, Virgo persons involved."

There it was again, finance and romance. I wished the stock market were as consistent as Sydney Omar. Rich I'm not worried about. People don't do what I do if they're interested in money—big money. But getting laid is becoming a serious worry, something I think about more when Shelly's not around. Anyway, so much for my daily lunar fix. I poured a bowl of bite-size Shredded Wheat and laced it with skim milk to make certain that my triglycerides behaved themselves. A breakfast like that goes down in no time, so I resumed surfing through the newspaper, considering the headlines that telegraphed the convincing message that the world was falling apart and the country was going to hell in a handcart.

The doorbell rang at precisely 9:20 A.M. and a uniformed postman handed me a large red, white and blue overnight mailer that bulged by an inch at the center. The door shut behind me. I snapped open the pouch and removed a small diary with a note that said:

"This was recovered in Faye's apartment after her death. It's better in your hands than in Nelligan's or Krall's. You'll know what to do."

Inside the front cover, Faye had inscribed her name and address and the date she began keeping score. There was also a small aging picture of her, like one of those wallet-size high school graduation shots that everyone in the class orders a dozen of and autographs for relatives and classmates. She appeared a lot younger, smoother and without worry lines. There was even kind of an innocent smile. Flicking through the pages, the diary contained nothing but dates and names and a letter or combination of letters beside each. Holy shit! Faye had kept a diary of everyone she'd ever had bodily contact with. Half the city had gotten into her G-string over the years and not just Joe Nelligan. In addition to Nelligan, there was Charles Sharkey's name and that of Judge Falcone. Joe Frank had congress with her on numerous occasions, maybe even in the next room while his son was mounted on Fern. Anthony Scarlatti had sliced her a number of times as did his patron, Gaetano Terrachio. Even the name of the U.S. Attorney for Maryland showed on several pages when he was a member of the state legislature. Holy shit! HOLY SHIT!

I pushed seven buttons, and after three rings Mulligan came on the line with a voice that sounded like a fork caught in a disposal.

"Dart, Buck. It's all over. We're going to kick ass tomorrow. I'll be there in twenty minutes."

"Slow down, kid. Watcha got?" Mulligan said.

"A diary. It's tough to explain. You've got to see it to believe it," I said.

"Draw me pictures, kid," Mulligan said.

"I'll show you the real thing in twenty minutes," I said.

My heart was ticking faster than a flamenco dancer's heels. I slipped the diary back into its mailer, grabbed my jacket and hotfooted it out to the car. I draped my jacket on the wooden hanger I keep on the back seat and hooked it on the handgrip. I'd rather be cold than wrinkled. Peeling rubber out of the driveway, I slammed the gearshift into drive and took off like a Lear Jet without wings. To avoid distractions, I turned off the radio so I could keep my eye on the prize. In this puzzle of angles and loopholes, the only thing that made sense was this: That Faye's diary was in my possession had to be the handiwork of one of the homicide detectives who searched her apartment. After all, there was a three-way contest over who had jurisdiction over the case and they were the only ones who had entered the flat after the fall. Krall had out-maneuvered Gallazio and Nelligan and Gallazio hated Nelligan's ass. So how better to tuck it to Krall and Nelligan at the same time than by slipping the diary to a reporter who could cost Nelligan his badge and Krall his cool, never knowing who administered the stiletto. This was a masterful stroke that would have been envied in a Medici palace. I never look a gift horse in the rictus, but if my flawless logic is correct, thank you Lieutenant Galazzio of Baltimore's finest, wherever you are.

One thing that didn't make sense, though, was Nelligan's audacious behavior. Being a big boy, he had to know that he was playing a dangerous off-duty game, that Faye could have tooted the tin whistle on him at any time. Nelligan was coming on like the people he chases: They become so arrogant they're convinced they'll never get caught. Or was Faye so dependent upon his heroin handouts that she really didn't give a damn. Yet somehow, she must have believed that keeping a diary was a kind of insurance policy that would set her free when the day of deliverance arrived. It never did. Now I was going to be her avenging angel.

It took the full twenty law-breaking minutes to reach *City Press* from my leafy warren in the outer reaches of the city, one of the joys of Baltimore when drive time is over. Inside the building, I flicked my ID at the guard and boarded an elevator for a lift to the third floor and my personal purgatory here on earth. Ignoring my desk, I headed directly for Mulligan's glass box, and through the cumulus of low-hanging smoke I saw the benign Buddha with rimless glasses contemplating a Styrofoam cup and two packs of cigarettes, one mentholated, the other straight-ahead unfiltered pack of carcinogens. By the time I will have finished this meeting and escaped Mulligan's second-hand smoke, I'd probably smell worse than the bottom of his ashtray and there'd be nicotine in my blood sample.

"Whatcha got, kid?" Mulligan said.

"What we've been looking for, the smoking gun that ties the whole story together," I said.

"So what is it?" Mulligan said.

"Faye's diary, more like her little black book. Lists all her action, everybody's she's ever diddled and how they liked their diddling. You're gonna be surprised by what you see in there," I said.

Holding the cardboard mailer upside down over Mulligan's desk, the story of Faye's life thunked out onto the first edition of *City Press* spread out on Mulligan's desk before mulligan could snatch it mid-air. He grabbed the book and began leafing the pages, alternately mumbling to himself and chuckling without saying a word, apparently amused by what he was reading and decoding for himself the meaning of the "O's" and "A's" and "F's" appended beside each name. Turning Mulligan onto this story was like selling sex to sailors.

"Good stuff, kid. Where'd you come up with it?" Mulligan said.

"I'll never tell," I said.

"This ought to lock up the story for good, blow those assholes out of the water once and for all, pun intended," Mulligan said.

"Should we name names?" I said.

"Goddam right. That's what the story's all about," Mulligan said.

"You've got the book with the names. What the hell more proof do you need? Besides, they're all public figures," Mulligan said.

"You know Krall's gonna start screaming his ass off and so's Nelligan, especially since he's one of the leading characters in this cozy little sex slave drama. We might have to turn this thing over because, technically, I'm in possession of evidence that's missing from the scene of a police investigation," I said.

"That's why I asked you how you got it," Mulligan said.

"I'm not sure, but I have a pretty good idea," I said.

"Gimme a helluva story for tomorrow," Mulligan said.

"Don't I always?" I said.

I secretly liked Mulligan because one of the joys of working for him is that he's so predictable. Talking about news and not the financial markets or the weather, he reacts from the gut and his judgment calls are a bull's eye ninety-nine percent of the time. Impressive for a man who started as a copy boy and probably never went beyond eighth grade. I backed out of Mulligan's office and exhaled several deep breaths to decontaminate my air tanks. I'm not a hypochondriac, mind you, but I believe the surgeon general and all of those reports that say cigarettes contain more than two hundred different toxins, some of them lethal. Why anyone would do that to a perfectly healthy blood-red lung is beyond me. Would they eat arsenic, chew lye, smell mustard gas or inhale anthrax? Hell no, but smoking's the same fatal trip that'll get them in the end.

At my desk, I shrugged out of my jacket and draped it over the unoccupied chair next to mine. I undid my cuff links and folded the shirt cuffs over twice, not only to preserve the cleanliness of the shirt but also to telegraph the look of a guy who really rolls up his sleeves and digs in. I liked the imagery. I clickety-clicked and tappety-tapped until I was logged on the computer and ready to write. This was the story of a lifetime.

> "The personal diary of the exotic dancer who plunged to her death after an overdose of heroin paints a lurid and graphic picture of high government officials and political power brokers and their connections to Baltimore's squalid sex-for-sale Block.
>
> The diary of Faye Madison, who danced at Pandora's Box under the name of Fabulous Faye, contains the names of judges, high City Hall officials, ranking police officers, political operatives, underworld figures, lawyers and many others whose names are unfamiliar. Also written in the ledger-style book were letters beside each name, apparently identifying the sexual preferences of her clients.
>
> The discovery comes at a time when a federal grand jury and the special prosecutor's office are accelerating their investigation into political corruption on the Block.
>
> Inside the front cover of the book was Madison's name, address and phone number, and tucked between two pages was a 3x5 photograph of a younger, fresh-faced Faye Madison and not the grim hard-knocks' mask she was wearing when she died.
>
> Among the names in the diary were those of Police Captain Joseph Nelligan, City Budget Director Charles Sharkey, Federal Judge Michael Falcone, political power broker Joseph Frank and his son Milton, well-known Philadelphia Mob boss Gaetano Terrachio and the U.S. Attorney for Maryland, Judd French.
>
> It was well known in police circles and on the Block that Nelligan had a relationship that went far beyond sex. As head of the police department's narcotics squad, Nelligan had easy access to confiscated drugs and it was rumored that he was Madison's supplier as well as her occasional lover. In exchange for illicit drugs, Madison was Nelligan's eyes and ears on the Block.
>
> In another ironic twist, Sharkey, an alcoholic before his epiphany as a born again Christian, had a sexual arrangement with Madison that spanned several years, according to entries in her diary. Now he is leading an emotional personal and media crusade to eliminate the Block to make room for more office towers despite a forty percent vacancy rate in existing Class A office space.

To accomplish this, Sharkey struck up an undercover business arrangement with Frank and indirectly with his son, Milton, who doubles as Frank's legal counsel. Frank, through various business entities, owns every building on the Block. Frank himself had a number of sexual encounters with Madison, and his son, Milton, has had a long-time relationship with Madison's best friend, Fern Royal, also a stripper at Broadway Brown's show bar.

There are several entries for Judge Falcone, who is in the awkward position of presiding over the grand jury that is investigating political corruption on the Block. But the relationship apparently broke off at about the time Judge Falcone, then a widower, remarried nearly a year ago.

The name of U.S. Attorney Judd French was a late entry in the diary and could explain why the investigation of the Block is being directed by the special prosecutor's office and not through the normal channels of the U.S. Attorney's office.

Terrachio's visits to Madison and the Block were infrequent, according to entries in the diary. It is known, however, that years ago, Terrachio attempted to muscle into Baltimore by offering to purchase nightclubs on the Block and use them to launder money obtained through his illegal activities in Philadelphia and New Jersey as well as other states.

Madison's bruised and broken body was found in an alley behind her East Baltimore apartment where she fell to her death in what the coroner said could have resulted from an overdoes of heroin….etc."

After another ten paragraphs of background, I wrapped up the story as tight as a drumhead and called it a good day's work. Good, hell. It was great. I zapped the story directly to Mulligan's file and retraced my footsteps back to his office. He read it and said with his customary nonchalance and his highest form of praise:

"Good work, kid."

When the story broke the next morning, complete with photos of pages with key names, I could imagine the phone lines humming and zinging through the alphabet, fiber optic voices beginning with asshole and working up to motherfucker, then really getting mad. I normally don't go out of my way to piss people off. In this business, it just happens as kind of an occupational hazard. I could also imagine a lot of people tut-tutting and laughing that evil "gotcha" kind of chortle, of all Frank's political rivals rummaging through their get-even lists, and the junkies Nelligan's busted giving him the finger and all the criminals Falcone has been tough on saying, fuck you, sucker, under that robe you're no different, no better than we are. I like being available when the shit hits the wall, so I'd arrived at *City Press* at about the same time the early edition began causing a serious case of heartburn.

Twenty minutes into my bivouac by the phone, the first call came roaring through the rickety system at *City Press* with a ferocity that melted the wax in my left ear:

"Newsroom, Dart speaking," I said.

"You fucking ninny, now you've gone and done it, and this time I'm going to bust your ass."

It was the unmistakable Irish whisky rumble of Joe Nelligan's voice, a troubled man swinging somewhere between a low boil and a blood pressure high. Then, again, he had something to be all hot and lathered about.

"I've listened to your shit long enough, Nelligan. You're not going to do a fucking thing to anybody, 'cause where you're going you won't be in a position to intimidate or threaten anymore. I'll personally recommend that you get a six-foot roommate named Jahmal. Take your drugs and your tin badge and shove them where the sun doesn't shine. This one's for Faye," I said.

"You common little sonofabitch, who the hell you think you're talking to?" Nelligan said.

"I know exactly who I'm talking to, a fucking pusher, just like the creeps you bust. You're no better than they are. I watched you help Faye shoot up, remember? Keep talking and that'll be chapter two," I said.

"Listen, asshole. I still run this town and I still control the Block. I'm gonna stick a couple of my men on you like flypaper. Your ass has had it," Nelligan said.

"You don't control a goddam thing anymore. You're through, history. Now get lost and stop hassling me," I said.

The needle shot into the excitement zone. I slammed the receiver down, astonished at what I'd just done. I had that watery feeling when every limb seems to quiver and go slightly limp. My giblets were pumping juices as fast as the municipal waterworks, while my heart did a tap dance against my rib cage. Reporting is the last blood sport. I hate bullies. Normally I don't carry on that way with people I write about because I couldn't care a fig about them. But Nelligan's roughneck attitude really pissed me off. I was fed up with his highhanded bullshit, the way he threw his considerable weight around and abused people. They're all a bunch of arrogant, abusive, lying incompetent assholes. All except my benefactor with the diary.

Call number two. Bingo! Another bear with a sore ass making an appearance. The squawk that served as Bob Krall's voice scraped across the telephone line as if it were in a static box attached to his vocal cords.

"Like to have a little chat," Krall said.

"You know the routine. You call me. I call the lawyer, the lawyer calls the judge. Except this time I believe we can eliminate the judge. That sound about right?" I said.

"The diary is evidence," Krall said.

"That's for somebody else to decide, not us," I said.

"I want the diary, or I'll go for a contempt citation," Krall said.

"The Constitution says We, the People. Not We, the special prosecutor, not We, the FBI. It says We, the People, and don't forget it," I said.

"You want to do it the hard way, fine. You know the process. There's more than one way to do this," Krall said.

This time Krall hung up on me, as If I gave a damn. Sensitive I'm not. He'd probably end up getting the book anyway, but let him earn his fat federal salary. Besides, I was finished with it, but I made a trip to the copying machine nonetheless. I planned to bury the copy in the bank vault along with the tape of Goodwin and Frank's conversation and the file memo detailing Nelligan's participation in Faye's drug-shooting session. There's no law against boffing a prostitute unless a hornball gets caught with his naked tool hanging out. But with the diary in hand, Krall would have another weapon to force Faye's clients into cooperating with him or risk the wrath of the grand jury. And bet the family jewels that he wanted the book as evidence of Nelligan's personal involvement with a known addict. Trouble with the feds is that they expect an army of willing volunteers to do their dirty work for them. They're used to dealing with informants and stoolies, people they've got a rap on, and other demented assholes who get their jollies (or money) snitching to the cops, and they think everybody else should play their trade-off game. The idea might be as American as apple pie, but I prefer blueberry myself. I had no intention of surrendering Faye's diary without a fight just to protect myself against the impression of cooperating with the investigation. Screw 'em.

Morning yawned on. The lack of sizzling telephone activity at my corner of the universe indicated that the objects of my attention in today's *City Press* had more important people to talk to than to hurl bolts of indignation at me— namely their lawyers and their wives, in that order. Usually I don't feel sorry for people who get their tits caught in a wringer. But I had a pinch of sympathy for an old codger like Judge Falcone, who's recently remarried, trying to find a little patch of happiness until he's toe-tagged. The real revelation in the diary, though, was the name of Judd French, the U.S attorney. He, too, had recently married, a fancy WASP lady with a horse farm in the Valley—what's known hereabouts as a First Family of Maryland. Poor bastard's going to be hounded by the notoriety of his *louche* life for a long while to come, knowing that every time he turns his back his associates are tittering and smirking *schadenfreude* over his misfortune. And his wife will probably carry on and cut him off for a while, complaining that she's too embarrassed to go to the hunt club for lunch, let alone have their friends over for dinner. Some philosopher, Schopenhauer, I believe, observed that since the beginning of time all of man's activity has been directed at a point centrally located between a woman's navel and her knees. Which reminded me, I could use a little activity myself.

By the time the last orange peel of evening sky slid over the edge, the Police Department issued a statement saying that Captain Joseph Nelligan was being relieved of his duties as head of the narcotics squad and being assigned to desk duty pending an internal investigation into allegations of illegal activities. Ditto Judge Falcone. The chief judge of the federal court announced through a spokesman that Judge Falcone was being replaced as the judge overseeing the grand jury investigation into the Block while a judicial disabilities commission determines whether he engaged in any improper conduct that might have influenced his decisions relating to the Block probe. There's an old story that goes like this: A cat was crossing the railroad tracks when a train came along and cut off its tail. The cat turned around to see what happened, and another train came along and cut off its head. Moral: Never lose your head over a piece of tail.

Hirings and firings are not my line of work even though I was the instrument that might cause their eventual decapitation. The reporters covering the police and courthouse beats had more background on Nelligan and Falcone than I had, so I convinced the night city editor to let them collaborate on the story of whatever difficulties the cop and the judge might have with their employers. Besides, it was late and I hadn't eaten all day. I slouched over to the men's room, thinking I'd go to Paisan's. I took a long laser-like whiz, washed and dried, and on the way out I folded down my cuffs and re-set the cuff links. Ignoring the elevator as a salute to aerobic activity, I put on my jacket and took the stairs, two at a time, down to the first floor.

At Paisan's, the first wave of spaghetti-and-meatball eaters was just breaking up and Tony Russo was at his usual observation post checking arrivals and departures.

"Hey, I'll be damned. If it isn't the Kamikaze pilot. Man, you really get a set of balls, showing your face in public after what you did today," Russo said.

"Fella's gotta eat," I said.

"I take that back. You haven't got a set of balls. You've got no brains, thinking about food when every gun in town's aimed at you," Russo said.

"I wouldn't be too sure of that, unless you know something I don't. A lot of people are going to be happy that Nelligan's finally going down. In case you haven't heard, he's been relieved of his badge and gun while they investigate him," I said.

"No shit. That oughta make him doubly pissed off at you. He lost his broad, he lost face and now he might lose his job. Nice work," Russo said.

Breaks of the game. Maybe he ought to learn how to play the piano. He can lead the sing-alongs where he's going," I said.

I wouldn't bet the family jewels on that. Guy's got nine lives," Russo said.

"We'll see. Hear anything I oughta know?" I said.

"Courthouse is heating up again. The way they're rolling, the thing oughta be over soon," Russo said.

"You heard from them again?" I said.

Not a word," Russo said.

I was as parched as the Bonneville Salt Flats, so I ordered an Absolut on the rocks at the bar and was eventually guided to a table in the main dining room. Seated back to the wall in my favorite corner, I scanned the crowd like one of those bank cameras. Over the rim of my glass I zoomed in on the opposite corner and freeze-framed the moment as one that I'd probably remember to include in my memoirs. Lieutenant Pete Galazzio smiled a knowing thin smile and gave me a thumbs-up sign. Some day I'd like to thank him in person, but discretion being the better part of protecting my ass, I decided to acknowledge the gesture with a vague nod and forego the hop to his table and handshake for now.

CHAPTER 24

▼

In journalism, as in life, you make your luck, but you do it with the help of people like Gallazio. I'd learned a long time ago that if I ever had to choose between talent and luck I'd take luck every time. It'd been a good day for homicide. Now that Nelligan's been mothballed, Galazzio was free to pick through the loose ends of Faye's star-crossed life (and Nelligan's as well) without interference from narcotics. Gallazio had reason to smile. He'd pulled off a knife-in-the-back that would have been admired in the Nixon White House.

Chow time! I was feeling expansive tonight, in search of something more celebratory that the plate of pasta and seafood that I usually eat. So I ordered a salad and the *zuppa de pesce*—the day's special—and a bottle of *Barbera d'Asti*, in Italy the peoples' wine, which I'd never finish, for sure, but I'd re-cork and take home in a bowser bag. The bottle of wine, slightly chilled and sweaty with condensation, arrived well before the food, and when the waitress popped the bottle I was presented with the cork to sniff, a pretentious gesture carried out with great ceremony by wine snots and know-nothings trying to impress their dates. I rejected the cork for an actual tasting of the wine. Not bad. Nice medium body and warm afterglow. Next came the salad, which I pushed aside, preferring to eat it with my meal rather than before, as they do in America, or after, as they prefer in Europe. Finally, a steaming soup bowl of tomatoey liquid serving as a fennel ocean for mussels, clams, shrimp, lobster chunks and a slab of heavy white fish. This is the stuff the gods eat when they can afford it. I finished off the vodka and shifted my taste buds up a sensation to food and wine.

I slurped, poked, picked—clinking the shells into a empty vessel presented on the side for that purpose—until I was down to a moat of amber fluid in the sump of the bowl. I mopped up the sauce with doughy bread and washed it all down with a great gulp of wine. Damn, I'd done more damage to the bottle of wine than I thought, so to prevent any further disrespect to my liver I corked the bottle and ordered a coffee, an *espresso,* which was thick enough for a mudpack. Before I'd finished the coffee, Galazzio and his partners got up to leave, and as he did he shot another quick curled-corner smile in my direction and just as quickly vanished through the archway into the night. I wondered if he paid the bill, or was billed at all, because in Little Italy cops are rewarded by restaurant owners for keeping the neighborhood safe and for not hassling customers with violations when they park too close to a fire hydrant or slop over a corner curbstone. Little Italy's a bustling neighborhood where parking can often be a problem, so residents lay claim to parking spaces by squatting bushel baskets on the street in front of their shiny-bright row houses with form stone fronts and green-and-white striped aluminum awnings.

Miracles do happen, and so, too, do accidents. For the first time that I could remember, Tony Russo was missing from the perch where he sat like a lifeguard presiding over a pool of swimmers. As I was leaving, I sought out the owner and host, the main *paisan* himself, and learned that, during my encounter with the *zuppa de pesce,* a couple of plainclothes detectives arrived with a warrant for Russo's arrest, busted again, it turns out, for making book on a company phone. Russo keeps forgetting that with the help of certain electronic enhancement devices attached to publicly regulated utilities, more than two people can listen on a telephone. So Russo was escorted, in elaborate style, by two of Baltimore's finest, in an unmarked municipal Ford Victoria, to police headquarters, where, for the umpteenth time, he'd be booked and scheduled for arraignment on charges of bookmaking. All of which set me to spinning a scenario in which Bob Krall would crowd in on the bust and try to squeeze Russo for information in exchange for a recommendation that the local prosecutors ease off on the punishment. But Russo maintains a curious code of morality. He'll yackety-yak his head off to anyone with a willing ear, but when it gets down and dirty in dealing with the law, he's no snitch. If I had to guess, he'll tell Krall to go screw himself, take his medicine and do thirty days, then get out and claim squatter's rights on the banquette at Paisan's and brag about being a con as if it's a badge of honor. Everyone seemed to take it all in easy stride, part of the decoration that gives the restaurant its sass.

Morning pitter-pattered in on cotton-ball paws. But the phone jangled my nerve endings before the clock radio could lull me awake by piping in the news and giving me a couple more minutes of slumber time. The bourbon-and-branch voice identified itself as belonging to John Doyle, attorney for *City Press*.

"You were probably expecting this call," Doyle said.

"More or less, but not in the middle of the frigging night," I said.

"Get dressed. We've got a date with Krall and the new judge who's presiding over the grand jury, real anal type, Cashman Fullwell the third, product of the circuit, Gilman, Princeton and Yale Law," Doyle said.

"What's it mean?" I said.

"The guy goes by the book, no street instincts like Falcone. But now that you've taken Falcone down, we'll have to adjust our strategy a bit. Christ, I've never seen anyone make trouble for himself the way you do," Doyle said.

"Well, look at it this way. Thomas Mann, the great German novelist, observed that every well-chosen word carries with it spite. So in that sense, I guess I can't help myself. What do you want me to do?" I said.

"Meet me at the office as soon as you can," Doyle said.

"I'll be there quicker than you can shake a stick at," I said.

After completing the usual watery morning ritual, I draped myself in a smug cocoon of gray pinstripes, white broadcloth shirt (French cuffs) and tie of squiggly silver, gray and black amoebas, topped off with a white pocket square and cap toe Allen Edmonds laced shoes of bourbon leather. Conservative yet with panache, something that even a Cahsman Fullwell the third would wear to a class reunion, except that he'd wear black shoes. On second thought, he might not go for a layered sperm tie, but would instead probably substitute a maroon tie with crossed tennis racquets and maybe even an oxford button-down shirt.

One hour and forty-five minutes after Doyle had called, I was in an elevator and on my way up to the high-rise hunting lodge-office of Swindle-Duff-Dander and Doyle, law firm of the great and near great. The receptionist had been told to scoot me to Doyle's office as soon as I arrived, no fancy conference room this time. By now, I was family. The receptionist offered me coffee, which I accepted, and Doyle motioned to a chair, which I claimed with my customary ceremony of adjusting creases and flaring out coattails to avoid wrinkles. Christ, if I lived in Dundalk and worked at Bethlehem Steel, I wouldn't have to worry about things like that.

"Where's the book?" Doyle said.

"In a safe place," I said.

"Christ, I'm on your side. Where's the book?" Doyle said.

"In a safe deposit box at the bank branch across from *City Press*," I said.

"How'd you get it?" Doyle said.

"Arrived at my house overnight express mail. But I received an anonymous phone call the night before alerting me that it was coming," I said.

"Any idea who called or sent the book? Doyle said.

"Only a guess, so I'd rather not say, and maybe you'd better not know, so I can protect the guilty as well as the innocent," I said.

"Fair enough—for now," Doyle said.

"Do you have any strong feelings about giving it up? Doyle said.

"None whatever. But I'd like to tweak Krall a bit and not surrender it without a little static. I don't want to make it appear as if I'm cooperating with those assholes in an investigation," I said.

"I believe that can be arranged," Doyle said.

"By the way, you should also know that I stashed a photocopy of the diary in another safe place just in case Krall wins and tries to get cute," I said.

"You're entitled," Doyle said.

Doyle and I walked the few blocks to the courthouse like Trappist monks honoring a vow of silence, a drift that I assume meant Doyle was confecting a strategy to save my naked ass once again. It was a pewter-shaded morning in Baltimore, and the commercial haze of the city was helping to blur the horizon, not to mention the size of the hole it was punching in the Ozone layer. A large boat of anonymous nomenclature honked its melancholy horn against a chorus of serenading gulls. The trouble with big cities is that everything and everybody cranks up at the same time, between seven and nine in the morning. On this morning, Baltimore rocked with the temblors of commerce. This creaking medieval town rumbled with trucks, clattered with cars, hummed with buses, shouted with horns, whistled with police, as masses of human chattel, burned-out and aching inside, dragging their shattered lives to work with them, undulated through the streets in tight huddles, slouching toward pigeon-pooped buildings where they'd spend the next eight hours hating everything about and around them. I love the sounds of cities in the morning. They sound like money.

We reached the entrance to the courthouse and Doyle snapped back from the bottom of his dark thought as if he were answering a trumpet call.

"Let's go deal," he said.

"Let's hear it for democracy in action," I said.

We retraced the familiar pathway up five floors to where grand juries are cloistered and judges are undisputed bosses, down long black-and-white diamonds of marble hallways, past doors with panes of frosted glass until we reached the one that was lettered with the name of Cashman Fullwell 3d, Associate Judge. Inside, a stern unsmiling secretary with the bearing of a private girls' school headmistress took our names and disappeared through a wall of oak paneling. Returning, she motioned us through the wall without so much as a tic of a smile.

The prick alert in my head shot all the way into the red zone like a tachometer on a Porsche, setting off imaginary bells, alarms, whistles and honks. Cashman Fullwell the third looked as if he ate law books for breakfast and washed them down with prune juice, the most constipated looking public official I'd ever seen, face screwed up tight like a raisin wearing horn rimmed glasses. And knowing that Krall got the drop on us by arriving earlier and having a chance to chat with the judge only added to my edgy sense of doom.

Judge Cashman Fullwell the third said: "Sit down, gentlemen. We all know why we are here. But just so there is no misunderstanding, let me spell it out for you. The special prosecutor, Mr. Krall, has formally complained that Richard Dart, of *City Press*, is illegally in possession of evidence that he believes is relevant to his investigation into the Block. He asked for this meeting because Mr. Dart has refused to turn over the evidence he is seeking, a diary that belonged to Faye Madison, which may have been unlawfully removed from her apartment after her unfortunate death. I'm hereby requesting that Mr. Dart surrender the document to this court so that I can review the material and determine whether it has any salience to Mr. Krall's investigation. Any resistance to my request could lead to a contempt citation and time in prison. Do I make myself clear?

"John Doyle, representing *City Press* and Mr. Dart, your honor. If I may, your honor, I'd like to remind the court that the law provides certain privileges and protections to reporters who uncover information in the pursuit of stories. I believe this is a case in which the material obtained by Mr. Dart while covering the investigation of the Block is privileged and therefore beyond the reach of the court and the special prosecutor," Doyle said.

Krall cleared his throat and chimed in:

"Your honor, based on my reading of Mr. Dart's story of the diary, I'm convinced that the document will contribute significantly to establishing certain patterns and connections among individuals who figure in this investigation in a substantial way."

Judge Cashman Fullwell the third rejoined: "Let me repeat myself, which I frequently must do. This is not a request to turn over the diary to Mr. Krall. This is an order to surrender the document to me so that I can review the contents and then determine whether the diary should be submitted to the grand jury. Mr. Dart, you have twenty-four hours to surrender the diary to your attorney, Mr. Doyle, who, in turn, will present it to me. If you fail to follow the instructions of this court, you will be cited for contempt. Do I make myself clear? You're all dismissed."

Clearer than a church bell on a cold night, you old fart. It was evident that there was no point in pursuing the argument, especially after being dismissed by a tight-ass like Fullwell, who'd likely issue a contempt citation to anyone who asked permission to use the courthouse plumbing. So the three of us, Doyle, Krall and I, rose in a self-conscience way, each trying to avert one another's eyes. But on the way out of my chair, I zoomed in for a quick shot of Krall and caught him smirking. Krall had had his day in court. What we call in the news business, a BFD—Big Fucking Deal—I thought. I get the shaft and he gets to read yesterday's news all over again. It was an ironic turn of the screw. Judge Falcone was my protector, and I brought him down, only to be screwed by his successor. If only he'd kept his pecker in his pocket.

Outside, Doyle rationalized and dissembled, recalling that he'd been apprehensive about being dicked over by Fullwell from the beginning. Nobody likes to lose, Doyle was saying, giving me the big picture bullshit. But in the cosmic scheme of things, in the overall framework of the law, in the grand fashion of what I'd accomplished so far, in this wonderfully fragile democracy, the setback was small potatoes. I'd already told Doyle I was resigned to giving up the hard copy of the diary. Either that or spending a few nights in the slammer with a room-full of butt-fuckers and drug-heads.

Comfortable with the temporary retreat, I invited Doyle to accompany me to the bank where I asked him to wait while I entered the vault and retrieved the diary. I presented the bestseller to Doyle with a great flourish and suggested that he tell Fullwell that, according to Faye's alphabet code, his associate on the bench, Judge Falcone, enjoyed doing his business in the fudge factory. See if he registers an emotion, any kind. Doyle frowned and stashed the book in his briefcase, saying he'd deliver the prize the next morning. I knew what he'd be reading tonight. It won't be the Gideon Bible.

The paper chase is a long winding trail that IRS auditors and FBI agents hope will eventually connect their prey to an illicit exchange of something of value. Krall and his investigators had earlier subpoenaed the appropriate records and files, both public and private—the usual assortment of phone bills, bank statements, income tax returns, records of purchases, credit card receipts, government office records—a form of autobiography that says what people do and how well they do it. They're the price tags of life that most people stuff in a shoebox in a closet until tax time rolls around. Now the word bouncing up from the asphalt had it that Krall had connected the dots in the finger painting, forensic point-illism with a point. As every political hobbyist knows, when the Fed sets out to get someone they're as good as got. The point was—get Goodwin!

To do so, the investigators had accumulated a storage roomful of boxes—the private papers of Goodwin, Joe Frank and Charles Sharkey—along with truck-loads of records of state and city government and, of course, the books and cash register receipts of every establishment on the Block and the businesses that supply them. Anyone who thinks finding a needle in a haystack is tedious work ought to try locating a bribe in a bale of paper. But, hey, that's why government pays accountants to do nothing but add and subtract. So finally, one fateful day when the numbers didn't add up, Krall decided to try something cute. He decided to scare the shit out of Sollie Stein, enough to send his pacemaker into a power surge.

It was around *yontiff* time, the autumn space between *Rosh Hashanah* and *Suk-kot* when Jews pay tribute to the dietary laws contained in the Book of Leviticus by stuffing themselves with all sorts of food with the consistency of a sash weight until they're in a cholesterol coma, that Krall knew Sollie Stein would be in Balti-more to celebrate the high holy days with his children. Krall was right. He offered Sollie Stein a deal. They could meet for a polite (taped) conversation at a subur-ban motel of Stein's choice, or the next day Krall would activate, through a U.S. Marshall, the original subpoena *duces tecum* and parade Sollie Stein, kicking and screaming, before the grand jury once again for all the world to see.

Sollie Stein decided to be heroic. With lightening swift wit, Stein said to the special prosecutor: "Fuck you, Krall. I got nothing to say. You want me, come and get me."

It was that last sentence that got Sollie Stein's necktie caught in a revolving door. For his loyal-soldier bravura, Sollie Stein was rewarded with the courtesy of a van, stenciled with the words U.S. Marshall, that arrived at his son's condomin-ium building the next morning and shuttled him to the courthouse in downtown Baltimore. Krall's a bully, but he's learned to do his homework. When prosecu-tors want to fuck over a witness with a vengeance, they put on a display of lynch-mob democracy for all the world to see. Krall had quietly alerted every reporter within the area code and beyond that he would be entertaining a very special guest this morning. So when the U.S. Marshall's van arrived curbside at the courthouse and deposited its passenger, the event was photographed by more cameras than recorded the All Star game at Baltimore's Camden Yards. Sollie Stein looked as gray as chopped liver in contrast to his bodacious plaid dou-ble-knit suit that was left over from the golden age of polyester. He *schlepped* along, kind of dragging himself between his two government-issue escorts. I felt sorry for the old guy, having to go through public torment, not to mention the ruckus it'll raise in certain publicly subsidized offices. All of which proves that whom the gods would destroy they first turn over to buttheads like Krall.

Once he entered, no one ever saw Sollie Stein come out of the courthouse. What he said, and how long he appeared before the grand jury, was the hot-wire gossip of the week. A stakeout at his condo failed to provide clues to Stein's where-abouts nor that of his wife. The smart money on the streets was betting that Sollie Stein had had his holiday chicken soup and matzo balls, his gefilte fish with red horseradish, his sweet-and-sour *kugel*, his brisket and capon and his honey cake, in a safe house under the watchful eye of the federal witness protection program. For Sollie Stein, it would not be a sweet new year.

Guilt-tripping is not my style, but the road to City Press is paved with unintended consequences. Write a story and watch the words zing like shrapnel to unlikely corners and doorways across the city. The same is true of investigations. They, too, have a tortuous route of their own, a zig here, a zag there, impersonal and not caring who or what they damage along their winding way. In journalism it's called objectivity. In the government investigations business it's called just doing a job. How many lives have been damaged by reporters' objectivity and federal prosecutors just doing job. Nothing personal, mind you. In both cases, it's probably a little sick, too. I worry about stuff like that.

Days telescoped into weeks. The background noise of the investigation gradually lowered its angry voice and became as quiet as the *adagio* movement of Beethoven's Symphony Number Six. It was almost as if the entire mass of the investigation had been suspended by invisible wires. No leaks. No subpoenas looping across town like paper airplanes. No signs of witnesses parading through the courthouse. At least none has been spotted lately. There were rumors about late-night meetings with witnesses in secluded motels and reports of witnesses being smuggled into the courthouse's underground garage in mail trucks and upstairs to the grand jury room in freight elevators. Such is the libido of the prosecutor that they'd probably choose figuring out how to get someone to talk over having sex. But for the sad-sack witness, there's no upside. The sudden hush was a sign that the investigation was cruising to an end. This is the point of no return, where investigators start pulling together all of the loose ends on the linguini plate, the months of testimony and mounds of paper, into a compelling story they can take before the grand jury and secure indictments. Nobody except those in the room really knows how many witnesses actually appeared or what they said. Trial time is also show-and-tell time.

On a clear, crisp, spun-honey of a day, during a brisk walk to the office, I detoured to the Block and shuffled past Broadway Brown's, where a Caribbean native was tapping out reggae tunes on a steel drum and two panhandlers, a man and a woman, were rattling money cups at indifferent passers-by who generally looked down at their shoes rather than make eye contact with the hapless homeless. The Block, too, was becoming a sign of the times. Once it stood for high times. Now it reflected hard knocks. The case of the street music was an upgrade, more lyrical than a barker's call in the night. The niche of the homeless, though, was etched on the urban lifescape like a municipal plague. Baltimore was beginning to resemble Calcutta. So prevalent and pushy have the street people become that the City Council passed an ordinance prohibiting panhandlers from cursing, following and otherwise hassling people. They've become the latter generation "squeegee kids." Polack Johnny's was still here, serving belch burgers the consistency of hockey pucks to customers with disposal stomachs. And so, too, was Pines Pharmacy, smudged and splat upon, anchoring the northeast corner of the Block. Other than the shushing of busses and the competing clatter of street sounds, the Block appeared heavy with indifference to Krall and his rogue band of gangbusters, a huge anthropomorphic jumble of bricks and juicyfruit neon offering up bottle and broad and the risk of a wide menu of contact infections. On the Block, life goes on whatever the curse, much as it has since the first visiting serviceman during World War II got a does of the clap, a sniffle, if you will.

The side trip revealed nothing of consequence. But just as I rounded the corner and re-set my compass needle for *City Press*, I came paunch to haunch with Fern, whose chipped edges were magnified by the butterscotch sun slats beaming down on her face like a bank of Kryptonite flashlights.

"Shall we dance?" I said.

"You know, I'm beginning to change my mind about you, even though I still have doubts about talking to you," Fern said.

"How so?" I said.

"If for no other reason than you took care of a lot of people who were using Faye, who saw her as nothing but a piece of meat," Fern said.

"With all due respect for the dead, she was no virgin," I said.

"No, but she was a person. And that counts for something," Fern said.

"Milton and Joe Frank mind if I buy you a cup of coffee?" I said.

"Look, let's keep them separate. Milton's been good to me and I've been good back in my own kind of way. But Joe Frank I owe nothing. You want my opinion, I think he's just another bloodsucker making money off other people's backs," Fern said.

"Know anything I shouldn't?" I said.

"I've seen him come around, go down to the office and spend time, then leave. Same routine every week," Fern said.

"What could it mean?" I said.

"I don't know and I don't want to know," Fern said.

"Heard anymore from the grand jury?" I said.

"Nothing I'm going to tell you," Fern said.

"About that coffee?" I said.

"Some other time," Fern said.

She smiled as if he meant it, then heels tapping across cement squares, hips fanning lazy air aside, knee-length skirt luffing in a steady fluid swish, Faye kicked her ass into high gear and headed for Pandora's box, ready to get down to business. She left me wrapped in a vapor trail of high-octane perfume that was part of her calling card, wondering what she meant by the grand jury remark.

CHAPTER 25

▼

The newsroom at *City Press* is like a fun house without mirrors, and Mulligan was its ringmaster. Survive this room and you could work any room in the country. The performers in the daily sideshows come in more flavors than Baskin Robbins has ice cream—moderate-to-cynical political reporters, dowdy old food page editors, frou-frou society reporters and softball features writers. On this day in the newsroom, the scoop *du jour,* if you will, what had everybody's pecker up, involved a contract worker at a leasing company who went to his ex-girlfriend's office, and with a .38 caliber revolver blasted her out of her pantyhose in front of twenty other employees for getting pregnant by another man. Such is the news these days because everybody's living on the edge and life's getting cheaper by the day. Flick on television or pick up a newspaper and read the overnight police blotter, people shooting up society out of anger or because their toast was burned that morning or somebody invaded their space, or in more current urban culture shock, somebody engaged a dude in a "hard stare." But stories such as this one make Mulligan's heart do a drum roll. Today, Mulligan was standing tall in high cotton. And when Mulligan's happy, so is everyone else because the pressure's off. The atmosphere was as lighthearted as if the newsroom was floating on laughing gas. Besides, it was payday and everyone had a check in his/her pocket. I draped my jacket over the empty chair next to my workstation and activated my voice mail.

"(beep)....Nice shooting, Dart. One of these days you're going to come up with the big one. Keep pushing....(beep)....This is the VISA Gold Card calling Richard Dart to say there are many more benefits when your VISA card is gold instead of the regular one you have in your wallet. We'll get back to you later….(beep)….Dart, this is a friend who shall remain nameless. A world of caution. Don't mess with Joe Frank. Remember the guy he killed with his bare fists? I wouldn't want to see him mess up your pretty face….(beep)Richard, it's Shelly. I called the office. I heard about the diary. I'm glad your name wasn't in it. The bombshell's going to drop any day. Don't let go. I miss you. I'll be home in a couple of days. Love and kisses. Behave yourself….(beep)….(beep)….click.

Decoding as best I could, that Shelly's coming home in a day or two must mean that her office sounded the all-clear buzzer. And the bombshell remark signaled that the investigation was accelerating toward a conclusion whose consequence was suspicious but nevertheless still very much unsubstantiated. What's more, it was exhilarating to know that in a couple of days I'd give up the celibate life of a monk and reclaim my wicked ways.

Knowing that the despot in Mulligan had been temporarily suppressed by someone else's untimely misfortune, I marched to his Jack-in-the-box office, determined that when the story of the Block ends I was going to make a total pest of myself by campaigning for a smoke-free workplace. But for now, using his (unfiltered) Camel as a baton, Mulligan waved me in with a grand flourish.

"Whatcha got, kid?" Mulligan said.

"It's more what I haven't got. I no longer have the diary," I said.

"Whadaya mean?" Mulligan said.

"Got a wake-up call from Doyle, telling me to get to his office lickety-split. Krall went to the new judge overseeing the grand jury, a tight-ass named Cashman Fullwell the third. I just came from the courthouse. The judge gave me twenty-four hours to turn over the diary or be charged with contempt," I said.

"So what'd you do?" Mulligan said.

"Roaches and winos are not my line of work, so I gave the diary to Doyle to turn over to the judge. But don't worry. I kept the copy I made," I said.

"Gimme a story on it," Mulligan said.

"I wish the stock market were as predictable as you are. By the way, one of my moles tells me the party's gonna be over any day now," I said.

"About time. Be ready," Mulligan said.

My eyes were watery, my clothes were smelly, my mouth was as dry as a dust mop and I thought I was going to vomit from the smoke as I exited Mulligan's office. I went to the men's room and emptied a tank full, washed my hands and revived myself with several slaps of eye-popping cold water. Next I visited the vending machine, where for two quarters the machine shot back a pack of peanut butter crackers. Thus armed, I returned to my computer terminal where I punched the buttons that entered my password that booted up my file that allowed me to begin writing. But not before the experience of gourmet dining at my desk.

The crackle of cellophane almost overpowered the approaching sound of Peaches' voice, as soft in its pitch as a tuning fork.

"Dear diary. I'd like to know if Richard Dart's name was in you," Peaches said.

"Nobody likes a smart ass," I said.

"Well, you've got to be awfully close to get that kind of information," Peaches said.

"Depends on who you know. Anyhow, I'm about ready to write a travelogue on where the diary ended up," I said.

"Where?" Peaches said.

"Read all about it," I said.

"Mister Personality. Read all about it. Sounds as if you're hawking newspapers on a street corner," Peaches said.

"Be a sweetheart and scram," I said.

"Be a sweetheart and go screw yourself," Peaches said.

"Be better than screwing you," I said.

I laughed, Peaches didn't. She took off as if she'd been shot out of a rocket launcher. Touch, touchy, touchy. Her thong must be hotter than four-alarm chili.

On a good day, a writer at the top of his form is all nouns and verbs. Or, put another way, as Voltaire observed, "The adjective is the enemy of the verb."

When the story of the diary was wrapped up as tight as a Christmas package, I zapped it to Mulligan's file. In about twenty minutes, a two-word message from Mulligan appeared on my screen: "Good job." Compliments such as "good story" and courtesies such as "thank you" are revolutionary talk in a newsroom where nobody's considerate and everybody's jealous. The cultural hallmark of journalism is cynicism, and once young reporters learn to fake that they've got it made in the news business, given, of course, that they have the rest of the equipment to go along with the attitude. Mulligan was at the head of the pack when it came to sneers and thus an exemplary role model and teacher in that department. But occasionally, as in this for instance, he lowered his guard and let the squishy-soft yellow yoke peek through.

Just as I was easing into the drowsy comfort of a lazy afternoon, the phone on my desk trembled. It was the news editor calling to advise me that the Associated Press had begun moving the text of a letter from Governor Goodwin to the attorney general of the United States that it obtained from a nationally syndicated columnist. It could have been leaked only by one of two people: My money was down on the beleaguered Goodwin.

"Dear Mr. Attorney General:

This letter is written as a private communication between the two of us and is not intended for public use until and unless either of us feels compelled by circumstances to reveal its contents.

A year ago, I spoke to you personally about the activities of federal law enforcement agencies operating in Maryland under the direction of the United States Department of Justice. At that time, you gave me your personal word that the activities of these agencies under your jurisdiction were in no way political, and you assured me that no political motives could be ascribed to the investigations or to the behavior of these agencies.

I accepted your word, and I was willing to accept it and your explanation as long as the activities of these agencies conformed to the Justice Department's highest standards of conduct, fairness and impartiality, and remained by your own admission and definition non-political.

Now, out of fairness to you, to the Justice Department's own high standards of integrity and to the citizens of Maryland, I feel compelled to inform you that recent developments and events in this state have drawn me to a different conclusion than you originally stated.

Regrettably, I have come to the inescapable conclusion that I can no longer accept either your personal assurances or the legitimacy of the agencies in Maryland under your direction now that their activities have begun to surface.

The activities of the agencies under the direction of the Justice Department appear to many elected officials in Maryland to be calculated and deliberate efforts to undermine confidence in government and to the officials who serve.

These agencies appear to be engaged in a well-planned and systematic campaign of innuendo and threat, and a conspiracy of leaks to the press of privileged information from their files and the files of the Justice Department.

Personally I feel that the antics of the Justice Department's agency in Maryland have gone beyond the limits of toleration. During the year that has passed since you were to have personally corrected this situation, I have been the subject of scurrilous remarks by members of your agency and of repeated attempts to link my name by innuendo to investigations and to persons who allegedly are under investigation.

I might also mention that the worst of the offenders are those who make up the Special Federal Strike Force. Not only do I resent this activity, but I also detest the harassment and intimidation that friends and associates of mine are enduring because of the widespread and unethical behavior or members of the Justice Department's Maryland agency.

In conclusion, I want to state as emphatically as I can that unless this despicable situation is rectified immediately, I will ask the Congress of the United States to undertake an investigation into the political activities of agencies of the Justice Department that are directly your responsibility.

Sincerely,

Marshall Goodwin,
Governor of Maryland

What a crock of shit! This must be the letter that Goodwin had discussed with Joe Frank on the tape recording. It sounded like the death rattle of a desperate man, although in a way I felt sorry for Goodwin, having the federal authorities up his tailpipe like a proctologist's wand. Better than anyone else, I knew that Goodwin was throwing up a straw man. Not a single story I'd come by during the investigation, and I'd written most of them, could be traced to the Strike Force and Bob Krall. Just the opposite. Krall had used every trick he knew to thwart me as a reporter. And the only leak from Krall's office that I was aware of was the photograph of Goodwin and Broadway Brown that had found its way to the television reporter. Goodwin was creating a diversion that he hoped would throw the investigation off stride, slow it down a little, maybe even end it, by going over Krall's head directly to his boss with charges that could create doubts about Krall's behavior in the public's mind. Pretty tough stuff for a small-state governor to confront the country's top lawyer with.

I moseyed back to Mulligan's smokestack office, told him about the letter and suggested that it told the story clearly enough by itself without any ramping up by a reporter. What he ought to do, I said, is to pair up the letter with my story and give the readers a neat little package. Two puffs on a Camel and he bought the idea. Now I wouldn't have to write another story, which is what I had in mind all along.

It was a snappy fall day under a buttermilk sky when at seven o'clock in the morning Shelly rolled over in bed, stuck her tongue in my ear and said:

"Today's the day the cropper comes."

"What's that?" I said.

"Krall's presenting the indictments to the grand jury. They'll probably be handed up by late afternoon," Shelly said.

Holy shit! I never look a gift horse in the mouth, to coin a phrase, but there was a note of authority in Shelly's statement that I didn't dare question. Goodwin's dead meat. One of his own lawyers had just said it. Instead, I took the appropriate steps to reward what's known in the news business as a reliable source. I reached under Shelly's gown and began to massage her stomach at the same time I slipped her a length of musky morning tongue. I worked my way upward and twiddled her nipples between my thumb and forefinger until I finally took the plunge into the damp and let my fingers do the walking. I've often thought that digital foreplay feels like feeding a horse. But I knew where Shelly liked to be touched. And when touching suddenly wasn't enough, Shelly slipped out of her nightgown, rolled over and straddled me, woman superior, inserted me into her sheath and slid down gently on my upright scabbard. Together we began riding the waves.

Shelly had returned, just as she said she would, two days after her phone call. I never asked where she'd gone. She never volunteered where she'd been. Since her return, we'd made up for lost time, catching up whenever we could, which was nearly every day. Now the waves were rolling in higher and faster, crashing, waiting for the crescendo as we surfed. I grabbed her buttocks and pulled her against me to give her more of my magic wand and suddenly the waves exploded into a rush of foam. The noise died down just as we crashed on the beach.

"God, we're good at this," I said.

"Because we work at it," Shelly said.

"Fucking takes years to perfect," I said.

"How come when you do it it's fucking, and when I do it it's making love," Shelly said.

"Don't go getting politically correct on me now," I said.

As a student of human motivation, I knew I probably wouldn't see my bed or press against Shelly's supple flesh for another twenty-four hours. But at least the day began with a bounce, getting it on the way we did. The worst thing about days like this is the waiting, waiting by the cheap Taiwanese phone on my *City Press* desk for a call from Krall's office. And some grand jurors can become damned defiant after being cooped up with the same twenty-one people for six months, further mucking up the works and causing delays. If everything played out according to the script, I figured Krall would call a news conference between four and five o'clock in the afternoon to distribute a list of the charges and wallow like a hog in slop over the indictment(s). Then I'd have to bust my ass half the night writing, one, two maybe even three stories, eating vending machine sandwiches and sucking high-test coffee from Styrofoam cups.

Shelly and I hit the shower together and immediately became engaged in some zesty lathering, scrubbing and all-around-rub-a-dub-dubbing. As one thing usually leads to another, being upright again so soon after having made a deposit was a salute to either my ego or my id or my general priapic nature. Shelly smiled that coy little smile of hers, pulled me by my stiffened stick and said:

"Come here, big boy."

Again I found myself slippery-dicking into Shelly's groove, sliding around on her Ivoryed body under a waterfall of fluoridated municipal water. After ten heart-pumping aerobic minutes that left me deep-breathing as if I'd been through a Jane Fonda workout, I uncoupled myself, unable to complete the job, but grateful for the opportunity to give it my best shot. Slowly I came unstarched and finished showering. Love is never having to say I couldn't come.

It was a dress-to-kill kind of day, a Bergdorf-Goodman, Paul Stuart, Saks Fifth Avenue Men's Club, Polo 72nd Street, Bloomingdale's, Alan Flusser kind of day. I settled on a charcoal gray-on-gray hound's-tooth check suit, paired it with a light blue-bodied *cum* white collar shirt, navy blue braces with tiny white hound's-tooth checks, a textured undertoned tie of alternate platinum and navy blue stripes, tasseled wing-tip loafers and a white linen pocket square. In a tight-assed understated way, the presentation said don't mess with me.

I was ready to kick ass, but not before having orange juice and spoon-size Shredded Wheat with skim milk, my breakfast fuel for the past dozen years. Eventually Shelly, in a warm-up suit, hair towel dried and brushed straight, joined me at the table for a glass of juice before driving to her condo to wrap herself in law firm *couture*. We walked to our separate cars, but not before a long warm kiss in the driveway that said: Let's do this again, soon.

"Don't wait up for me," I said.

"Good luck. It's going to be an interesting day," Shelly said.

I fired up the Volvo and eased out of the driveway, flicking the dial to the AM band of the radio to get a reality check on the urban lifescape. I recalled the old Beatle's song, "I heard the news today, Oh, boy!" As soon as it came on, the bullshit detector in my head went off so loud that it sounded like the brass section of the Marine Band blasting "Hail to the Chief" in my ear. I damned near drove off the road. Knowing what I know could get me a bullet in the back just for thinking it, but here's a guy who's close to visiting the prison tailor to get measured for penitentiary denim and he's farting in their faces instead of kissing their asses. Charles Sharkey, you asshole. You should have stayed on the bottle instead of peddling your epiphany as if you're Saint Paul being zapped in the backside by a zigzag of lightening issued from the hand of God. Saint Paul you're not. Maybe the Elmer Gantry of the anti-Block lobby. But there's no room on the hagiographic charts for you, if that's what you're thinking. Why Sharkey's running that commercial on a day such as this one could turn out to be something only God and Sharkey knew. But, then, maybe Sharkey hadn't bothered to clue God in. Either that or God hadn't answered Sharkey when he asked for advice.

The first edition of *City Press* was already on the streets when I wheeled into my parking space, written mainly last night in the fashion newspapers have adopted to save time and money. So it was flex time in the newsroom, time for phone calls to start gathering the same platter of shit for the next day's paper—murder, mayhem, war, drug deals, gun thefts, riots, the Block, the Administration in Washington, Congress, warring hotspots and starvation around the world—the music of democracy. A newsroom on down time is like the local loony tunes asylum during recreation hour—a playpen of cynical jokes, arguing over who gets which donut, misdirected mischief and hard-headed realism because the subject matter of a newspaper that's squeezed between the comics and the obituaries doesn't exactly fall into the category of random acts of kindness. But, then, show me a happy newsroom and I'll show you a dull one. In journalism, as in life, all in a days work meant worming along with society's underlife and in some wack-a-do ways enjoying it because it was bizarre. A generous ration of the antic behavior, too, can be ascribed to arrested adolescence. Nonetheless, reporting sure beats working.

I draped my suit jacket over the chair next to mine and humped it back to Mulligan's office, his cubicle resembling a Virginia ham smoke house. And here I was, only an hour out of the shower, deodorized and cologned, about to assume the acrid stench of a stubbed out end of a cigarette butt.

"Has anyone ever told you that the surgeon general has determined that cigarette smoking is hazardous to your health, especially if you're pregnant?" I said.

"What's up, kid?" Mulligan said.

No use toying with Mulligan.

"Today's the day Krall's going for the kill. With nothing unforeseen happening, the grand jury's decision should be out between four and six o'clock," I said.

"Where'd you hear that?" Mulligan said.

"Trust me," I said.

"Why should I stop now?" Mulligan said.

"Here's what I suggest. I'll spend the day writing background biographies on the principal's that we know are involved so we have them ready. Next I'll prepare a chronology of the investigation. And finally, I'll be waiting, if there's any time left to wait, for the indictments," I said.

"You said indictments," Mulligan said.

"That's right, Buck. You gotta have faith. Does my program have your imprimatur?" I said.

"Get to work. And by the way, have a good time licking your chops. You had more to do with this than Krall did," Mulligan said.

"Don't go getting all wet on me," I said.

I jitterbugged back to the library and rummaged through the file drawers for clippings on Goodwin, Frank, Sharkey, Falcone and Nelligan, remembering, suddenly, that most of the envelopes on Frank had disappeared long ago except for what I'd been writing since I'd returned to Baltimore. News clippings are a form of autobiography: The thicker the file, the larger the presence. In the pale fluorescence of the *City Press* reliquary, there were several shoeboxes full of envelopes on Goodwin, one envelope containing Falcone's climb up from the streets to the federal bench and mention of a couple of flamboyant cases he'd handled, a few drug busts and the usual bluster about drug crackdowns for Nelligan's resume, and virtually nothing on Sharkey beyond his freaky religious rantings of Apocalypse and nut-bar entropy and lately his curlicue screeds attacking the Block. True to the legend, Sharkey was one of the most powerful officials in Baltimore, yet he'd managed to remain virtually anonymous except to a few political rubberneckers and the in-crowd of swells and City Hall elitists. While I was in the morgue, I also roamed through the picture files for photographs of the objects of Krall's affection. The photo files are always fun. They can take you through the seven ages of man, from bar Mitzvah and Baptism to balding and near blindness—you enter the world drooling and you exit drooling. I sniggered as I searched for pictures that would render my quarries in a particularly sinister way, matching pictures with the words I'd be writing later today. To complete the mosaic, I fortified myself with several packets of clippings on the Block. Thus armed, I was ready for action.

By now, the fiber optic loop around the city was sizzling with the hurdy-gurdy voices of high-bracket lawyers massaging their clients at a cost of $250 an hour and six-minute fractions thereof. It was a backhanded courtesy extended by Krall that he notified each of the target's lawyers that he was appearing before the grand jury to seek indictments. And in their turn, the attorneys counseled their hapless clients to be stouthearted men and hope for the best but to be ready for the worst. As many a jailhouse lawyer will attest, no prosecutor has ever lost a case before a grand jury. In Annapolis, the ten-button phone on Governor Goodwin's massive oak desk was blinking like a short-circuited pinball machine, one call a-taking, nine calls a-waiting. Up in Joe Frank's private office, the major domo of Maryland politics sat staring at the gallery of framed newspaper cartoons decorating the clubby wood-paneled walls. At police headquarters, the recently disarmed Captain Joseph Nelligan was bouncing off the walls, so to speak, in his new administrative assignment as supervisor of the fingerprint department. Fingerprints were about as close as Nelligan ever got to a drug dealer since his decapitation. For his part, Judge Michael Falcone, left with a blank docket and time to spare since his suspension from the bench, was spending quality time at home tucking it to his new wife, who really didn't care very much about his earlier detours to Faye's basement bunk at Broadway Brown's. And in City Hall, the duke of devilish dithyramb, Charles Sharkey, sat at his work table in front of an open Bible, reading from the Book of revelations: "And I beheld, and heard an angel flying through the midst of heaven, saying with a loud voice, Woe, woe, woe, to the inhabitors of the earth by reason of the other voices of the trumpet of the three angels, which are yet to sound."

Back at my workstation, I began loading background material—what is known in the news business as A-matter—into the word processor. It was at the precise moment that I was punching in the outline of Goodwin's career that the heart-shaped *tush* of Peaches wriggled by in her signature second-skin jeans and silk shirt. She plopped a peach on my desk.

"What's that for?" I said.

"A peace offering," Peaches said.

"How are you spelling peace? P-e-a-c-e, or p-i-e-c-e?" I said.

"You really are a cynical bastard," Peaches said.

"Not really. Inside, I'm as soft as cotton candy," I said.

"The treatment I've gotten from you says that's B.S.," Peaches said.

"Besides, I couldn't make peace today, either way. I've got a busy twenty-four hours in front of me," I said.

"How so?" Peaches said.

"Read about it tomorrow," I said.

"There you go again," Peaches said.

Touchy, touchy, touchy. For someone who's so aggressive at asserting her lust, Peaches is as sensitive as she is eager. She stormed away in a bloodshot rage, muttering something barely audible that trailed off into words that sounded vaguely like "conceited ass." I inhaled the vapor trail of Peaches' fresh-from-the-shower dew, admiring the fact that she always had the look and smell of being freshly laundered and starched. I watched her twist and grind those wickedly inviting hips through the aisles of filing cabinets and finally disappear behind a mountain of outdated newspapers that would send the fire marshal into six-alarm shock.

Swiveling back to my computer terminal, I re-focused my attention from naughty thoughts of Peaches on the half-shell to the tedium of reconstructing the lives of five of the best potential felons that our town had to offer. Anyone searching for anything better would have to go to New Jersey. After an hour of tippety-tapping on the computer keyboard to the aggravation of my mild case of carpel tunnel in both wrists, I finished the text for the rogue's gallery of portraits of Goodwin, Frank, Sharkey, Nelligan and Falcone. I took a ten-minute break to give my wrists a rest before I addressed the Block itself, the durable symbol of the seedy and rundown nickel city of yesterday's bare-breasted Baltimore.

Here was the Gayety Theater, the entertainment anchor of the Block, playing host for belly laughs to the likes of big-foot Vaudevillians Milton Berle, Sophie Tucker, Don Adams, Bob Hope and Phil Silvers. And for seamless skin, the smorgasbord offered top-of-the-line strippers Gypsy Rose Lee, Ann Corio and Sally Rand. And it was Blaze Star's Two O'Clock Club that was celebrated for uninhibited raunch and for udderly beautiful boobs out to here. And in its early days, the Block was known as much for gambling and prostitution—politely referred to as "business ladies" in the old days—as it was for body language that was universally understood. There had even been a proposal to move the entire Block to the Inner Harbor's Pier Six, where it was thought to have the promise of becoming another Bourbon Street. Then, Suddenly, a major fire snuffed out the Gayety and the Block lost much of it strutting stuff. It never fully recovered. The entertainment center was encroached by X-rated peep shows and porno book stores along with fat cat developers with close ties to City Hall, and Charles Sharkey attempting to drown the Block in a downpour of holy water.

CHAPTER 26

▼

But miracles happen at Fatima and Lourdes, not in the nooks and crannies of City Hall. So it began to appear as if Sharkey was floating on his own gases. In politics, as in physics, every action produces a reaction. Elected official were chipping at the Block as deliberately as the death of a thousand cuts. Overhanging signs were outlawed. Barkers were no longer permitted to hustle customers on the sidewalks outside the clubs. Liquor license applications were denied. But around the city, neighborhood organizations, the not-in-my-backyard banshees, were mobilizing out of fear that if the Block were dismantled the contagion would spread across other areas of the city, possibly into their own neighborhoods. Sharkey's referendum to obliterate the Block was only days away, and the question titillating political hobbyists was, how the juxtaposition of the pending indictments and the ballot question would resonate in the voting booth.

Three hours into the workday I had finished all of the background music that was necessary to flesh out the main body of the story. I ran the material through spell-check and stored it in my file, not daring to let Mulligan or any other editor see it in the event of a grand jury misfire. Satisfied, I decided to let *City Press* treat me to a decent lunch since there was slim to no chance that I'd be having dinner tonight. Inviting Shelly was tempting but not an option. If there were a sighting, we'd be dog meat not only for the prosecutors but for the team of defense lawyers as well, with both sides trying to establish a pattern of leaks detrimental to their cases. That being decided, I went to the men's room to whiz and freshen up, remembering wickedly how the union once charged the publisher with watering down the liquid soap to save a couple of bucks. That's what dickhead publishers do. On the way out, I slipped into my suit jacket and directed my Ferragamos down the stairs to eliminate waiting for the elevator.

It was later, during lunch at Paisan's, halfway through a plate of spaghetti with crab sauce, that the owner of the restaurant, the *paisan* himself, delivered a cordless phone to my table and said my office was calling. Christ, I was becoming predictable. It was the tobacco-tarred voice of Buck Mulligan calling with a bulletin.

"Having a nice lunch, kid?" Mulligan said.

"You'll get the bill later and see how nice it was," I said.

"In case you're interested, Krall's office called. News conference is scheduled for five o'clock, if you're finished dining by then and are available to cover it," Mulligan said.

"Wouldn't miss it for the world. See you after coffee," I said.

What I hate about news conferences is the spectacle of pack journalism, not only having to run with the crowd but having to share a story—my story—as well. I had midwifed this sucker from the very beginning in gonzo kick-ass style, most of the time beating the prosecutors as well as the competition. Now every back-seat reporter in town was going to get a piece of the action and name recognition to boot. What pissed me off the most, though, was that the story would be handed to them in the form of a news release without even having to scratch the surface, let alone do any deep digging. I remembered all the nights I had spent busting my ass, chasing Governor Goodwin and Joe Frank across town, being hunted down by Joe Nelligan's goons, then spending half the night with the lice in Nelligan's sweat-box office, swapping insults with Bob Krall, facing down judges and lawyers, watching Broadway Brown disintegrate until he snapped, coming face-to-face with Nelligan while he helped Faye Madison shoot up then deny knowing her at the sidewalk blotch of her suicide, ducking bartender big-hands' flying fist—that's the stuff of the story that counts. But I try not to let shit like that get me down.

I wound the last strands of spaghetti into a tight tomatoey knot on the fork, careful not to slop up my tie, and bade it goodbye. Then I mopped up the remaining sauce and flakes of crabmeat with a squeegee of crusty bread. Expense account lunches always taste good to the last crumb. A cup of coffee arrived almost as if by telekinesis, my eating (and drinking) habits being well known at Paisan's, where the waitresses still call me "hon." I paid by credit card so I'd have and expense account receipt to present to Mulligan. On the way out of Paisan's, I encountered, as I expected I might, the redoubtable rapmaster, Tony Russo, his watery gray eyes scanning the racing form for promises of money on the hoof.

"What's the word, my man?" I said.

"You tell me, hot shot," Russo said.

"The buzz on the street, what's bouncing up from the asphalt?" I said.

"Word on the street's that heavy shit is coming down," Russo said.

"Like what?" I said.

"Good horse at Pimlico in the third, Daniella's Delight," Russo said.

"How heavy's the shit?" I said.

"You been shoveling it all these months, you oughta know," Russo said.

"You been up to see Krall lately?" I said.

"They're past that. It's last roundup time," Russo said.

"What I hear, too," I said.

"You got good ears," Russo said.

"Thanks. Gotta go to work now. Could be a long night," I said.

"*Ciao*, and *bona fortuna*," Russo said.

In a newsroom, there's an audible difference between a dull news day and one that's crackling with anticipation. The energy sizzles like static. You can feel the great machine of a thousand disengaged parts rumble into action and become a single well-oiled engine. No one has to tell anyone what to do. Everyone knows by instinct. Like the day John F. Kennedy was shot. And when Robber Kennedy and Martin Luther King took assassins' bullets. And the day Richard M. Nixon was forced to give up the presidency or be booted out of office. And the morning when the satellite Challenger exploded before our very eyes. No time for instructions. Everyone simply swings into action, all glands and synapses. They are the days and nights that reporters talk about when they get smarmy and sentimental (and drunk) at White House Correspondents' dinners and Gridiron Club get-togethers. They are the big books and little books inside every reporter that go largely unwritten. Today was that kind of a day, one for the history books and the reference room at the Enoch Pratt Library.

Whom the gods would destroy they first give voice mail. The blinker on my phone was flashing its steady urgency like a ruby silent alarm. "(beep)....This is Dr. Merrill's office calling to remind Richard Dart that he has a dental checkup scheduled for Thursday at nine o'clock....(beep)This is the Alan Flusser shop calling to invite Richard Dart to a preview of our new fall suitings for preferred customers on Saturday at two o'clock. Please call and let us know if you can attend....(beep)Dart, you asshole, this is Joe Nelligan—Captain Joseph Nelligan to you. If you have the guts, give me a call. I want to talk to you. You've got the number....(beep)Richard Dart, this is Fern. I'm calling to let you know that Joe Nelligan was in here earlier talking with the bartender and Joe Frank. It got kind of loud, and I heard the bartender say he's not taking a fall for anyone. Hope that helps….(beep)You don't know who this is, but I want you to know that you're a real ferret. Keep digging…."

Thanks, friend, but the archeological dig is over and by sundown a few folks are going to be deader than the Dead Sea Scrolls. I flipped through my Rolodex until the name and number of Joe Nelligan popped up. Three rings and the call was intercepted by a bullyboy voice that said, simply, "Nelligan," as if the tone was expected to bring everyone within earshot to attention.

"Dart, here. You wanted to talk to me?" I said.

"You got balls, Dart, big balls," Nelligan said.

"You want to talk, so talk," I said.

So Nelligan talked: "All I want to say is this. No matter what goes down today or whenever, I won't forget. I'm gonna carry this with me for a long time, and if it takes me twenty-four hours a day, seven days a week for the rest of my life, I'm gonna bust your ass if so much as rip a label off a mattress. Twenty-seven years on the force isn't going to end like this. And you're going to spend the rest of your life looking over your shoulder, wondering where the hell it's going to come from. You've had your fun, big shot, now I'm going to have mine."

I said: "While I've got you on the line, what were you and Joe Frank discussing at Broadway Brown's club earlier that got the bartender all lathered up?"

"Ask the bartender," Nelligan said.

"Nice chatting with you," I said.

Nelligan sounded as if he hadn't had his Ovaltine today. Developing a case of the fidgets is an occupational disease that afflicts reporters who're always rushing in overdrive toward some arbitrary curtain call. The clock on the newsroom wall was spinning relentlessly toward press conference time. The warm-up jitters, sort of like a pitcher tugging his cap brim or a manager irrigating a dugout with tobacco juice, included making certain that I had a blank notebook so I wouldn't run out of pages, and inserting a back-up BIC pen in my inside jacket pocket in the event the primary pen ran dry. Next I paid honor to the ageless dictum: "Eat when you can and pee when you can, because you never know when you'll get another chance." I went to the men's room. Before leaving, I made certain that my tie was precisely dimpled and centered. I worry about things like that.

Energy up! Under a bloodshot evening sky, with the chilly fingers of autumn tickling my cheeks, I strutted a manly cock-'o-the-walk strut up the dingy Calvert Street corridor, my compass pointing directly toward the courthouse, where Krall would soon be king for a day. I was feeling my oats. I wondered what Krall knows that I didn't, what he'd learned by squeezing people before a grand jury or in motel rooms when I couldn't because I lacked subpoena power and five million federal dollars to conduct a big-bore skunk-hunt investigation. The federal government can afford to be patient. Because government resources (in the eyes of the government) are a great bottomless maw, investigations can be an endless exercise in pointillism without a discernable point until sooner or later a pattern or a purpose emerges. When they want you, they'll get you. This investigation had dragged on for months at a cost of who knows what in money and manpower.

Preparing for a major news conference is organized mayhem. In the near distance, on the brick island in the center of Court Square, the television live-trucks circled the statue of Lord Calvert like electronic covered wagons, parked and zooming up their antenna poles and aiming their satellite dishes toward home base high on a hill in the middle of the city and another in the grassy suburbs to the north. For this event, there were even a couple of satellite trucks from District of Columbia stations to beam the images of the day to the Maryland suburbs forty miles away. Technicians were shouldering cameras, two thousand pound pencils, someone call them, while a couple of female reporters were teasing their hair and camouflaging their imperfections with pancake makeup. Up close, I saw a male reporter powdering his nose. Christ, if anyone had seen a man putting on make-up in public thirty years ago they'd have called the vice squad. I pondered all the fuss and the electronic gear, the cameras and the cables, the portable lights, the microphones and the tape recorders, and considered myself fortunate for being able to travel light and untethered. The only baggage weighing me down was a cheap ballpoint pen and a No. 801 reporter's notebook that fit conveniently into my back pocket.

Show time! The podium in the courthouse's main conference room was a thicket of microphones, each one identifiable by a station logo. Television lights were in place like a track-light bank of halogen halos. Photographers were adjusting the white balance on their cameras—"testing, one, two, three....testing, one, two, three...." Suddenly there was a piercing squeal on the public address system, loud enough melt the candles on the altar of the Basilica of the Assumption eight blocks away, as a man, presumably an assistant of Krall's, announced that the special prosecutor himself would appear shortly. Meantime, he said, a secretary would be passing out news releases so the assembly of reporters would have a few minutes to review the material. Finally, I'd find out what down-and-dirties I'd missed.

The rules of politics are the rules of the marketplace. The four-page news release finally reached me, and I put my speed-reading lessons to the test. Holy shit! Holy shit! Under the RICO statute, four of those under investigation— Governor Goodwin, Joe Frank, Charles Sharkey and Joe Nelligan—were indicted by the grand jury on twenty-one counts of bribery, extortion, money laundering, malfeasance, drug trafficking, income tax evasion and wire fraud. Judge Falcone was an unindicted co-conspirator, recommended for defrocking for consorting with, and leaking information on the investigation, to known criminal figures. According to the indictments, Frank had masterminded an elaborate scheme of money laundering through which hundreds of thousands of dollars were washed, starched and dried and returned to him in the form of cash. Liquor distributors and other suppliers of goods and services to establishments on the Block were forced by Frank to mark up their bills by ten percent. The club owners paid the bills by check, and the checks were cashed by the vending machine operator whose cigarette machines are standard appliances in Block clubs. The ten percent was skimmed by the vending machine operator and returned to Frank in the form of cash. Frank, in turn, made regular cash payments to Goodwin, Sharkey and Nelligan. Using the vending machine owner as a banker was a stroke of Frank's genius. First, it's an all-cash business. Second, the transactions didn't have to be reported to the IRS as is required of all bank transactions of ten thousand dollars or more. No wonder they refused to let the mob muscle in. Frank was slick, all right, but the trouble is the slick ones think they'll never get caught.

Nobody ever said democracy in action comes cheap. Goodwin was on the grab, because, as governor, he was able to manipulate the courts and the state's law enforcement apparatus and thereby protect the Block. For his part, Nelligan was the enforcer in the scheme, paid to keep peace and to run intruders out of town. In addition to the bribery and income tax charges, Nelligan also faced other charges of drug trafficking and malfeasance in office. And Sharkey, despite his holy roller caterwauling, was being taken care of to make certain Frank's real estate investments were protected. What Sharkey's crusade was actually accomplishing was driving up the price of Frank's property portfolio. What a fucking fraud. Goodwin and Frank were public enemies but still very much private bedfellows. And Sharkey's epiphany was all public relations bullshit. Under that sanctimonious born-again bureaucrat's shiny serge suit lurked the heart of a common thief, proving once again that money talks, bullshit walks.

Robert Krall arrived in the conference room as point man of a phalanx of look-alike lawyers and others whom he introduced one-by-one as members of the team that had cracked open the case of political corruption and payoffs. The long gray line of somber suits and button-down shirts included members of the special Strike Force, the FBI and agents of the IRS. Working together, he explained, they were able to trace the pattern of kickbacks and bribes by checking income tax returns, invoices, receipts, bank deposits and company records, all of which had been subpoenaed over the course of the investigation.

Krall continued his jabber: "This could only have been accomplished by team-work, the various agencies and instruments of the federal government working together. This is not a victory for the government, but a triumph for the people of this state who were being systematically defrauded by a tight little circle of corrupt public officials and others. They abused the public trust by denying the citizens of this state an honest and decent government to which they are entitled. They have violated the law. By now, you've all had a chance to read the news release that was prepared for you. I'll be happy to answer your questions, if I can."

Reporter: "Mr. Krall, how did you first learn about the crimes you're accusing these men of?"

Krall: "Our conclusions are the result of a systematic investigation and a matter of inquiry by the grand jury."

Reporter: "Did any of the subjects appear before the grand jury or cooperate with the investigation?"

Krall: "For the record, I can only say that the results speak for themselves, and in due time a number of aspects of this investigation will reveal themselves in court."

Reporter: "Mr. Krall, what are you feeling right now as you stand here with the lives of four men in your hands?"

Krall: "As I said earlier, this is a moral victory for the people of this state, and nothing personal."

Dart: "Mr. Krall, it strikes me that there's too much of a coincidence here. Did you stumble into the kick-back arrangement, or did someone, a witness maybe, point you to it?"

Krall: "Mr. Dart, you know I can't comment on any proceedings that occurred before the grand jury."

Dart: "It's a simple question. Did you have help?"

Krall: "The simple answer is, no comment."

Dart: "No disrespect, sir. But information like this just doesn't fall out of the sky and land on your desk with your name on it. You and your colleagues worked hard, I'm sure, but did you have an informant, somebody you might have threatened or scared, who doped out the whole scheme for you?"

Krall: "One more time, Mr. Dart. No comment. End of news conference."

Why do I always feel as welcome at news conferences as nuclear waste. Not only had I managed to piss off Krall one more time and deny him his moment of glory. But more important, I had angered the television reporters because Krall cut the conference short and they were unable to get the camera shots they wanted. I left the news conference in a trail of expletives such as "shithead," "showboat" and "hot dog." But hey, that's what reporters are for. On the way back to *City Press*, I began composing leads and organizing the story in my head. By now I wished I had worn a coat. A new blast of wind was stirring up funnels of dirt and whipping around debris left behind by the hokey-pokey man as if it were urban confetti. The dirt put a sting in the wind as if it had teeth and gave it the feeling of standing on the beach during a sandstorm in Ocean City. A ten minute walk against a headwind is hard work, and by the time I reached *City Press* I felt as if I'd been torn apart by a pack of hungry wolves.

The sound of Maryland on the move is the *City Press* newsroom's burlesque of whirs, buzzes, dings, clicks, taps, rings, squawks and voices that produce the first draft of tomorrow's heartburn. Before joining in the jumble of polyphonic sounds, I purchased from the vending machine cafeteria a tuna salad sandwich (on white) and a cup of coffee (black.) The toothsome irony crossed my mind that the coins I fed into the machine might somehow find their way into Goodwin's pocket in the form of newly sanitized currency. At my desk, I spread out dinner along with the news release and my notebook. I tapped-tapped into the computer system and when the cursor winked back I slugged the story "crooks" and began writing. It was a story of money in motion:

> "Governor Marshall Goodwin and three others were indicted yesterday in an elaborate scheme of kickbacks and bribery that reached from Baltimore's notorious Block to the highest levels of city and state government, the city police department and the most powerful political clubhouse in Maryland.
>
> Indicted along with Goodwin were his one-time mentor, political major domo Joseph Frank, City Budget Director Charles Sharkey and Police Captain Joseph Nelligan of the narcotics squad. A fifth person, Federal Judge Michael Falcone, was named as an unindicted co-conspirator and recommended for removal from the bench.
>
> The charges allege that Frank organized a system of kickbacks and skimming from Block club receipts and vendors in order to obtain cash that was routinely paid to Goodwin, Nelligan and Sharkey. The vendors were also listed as unindicted co-conspirators but the indictments were sealed to protect their identities.

The charges were brought by a special federal grand jury after a lengthy investigation by the federal Strike Force into the relationship between Baltimore's randy Block and political corruption among public officials. The indictments were announced by Robert Krall, the U.S. Justice Department attorney who heads the Strike Force....etc."

Within an hour after the bulletins flashed out on the evening news, Goodwin's office reacted with the predictable political twitch—a statement declaiming his innocence, welcoming his day in court and attesting that he will fight the charges and eventually be vindicated. Sharkey was unavailable for comment as was Frank. And the police department issued a statement saying that Nelligan had been suspended without pay pending the outcome of the trial and the department's own internal investigation.

One suicide, one questionable death, a shot-gunned *schlepper* in a duck blind, a defrocked judge and four indictments—all so that Frank's real estate was protected on all four corners. Bribery ought to be legalized in this country the way it is in some others. Spell out exactly the cost of doing business with government and politicians and who gets the kickbacks. But, then, the lawyers in the legislatures would probably oppose the idea on the grounds that there'd be one less crime on the books for them to cash in on.

The one who surprised me, but shouldn't have, was Sharkey. Goodwin, yes. Nelligan, for sure. Frank? Why, he not only invented the system, but also thought he'd perfected it. But Sharkey? A fork-tongued bag of bones in a cheap suit, yes. A vendible public official, no. In the early days, Sharkey's fidelity was secured for an occasional blow job. But apparently, as the price of Frank's real estate escalated, so, too, did the cost of Sharkey's services to help inflate the value. As it turned out, like the old joke, it was simply a case of establishing what he was and then negotiating the price. Would I sleep better at night knowing that within twenty-four hours the gang of four would be relieved of their fingerprints, mug shots, passports and gun and hunting licenses (if anyone had them)? I doubt it.

Mulligan stayed late to personally edit the story. By the time I wrapped up the whole sordid tale and flashed it to Mulligan's file, the clock on the wall said I'd been working several hours without a break. The anxiety band around my head was tightening like a giant watch spring. I was groggy. My mouth felt as if I'd swallowed half the dust in Baltimore. Writing is headachy business. I dialed my home phone and heard my voice on the answering machine. I dialed Shelly's condo and heard her voice on the answering machine. No Question. She must be working late, too. Goodwin's no longer my problem. His ass now belongs to Shelly's law firm. I slouched back to Mulligan's sot weed surround.

"Wipe that shit-eating grin off your face," Mulligan said.

"You do the same," I said.

"Good work, kid," Mulligan said.

"I suppose I'll have to cover the frooping trial, too," I said.

"Nice if you would," Mulligan said.

"Christ, it's been a long jittery day. If there's nothing else, I'm heading home for a shower and some brandy to make sure I'm comatose for the night," I said.

"Drink to yourself, kid. Nice shooting," Mulligan said.

"Don't go getting all wet on me," I said.

CHAPTER 27

▼

Sollie Stein's blue and bloated body, his chest ripped open by a shotgun blast and his clipped cock cut off and stitched in his mouth in the time-honored signature of a snitch, was found bobbing ass down among the reeds and grasses in duck-blind swamp water, two days before he was to appear as the opening witness in the spectacular media festival trial of the cash-flow four. The person who triggered the buckshot blast that short-circuited Stein's pacemaker was never identified.

The separation of Sollie Stein from earthly worries was made to appear as a copycat gangland execution—clumsy, crude, following almost a mob prescription hit. The dick-in-the-mouth thing was a nice touch, if you get my drift. But the only people with access to Stein after his sudden disappearance from Baltimore were the FBI agents who were assigned to protect him from any mortal harm or vengeful germ. Now here he was, presumably Krall's show pony, as dead as medical waste. Could it be, then, that some of Frank's funny money had found its way upstream and into the pocket of some rent-a-fed, pay-as-you-go Elliot Ness? Trust me. Shit like this happens. For it became apparent on the first day of the trial in Krall's opening statement, Sollie Stein or no Sollie Stein, that someone, or several someones, had talked too much. Before Stein's retirement to his Florida condo, he had to have been in on, or at least aware of, Frank's cash stream scheme. For the skim scam pieced together too easily for Krall to have decoded it on his own. I remembered the question I'd asked him at the news conference: Did any witnesses provide information that helped you follow the yellow brick road? If I had to guess, I'd say it was Stein, scared out of his Jockey shorts and too worn out to say, "fuck you," which is the only way to handle tin-star, secret-decoder-ring assholes like Krall and the FBI. I was on a downer, too, because in a way I'd sucked Stein in, used him as an information pathway to stories in the same way Krall had. Except I'm not the law, and I can't make him a star witness to be used as target practice.

The trial lingered on like a stubborn sinus infection for about six weeks. It was neat-o seeing Shelly in court every day as one of Goodwin's team of defense lawyers. Because most of the trial preparation and research was conducted at night, I'd been getting it on with Shelly only on weekends for the past couple of months. I, too, had been working long hours, covering the trial by day and writing about it well into the night.

But all of a sudden, headlong into the seventh week, the shit hit the fan and the trial hit the skids. During the interval between Krall's toddling out Fern to the witness stand and his introducing Faye's diary into evidence, Charles Sharkey stood up, writhed and twitched, eyeballed the ceiling, collapsed on the defense table, and died instantly of a massive heart attack. The unexpected croaking of Sharkey thus spared him the public embarrassment of being exposed as an entry in Faye's diary as one who was a fancier of fellatio.

Judge Cashman Fullwell (the third) was such a tight-assed prig that he refused to suspend the trial until Sharkey was fast asleep in the ground among the tree roots and ant colonies. The defense attorneys issued the appropriate roll call of noises, a great bloviation of words that failed to budge Judge Fullwell even a nanometer on the compassion scope. He looked all the while as if he had sat on a suppository. The lawyers had tried earlier during the opening motions to separate the trial into four individual cases, But Judge Fullwell ruled in favor of the gang-bang approach, a clear victory for Krall and his band of prosecutors. Trying Goodwin, Frank, Sharkey and Nelligan together as a single hogtied bunch would demonstrate, from the prosecution's vantage, a stronger pattern of conspiracy and corruption as well as a more compelling smack of sleaze to a jury of hoodwinked taxpayers.

So it came as no surprise that, in one of those remarkable thumbs-to-the-nose, in a bizarre up-yours kind of gesture aimed like a stinger at Fullwell, the cohort of Citizens for a Christian Baltimore had a new commercial on the air within eight hours after Sharkey's departure as airily as if they were singing a chorus of "Nearer My God to Thee."

"Charles Sharkey is gone but his work and his legacy live on with us. His mission in life was to cleanse Baltimore by eradicating the Block, its moral and physical filth. Ask yourself this question. Would you let your daughter work on the Block? Of course you wouldn't. Neither would Charles Sharkey. Remember

Charles Sharkey and remember his work to clean up Baltimore. Support Question Six on election day. Paid for by Citizens for a Christian Baltimore."

What a crock of shit. Sharkey had even suckered in the true believers with his phony-baloney clean-up Baltimore front for his real estate scam. Here's a guy, if the truth were known, who'd sell out his mother for a quick oral fix and probably his daughter, too. It was another one of those hairpin turns at the intersection of laughs and cries, giggles and chokes that compete for the proper emotion. Sharkey, by all accounts, had a good mind and a good mouth. Trouble was, they didn't engage together. Nonetheless, Sharkey was laid to rest in the damp brown earth, tilled by worms and gophers, in Green Mount Cemetery, in the heart of the city he had simultaneously helped to govern and loot. As is customary on such occasions, a minister of ambiguous affiliation read over Sharkey's open grave the comforting words of the Twenty Third Psalm, while members of the Citizens for a Christian Baltimore passed out handbills at the cemetery gates urging support for Question Six. In politics, life often imitates handouts.

In another corner of the city, the trial that had been punctuated by Sharkey's dramatic but inconsiderate courtroom display, dragged on for another two weeks until it finally lurched to a conclusion and went to the jury after a tortuous instruction by Judge Fullwell. After four days of haggling, name-calling and threats of physical violence, the jury finally returned verdicts of guilty on the remaining counts of bribery, extortion and racketeering after several other piss-ant charges had been dropped. The convictions were followed by the customary statements about appeals, vindication and that bedrock of American jurisprudence—justice.

Sentencing day arrived on a magic carpet of snow flurries, early this year for Baltimore where soupy summers usually last until Thanksgiving or beyond. In the courtroom, looking somber and gray, all wearing the appropriate dark suits of varying penitential tones, Goodwin, Frank and Nelligan, each in his order, rose to appeal for leniency, relying on friends, religious leaders and community Big Cheeses to sound the convincing high notes to reinforce their pleas. In the end, Judge Fullwell, as was customary for stiff-upper-lip WASPs, was unmoved, indisposed to show even a modicum of sympathy here in the land of the thief and the home of the knave. Goodwin and Frank each received three-year sentences, while Nelligan drew five years because of the added drug charges. Sharkey had already been sentenced to death. The big loser was Goodwin, of course. He had to give up the governorship upon being sentenced and surrender his law license to boot. I felt kind of sorry for the jerk for being to weak to say no.

It had been a bell-ringer of a ding-dong year, mood elevating, Shelly and I recalled over broiled rockfish and a bottle of *Sancerre* on a celebratory night not long after the legal noise had faded away to a dim flicker. The roller coaster ride was over. The appeals mish-mash had been an expensive backfire, and three of the best politicians money can buy were headed for the federal campgrounds, soft time in a cushy minimum security prison with only an imaginary fence around it to hem them in. Sharkey's ballot question, Number Six, was in the trash compacter. The voters gave it a whoopee-cushion reception, rejecting it by a two-to-one vote, leaving sex and sin alive and well in Baltimore just the way the home folks like it. Mess with anything else, but don't fool with their poontang. God's in his heaven and all's well with the world. I was wearing a new suit from Alan Flusser, and Shelly was swaddled in Bill Blass crepe. I was easy to please.

"Did you ever think Goodwin really had a chance?" I said.

"Not a shot. They left a paper trail from here to Las Vegas and back, and once Krall cracked the scheme it was only a matter of time. The other thing in Krall's favor was the judge. When Fullwell got the case, we knew Goodwin was a goner," Shelly said.

"Krall got lucky," I said.

"Doesn't matter how he got it. The fact is he had it and that's all that matters in court," Shelly said.

"Did you ever find out during the proceedings who the songbirds were, who did the painting-by-the-numbers for Krall?" I said.

"You were right about one thing. Sollie Stein became scared and opened up. But toward the end, Fern got religion because she was angry at Nelligan. She handed Nelligan to Krall," Shelly said.

"The bully deserved it, all that bluster and intimidation. I feel bad about Sollie Stein, though. Poor *schlemiel* deserved better than dying up to his ass in swamp water," I said.

"What about Frank's son, Milton?" I said.

"It's the old story about famous sons of famous fathers. They never live up to the expectations, and that was true of Milton. He knew nothing about the scheme, only liked to pretend he was in on the action," Shelly said.

"I had him pegged for a dimwit from the beginning," I said.

"By the way, where'd you ever come up with Faye's diary?" Sherry said.

"The bluebird of happiness left it on my windowsill," I said.

"Not to end this shaggy dog story, but coffee's finished and the bill's paid. So let's go home and play catch-up," Shelly said.

"You know, my name's been in maybe a billion newspapers, but never on a book cover. It's a helluva romp. Maybe I'll write a book about it some day," I said.

A F T E R W O R D

▼

On the subzero Friday of January 14, 1994, one day after the original manuscript of "Hooked" was completed, five hundred Maryland State Policemen and National Guardsmen stormed the Block and raided twenty-four nightclubs and businesses in what was largely viewed as an urban land grab.

The raiding party arrested employees and patrons alike, carting them off in handcuffs to five waiting school buses. The troopers and Guardsmen arrived in Ryder rental trucks, armed with sixty arrest warrants charging six hundred violations, and were led by the governor of Maryland, William Donald Schaefer. Mr. Schaefer said:

"We saw drugs, we saw prostitution, we saw liquor. It's just not right."

Before becoming governor, Mr. Schaefer had been mayor of Baltimore for 16 years, and before that a City Council member and its president. His City Hall office was one block north of the Block, and across the street from the Clarence M. Mitchell Jr. Courthouse, which is the heart of the city's central red light district.

The raid was conducted in the shadow of the Baltimore Police Department headquarters, located one block from the Block. City police were not involved in the show of force.

The state Police blitzkrieg closed down the Block for one night. A judge ruled the next day, however, that the liquor licenses had been illegally confiscated and ordered them returned to the licensees for a fee of one dollar each.

State Police spent three hundred sixty thousand dollars of taxpayers' money on the investigation and raid. Yet within three months after the storming of the Block, prosecutors dropped dozens of the drug and felony distribution charges because the cases were tainted by improperly obtained evidence and sexual misconduct charges against undercover state troopers.

One trooper spent the night in a hotel with a female bartender who is married to the owner of a Block bar. Another trooper tipped a dancer one hundred dollars to have sex with his friend—a trooper assigned to the investigation. A third trooper paid a dancer one hundred fifty dollars to have sex in the basement of one of the bars under investigation.

As a result, the supervisor of the Maryland State Police drug bureau, a twenty-three year veteran of the force, was demoted two ranks to a low-visibility administrative post, from lieutenant colonel to captain. Two other officers were also transferred in the shake-up, while administrative charges were prepared against the three troopers involved in the exchange of money for sex scandal.

The arrests were made for gambling, prostitution, narcotics and weapons violations. Colonel Larry W. Tolliver, the State Police superintendent at the time, said twenty-six handguns and a pound of cocaine were seized from one man who was described as a drug kingpin, who used the Block as a drug dealership.

Police also hauled off a number of video poker machines, which they said were being used for illegal gambling.

At the time of the raid, most Baltimoreans sneered and viewed the show of force as overkill and, at best, a Keystone Kops comic opera. More manpower descended on the Block than is usually dispatched these days to foreign nations in military operations.

The investigation and subsequent raid were said to signal the beginning of a new era of law enforcement cooperation that was agreed to by Governor Schaefer, then Baltimore Mayor Kurt Schmoke and Colonel Tolliver. When Schmoke took office in 1987, he vowed to redevelop the Block. But a forty percent vacancy rate in class-A commercial office space (at the time of the raid)—2.3 million square feet—had slowed the mayor's bricks-and-mortar campaign and allowed the Block to continue as a municipal Sodom to some and local lore to others.

The Block came under fire from city legislators in 1992. They had threatened to shut down the Block entirely, but club owners beat back the challenge.

In 1977, the city created an adult entertainment district around the Block. The move was designed to contain the clubs as well as to recognize the Block as a tourist attraction.

Block business owners agreed to clean up their storefronts, and show bar operators consented to upgrade the quality of the entertainment they offered. The city's Office of Tourism touted the Block in its promotional brochures. The attitude of the current mayor, Martin O'Malley, is to discourage any further expansion of business on the Block. Yet in November 2003, Larry Flynt, the pornographer, opened Larry Flynt's Hustler Club on the second and third floors of the restored Gayety Theater as an elaborate and posh gentlemen's skin club. Among its architectural features is a glass dance floor that allows patrons on lower levels a bottoms-up view of female dancers. Owners of established clubs initially opposed the arrival of the upscale intruder, but later accepted Flynt's club as a magnet for cultivating a new generation and class of clients. All the while, city leaders adopted a posture of winking at the Block's minor legal and moral transgressions. In February 2000, for example, the Baltimore Liquor Board issued $105,450 in fines for adult entertainment and liquor law violations, according to the Baltimore *Sun*.

On the night of the raid, Governor Schaefer said: "I'm disappointed in the Block. Years and years ago, when Charles Center was first developed, the Block was left in, simply because it was a safe place. There wasn't crime, there wasn't drugs, there wasn't problems with alcohol. But what I saw tonight, it's gone down. It's really gone down"

And so, some say, will the buildings eventually come crashing down. But through wars, legal challenges, creeping development and the moral taunting of religionists and social activists, the Block has remained a durable prop of downtown Baltimore's midsection and a kitschy artifact of cultural life here on the lip of the Patapsco drainage basin.

Finis

About the Author

Frank A. DeFilippo is an award winning reporter, columnist and political commentator who lives and works in Baltimore. He has been writing about the comic opera of politics for more than 40 years as a reporter, White House correspondent and columnist for The *News American,* and as a contributing columnist and writer to The *Evening Sun,* The *Sun, City Paper, New York Press* and a shelf of regional magazines. DeFilippo has observed and reported on eight Maryland governors over his career as well as a cast of the great and the near great. He is also the political analyst and a talk show co-host for WBAL-AM in Baltimore as well as a frequent television commentator. His only detour from journalism was a hairpin turn as press secretary, speechwriter and chief of staff to a governor of Maryland. This is his first work of fiction, other than writing about politics, of course.

978-0-595-34017-0
0-595-34017-2

LaVergne, TN USA
02 November 2009
162714LV00003B/150/A